S0-AQH-782

TEMPTED
ALL NIGHT

ALSO BY LIZ CARLYLE
FROM POCKET BOOKS

Never Romance a Rake
Never Deceive a Duke
Never Lie to a Lady
Three Little Secrets
Two Little Lies
One Little Sin
The Devil to Pay
A Deal with the Devil
The Devil You Know
No True Gentleman
Tea for Two
A Woman of Virtue
A Woman Scorned
My False Heart

TEMPTED
ALL NIGHT

LIZ CARLYLE

POCKET BOOKS

New York   London   Toronto   Sydney

Pocket Books
A Division of Simon & Schuster, Inc.
1230 Avenue of the Americas
New York, NY 10020

This book is a work of fiction. Names, characters, places, and incidents either are products of the author's imagination or are used fictitiously. Any resemblance to actual events or locales or persons, living or dead, is entirely coincidental.

Copyright © 2009 by Susan Woodhouse

All rights reserved, including the right to reproduce this book or portions thereof in any form whatsoever. For information address Pocket Books Subsidiary Rights Department, 1230 Avenue of the Americas, New York, NY 10020

POCKET and colophon are registered trademarks of Simon & Schuster, Inc.

For information about special discounts for bulk purchases, please contact Simon & Schuster Special Sales at 1-800-456-6798 or business@simonandschuster.com.

Cover art by Alan Ayers. Lettering by Ron Zinn.

Manufactured in the United States of America

ISBN-13: 978-1-60751-829-7

TEMPTED
ALL NIGHT

Prologue

❦

Fortune, good night;
smile once more, turn thy wheel.

*I*t's generally said that a man can be known by the company he keeps, and Tristan Talbot was likely the only fellow in London who went dicing with his manservant. That his servant disdained the Three Shovels as beneath his dignity served only to further illuminate the level to which Tristan sometimes sank. And illumination was direly needed at the Shovels, for the place was dark as a den of thieves.

Actually, it was a den of thieves. And rogues and sharps and bawds—even the occasional gentleman out for a low-class lark. From somewhere deep inside the low-ceilinged alehouse, raucous laughter rang out—one of the sharps, Tristan noticed, who was rapidly plucking his evening's pigeon with a slick hand and a pack of marked cards.

Distracted, Tristan shoved his tankard away, and passed the dice to the chap who sat opposite. Across the room, the door burst open. Through the miasma of smoke and gloom, he looked at the woman who darted in, slamming the door behind her. She was little more than a shadow on the threshold, lingering in a puddle of feeble, bilious lamplight, and looking faintly unsteady on her feet—not that he was any arbiter of sobriety, mind.

He tried to listen to the ribald joke someone farther down the table was telling. But the girl—something in her posture—nagged at him, drunk and detached though he was. Then he realized. It was *fear*. The constant glancing over her shoulder. The gray cloak pulled tight about her, as if she might shrink from view. Lord knew he'd seen it all often enough on the battlefield. Could he have but seen her face, he knew it would have been stark. Pale.

But what business was it of his? Most of the females who chanced to come in here were just birds of the game, looking for a warm hearth and a dram of gin. On the other hand, she wasn't flashing her wares, he thought, flicking her another glance. Instead, her gaze searched the dingy room as if it were the bowels of perdition.

The Bowels of Perdition.

Now that, Tristan decided, was the perfect name for a public house. Especially in this part of town.

He had a sudden notion to buy one, just for the pleasure of naming it. But like most anything remotely approaching ambition, it would not likely see the morning still in Tristan's head.

He drained what was left of his porter, and watched the girl approach the tapster. She set her hands on the edge of the bar and leaned tentatively across, pleading in a voice so quiet the tapster had to bend over it to hear. He shook his head, and turned away.

Tristan forced his attention back to the game. Foresby

had pushed the dice away, his face red with drink and dissatisfaction. The smithy from Clerkenwell—Tristan was too sotted to recall his name—sent them rumbling down the rough wooden trestle table with an artful flick of his wrist. The crowd roared, Foresby dropped his head into his hands, and the smithy swept up a pile of coins, his mouth curling into a stump-toothed grin.

The play went on and Tristan wagered again, but he couldn't keep his eyes on the table—an invitation to be rooked, and he knew it. By God, the chit was quarreling with the tapster now. Beneath his coat, Tristan's skin prickled.

Foresby cursed, and shoved away from the table. "Damn my luck," he said, jerking to his feet.

Tristan looked down at the two single dots. Foresby was plagued by the twins tonight, that was bloody certain.

"Sorry, old boy," he managed, thumping Foresby's back as he went. "You—Clerkenwell—cast 'em down."

The smithy snatched up the dice again. The play went on as the argument at the bar escalated. The tapster walked away, the set of his shoulders rigid. Somehow, Foresby had joined in. Tristan looked up to see him catch the girl by the upper arm. She flinched and jerked back, but Foresby followed her, pressing her up against the bar.

Tristan had shoved back his chair before he knew what he was about. "I'm out," he snapped. "Play on."

In six strides, he was there. Foresby had his face in the wench's, leering.

"Take your hands off me." Her voice quaked. "This instant, or I shall—"

"Or you shall what?" Foresby whispered.

Tristan shoved himself between them. "You're casting next, Foresby," he said amiably. "Quit your wenching, and get back to business."

Foresby smiled over Tristan's shoulder. "Oh, I think I've found something to occupy me right behind you," he said. "That saucy piece has quite a mouth."

Though he couldn't quite see the girl, Tristan could feel her fear rising. "Just let go of her arm," he suggested. "The lads are waiting."

"Mind your own business," said Foresby. "I'm pockets to let, and in the mood for some cheap amusement."

Uglow, Tristan's man, had risen from his chair and moved to the door, his massive form blocking it, his arms implacably crossed. Tristan shoved his leg harder and dropped his voice to a whisper. "I asked you to leave the wench alone," he said quietly. "Now, do you really want to take me on? In this shite hole?"

"You're drunk, Tris," he growled. "Go back to your dice."

"Aye, drunk as a lord," Tristan agreed, setting a heavy hand on Foresby's shoulder. "But sotted and staggering, Foresby, I'm still twice the man you are. Now, shall we step outside? Or will you let the wench pass?"

Foresby let the girl go long enough to shove Tristan. "Bugger off, Sir Galahad."

"*Tut, tut,*" said Tristan. "The unanticipated hazards of an Eton education—" Here, he paused to strike Foresby an upper cut that snapped his head so far back he fell, cracking it against the bar. "—can make a chap too brash with his tongue."

Foresby shoved himself up on one unsteady arm, and touched his bleeding mouth with the back of his hand. "By God, name your second, sir. I demand satisfaction."

Tristan grinned, and waved him up. "Come get it now, old boy," he suggested. "Duels at dawn come too bloody early for me."

After a moment's consideration, Foresby came off the floor and launched himself, fists and elbows flying. It was a short-lived fight. Though neither of them was sober, Foresby was mismatched in height, reach, and suicidal inclinations. He managed, however, to land a blow that swelled one eye and sent blood spurting from Tristan's nose. But when it was over seconds later, Foresby was on the floor holding what looked to be a broken jaw and cursing Tristan to the devil. The girl had vanished.

Tristan dragged a sleeve across his nose and looked round to see her cowering deep in the shadows, her face half turned to the wall. The tapster went back to his tankards. Uglow abandoned his guard post. And everyone else went back to their dice and their drink and their cards, shrugging.

Foresby got up and cast the girl a vengeful look. "Slut," he said.

In the gloom, the girl startled like a rabbit. Realizing Uglow no longer blocked the door, she turned to run, but Tristan caught her by the arm and hauled her hard against his side.

"You're going with me," he said, giving her no choice.

He dragged her back through the faint yellow light and into the damp of the unlit alley beyond. Near the door, a barefoot boy sat cross-legged in the thick brume. Tristan dug deep into his pocket, then tossed down a coin. "That you, Lem? Fetch my horse round—and be quick about it."

"Straightaway, gov." The boy leapt up, and vanished into the fog.

Unsteadily, Tristan leaned back against the building and studied her—not that he could really see much. He still gripped her hand, and could feel her quaking with terror. "Haven't been about much in this part of town, have you, love?"

She shook her head. "I—I need ter go," she said, her voice oddly gruff.

He let his gaze drift over her. Something . . . something just didn't fit. But damned if he was sober enough to know what. "Stay put," he said quietly. "I'm taking you home."

"No!" She jerked, and darted away.

He dashed over the cobbles after her and drew her back, surprisingly steady on his feet as the fog swirled around them. "Whoa," he murmured. "To *your* home, love. Foresby's actually one of the nicer chaps you'll meet in this part of town, if you take my meaning."

He felt the fight go out of her then. "Oh. Th-thank you."

Though he couldn't really see her, he cast an appraising glance in the direction of her face. "Now what was it, I wonder, that sent you bolting into the Shovels? The devil at your heels?"

He heard her swallow hard. "It felt like it," she confessed. "Someone . . . followed me here. I could hear their footsteps in the fog and—" She stiffened again with alarm.

Callidora. The great black beast materialized from the fog, her footfalls muffled and disembodied, Lem's head barely reaching her breastplate.

Tristan let the girl go long enough to fling himself up into the saddle, then leaned over and offered down his hand. She looked at it, then flicked a hesitant glance up at him. "Oh, I'd suggest to you take it," he said softly. "I'm drunk, aye, but I'm at least half a gentleman—and that's the best offer you'll get round here."

With a quick nod, the girl dropped her gaze and let him haul her up.

"So you had business in the Shovels?" he asked, lightly tapping Callidora's flanks.

"Just looking for someone."

"Aye, well, you found someone," he remarked. "Got a name, love?"

"No."

"Odd, neither do I," he said lightly. "So, where shall I set you down?"

For an instant, she hesitated. "In the Haymarket, if you please," she finally said, ". . . if that's not too far?"

"Precisely where I was headed," he lied.

The girl said not a word but sat sideways before him, her spine stiff as a duchess. Unable to resist, Tristan leaned forward and drew in her scent. She smelled rather like a duchess, too—and he'd smelled one or two rather intimately. Not even the faintest hint of sweat or must clung to her skin, and her hair held the distinct fragrance of lavender.

She must have sensed his nearness, and glanced back, eyes widening disapprovingly. It was a good thing, he decided, that the gloom obscured his face for he likely looked a horror. He drew back, and spent the remainder of the journey blotting the blood away.

It was rather a miserable ride, too, with her amply rounded arse pressed altogether too near. Despite his inebriated state, Tristan felt Old Reliable starting to rouse, and visions of how he might otherwise have spent an evening with the chit began to dance in his head. Not that he wasn't enamored of Callidora, for he was. But there was much to be said for a good feather tick and a round-arsed wench beneath you.

In the Haymarket, she stopped him near an especially dark corner. He dismounted before her, then lowered her to the pavement with his hands set firmly at her waist. He misjudged the distance, perhaps, lowering her a little closer than was strictly necessary, and a pair of exceptionally well-endowed breasts brushed lightly down his coat front.

Oh, Lord. Old Reliable indeed.

"Thank you," she said in her odd, rough voice.

"It was my pleasure." *Or could be*, twitched his cock. "Look, I don't suppose—"

In the gloom, she lifted her gaze to him. "Yes?"

"I don't suppose your gratitude would extend to warming a chap's bed tonight?"

The girl drew back. "Certainly not."

"Ah, a pity." He flung himself back into the saddle. "I'm a handsome devil, you know, in the daylight—when my nose isn't swollen."

"I'm sorry you're bloodied," she said hesitantly. "I do fear you'll be in pain when you sober up."

Was that a hint of sympathy in her tone? On those rare occasions when his charm failed, he could sometimes persuade a woman to capitulate out of pity. "Listen, are you quite, *quite* sure?" he asked, glancing back down. "I was awfully damn brave back there."

"I said *no*," she replied more firmly.

He set his head to one side, and looked down at her a little wistfully. "Aye, well. It was worth a shot."

"I daresay." She darted into the fog, then looked back at him. "But . . . But I thank you, sir. For your kindness."

Somehow, he managed to grin and tip his hat with a grand, sweeping flourish—while *not* tumbling back off his horse. At that, she turned round and walked back again. "Tell me, do you just *do* that?" she asked, her voice quizzical. "Just . . . drunkenly proposition every female you meet? And do they actually say *yes*?"

Atop the horse, he nodded, the reins draped lightly through one hand. "A great many, aye—and often when I'm sober."

Clearly this escaped her. "Old? Young? Ugly? What are your criteria for these propositions?"

The fact that the word *criteria* didn't precisely belong in a servant's vocabulary sailed right over his leaden head. "I ask the ones I like," he said after considering it. And after all, he consoled himself, there were plenty of other women who would say *yes* if she did not. The girl, too, seemed to know this. She nodded pensively, then set off up the Haymarket again.

Yes, *plenty of others.*

But she was a lush little morsel, he thought, glumly watching her walk away. There was something about her that was significant in a way he couldn't quite put his finger on. And the hell of it was—for all that she had an exquisite backside and a fine pair of charms—he was probably too drunk to remember her.

Suddenly an odd frisson ran down his spine—an old instinct he'd thought long dead. He sensed a foreboding stillness in the air. Disembodied footsteps in the fog behind him. He looked about. But there was nothing. Nothing but a soldier's intuition . . .

"Miss?" he called after her into the heavy brume.

He sensed rather than saw her turn. She did not speak.

"Be careful," he said. "Won't you?"

There was no answer save the rapid click of her heels vanishing into the fog.

Chapter 1

'Tis a vile thing to die, my gracious lord,
When men are unprepar'd and look not for it.

LONDON, APRIL 1830

*L*ady Phaedra Northampton made her way down to Charing Cross, her strides long and purposeful—mannish, her mother would have chided—as she weaved her way through the afternoon jumble of bureaucrats and shopkeepers. All of them had seemingly set off in search of luncheon at once, crisscrossing her path in a sharp-elbowed frenzy as if conspiring to impede her march across Westminster. But sharp elbows were the least of her concerns.

Desperation—and a rash, reckless idea—had driven her from the house, and despite the chill, Phaedra had left Mayfair without a hat. How foolish. And how unlike her. Now she pushed back the high collar of her heavy gray cloak, cutting a glance over her shoulder. Just behind Phaedra, her maid scurried along, a hand clasped to the top of her bonnet against the wintry gust. Other than that, there was nothing. Why, then, did the hair on the back of her neck keep prickling so? Phaedra tucked her portfolio closer, and picked up her step.

"Ooh, miss, do slow down!" Agnes complained. "I want to find Millie as bad as you, but I'm taking a stitch."

Phaedra glanced back, realizing in some shame that her maid had been practically trotting since they'd left Brook Street. Checking her pace, she noticed a familiar black and yellow barouche pulled to the pavement ahead. *Drat.*

Agnes, too, saw it. "That'll be Lady Blaine, miss," she said warningly.

Lady Blaine, indeed! To Phaedra, she was still Eliza, a little slip of a girl from their home village. Unfortunately, there was no avoiding her.

"Do you think she knows the truth about Priss, ma'am?" Agnes's voice trembled. "Or that Millie's gone missing?"

"She could not possibly," said Phaedra with more confidence than she felt.

"Phae! Oh, Phae!" The wheedling cry rang from the door of a milliner's shop. Eliza came with unfashionable haste toward them, her husband staggering in her wake with a stack of bandboxes which nearly reached his nose. The girl wore a dress of yellow trimmed in deep green, and a green cloak which was a bit insufficient for the weather. The cloak's collar was turned up at a jaunty angle, and embroidered with a chain of white and yellow daises which, Phae inwardly considered, looked hideous, and a little silly.

"Phae, what luck!" said Eliza. "When did you arrive in London? Why did you not tell me?"

"Good afternoon, Eliza." Phaedra spoke cordially if a little hurriedly. "We came up some weeks past."

"Oh, how *exciting* for you!" Eliza had drawn up in front of them, eyes wide. "How very weary you must have been of being stuck in Hampshire the whole winter."

"Actually, I prefer Hamp—"

"But *London*, Phae!" Eliza interjected. "And the *season*! I have scarcely left Town, you know, since my marriage last autumn." She shot a doting glance back at Blaine, a minor baronet so young his forehead was still pimpled. Phae almost suggested he lift the bandboxes higher.

But Eliza was quivering with excitement. "Listen, Phae! I have quite the greatest news ever. Guess! Guess!"

"Why, I could not possibly," said Phaedra.

"Oh, just try!" Eliza was almost hopping up and down with excitement.

This was the point at which, of course, Eliza would announce that she was *enceinte*. Phaedra had been through this little post-season ritual many times. "Just tell me, Lizzie." She forced a smile. "I know I will be very happy for yo—"

"We're to give a ball!" Eliza interjected, giving Phaedra a swift, explosive hug. "The last Thursday in April!" She set Phaedra a little away. "Now you all must come, Phae! Do say that you will?"

"You know I do not go out much, Lizzie," she said quietly. "I thank you for asking. Mamma and Phoebe will be thrilled to come, I am quite sure."

Eliza's lower lip came out. "Phae, you really are not so firmly on the shelf as all that!" she said. "Indeed, I am quite persuaded that *this* shall be your year."

"I do not need a year." Phaedra smiled. "Besides, Eliza, this is to be Phoebe's year."

"I cannot think, then, why you bother to come each season if you think Town pursuits so very silly."

"And let Mamma come alone?" The words slipped out before Phaedra could bite them back.

"But she would not be alone." Eliza blinked innocently. "There's Phoebe. They would be together."

Yes, thought Phaedra grimly, *and together they would find twice as much trouble.*

But she was being churlish. She gave Eliza another hug. "Do get in your carriage now," she said, urging the girl toward it. "That cloak is not warm enough to stand here gabbing. Come round for tea next week. Phee will wish you to see all her new finery."

Eliza's eyes lit up. "Why, I should be pleased to offer my sense of Town style," she said, stroking her gloved fingertips over her daisies. "How excited the dear child must be. Why, I remember my first season as if it were yesterday."

"That's because it *was* yesterday," Agnes muttered behind her.

In short order, Lord Blaine had tucked his bride back into their carriage, and secured a rug across her knees. "She's still just a flighty little chit in an ugly cloak," Agnes complained as the carriage drew away. "But she's right about one thing."

"I can't think what," said Phaedra, resuming her march toward the Strand.

"This *could* be your year."

Phaedra cut a stern glance over her shoulder. "Don't be ridiculous, Agnes," she said. "Every year is my year."

She was distracted suddenly by a figure in a dark top-coat and an odd, fur-trimmed hat. He pushed away from the shelter of a doorway far to her right, then his head turned toward Agnes and he stiffened. At that instant a black and red mail coach came clattering up from Charing Cross, fresh horses prancing wildly, passengers clinging to the roof, the box, and all but bursting out the doors. When the dust and clatter were gone, the doorway—a tobacconist's—was perfectly empty. She had not even seen his face. "Did you notice that man?" she asked Agnes.

"What man, miss?"

"I thought—" Phaedra shook off the ill feeling. "No, it was no one, I daresay."

Good heavens, she was becoming as fanciful as Phoebe and Mamma. Phaedra forced herself to stroll down to the Strand. She passed her favorite bookseller's—a tatty little shop that sold musty volumes of history and geography. Beyond that was a brass shop where one could buy candlesticks, pokers, and firedogs. A stationer's. A coffin maker and, next door—incongruously—a pie seller, his window trays rapidly emptying. Phaedra turned right into the doorway of a bay-windowed shop, pausing just long enough to read the shop's only marking, a discreet brass plaque:

MR. GEORGE JACOB KEMBLE
PURVEYOR OF ELEGANT ODDITIES AND FINE FOLDEROL

Agnes, too, hesitated. "He might be dining at such an hour, mightn't he?"

"Then we shall simply wait." Phaedra grasped the cold brass handle and pushed in the door. "Have faith, Agnes. It is possible Mr. Kemble can help us find your sister."

Overhead, a discreet little bell jangled as Phaedra's feet sank into an impossibly thick Turkish carpet. Inside, the shop smelled faintly of camphor, polish, and of the vinegar which was doubtless used to shine the glistening acres of glass cases. Phaedra's gaze swept over a row of Imari vases, a collection of Meissen figurines, and an entire shelf of bejeweled perfume flacons. Oriental carpets hung from the walls, chandeliers dotted the ceiling, and suits of armor were tucked into the corners.

"Mercy," said Agnes. "Looks as if half o' Blenheim Palace got shoved in here."

Just then Phaedra's quarry appeared from the rear of the shop, throwing open a pair of heavy velvet panels with more drama than was strictly necessary, and setting the brass curtain rings to jangling. Mr. Kemble was a lithe, elegant man of indeterminate years with quick, dark eyes which always set Phaedra's nerves a little on edge. "Good afternoon, Kemble."

A strange expression passed over his face. "Lady Phaedra Northampton!" he said. "And in my humble shop, no less."

"I wish a moment with you privately, Kemble," she said, laying her portfolio atop one of the glass cases. "A pressing personal matter which—"

The door jangled again. All eyes turned to the slight,

dark young woman who entered, her jet eyebrows snapped together. She wore a gown of striped yellow muslin under a sweeping green cloak. Her maid had been left standing just outside the door.

"Hullo, George," she said, nodding at Phaedra as she passed.

"Miss Armstrong," said Kemble smoothly, coming at once from behind the counter. "To what do I owe the pleasure?"

"George, I want another of those heads," she said bluntly.

Kemble folded his hands neatly together and smiled. "My dear Miss Armstrong, you already have a head," he answered. "God only knows the trouble you'd get into if you had a second."

"Lud, not that sort of head," she said, passing easily over the insult. "The white china sort, like the one Papa pitched through the window last year. It was one of the Georges, but I can't think which."

"Ah, the Chaffer bust of George II," said Kemble knowingly. "My dear child, I do not uncrate those by the box load, you know. The Chaffer was rare. And since the marquess saw fit to destroy it in his little temper tantrum, I fear you must all bear its absence stoically."

"What, you can't just get us another?" The girl's black brows snapped back together. "Good Lord, George. It's his *birthday*."

A sort of verbal fencing match ensued, the girl insisting rather tongue-in-cheek that perhaps Mr. Kemble could conveniently *steal* her a head if he hadn't one in stock, and Mr. Kemble parrying just as tartly that he might as easily steal the Marquess of Rannoch a modicum of self-control, and they'd all be the better for it.

Bemused, Phaedra watched, making several observations at once. Firstly, that the girl had a temper—probably got honestly from her father if he'd thrown such a masterpiece as a Chaffer porcelain through a window. Secondly, that the girl was called "Miss" but her father was a marquess, which meant she was either adopted or illegitimate. And lastly, that the girl was dressed to the nines in Parisian fashions which had cost someone a bloody fortune—but unfortunately, she had topped the gorgeous ensemble with a cloak embroidered in daisies just like Eliza's. It seems so oddly incongruous on such a dark, elegant creature, and with her nerves already on edge, Phaedra let out a little burst of laughter. Swiftly, she slapped her hand over her mouth.

Too late. The argument sputtered away, the girl and Mr. Kemble turning to look at her.

But Phaedra was saved by the ring of another bell, this time not the door, but a loud *clang-clang-clang* that seemed to come from above. A hand bell, Phaedra thought.

"George—?" boomed a disembodied voice from somewhere above them. "George? What's Jane done with my book now?" There was a muffled series of bumps, then the sound of glass shattering.

"Oh, Lord!" Kemble cast an exasperated gaze upward. "The Sevres teacup."

"It's Maurice again," said Miss Armstrong irritably. "I swear, George, I have never seen a man savor a broken ankle so."

As Phaedra wondered who Maurice might be, Mr.

Kemble gave a tight smile, and turned to bow toward Phaedra. "Ladies, I do beg your pardon. It is the house-keeper's half-day and Jean-Claude is at the post office. I shall be but a moment."

He returned through the green curtains, this time leaving them open to reveal a staircase to the right. Through the curtains Phaedra could see a rear entrance flanked with windows, and several worktables set about a cavernous back room. They watched as Mr. Kemble's elegant trouser hems disappeared up the steps.

Miss Armstrong turned to Phaedra and smiled warmly. Phaedra returned the greeting, but hers was a perfunctory smile. She knew Miss Armstrong's type. Pretty and vivacious. Fashionable and flirtatious. The *ton* was littered with their beauty, and with the almost-beauties like Eliza, none of them with two thoughts in their heads worth speaking aloud. Amidst her contemplation, however, Phaedra realized Miss Armstrong was . . . well, *quivering*.

"You were laughing at me!" she declared.

Heat washed over Phaedra's face. "I beg your pardon?"

"You were *laughing*," Miss Armstrong repeated. "At my cloak, I daresay."

"Why, I—I was not," Phaedra fibbed, face flaming.

"*Liar*," the girl answered on a strange gurgle.

"No, please, I—" Phaedra realized the girl was choking back laughter.

Miss Armstrong burst into giggles. "I daresay I cannot blame you; it's perfectly hideous." Her eyes danced with merriment. "But my aunt Winnie chose it, and I haven't worn it once, and now she's taken notice. So I said to myself, well, it's only George, and after all, *he* must have something to poke fun at, mustn't he?"

"Oh," said Phaedra vaguely. "Yes, I daresay."

But Miss Armstrong was surveying her more closely now. "I'm sorry," she managed. "Have we met?"

"I think not." But politely, Phaedra extended her hand. "Lady Phaedra Northampton. How do you do?"

To her shock, Miss Armstrong squeezed her hand almost affectionately. "So pleased to meet you," she said. "I'm Zoë. Zoë Armstrong—and I *do* know you, come to think on it. Your mother lives opposite Aunt Winnie in Brook Street. I often stay with her during the season."

"Yes, we reside there when we are in Town," Phaedra replied. "Along with my brother, Anthony Hayden-Worth."

"Oh, yes!" said Zoë brightly. "Mrs. Hayden-Worth left him and went back to America, did she not? A pity, that. One hates to see such a *desperately* good-looking man going to waste."

Phaedra blinked at the girl uncertainly. She was frightfully plain-spoken, but what she said was perfectly true—except that Tony wasn't exactly going to waste. It might be better for all of them if he were. Then Phaedra and Agnes would not be here, dealing with the aftermath, and searching for a needle in a haystack. "Actually, Tony has gone to America, too," said Phaedra abruptly. "I believe his wife wishes a divorce."

"Indeed?" Zoë did not look shocked. "Such things are easier done there, I daresay."

Suddenly Phaedra's thoughts were distracted by something—a shadow, she thought, hovering at one of Mr. Kemble's rear windows. She glanced toward it, and just as quickly, it was gone. Perhaps there had been nothing at all.

But Miss Armstrong was still speaking. "In any case, I used to see you coming home from your morning walk," she continued. "How refreshed and brisk you always looked. At that hour, I am still languishing in my nightclothes, of course, and drinking my chocolate. But I do so admire your zeal."

Phaedra was still trying to figure out Zoë Armstrong when a faint noise sounded at the back door—a sort of whimper and scrape, like a dog wanting to be let in. A vagrant in the alleyway, perhaps. She turned back to Miss Armstrong. It was very odd. Dashing girls like her rarely gave Phaedra's sort a second glance, writing them off as bluestockings, wallflowers, or just hopelessly unfashionable.

Phaedra was all of those things, she supposed. Indeed, she had embraced them.

But Miss Armstrong seemed to find her interesting, and was rattling off an almost apologetic story about how her father had come to break the Chaffer bust in a fit of temper over her cousin Frederica's having fallen for a terrible rake. But Frederica and the rake had married and, it seemed, were living happily ever after. Phaedra had missed most of the details in between.

"And now that my stepmother is with child again," Miss Armstrong finished brightly, "I'm to stay with Aunt Winnie for the season. Papa is hoping quite desperately

that this year I will *take*—but this is my second season—
well, my third, almost. And I've been in Town most of my
life. I really do think it is quite hopeless."

This last was said with a beaming smile which suggested Miss Armstrong was in no way cast down by her
lack of marital prospects. The girl went up another notch
in Phaedra's eyes. As to Zoë's eyes, they were not just ani-
mated, but sparkled with a keen intelligence with which
Phaedra would not first have credited her.

"I daresay I could go in the afternoons," Phaedra
blurted out.

Miss Armstrong lifted her eyebrows. "Could you?
Where?"

"For my walk, I mean," she answered, feeling a little
silly. "If you wish to take some exercise, I could go in the
afternoon. I . . . I no longer walk in the mornings anyway." That was not wholly true, but Phaedra did not elab-
orate.

Miss Armstrong's face lit with pleasure. "Why, how
very kind you are."

"And I wasn't laughing at your cloak," Phaedra hastily
added. "It's just that, well, a friend of my sister's—a rather
silly friend, actually—was wearing one just like it not ten
minutes past."

"No—!" said Miss Armstrong hotly. "You can't mean it."

"I fear so," said Phaedra, edging ever so slightly into
the girlish spirit. "And the two of you are as different as
chalk from cheese."

Miss Armstrong's face had darkened. "Devil take Madame Germaine!" she swore. "I knew that old hag had
shifty eyes. An original design, indeed! She knows very

well I shan't wear so much as a garter if someone else has one like it."

"I'm very sorry," said Phaedra contritely.

"Well, don't be," said Miss Armstrong. "Now I have a reason never to wear the silly thing again. Daisies, indeed!"

Just then, the bump at the door came again—several bumps, in fact, like a slow dirge.

"Oh, bother," said Zoë, walking through the green curtains to call up the stairs. "George—? *George!* I think you've got a delivery at the rear."

Phaedra followed her into the back, looking curiously over the workroom as Agnes tentatively trailed behind.

Zoë had a hand on her hip, glowering up the stairs. "Oh, bother," she repeated as the thump came again. "Let's just open it."

But as Zoë stepped toward it, the door suddenly gave, the hasp flying back with a *crack!* A hunched form in a dark coat came staggering in. A gray muffler slithered to his feet, stained blood-red. Eyes wide and glassy, the man collapsed, his knees buckling. He toppled onto the floor along with his fur hat, something tumbling from his outstretched hand as he fell.

Behind them Agnes stifled a scream.

A thick wooden knife handle protruded from between his shoulder blades.

"Good God!" said Miss Armstrong, drawing back. Then, less steadily, "George!" she cried. "Oh, George! You'd best get down here *now!*"

Her hand over her mouth, Phaedra sank down beside the bleeding man. *The man near the tobacconist.* The hat . . .

and his face. Oh, dear Lord. Fighting down a surge of panic, Phaedra stripped off her glove and set her fingers beneath his ear.

"Oh, lawks a'mighty!" whispered Agnes. " 'E looks like 'e's . . . oh, gawd!"

"Hush, Agnes," Phaedra ordered.

"But, oh, miss!" Agnes wrung her hands. "Is 'e dead?"

Phaedra could see an ominous pool of blood oozing from beneath the man's shoulder.

Zoë Armstrong knelt beside her. "Good God," she said again. "Poor devil."

"Yes, he's quite dead, I fear," Phaedra answered, withdrawing her hand.

"Who do you think he is?" Zoë whispered, turning the man's head with one finger to better show his face.

Phaedra swallowed hard. "I . . . I'm not sure."

"Should we roll him over?" asked Zoë. "Go through his pockets? That's what they do in novels, you know."

"What on earth is going on?" Phaedra whispered, almost to herself. On impulse, she reached for Zoë's hand. "Miss Armstrong, I think we should call Mr. Kemble again. We shall need a doctor—or a constable, perhaps."

But Mr. Kemble was already clattering back down the stairs. "Good heavens, Miss Armstrong, what have you done n—" Then, upon seeing the prostrate body, he said, "My God! What's happened?"

"George, he just staggered in!" Miss Armstrong rose. "I had nothing to do with it, I swear."

"I cannot feel a heartbeat." Phaedra's voice was surprisingly calm given the terror rising in her throat. "Have you a doctor close at hand, Mr. Kemble?"

"Yes, yes, just round the corner." Kemble was peering down at the body.

"Who is it, George?" asked Miss Armstrong stridently.

Slowly, Kemble shook his head as he studied the man's profile, stark white against the dark, polished floorboards. "No one I know," he said almost disbelievingly, "—and I know *everyone*."

"Everyone who's apt to turn up murdered, you mean," Miss Armstrong added.

Kemble seemed not to have heard her. "My dear ladies, I do beg your pardon," he said. "You must go upstairs at once." Then, springing into motion, he snatched a Holland cloth off a tarnished suit of armor and tossed it neatly over the dead man.

The next half hour passed in something of a daze. Miss Armstrong's maid, who looked to be made of stern stuff, was sent at a run to the Bow Street police station. Despite their protestations, Mr. Kemble whisked Phaedra and Miss Armstrong to his flat upstairs where he seated them in an elegantly furnished parlor, and busied Agnes with the making of tea.

Miss Armstrong glumly watched him go. "This is nonsense," she said, tossing her green cloak disdainfully over a leather armchair. "Tea, indeed! As if we were swooning, faint-hearted females."

"It is rather silly," Phaedra replied, chewing at her thumbnail, her mind racing.

"Now we're missing all the excitement." Miss Armstrong flung herself into a chair and crossed her arms over her chest. "I mean, I'm terribly sorry the poor man is dead, to be sure. But there will be constables now, perhaps even a magistrate. Perhaps we shall have to go and give a statement? He was a gentleman, don't you think, Lady Phaedra? Or something very near it?"

"No, not precisely a gentleman." Phaedra's voice trembled a little. "An upper servant, I daresay."

"Or—or a bank clerk!" said Miss Armstrong. "Or perhaps just one of George's disreputable friends. Perhaps he lied to us."

Phaedra lifted her gaze to meet Miss Armstrong's. "Does Mr. Kemble know a great many such people, Miss Armstrong?"

"You must call me Zoë," she said swiftly. "Especially after *this*. Oh, yes, lots of George's friends are rotters."

Phaedra managed a shy smile. "Have you known him long?"

"Oh, all my life!" she said, waving her hand airily. "When I was little, George was Papa's valet."

"Was he?" said Phaedra, surprised.

"Well, it was mostly an act of mercy on George's part," said Zoë. "To be frank, Lady Phaedra, Papa hadn't any taste."

"Please call me Phaedra," she suggested. "Or just Phae, if you prefer."

Zoë's eyes brightened. "Do you think, Phae, that there shall be something in the *Times* tomorrow about this?" she asked, clutching her chair arms. "Won't that be exciting?"

"I fear your family will not find it so," Phaedra warned. "My mother shall be mortified. Certainly she will not wish me to speak with a policeman. She would think it much too far beneath us."

A grin tugged at Zoë's mouth. "Yes, just think of the scandal!"

Just then, a commotion rose up from below. Zoë leapt up, and strode from the parlor in a swish of muslin. Curious, Phaedra followed.

A man stood at the foot of the stairs—a short, red-faced man wearing a bright green waistcoat fit so snugly across his ample belly it looked as if the buttons might explode. He was trying to push his way past Kemble, who was blocking the steps as they snarled at each other.

The red-faced man pounded a beefy fist on the balustrade. "Aye, an' I 'ave a right ter speak wiv any witness ter a murder," he was shouting. "Stand aside now, Kem, and let me do me job!"

"They did not witness a murder, you dolt." Kemble stuck out a well-shod foot, nearly tripping the man. "The knife was already in his back."

"Even worse!" roared the man, his color deepening. "Now I don't give a cock's tail feather wot manner o' fine ladies these are, I'm ter speak wiv 'em, and speak wiv 'em now!"

"Not in my shop, Sisk," Mr. Kemble retorted. "I shall give you their names as the law requires. Then you may call upon their families and ask permission."

"Aye, and that'll be the end of it," the police sergeant growled. "I'll be sent round back an' left ter cool me 'eels till kingdom come."

"So you would have me permit what their families will not?" Kemble demanded. "You'll rot in hell first, *Sergeant* Sisk."

Her mouth set in a peevish line, Zoë Armstrong started

down the steps. "George, don't be ridiculous. We are perfectly happy to—"

"*You*, Miss Armstrong, will not put one more foot down
those stairs," Kemble interjected. He half turned on the
staircase, his face suddenly unrecognizable in its wrath.
"Get back in that drawing room, miss, or by God I shall
come up there and put you in it—and your father will
thank me for it, too."

Something in Mr. Kemble's expression must have persuaded her. For the first time, the wind went out of Zoë's
sails. She turned meekly, and darted back down the corridor, Phaedra on her heels.

Chapter 2

A woman is a dish for the gods,
if the devil dress her not.

Despite being on the far side of forty, and possessing a vast quantity of unruly red curls, Lady Swanstead was generally considered a fetching creature. She looked especially fetching, thought Tristan Talbot, with a grape stuck in her navel. A succulent, swollen, sleek-skinned grape just on the verge of being past its prime—and all the sweeter for it. Much like the lady herself.

Just then Lady Swanstead shuddered with pleasure, dislodging Tristan's fine metaphor. The little green orb rolled down her belly, caught the crease of her thigh, wobbled south, then vanished into the soft nest of red between her legs and left her giggling.

"My God, madam!" said Tristan, lifting his head from the breast he'd been nuzzling. "You do know how to challenge a man's viticultural expertise."

"Viti— *What?*" The lady's words ended on something of a shriek, for Tristan was already retrieving his grape. Without the use of his hands.

For Tristan, it was an easy task—and one which took a while. With the morning sun warming his lover's tender skin, and the softness of her expensive bed beneath him, he saw no need to hurry. His fingers, languid upon her thighs, were dark as sin against her pale, pink flesh. She watched him, mesmerized with pleasure, as she had done almost the whole of the night.

Lady Swanstead had begun to cry out most charmingly when the tentative knock came upon her bedchamber door. Fleetingly, Tristan hesitated, lifting his head to look up at her. Her eyes rolling heavenward, Lady Swanstead moaned, and pushed his head back down. Tristan cheerfully obliged her. He was in the business, really, of cheerfully obliging women. It was very nearly the only skill he honed nowadays.

The desperate whisper, however, was harder to ignore.

"My lady!" said a soft, female voice through the door. "My lady, a message."

"Oh, bother!" said Lady Swanstead, rolling up onto her elbows. "Did I not say, Jane, that I wasn't to be disturbed tonight?"

There was an embarrassed pause. "But it's morning, ma'am," came the whisper. "And Lord Hauxton's come—his footmen, I mean—and he's sent his carriage."

"Blast!" Tristan swore, letting his head roll back onto Lady Swanstead's thigh. "How the devil did he run me down?"

But Lady Swanstead was grappling with the message's implications. "Dear heaven, *Hauxton*?" Unceremoniously, she shoved Tristan off, pushed away the fruit platter, and sat abruptly up in bed. "He knows you're *here*? With *me*—?"

Tristan cast a bereft glance at the fruit, especially that rare, hothouse banana. Yes, he'd had some particularly wicked thoughts of . . .

But his lover was scrabbling about for her dressing gown, which had vanished in the tangle of bedcovers.

"Come, love, don't fret," he cooed. "Perhaps my father has discovered I'm here, but that does not mean he knows *why*."

Lady Swanstead cut him an exasperated glance. "Oh, for pity's sake, Tristan, don't be a fool." She had risen, and was winding her pink satin bedsheet about her creamy breasts. "When you call upon a lady of the *ton*, everyone knows *why*."

Tristan let his hand fall. "So it's not my erudite conversation, then?" he said a little flatly. "Well. I am crushed to hear it."

She was gracious enough to blush. With a yawn, Tristan stretched, and rolled onto his belly, sprawling languidly across the lady's bed.

"My lady . . ." came the whisper again. "What must I tell his lordship's men?"

Lady Swanstead gave up all pretense of propriety. "Oh, very well, Jane!" she said tartly. But her eyes, Tristan noticed, had strayed back to his bare buttocks as he plucked another grape from the platter and languidly chewed it. "Lord Hauxton's beloved son will be down in a trice," she finally said. "Tell them they must simply wait."

* * *

Drawing her favorite woolen blanket tighter around her knees, Phaedra sat by the hearth in her bedchamber and let her head fall back against her chair. Good God, she was so cold this morning. Utterly bloodless, despite the roaring fire she had ordered built up at dawn.

The stirring of a new day ordinarily heartened her—the hum and clatter of a house coming smoothly to life beneath the touch of a well-trained staff. Phaedra busied herself by overseeing the running of her family's households, and ordinarily took great satisfaction in its success, for in life, she philosophized, one must find satisfaction in what one had, not what one dreamed of.

Behind her, servants were pouring brass cans of steaming hot water into the old slipper tub. Below, in the street, she could hear the wooden rumble of the costermonger's cart drawing up to the kitchen stairwell to unload the day's vegetables. Everything was normal—and yet, nothing felt right. Her trip to Mr. Kemble's had served only to make matters worse.

"Phaedra, darling!" Her mother, the Dowager Lady Nash, popped her head into the room, and made a *titch-titching* sound. "Oh, dear. You've dark circles again. It's that murder business, I do not doubt."

"No, Mamma, I was up reading." Phaedra sat up a little straighter. "Was there something you needed?"

A frown creased Lady Nash's high, beautiful brow. "Yes, I wish to know if we're still short a footman." Her voice was edged with petulance. "Phoebe and I are to go shopping with Aunt Henslow this afternoon. We shall need help carrying our packages."

"We cannot justify four footmen, Mamma, with Tony

away." Phaedra dragged a hand through the heavy, brown-gold hair that still hung loose to her waist. "You must make do with one today. I'll find a new groom in the summer, and move Litten to the household staff. I promise."

But Phaedra's mother believed that a lady's station in life was measured by the number of footmen trailing her through the Burlington Arcade. "By autumn we'll be back at Brierwood. What good will he do us then? Heavens, Phae. We are not precisely *poor*."

"No, we are quite rich." Phaedra forced a smile. "And with just a nip here and a tuck there, we shall stay that way. You must think, Mamma, of your grandchildren, not about impressing your elder sister."

Her mother's lips twitched with irritation. "Oh, very well!" she finally said. "Pinch your brother's pennies to your heart's content, then."

"Thank you, Mamma."

Lady Nash paused to shake a finger at her daughter. "And you, miss, need to keep better hours," she chided. "Reading all hours of the night until you look haggard as an old crone! We might hire three or four footmen, I vow, on what you spend for candles and oil."

When the door thumped shut, Phaedra let her head fall back again. Though she was not quite two-and-twenty, she felt suddenly very old. Yesterday she had watched a man die. Worse, there was a little part of her which could not escape the fear that perhaps, to some small degree, he had died at her hands.

Oh, surely, surely not? Phaedra had wanted only to right a sin; a sin of the flesh and of human weakness. Not

her own, no; that one was long beyond her. But God knew
the world was rife with others—and this one had fallen to
her. Yet thus far, she had failed.

"Miss, are these yours?" Her brow furrowed, a housemaid approached, a folded pile of clothing in her hands.
"Shall I put them away?"

Phaedra glanced down at the brown twill gown and
rough cloak, and realized her error. "No, Helen," she
calmly lied. "Agnes and I were mending yesterday. Leave
them for her."

The housemaid bobbed. "Your bath water's ready, miss,
whenever you like."

"Thank you, Helen. I'll be but a moment."

Phaedra opened the folio which lay across her lap, noticing as she did so that her hand shook. The eyes of a
dead man looked up at her, narrow and faintly exotic in
appearance. Mr. Gorsky, perhaps, had possessed a hint of
Mongol blood.

Alas, no more.

Phaedra pulled the charcoal sketch from the portfolio.
She dared not show it to anyone now. After a quick glance
over her shoulder, she tossed it, unseen, onto the fire. The
red and gold flames licked up the corners first, curling
them into spirals of black ash. Then the center burst into
color, exploded, and was gone. Gorsky was beyond helping Priss—or anyone—now.

Twenty minutes after leaving Lady Swanstead—having
persuaded her into bed for one last effort at sealing his
reputation—Tristan was seated inside the shadowy depths
of his father's coach, retying his cravat as they rumbled

from the white-walled elegance of Belgravia toward the staid streets of Marylebone.

Despite his having taken his pleasure long and hard with Lady Swanstead, Tristan's mood was a black one. He did not like this business of being run to ground like common prey. But by virtue of his lofty position within the Government—not to mention his nearly incalculable wealth—the Earl of Hauxton's resources were many, and his will nearly inflexible.

In the past, however, that iron will had done him little good where Tristan was concerned. But things changed, Tristan ruefully acknowledged. Boys grew into men, green recruits into hardened soldiers. And old men died. Thus, as it had ever been said, to everything there was a season— even, perhaps, Tristan's obedience to his father.

Tristan stared through the window at the muted morning sunlight and considered it. Yes, now he was at Hauxton's service, though in the past he had been quick to refuse his father anything—sometimes even the smallest of things, and often out of petty spite, too.

Tristan was not proud of it. He was not by his nature a mean-spirited man. Quite the opposite, in fact. His father himself had often suggested Tristan's greatest fault was his breezy nature—his mother's shocking *joie de vivre*, his father often called it—which was a rather poor choice of words when his mother had been not French, but a hodge-podge of itinerant Mediterranean peasantry. Sadly, her *joie de vivre* had not long survived her marriage, and the only shock—so far as Tristan could see—was that his haughty father had ever deigned to marry her to begin with.

In Cavendish Square, Lord Hauxton's massive mansion sat glowing white in the sun, as solid and impervious an edifice as the man himself had once seemed. The portland stone of its façade reflected not just light, but warmth as well, Tristan noticed as he climbed down from his father's carriage. At the wide, pedimented door, Tristan forced aside his old frustrations and went up the steps. Pemberton, his father's butler, awaited him in the hushed entrance hall.

"My lord." The servant bowed and hastened toward him, his expression relieved. "You have come."

"Afternoon, Pemberton," said Tristan, sliding out of his greatcoat. "How does he go on today?"

In one smooth motion, the butler caught the coat and thrust it at a waiting footman. "Little changed, sir," he answered, waving Tristan toward the grand staircase.

Pemberton's shoes clicked neatly on the polished marble floor alongside the swift, heavy ring of Tristan's boot heels. "The doctor bled him again this morning," he continued, "and left a tincture of laudanum to be taken every hour."

Tristan cut a knowing glance at the servant. "Aye, but he's refused it."

Pemberton's smile was wan. "His lordship says it is merely his body which is failing him," he dryly remarked, "and that he refuses to hasten his mind along with it."

A prudent choice, Tristan considered as he mounted the sweeping staircase. God knew his father's brain was well worth saving. Brilliant and cunning. Incisive. Calm. Utterly Machiavellian. Which made Lord Hauxton one of England's most valued statesmen.

Inside the earl's stately bedchamber his personal secretary and three of his aides were hovering near the bed. Ink pots, papers, and files were everywhere. At the sound of Tristan's heavy tread, the earl lifted his gaze to the door, his expression instantly sharpening. But his face was the color of death, his eyes drawn. And when their gazes caught, Tristan felt a sudden and unexpected rush of some nameless emotion—grief, perhaps, muted and distant though it was.

Hauxton broke the contact and turned to the others. "Leave us," he commanded, lifting a regal hand from the counterpane.

His black-coated staff leapt to attention, fluttering out like a flock of crows flushed off a fencerow, taking their papers and files away with them. One of them paused before Tristan on his way out. "My lord," he said, bowing stiffly at the neck. "You are well, I trust?"

"Well enough, Nebbett," said Tristan. "And you?"

"Quite, thank you," he answered, tucking a leather folio under his arm. His eyes, Tristan noted, were less than warm.

With a lazy smile, Tristan watched him go. "Oh, and give my warmest regards to your wife, Nebbett," he added when the man reached the door. "I have not seen her in an age."

Nebbett looked at him, his mouth tightening. "You are too kind, my lord."

When they were gone, Pemberton closed the door with a quiet *click*, leaving Tristan alone with his father.

"Nebbett doesn't like you," remarked his father dryly. "I wonder why."

Tristan smiled. "I can't imagine."

Hauxton cut him a chiding glance. "Kindly do not antagonize my staff, Tristan," he said. "Nebbett may be a pompous prig with an indiscreet wife, but he is like my right hand—and I can ill spare it just now."

Tristan refused to be baited. He strolled toward the massive half tester bed which was hung with heavy crewelwork curtains. "I collect, sir, that Whitehall cannot function in your absence," he said lightly.

"It seems not." His father's eyes swept up Tristan's length.

"So they must send half your staff up here to bedevil you whilst you're bedridden?" Tristan pressed. "What you need, sir, is to rest and to recover."

"Balderdash!" said the old man, twisting restlessly. "You sound like Pemberton. I am not going to recover, Tristan. We both of us know that. Indeed, I cannot hope to hide it much longer."

Tristan's father had never been one to mince words. Nor was Tristan. "Perhaps not, sir," he acknowledged. "Well. You have my undivided attention now. How do things go on at the Foreign Office?"

"Poorly, sir, very poorly." His father's shoulders seemed to roll forward from the stack of pillows, and even his nightcap seemed to sag. "The Belgians grow unhappier by the day, and now there is trouble brewing in Poland—talk of revolution. Mere murmurings so far, but disconcerting nonetheless."

"Revolution?" Tristan echoed. "Good God, another? Is no one on the Continent happy with their political lot in life?"

"The Poles find the Russian yoke a heavy one, I fear," said his father.

"Have they any chance?"

"None," said his father a little bitterly. "The Russians will mow them down like winter wheat."

Fleetingly, Tristan considered the implication of his father's words. More war, and all the inhumanity it brought with it. Oh, *revolution* was a lofty-sounding word—sometimes even a noble concept—but it was war just the same. The blood of the innocent was just as red. The end result was always the same.

But it was no business of his. Not any longer. Roughly, Tristan cleared his throat. "I am sorry for your troubles, sir," he said. "Nonetheless, I fail to see what could be so urgent as to call me—"

"—from Lady Swanstead's bed?" his father interjected. "A matter which is a vast deal more important than a woman's pleasure, Tristan—something which you might, by the way, consider leaving to *Lord* Swanstead? Pray sit down."

Tristan folded himself rather awkwardly into the small chair by the bed.

His father's gaze turned inward for a moment, as if he saw not the vast, luxuriously appointed bedchamber, but another time and place. "The Home Office is looking into a stabbing which occurred yesterday afternoon in the Strand," he finally said, his voice edged with fatigue. "It is a death which greatly concerns me."

"My sympathies, sir."

"Not that sort of concern," his father snapped. Then, as if remembering to whom he spoke, Hauxton gentled his tone. "It is a matter of some political importance—possibly."

It was on the tip of Tristan's tongue to tell his father he didn't give a damn about politics—*anyone's* politics. He had learned at an early age the treachery of men and their governments. But today his father's color was ashen, his hands tremulous, though he tried to conceal it.

"Of whom are we speaking?" Tristan asked quietly.

"A man called Gorsky," said his father. "A Russian. But his name is being kept quiet for now."

"He was attached to the Russian embassy?" Tristan suggested.

"God, I hope not." Hauxton scrubbed a hand down his long, thin face. "Ostensibly, he was a . . . a sort of business agent."

"Indeed?" Tristan tried to look as if he cared. "For whom?"

"For a rather infamous brothel in Soho, as it happens."

A sour smile curved Tristan's mouth. "Is that why you called me here?" he asked. "My expertise in brothels? I assure you, Father, I need rarely resort to whorehouses. The Lady Swansteads of this world are all too willing to oblige me."

The earl's tremulous hands fisted angrily. "Good God, Tristan, I do not need your frivolity just now."

Tristan paused. "No, you never have, have you?" he murmured, fighting down the urge to walk out. There had been enough of that already, he supposed. "Well, go on. Your dead Russian brothel chap—your concern with him is . . . what, pray?"

His father seemed to shift uncomfortably. "Nothing,

perhaps—or perhaps a vast deal," he finally said, his voice still strident. "Damn it all, I hate being confined to this blasted bed!"

Against his better judgment, Tristan took one of his father's cold, thin hands into his own. For a moment, he stared at the contrast, his dark olive skin against his father's pale, bloodless fingers. They could not have been more different—and in more ways than coloring. And yet now, as the end of his father's life neared, Tristan was beginning to feel the faintest stirring of kinship. Not belonging, no— that he would never feel—but it was instead the sense that a part of him was leaving this cold, mortal coil, and the understanding that his life would be forever altered by it. How strange it felt after all these years of believing it did not matter.

"I'm sorry you are ill, sir," he finally said, then tactfully changed the subject. "What does the Foreign Office care about this dead man?"

To Tristan's surprise, Hauxton did not remove his hand from Tristan's grasp. "Do you know the Russian states-man, Czartoryski?"

"The Polish prince?" Tristan acknowledged. "I know of his work at the Congress of Vienna, of course. You are acquainted with him, are you not?"

"I once was," he answered, "when he resided in London as a young man. At that time, there was amongst his en-tourage a young courtesan named Vostrikova. Some said she was a spy planted by the Russian empress to ensure the prince's loyalty."

"She did not trust Czartoryski?"

His father's smile was dry. "The Russians trust no

one," he said. "A wagonload of tinkers could scarce leave Mother Russia's domain without a spy planted in their midst."

"And all this has something to do with the death of this Gorsky fellow?"

Hauxton looked pained. "I am not sure," he confessed. "When the prince last left London, this courtesan remained behind. That was years ago, of course. Over time, she inveigled her way into a great many Government beds, and when her looks began to fail, she opened the brothel in Soho."

"Indeed." Tristan lifted one eyebrow. "How the mighty have fallen."

His father managed a sarcastic smile. "Oh, Vostrikova's is no ordinary brothel," he answered. "It is a very private affair, offering things . . . well, things money can rarely buy. And catering only to those men amongst the highest echelons of power and privilege."

"Ah," said Tristan softly. "Which further explains my knowing nothing of it, then."

Hauxton's smile faded. "No, men of your sort are not invited there."

Men without influence or power—that's what his father meant. Tristan took no offense. He was what he had chosen to be, whether his father liked it or not.

He released his father's grip, and relaxed in his chair. "I do not see how I may be of help to you, sir," he said, casually opening his hands. "You obviously suspect this Gorsky fellow of some sort of duplicity, but as I said, I do not know him."

His father stared into the shadowy depths of the room.

"Gorsky was assassinated in broad daylight," he finally said. "And there were witnesses. Two young ladies of good family."

"Most unfortunate," Tristan murmured. "Did they see the killer's face?"

"I am not perfectly sure what they saw," his father acknowledged. "That is what I wish you to discover."

Suddenly, Tristan understood why he had been summoned. "No," he said firmly. "No, I am sorry, sir. That is what all these new police constables and magistrates are for, I believe."

"Bah!" said the earl. "Utter fools, the lot of 'em."

"You've often said the same of me, sir."

At that, the earl began suddenly to fidget with the gold brocade coverlet, picking almost nervously at a loose thread. "I have never believed you a fool, Tristan. You have a great mind if you would but use it. And your exploits in Greece have proven your instinct for . . . well, let us call it *reconnaissance.*"

Tristan jerked from his chair. "Greece proved nothing but my naïveté, sir," he countered. "And persuaded me to mind my own damned business. What do you want of me?"

"Only that which I have wanted these last three years, Tristan," said his father. "I want you to accept a position at the Foreign Office. I want your help."

His father wished him to become one of the black-coated, file-toting crows. It was not the first time his father had pressed him; indeed, it had become a point of contention between them.

"One might better make a silk purse out of a sow's ear,"

Tristan muttered. "It is out of the question, sir. I've no stomach for politics. You will not persuade me."

"I long ago gave up in trying to persuade you to do anything."

Hauxton watched in silence as Tristan began to roam the room, going from window to window, and then to the small bookshelf by his father's writing desk, lined with volumes of history and politics. As always, he felt trapped in this house. Caged, like a beast, by bars made, not of metal, but of his own childhood longings. His father's unmet expectations. His mother's grief. Oh, he could leave, of course. Nothing held him here—nothing but a sense of duty, a new and somewhat unwelcome sentiment.

He looked down and realized he had wandered to his father's burnished mahogany dressing table; the same dressing table which had doubtless served two or three generations of Talbots before him. His father's pocket watch, seal, and cravat-pin were laid out as if they had just been taken off to await the morrow, when the earl would put them back on again, and return to his office in Whitehall, or to the king's side, or to some foreign nation caught in the throes of a political upheaval which wanted sorting out.

But Lord Hauxton would not be returning to Whitehall. And when next he wore his cravat-pin, it would likely be the undertaker's doing, not his valet's. The knowledge saddened Tristan far more than he might have expected.

It was his father's voice which pierced the silence. "Then at the very least," he said, his voice weary, "will you speak with the families of these girls, get permission to interview them, and see what you can learn? You are charming and handsome—someone whom they won't find threatening. I need to know what they heard. What they saw. Or even sensed."

"Murder is the concern of the Home Office," said Tristan, still looking at the dressing table.

"Indeed, and they have assigned someone," said the earl. "One of Peel's henchmen—a quite competent fellow by the name of de Vendenheim. But the Home Office wishes only to know *who* so that they might provide the killer with a speedy trial and a swift execution."

"And your objectives are different?"

"Quite," said the earl. "I wish to know *why*. And at whose behest."

"And if it was a random killing?" Tristan suggested. "A raving lunatic? Some common cutpurse turned violent?"

The earl fell back into the plump softness of his pillows. "Then I would be deeply relieved," he confessed. "But it is not. I sense it with every fiber of my being."

Tristan picked up the cravat-pin and rolled it pensively between his fingers. "Your political instincts, sir, are unfailing," he said. "But your choice of emissary is not. I fear I cannot oblige you."

The earl swore softly beneath his breath. "God's truth, Tristan, have you no sense of duty?"

The question stung, especially when it had been duty which had driven him here. "Why the hell should I?" he snapped, turning from the dressing table.

His father seemed almost to shrivel before his very eyes. He clutched his hands, an almost childlike gesture, and Tristan felt something rend inside his heart. "Perhaps because I am your father, and I am begging you?" said the earl quietly. "There. I have said it, Tristan. I am begging. Does it please you?"

Strangely it did not. And it struck him that this was perhaps the first time in his life that his father had asked— rather than ordered—him to do anything. Tristan looked again at the withered and ashen man who had thinned to a mere caricature of himself these past few months, and felt the one thing he had never wished to feel for him. Pity.

Or perhaps his father was merely playing clever politics again. A direct order Tristan could flout. But a request from his aged and dying father? No, that he could not.

"Very well," he said at last. "Tell me everything you already know."

The Marquess of Nash was not a happy man. His hands clasped tightly behind his ramrod-straight spine, he was standing before the massive desk in his wood-paneled library, and trying not to curse aloud in front of the ladies, which this afternoon included his flighty stepmother, Edwina, the dowager marchioness, and his two younger half sisters.

"A most unfortunate business," he said, watching his stepmother pour tea. The news of yesterday's unpleasantness in the Strand had fallen upon the marquess's ears early this morning, and he had summoned Edwina and his sisters to his house in Park Lane at once so that he might get to the bottom of it.

His stepmother set down the silver teapot. "Well, I think it perfectly sordid, people getting themselves stabbed in public," she twittered. "I vow, I very nearly fainted when I heard."

Phaedra's cup chattered as she picked it up. "Mamma, pray do not start again," she murmured. "I scarcely think the gentleman meant to flout etiquette by falling dead of a stab wound."

The dowager turned on the narrow settee. "Well, at the very least, Phaedra, they should keep such vile business to the East End where one expects it," she declared. "Phoebe had to fetch my hartshorn—didn't you, my love?"

"Just so, Mamma." Phoebe's eyes were lowered—spuriously, the marquess was sure.

"—and to think that there was Phaedra!" his stepmother went on. "Caught in the middle of it! And poor Phoebe getting ready to debut."

"I daresay no one will come to my ball now," Phoebe complained, poking out her lower lip. "Phae has ruined everything for me."

"What nonsense, Phee!" Phaedra groaned.

Nash wanted to groan, too. The sad truth was, Phoebe and Edwina hadn't an ounce of common sense between them, and Nash knew it. For years he had depended—perhaps unfairly—upon Phaedra's looking after them. And before that, Edwina's sister, Lady Henslow. Otherwise, God only knew what would have become of the pair. They would have fallen down a well, starved to death, or mortgaged the family estate to buy new hair ribbons. And Tony—for all his political savvy—wasn't much better. Phae was the steady one, and the fact that it had been she in the wrong place at the wrong time was just damned bad luck. He hoped.

"Pray do not be so dramatic, Phoebe," said the marquess. "People love nothing so well as a scandalous story. Now we may oblige them."

"Still, the situation *is* awkward, Nash." His stepmother relished drama. "I daresay Phaedra shall have her name in the newspapers."

"No one in this family," said the marquess tightly, "shall have their name in the papers. I have already spoken to Lord de Vendenheim at the Home Office."

Phaedra hung her head. "Thank you, Stefan."

Lord Nash felt something inside him soften. "You are welcome, Phae." He smiled across his teacup. "No harm has been done, has it? Well, save for that poor devil with the knife in his back. He was Russian, by the way. You doubtless had not heard."

Something strange sketched across Phaedra's face, and was just as quickly concealed.

They passed the remainder of the hour talking about Phoebe's come-out ball, his stepmother darting from topic to topic—food, wine, hemlines, gossip—like the rattle she was. But it was an almost comfortingly familiar sort of blither to which he'd grown accustomed—perhaps even fond of.

"Well!" said Lady Nash, rising once the tea was cleared. "Phoebe has a fitting for her ball gown shortly, and Aunt Henslow will be waiting."

Nash turned his gaze on Phaedra, and steepled his fingers pensively. "What of you, my dear?" he asked quietly. "Are you to have something new to wear to Phoebe's come-out?"

His sister shook her head. "I had not thought to go to any balls this season."

"It would be my greatest pleasure, Phae, to purchase a lavish new wardrobe for the both of you," her brother pressed. "Do please consider it. We shall call it a gift from a doting brother."

"Thank you." Phaedra looked away. "I have considered it already."

Lady Nash pursed her lips and shot her elder daughter a dark, cutting look, but said no more.

Nash forced a smile. "Then if you've no fitting today, my dear, perhaps you can be persuaded to remain behind?" he lightly suggested, motioning toward the nearby chessboard. "I haven't had a worthy partner in an age."

"Oh, Nash!" His stepmother patted his hand affectionately. "With a child in the house and another on the way? You cannot possibly have any time for chess!"

"Very little, 'tis true." Nash rose, his smile still muted. "Will you stay, Phaedra?"

"Yes, of course," Phaedra was wise enough to recognize an order from the head of the family, however politely it might have been issued.

Soon, in a bustle of reticules, hats, and shawls, with cheeks kissed all around, Lady Nash and her youngest daughter took their leave. Her spirits low, Phaedra followed her eldest brother to the back of the library, to the elegant marquetry table beneath the windows at which they had so often played. Phaedra scarcely spared it a thought, for her mind was elsewhere, numbed by worry, and by a measure of grief for the dead man. Whatever else he might have been, he was a human being—something others seemed all too willing to forget.

"Is there anything else, Phaedra, which I should know about what happened in the Strand?" asked Stefan quietly. "Something, perhaps, you did not wish to say in front of Edwina and Phoebe?"

Fleetingly, she hesitated. It would have been such a relief to unburden herself to her elder brother. But she dared not. "No. There is nothing else."

"Good." Nash smiled wolfishly.

Oh, she was in trouble. She knew it.

His hands were clasped rigidly behind his back again as he strolled along a wall of paintings. Phaedra knew it had always fallen to him to be the disciplinarian. The one who fixed their scrapes and covered over their scandals. He also put roofs over their heads and paid their allowances, and the fact that Stefan was eldest had little to do with his position of leadership. He was by his nature a strong man, a man one did not willingly anger. And to almost everyone—even to her mother, Tony, and Phoebe—he was *Nash*—more title, it often seemed, than mortal man.

Was she in trouble? Was Stefan to scold her for what had happened at Mr. Kemble's?

No, she thought not. Her brother was a fair man. And he, above all of them, understood her, though he was many years her senior. Even her mother had often remarked that of the four of them—Stefan, Tony, she, and Phoebe—only Phaedra and Stefan were remotely alike. Phaedra often knew what Stefan was thinking— sometimes before he did. Moreover, he confided in her.

Trusted her to help him guard the family. And until now, they'd had no secrets from one another.

"This isn't about yesterday, is it?" she said, clasping her hands in her lap.

He stopped pacing. "No, it is about the gown, actually."

"The gown?" Her brow furrowed.

"The gown you are *not* being fitted for this afternoon," he clarified.

At that, Phaedra leapt up. "Oh, please, Stefan, not you, too."

He closed the distance between them swiftly, and caught her shoulders in his hands. "Phae, why not? I . . . I could work something out. Lady Henslow, perhaps, could help us?"

"*No.*" Her voice was bitter. "Aunt Henslow has helped quite enough already, don't you think?"

His lips thinned, and still holding her shoulders, he shook his head. "God's truth, I blame myself for all this," he said. "Phae, my dear, you are not yet two-and-twenty. Your whole life—a normal life—could be before you. Marriage. A family, perhaps."

She jerked from his grasp, and went at once to the window which looked out over Park Lane. "Yes, now that you have Xanthia, your notions about wedlock have rather altered, haven't they?" Her voice was laced with bitterness she could not hide. "You have become conventional."

"You say that as if it is a dread disease."

She shook her head. A deep, boundless sorrow seemed to swamp her, dragging her heart into the pit of her stomach and leaving her awash in grief and shame. Instinctively, as it so often did, her hand went to her belly, resting over that dark void inside her womb. Yes, it was easier to pretend. To pretend that it did not matter. To cloak herself in her wit and her intellect, and tell herself that she felt whole and happy as she was. That a part of her was not missing. Her face must have crumpled a little.

"May I no longer count on you, Stefan?" she whispered. "Will you gainsay me now—after all these years of standing by me?"

His expression suddenly altered, his brown eyes going soft. He drew her into his arms, and she went willingly. "Never, *zaichick*," he murmured against the top of her head. "But just know that—if you wish, and only if you wish—I will arrange things for you."

Phaedra was glad Stefan could not see the tears which had sprung to her eyes. "Arrange what?" she snuffled, clinging to him as she had not done since she was fifteen.

"A husband, Phae," he murmured, tightening his embrace. "Someone good and kind."

Phaedra laughed through her tears. "You mean some desperate old widower with eight children."

"No, I mean someone who might give you children of your own."

She shook her head, her hair scrubbing his chin. "It won't work, Stefan."

"A marriage can be arranged, my dear, at the very least."

"Stefan, you *promised*," she whispered.

"And I shall keep that promise," he said quietly. "Do you wish me never to speak of this again?"

"That is precisely what I wish."

She felt his arms begin to slide away. "Very well." His voice was sad. Resigned.

"I know you mean well," said Phaedra, dashing away her tears with the back of her hand. By God, she would not be a weak and sniveling thing—not even in the face of Stefan's sympathy.

Her brother tipped up her chin. "But do buy some new gowns, Phae," he said firmly. "A whole wardrobe, actually—one with a little color this time—or at the very least, a gown for Phoebe's come-out, and another for Xanthia's gala in June. Please do not disappoint me in this."

"And that is an order?"

He ran the pad of his thumb beneath one teary eye, taking care not to smudge her spectacles. "For your sake," he repeated. "Your not being seen about town with your sister might well cause more speculation than the alternative."

"If you insist, then."

"I do," he said. "Now, chess?"

Phaedra shook her head. "You are very kind," she said. "But I have much at home to do."

"Ah, linen to sort or a housekeeper to chide, I do not doubt." Her brother smiled warmly, and much of the tension seemed to vanish from the room. "Or a book, perhaps. Busy Phaedra, always obsessed with your duties and your dusty tomes."

"Today it is a book." Phaedra brightened her expression. "I am rereading the Langhornes' translation of *Plutarch's Lives*. I feel a little guilty, for it is much faster-going than the original Greek."

But it did sound desperately dull, she inwardly admitted, when said aloud. And later, looking back on it, Phaedra realized that her entire life had become dull—that she had made so, for there was a sort of comfort in predictability. What she did not know, however—and what was to prove utterly *un*predictable—was how swiftly and how thoroughly that quiet life was about to end.

Chapter 3

❦

Mark how his virtue, like a hidden sun,
Breaks through his baser garments.

In Long Acre that afternoon, Tristan dressed with a good deal more care than usual, biting back impatience as he did so. The day was to take him to staid Mayfair instead of boat racing upriver on the Thames with some raucous, rough-elbowed companions as he'd planned. There, they would have tossed out blankets in a sunny, sheltered spot along the riverbank, and spent the afternoon skulling against one another, and wagering as to which of them would have the day's strongest back.

There would have been tankards of cool ale from the nearby public house, and undoubtedly one or two of the tavern wenches would have come out to cheer them on. But today, instead of old breeches and a nice, baggy shirt worn soft with age, he was to rig himself out as a gentleman. There would be no buxom wench with her round, squirming rump planted squarely in his lap and her arms twined round his neck.

Instead, he was to call upon the elder of the two ladies

who had had the grave misfortune to witness the murder in the Strand—a bluestocking of uncertain age. Tristan sighed, and reached out his hand for a fresh neckcloth. He hoped he did not end the day strangled with it. Lady Phaedra Northampton, he was forewarned, was the younger sister of the Marquess of Nash, a hard-eyed, unrepentant turfite whom Tristan knew from racing circles. And Lord Nash, though reportedly mellowed by his marriage, was not a man whom one lightly angered.

Perhaps Tristan was destined to become the diplomat his father had long dreamed of. He finished off the knot, and let his hands fall.

"Crumpler-peg, m'lord?"

Tristan looked around to see his man, Uglow, thrusting something out between his sausage-like fingertips. "Thank you."

The cravat-pin stabbed securely into place, Tristan peered at himself in the old, mottled mirror which hung haphazardly above his washstand. He had never bothered to purchase a proper cheval glass or any other decent sort of mirror in which one might examine oneself. Other than to pay his tailor's bills in a relatively timely fashion, and to forswear the wearing of any shade of pink, Tristan had never given much thought to his wardrobe. Suddenly, it occurred to him that relying solely upon Uglow's somewhat dubious opinion today might be a mistake.

"How do I look?" he nonetheless asked, giving his cuffs a neatening tug.

The crease in Uglow's slab of a brow deepened. "Togged out ter the nines, sir," he finally decided. "A right proper gent."

Tristan laughed. "First time the phrase has been applied to me, I daresay," he remarked. "Now check the boots. Like mirrors, are they? Today, old boy, they'd better be."

"Aye, but not like *your* mirror," said Uglow with umbrage. "I thinks I knows, sir, 'ow to give a boot a proper lick by now."

"Sorry, Uglow," he said. "Guess I'm out of sorts."

Uglow grunted, and handed Tristan his coat. He slid it on; then, at the last possible minute, Tristan returned to his makeshift dressing table, and pawed through the top drawer until he found his small leather jewelry case. The trefoiled and befeathered crest of the oh-so-noble Talbot family winked up at him in solid gold. Tristan slid his signet ring on a finger of his right hand, marveling as he did so that he could not even remember the last time he'd worn it.

Ten minutes later, Tristan was thundering down the narrow flight of stairs which led from his maisonette to the street. At the livery stable near Covent Garden market, Callidora was saddled and waiting. It was but a short walk to the home of Anthony Hayden-Worth, Lord Nash's stepbrother, with whom Tristan's quarry made her home in London. But Callidora made a striking first impression with her black satin coat, flashing hooves, and wide, snorting nostrils. She was big, too, for a mare so elegantly boned; sixteen hands of broad-chested, long-legged, sidestepping witchery.

A former cavalry horse, Callidora had come home with him from Greece, in part because Tristan could not bear to leave her behind. She was half Arab, the black part— and half Andravida, the big, broad part. And as with

Tristan himself, perhaps, her looks were deceiving. Despite all the flash and show, Callidora was no longer young. She was also tame as an overfed housecat, and totally subservient to his commands.

Usually. Which just proved a man could never entirely trust a female.

In Brook Street, he had almost reached Grosvenor Square when Callidora went prancing sideways, eyes inexplicably shying at two newsboys on the corner. Suddenly, a cry rang out. Newsprint and fists exploded. One chap shoved the other up against a costermonger's cart, flailing unmercifully. Wind sent a sheet of newspaper flapping low across the street. Still dancing, Callidora tossed her head and skittered across the road into the path of a coal wagon turning the downhill corner from Duke Street.

"Whoa!" cried the driver, drawing up hard. A scuttle's worth of coal went cascading over one side.

Across the square, a tall, elegant lady in a gray dress froze in midstep, then drew back onto the pavement, her eyes rolling.

As Tristan tried to settle his dancing mount, the costermonger leapt down. He tried to part the two chaps—the larger of which was rather a brute. But the costermonger was old and bent. The big fellow swung at him. The costermonger jerked, hitching up against his barrow, dislodging a peck basket laden with parsnips. A cabbage tumbled down with it. Coal, cabbage, parsnips; all of it rolled beneath Callidora's feet as the men fought on. The horse reared high, coming down mere inches from the cart just as blood exploded over the old man's coat.

In a trice, Tristan was out of the saddle, stripping off

his gloves as he went. "Keep her head," he ordered, pressing the reins into the old man's hands.

Wading into the fray, Tristan yanked the larger fellow off the small chap effortlessly. The brute whirled and gave him a fist in his face for his trouble. "Bugger off!"

Head snapping and blood stirring, Tristan threw back a good left. He caught the chap square in the right jaw. "By God, I'll teach you to pick on someone smaller," he said, grinning.

The thug grinned back, and came at him.

The coalman jumped down, shaking his fist. As Tristan and the brute circled about, throwing punches, the coalman began to shout that someone needed to pick up his lost wares. Callidora was still wheeling her hindquarters, her eyes wild, her velvety black nostrils big as the parsnips she trod upon.

Just then, the big chap lunged. A tactical mistake. Tristan was slender, but he was tall and strong—and a much better wrestler than boxer. After a few flips and flops, and a great deal of grunting, he had the bully down if not out.

"Ho, there!" a deep voice boomed behind Tristan. "What's all this?"

Tristan was astride the chap, trying to wrestle him into submission, but the smaller fellow had plucked up, and began kicking his assailant repeatedly in the ribs.

"Ow, ow!" The bully tried to roll Tristan off. "Le' me at the li'l shite!"

The small chap kicked him again.

"Stop, damn you!" Tristan ordered, cutting a glance up at the lad. "Stop kicking hi—"

It was his last clear, conscious thought. Tristan collapsed, rolling to one side. A great, roaring blackness rushed in.

When he awoke—mere moments or perhaps even days later—it was to find the rooflines of Brook Street wheeling above him like a giant jigsaw puzzle, interspersed with shafts of twinkling sunlight, and an oddly split vision of the lady in gray. She looked down at him indignantly, lips wordlessly moving, blue eyes swimming behind a pair of stern gold spectacles. Tristan decided to blink until the vision went away. Christ, his head hurt.

"Oi, Mr. Pimkins!" said a cockney voice through the haze. "Wot a constable you are! Yer clouted a proper gentry-cove."

The swish of skirts rattled near Tristan's ear. "Stand back, you fools," said a sharp, female voice. "Stand back, I say. Mr. Coalman, get this gentleman up, if you please."

Someone—perhaps a pair of someones—hefted Tristan up beneath his arms and hauled him to his feet. The lady in gray appeared to be gone, and so was his hat. Light, cool fingertips were riffling through the hair on the back of his head.

"Well, this is rather a mess." Ah, the tart-tongued female was behind him now. "And it's going to need a stitch."

Tristan moaned, and tried to sit down, but he was hitched back up again.

"Oh, Mother Mary and Jesus!" A man in a blue police uniform swam before Tristan, all bulbous nose and fretful eyes. He still clutched the tool of Tristan's undoing—a heavy tipstaff, its royal coat of arms glittering in the sun. "Gawd, they'll 'ave me job for this!"

"Stop whimpering, Pimkins," said the female, stepping round. Her voice was husky; a seductive bedroom sort of voice.

Tristan shook his head, and the newsboys came fully into focus. So did the female. Yes, it was the lady in gray who'd been rolling her eyes on the corner. Her throaty voice aside, Tristan did not like disapproving females; he much preferred the cheerful, willing sort. He leaned back against the costermonger's cart and tried to blink her away again.

But the lady in gray was in command now. "Clear these lads off Brook Street, Pimkins," she ordered, stabbing her finger at the pair. "Brawling in the street, indeed! If I ever see either again—"

"Oi, it's my corner!" the larger lad interjected.

"Is not!" cried the second.

"*And if I ever*," the woman ground out, "see either of you this side of Grosvenor Square again, my brother shall have the both of you before the magistrate. Do I make myself plain?"

The smaller of the two hung his head.

"Well, go on!" The police constable pointed up Duke Street. "You 'eard the lady. Off with you."

With one last resentful, sidelong glance, the hulking bully slunk away, seizing up his bundle of newspapers by its twine cording as he went.

"But it's *my* corner, m'lady," cried the smaller chap, shuffling one foot. He was a slight lad of perhaps seventeen in a shabby brown coat, a head shorter than the lady in gray, with the heels of his boots worn down to nearly nothing. "You know it's my corner, for you see me out 'ere every day."

Tristan had given up trying to blink the woman away and was watching her now, mildly fascinated. Her heavy chestnut-gold hair was twisted up in a simple arrangement, but despite her dull gray gown, she could never have been mistaken for a servant. No, she was every inch a wellborn lady—a lady who was still tapping one toe. The angry glint in her eye, however, was relenting.

"You shouldn't have been kicking a man when he was down," she finally said to the newsboy. "That's hardly cricket, is it? If you'd fetched Pimkins to begin with, we would not have this—this *addled gentleman* to deal with."

"Aye, m'lady," said the fellow glumly.

"I'm not addled." Tristan tried to prove it by shaking himself off and standing up straight.

The woman cut him a disdainful glance. "You may go up to Oxford Street for the rest of the month," she said, still addressing the newsboy. "Hawk your papers there."

"Aye, m'lady, but there's a score o' blokes hawking Oxford Street," he said. "This is my corner. An' I got a sick mother and three starving sisters ter feed as is."

The lady glowered. "Have you indeed?" she said. "And do not lie to me, for I shall discover the truth."

"Aye, she will, too," Tristan muttered grimly. "They always do."

The lady shot a disdainful glance at him, lifting one brow. "What do you know of horses?" she asked, returning her gaze to the lad.

Again, the shuffling feet. "A bit, m'lady."

Aye, the arse from the ears, perhaps, thought Tristan.

The lady sighed. "Well, you can shovel manure as well as anyone, I daresay," she muttered. "Go round to the mews and ask for Feathers, the coachman. We've need of a groom."

"Yes, m'lady." The fellow's eyes widened, and he tugged on his forelock. "Th—Thank you. And God bless you." Then he darted away as if he feared she might change her mind.

Tristan dragged both hands through his hair. The throb in his temples was fading, only to be replaced by a deep, settling ache at the base of his skull. Oddly, a pair of footmen had come down from a nearby house. One had gathered up the coal and the vegetables, and the other had taken charge of Tristan's mount.

Suddenly, the lady's gaze turned to Callidora, narrow and oddly assessing. "Go back to your watchbox, Pimkins," she said absently. "I shall see to this gentleman's head."

"Aye, my lady."

At last, she looked back at Tristan. Whatever it was about the horse which had distracted her was apparently forgotten. "Can you walk, sir?" she asked, her voice perhaps a little gentler. "Or may one of the footmen help you?"

"I'm fine, ma'am," he muttered. "Thank you."

"You are not fine." She set one small fist on her hipbone. "You are bleeding. And likely concussed—if you actually have a brain in that pretty head of yours." This last was added under her breath.

"I heard that," said Tristan, rubbing one temple with his fingertips.

She narrowed her eyes. "Come with me, sir," she said more authoritatively. "That wound must be seen to."

Tristan was looking about, trying to get his bearings. "Thanks, but I've a call to pay hereabouts."

"Very well, suit yourself," she said, lifting both hands. "You are obviously hardheaded. But I do hope, sir, that you are aware you look a fright. Your hands and knees are filthy, and blood has soaked the back of your collar."

Tristan had not been aware. He looked down to see that Uglow's fine boot polishing had been all for naught, too. *Damnation.* He considered walking to his father's. No, better to take his chances with the lady in gray. His father might become apoplectic, and in his weakened condition . . .

"If I might just wash up a bit, ma'am?" Tristan suggested, returning his gaze to her sharp blue eyes. "I daresay I should forgo my call for today."

Her mouth twitched almost charmingly. "I would recommend it, yes." She lifted her hand and one of the footmen came running.

"Yes, Lady Phaedra?"

"Be so good as to help this gentleman into the house, Stabler," she said. "Then fetch a basin of hot water and some towels. The back parlor, I think, will do nicely."

But Tristan barely heard the last.

Lady Phaedra.

Wasn't that the name? Or was he indeed addled?

He cocked his head a little to one side. "You are—" he began uncertainly.

She looked at him, and arched one delicate dark eyebrow. "I am what?"

"You were in the Strand yesterday," he said more certainly. "When—yes, when that foreign chap got himself stabbed."

She lost a little of her color then, and visibly stiffened. "Indeed," she murmured in her low, throaty voice. "One begins to wonder if one has become a magnet for violent lunatics."

With that, she whirled about, the hems of her gown furling out to reveal a pair of slender, well-turned ankles, and just a hint of a lace-trimmed underskirt. Intrigued, Tristan followed her across the street to the town house from which the footmen had come. Her spine remained stiff as a poker.

Lady Phaedra went up the steps before him, and to his pleasant surprise, her gray skirts slithered nicely over a lush, round arse which seemed somehow out of character, given her dowdy gown and disapproving expression. And something about her . . . yes, there was something vaguely familiar.

She turned to thank the footman, who now held the door, and Tristan realized in some shock that she really was quite remarkably pretty, with legs that must have gone on forever. As if it were second nature—and it was—Tristan's mind began to consider his options. Or perhaps it was not his mind, but another part of his anatomy altogether. But to Tristan's way of thinking, all women had potential. This one, perhaps, a great deal of it.

Yes, divested of that drab dress, with her thick, chestnut-gold hair down around her waist . . .

Oh, good Lord! His head still hurt like the devil. He still had the burden of his father's mission hanging over him. And Lady Phaedra Northampton was still Lord Nash's younger sister—younger *unwed* sister, he added. Indeed, the girl could not have been five-and-twenty, despite what he suspected were her efforts to appear otherwise.

She escorted him into a small parlor. "The light will be better in here," she explained.

Though the front rooms of the house, Tristan had noticed, were grand indeed with French furnishings and a generous amount of marble and gilding, this room was furnished with soft, well-worn chairs, an ancient game table, a great many books and magazines, along with a rug in shades of deep red and gold which was comfortably worn.

Once inside, she wisely left the door open, and went at once to draw the brocade draperies wide to the sun. Her motions were quick and neat, he noticed. Efficient. But not unpleasant. The actions of a woman with much to do—and a vast deal of experience doing it, he thought. A serious-minded woman. Oh, far too serious. Tristan considered *that* a challenge.

"Kindly remove your coat, sir," she said, going to an old walnut cupboard and throwing open the doors. Tristan did so, watching her assessingly. She seemed awfully comfortable ordering a chap to take his clothes off. And not the least afraid of him. Perhaps there was hope . . .

No. There was no hope. None. *Stop!*

But the devil in Tristan goaded him. "Lady Phaedra, this is frightfully risqué."

She turned about, skirts whirling again. "I beg your pardon?" she said stiffly.

"A gentleman never undresses in front of a lady to whom he's not been properly introduced." Tristan flashed his best shameless grin—the one which never failed to charm.

It worked. A faint glow flushed up her cheeks. "You already know my name, I collect," she said coolly. "What is yours?"

Tristan swept off an imaginary hat, and made her a presentable leg. "Tristan," he said. "Tristan Talbot, ma'am, at your service."

For an instant, she froze. "Tristan?" Lady Phaedra murmured. Then, lifting one shoulder almost imperceptibly, she retrieved a basket of mending from the cupboard and swept across the room toward him. "Pray be seated. I wish to look at your head."

She tilted her head toward a low-backed chair which was turned opposite the bay window, but he was fleetingly distracted. A little yellow garter trimmed with white lace lay atop the neatly folded mending, the little silk rose in its center hanging by a loose thread. He flicked a quick glance up at her, saw her rush of color deepen, and looked back again. *Hers.* Yes, as incongruous as it seemed, the delightful confection was hers. Now that was interesting.

"Just some warm water, ma'am, and a little privacy in which to tidy myself will do," he said more seriously.

"Nonsense," she answered. "You are going to need someone to gently cut your hair and bathe away the blood. And then, I think, a surgeon will be in order. You are going to need a stitch or two to pull the wound together."

"Thank you, but I haven't time," said Tristan. "Besides, I'm sure I've suffered worse."

"You've taken multiple blows to the head, then?" she remarked. "Why am I not surprised?"

"Aye, a great, thick-headed skull like mine is occasionally good for something," he answered, a wry smile tugging at one corner of his mouth.

"Nonetheless, you must be stitched."

"I wouldn't bother," he said. "After all, as you point out, there's probably not much of a brain in there. And all that brawn's likely padding it."

She tilted her head, and eyed him like an irritated governess. "Come now, Mr. Talbot," she said. "One mustn't be a coward."

Tristan laughed. "I'm no coward," he said. "I'm in a hurry."

The lady pursed her lips. "Very well," she said. "Then I shall do it."

That gave him pause. Then, "Fine," he said. "Have at it."

At that, Lady Phaedra faltered a little, and set the basket down.

He'd called her bluff, he realized. "Have you ever stitched anyone up?" he asked more gently.

"No," she admitted.

Tristan shrugged. "I have," he said. "It's no great thing. Have you any brandy?"

Her countenance brightened. "Yes, that might dull the pain, mightn't it?"

"Actually, I meant for you." He looked at her and grinned.

She pursed her lips again, but humor glinted in those keen blue eyes. "Sit," she said as if he were a disobedient mongrel.

Well, what harm was there, really, in playing along? After all, he *had* come to talk to her. And she was dashed pretty in a classic, somewhat rigid way. The door was open, and servants were passing back and forth. Perhaps because of her age—or her demeanor—no one seemed alarmed at his presence in her company.

She was tapping one toe, her gaze pensive. "I'm curious, Mr. Talbot," she said. "Have we met before?"

"I can't think where," he said honestly. He would have remembered those gorgeous eyes. That bedroom voice.

Just then, the footman returned with a basin, a brass water can, and some small white towels draped across his arm. A second servant followed with Tristan's lost hat, now freshly brushed, and placed it top down upon a small table behind the door. The gloves Tristan had so impulsively stripped off lay neatly draped over the rim. When the water and towels were set down, Tristan's coat was wordlessly whisked away—to be shaken and brushed, too, no doubt. Someone had trained the staff very well indeed.

"Mr. Talbot?" his hostess pressed.

"Oh, why not?" he said when the servants vanished. "A chap ought to play his weakened condition for all it's worth, I daresay. After all, a pretty girl's ministrations could hardly go amiss."

At that, her face warmed fiercely. She stabbed a finger at the chair. "Sit, please, with your back to the light."

This time Tristan did as he was told, though he

was loath to give up his vantage point. Lady Phaedra
Northampton had a beautiful blush—the innocent sort of
pinkish rush which started along her cheekbones, then
deepened. The sort of blush which the ladies of his acquaintance were scarce capable of, unless it came out of a
paint pot.

That thought brought home to him again his hostess's
marital status. "Is your mother at home, Lady Phaedra?"
he gently probed. "Perhaps you ought to fetch her."

She stood behind him now, pouring the water into the
basin. "Untie your cravat, please," she said. "Then bend
your head forward, but gently."

He did so, their hands brushing as she reached around
him to unfurl the cravat from about his neck. Her touch
was cool as she unwrapped it, her warmth hovering just
behind his back. She stepped to his side, neatly folding the
linen strip, the center of which was indeed badly blood-
stained, and laid it gently across a chair. Her fingers, he
noted, were long and thin, her nails cut short.

"Your mother, Lady Phaedra?" he repeated.

She returned to tuck one of the towels round his
neck. "My mother is out, Mr. Talbot," she said, stabbing
the cloth round the inside of his collar. "And the door is
open, with servants going to and fro. So if the two of us
remain here together—even given your shocking state of
dishabille—I think I can safely assure you that no an-
nouncement of our betrothal will be forthcoming."

"And you don't even sound disappointed about it,"
Tristan teased as he listened to her wringing out the towel.
"Are you this unaffected by all the gentlemen who come
calling on you, Lady Phaedra?"

For an instant, she hesitated. "Do you mean to mock me, Mr. Talbot?" she finally said, sounding a little breathless. "You are hardly a gentleman who's calling—well, not in the way you suggest. Indeed, nothing could be more ludicrous."

"Ludicrous?" he countered, not even sure why he goaded her. "How you do wound me, Lady Phae— *Ouch!*"

She had touched him lightly with the moistened towel. "You have wounded yourself, Mr. Talbot," she returned. "You were wrestling in the street like some common thug. Some would say you got what you deserved."

"Well, perhaps I am a common thug," he suggested lightly. "But I wasn't about to let that big chap beat the smaller one senseless."

Lady Phaedra kept bathing his wound. Could he but see her, Tristan was sure her lips would have been pursed again. "Now why do I suspect," she finally said, "that you are the sort of fellow who rather enjoys a good round of fisticuffs?"

"And why do *I* suspect," he returned, "that you are a good deal more tenderhearted than you let on? After all, this common thug sits comfortably—*ouch!*—ensconced in your parlor, and you do not know me from Adam, do you?"

Again, she hesitated. "No, but I know a solid gold signet ring when I see one." He could feel little bits of his hair being snipped away at the nape of his neck, but her touch was gentler now. "And, to be perfectly honest, I recognized the Talbot crest whilst you were out senseless."

"Did you, by Jove?" Perhaps that explained why she'd let him in the house. The Talbots—save one—were notoriously high in the instep.

She set her capable, long-fingered hands to either side of his head, the tips of her fingers touching his cheeks. Something soothing and cool seemed to emanate from her touch. He closed his eyes and gave himself over to it, the throb in the back of his head instantly easing.

"Tilt your head a little lower, please," she said, gently urging his chin down. "Now which of the Talbots are you, pray?"

She released her embrace, and Tristan reluctantly opened his eyes. "Ah, now *that* is a part of my reason for being here."

"I can't think what you mean." He heard her dunk one corner of the towel into the warm water again and steeled himself. "Your reason for being *here*?"

"Just so," he said. "My call, you see . . . well, I was coming to call upon you."

He heard her hand stop. "Upon me?" Her voice was no longer soothing, but sharp. "But I do not know you, Mr. Talbot."

"On behalf of my father," he belatedly added. "I know it's irregular, but I thought your mother would be in. My father, the Earl of Hauxton, sent me."

"I . . . I know who Hauxton is." She sounded breathless again, and he wished to the devil he could see her face. "But he does not know me, I do assure you. Moreover, he has but one son."

"Aye," said Tristan a little sadly. "And that would be me."

She came round to stand in front of him, one hand on her hip. She looked a little peevish. "So you . . . *you* are the

Viscount Avoncliffe?" she said. "Why did you not simply say so?"

Avoncliffe, indeed! What a wretched title. It sounded like something out of one of those overwrought novels he saw the ladies whispering over. It sounded silly. Romantic. Besides, he wasn't really the viscount *anything*.

"My reputation precedes me, does it?" he said, vaguely annoyed. But why? He'd earned his black name honestly. "Avoncliffe is just a courtesy title, as I'm sure you are aware. To the people who know me, I am just . . . Tristan."

"How perfectly absurd." But she dropped her fist, and circled behind him again. "In any case, returning to your earlier statement—what could Lord Hauxton possibly want of me?"

Tristan cleared his throat, then winced against the pain. She was blotting the blood from his hair again. "Well, it's like this," he began. "My father is in the Foreign Office, and—"

"Your father *is* the Foreign Office," she corrected. "And the king's Privy Council. And half a dozen other things. Everyone knows that."

"Yes, well, one does not like to presume," said Tristan wryly. "In any case, he's got a bee in his bonnet over that chap who got killed yesterday—I can't explain it, something to do with his being Polish."

"Polish?" she said sharply. "I thought Gorsky was Russian."

"Aye, Russian," said Tristan smoothly. "Whatever the difference is."

"There is a vast deal of difference," said Lady Phaedra

irritably. "Especially if one is Russian or Polish. Now do be still, Mr. Talbot. I have reconsidered my faintheartedness, and decided to stitch you up after all."

"Have you?"

"Yes, I begin to think I should enjoy inflicting a little pain upon you."

Behind him, he heard her rummaging through the wicker basket. "I am sorry," he said, genuinely contrite. "It must have been perfectly dreadful for you. I never thought—and your family—of course they will not wish you to have to think about what you saw."

But in truth, she did not seem like the weak, weeping sort. He looked around, and saw that she was threading a needle with some sort of heavy black thread, but her hand was shaking ever so slightly.

On impulse, Tristan turned in the chair, and set one hand over hers. "I am sorry," he said again. "My father . . . I wish he did not find this necessary. But he does, and he's ill and cannot come himself. I make a poor emissary in his stead, I do assure you."

Lady Phaedra exhaled a little tremulously, and let both hands fall. Tristan did not release his grasp. "It's all right," she said a little wearily. "Now, I am going to take three stitches in this cut, because I know that if I don't do it, you shan't get it attended to at all."

She was right about that, but he did not admit it.

"And when I am done," she continued, "I shall answer all your questions, Mr. Talbot, then send you on your merry way—provided you promise never to trouble me with this business again."

Suddenly, it didn't seem such a bad bargain. A little

discomfort for a few more moments in her company. Besides, pain did not much bother Tristan. He had learned to endure it.

"All right," he said quietly. "If you think stitches necessary."

"I do." She lifted her gaze to his eyes, her expression a little sad. "I'm afraid Mr. Pimkins's blow has cut quite deep. If you are sure you won't see a proper surgeon . . . ? "

Tristan smiled, and turned back around. "I trust you, Lady Phaedra," he said. "I don't think it will be too bad a job. I'm pretty stoic about such things."

True to his word, Tristan sat perfectly still whilst her work was done, hissing through his teeth a time or two, and wincing at every stick. Funny how a chap could get himself bayoneted in the heat of battle and scarce notice the pain, then whimper like an abandoned pup over a darning needle. But the work was soon done, and the scissors and needle restored to their basket. Tristan's freshly brushed coat was returned and draped carefully over the chair from which it had been taken. Then Lady Phaedra asked the footman to fetch tea to, as she put it, "buck him up a bit."

What Tristan really wanted was the brandy, but he didn't say so, and when the tea came, he drank it as if it were the elixir of life, just to please her. She was not smiling back at him yet, but some of the disapproval had lifted from her eyes.

"Now," she said when the saucers were set down again. "I should like to ask you just one thing, Mr. Talbot—is that *really* what you prefer to be called?"

Tristan dropped his voice. "I think I should permit you

to call me anything you pleased, Lady Phaedra," he teased.

The irritated governess look was back. "Very well," she said tartly. "What does Lord Hauxton care about the death of a man he cannot possibly know?"

"Very little, most likely." Tristan waved his hand vaguely. "It is just that there is some diplomatic issue with the Russians—something almost certainly unrelated to this dead man—but my father just wishes to be sure. The Russians might come round asking questions. One of their citizens turning up dead and all that."

Lady Phaedra seemed to accept his answer. "Yes, I see," she murmured, smoothing her hands down the front of her skirts. "What did he wish you to ask me?"

"My father should like to know just what you saw," he said. "Describe it exactly—particularly what the man said and all that."

"Why, he said nothing," she answered. "Indeed, I think he was all but dead when he fell through the door." She proceeded to describe the scene in what sounded like exacting detail.

"Yes, yes, I see," said Tristan when she was done. "And Miss Armstrong, was she there the entire time?"

"Indeed, but she can tell you no more than I," said Lady Phaedra. "Then Mr. Kemble covered the body, and sent us upstairs to his parlor. A policeman came—a sergeant, I believe—but Mr. Kemble wouldn't let him speak to us. I thought the sergeant might come by here later, but as yet he has not."

"No, I believe this matter has been sent down to Whitehall," said Tristan, scrubbing his chin. "Might I ask what took you to the Strand at that time of day?"

"Oh, just shopping," she said swiftly. "Isn't that every lady's favorite pastime? Mr. Kemble owns a sort of curiosity shop—a very elegant sort of place, I might add."

"I see." Tristan would not have taken Lady Phaedra for a lady who shopped for sport. But most of the upper-crust females whose beds he warmed did so. Why should she be any different? "This Mr. Kemble—he is an agreeable sort of man?"

"Well, I don't know quite how to answer that," said Lady Phaedra. "He is a man of strong opinion, certainly. And he has quite good connections, I know, in the Home Office. I believe his friend there, Lord de Vendenheim, has been put in charge of the matter."

Tristan was silent for a moment. He wondered if Lady Phaedra was somehow protecting this Kemble chap—a man who, his father had already informed him, had connections in a great many places, most of them far less savory than the Home Office. After all, it was his back door through which the dead man had come crashing, and in Tristan's experience, there was no such thing as coincidence. No, Gorsky had been looking for someone.

His father would likely send Tristan next to see de Vendenheim—either that, or summon the poor devil up to his sickbed for interrogation. Then again, Robert Peel mightn't wish Hauxton to run roughshod over one of his own. It would not be the first time the Foreign Office and the Home Office had bumped heads.

But none of this was Tristan's problem. Finding no further excuse to linger, he set his hands on his thighs. "Well," he said, rising. "I thank you, Lady Phaedra, for your candor. I hope that your family will not object to our having spoken."

Phaedra rose as he did. "I am of an age, Mr. Talbot, when I am afforded more than a little latitude in what I do and whom I see," she said quietly.

He pulled a chagrinned expression. "Nary a breath of scandal, then?" he said. "You are quite certain no one is going to demand I make an honest woman of you?"

Now why the devil had he said that? The notion was ludicrous, and Lady Phaedra did not look pleased. "Mr. Talbot, pray do not poke fun at me," she said. "I wish to ask you something quite serious."

Tristan sobered his expression. "Yes, of course."

She opened her mouth, then closed it again. For the first time, she looked a little uncertain of herself—and quite breathlessly beautiful. "I wish to know what you mean to do about Mr. Pimkins," she finally said, her hands fiddling nervously with bit of trim on her cuff.

"Mr. Pimkins?" Tristan watched her long, elegant fingers, wishing, oddly, that she still touched him. "Why? What the devil does he want?"

Her lips thinned. "Do you mean to make a complaint?" she clarified. "He was quite careless, it is true—he wasn't aiming at *you*—but he really is not a bad sort."

"Oh, that!" Tristan jerked his gaze from her hands and laughed. "No, no, once one leaps into a mill like that, one must simply take one's licks. I'll heal up quickly enough."

He heard her exhale slowly. "Thank you," she said quietly. "Mr. Pimkins thanks you. He . . . he has a wife and a large family."

Despite her tart tongue, she really had been concerned for the poor devil, he realized. And he supposed, given who his father was, he likely could have had Pimkins's head on a platter. But Tristan had never invoked his father's name for a damned thing, and certainly didn't want to do so now.

Some of her worries eased, Phaedra sent for her guest's horse to be brought round, then watched as Talbot wound his ruined cravat back around his neck, and shrugged into his coat. She felt a little drained. Shaken, perhaps. But what, really, had he learned from her? Oh, he was a handsome, charming devil—and he knew it, too—but from what little she'd heard, the Earl of Avoncliffe was not known for his intelligence. He was a pretty face, and no more. His father must have been desperate to send him.

His attire restored to relative order, Talbot followed her to the threshold. Phaedra stepped slightly behind the door to pick up his hat from the table where Stabler had left it. But when she turned back, she realized he had pushed the door half shut and followed her. In the small, confining space, he stood so near she could smell a hint of soap and something like bergamot swirling in his enticing male heat. Her heartbeat ratcheted up. Awkwardly, she handed him the hat.

"I fear you are going to have a bit of a bald spot near your nape, Mr. Talbot," she managed. "I—I had to cut some of your hair off."

I had to cut some of your hair off? As if he would not have noticed her snipping at it! Suddenly, Phaedra of the sharp tongue and even sharper vocabulary felt on the verge of stuttering. Tristan Talbot was watching her with a strange new glint in his eye.

"Well, then," he finally said, "there is but one more thing I should like to do."

"Yes?" The word came out breathlessly. "What?"

He held the hat behind his back now. "I should like to thank you properly," he said. "Or perhaps I should say *im-properly*?" And with that, he leaned in to her and set his mouth to hers.

It was a sweet, ethereal thing, hardly a kiss at all. His lips, smooth and pillow-soft, settled gently over her own. His eyelashes lowered in a sweep of soft black fringe.

The room stilled, and for an instant, there was just the two of them on earth. Phaedra stood stock-still, something bottoming out in her stomach, then bursting into a faint warm heat as his mouth lingered, almost molding over hers. That a man so uncivilized could be so tender—oh, the sweetness of it sent her reeling.

Then just as suddenly, it was over. He drew back, the ever-present grin upon his face, the mischievous twinkle back in his eyes. Save for his lips, Talbot had not even touched her. Nonetheless, Phaedra stood there like the veriest idiot, swaying ever so slightly on her feet.

"There," he said quietly. "Let that be a lesson to you."

She felt her face color. "A . . . lesson?"

The man had the audacity to wink at her. "It's never safe for a pretty girl to be alone with an arrant scoundrel," he said. "Even a slow-witted one such as I. But I thank you, Lady Phaedra, for your kindness—and for that most memorable kiss. I think it will warm my heart for a day or two, at least."

Then he stepped from behind the door, and started down the hall. Jerking herself into motion, she darted after him. His hat tucked neatly under his arm, Talbot was pulling his gloves on as he went striding through her house, acting very much as if he owned it.

He was right, she told herself, watching him. He was nothing more than a charming rapscallion with a handsome face. There was no need to sway on one's feet. It was hardly enough of a kiss to warrant a good slapping. Besides, she had invited it. Something about her—something wrong, and all too apparent—had assured him he could get away with it. Still, she was angry.

She stepped before him, yanked open the door, and shot him one last chiding look. "I would box your ears, sir, if I thought it would do a bloody bit of good," she said, her voice low and tremulous. "Now good day to you, Mr. Talbot."

To her consternation, Talbot threw back his head and laughed. "Lady Phaedra!" he said. "What shocking language!" Then he dashed down the stairs whistling, his long, limber legs so steady one would never have guessed he'd taken a stupefying blow to the head.

But then, as if to torment her, he hesitated on the last step. With his gloved hand still resting along the wrought-iron railing, Tristan Talbot turned back, some dark, inscrutable emotion sketching across his face. "Just one last question, Lady Phaedra, if I might?"

"Have I any choice?"

His eyes snapped to hers, suddenly black and utterly

penetrating. "The dead man," he said quietly. "You called him Gorsky."

The mood had shifted ominously. Phaedra felt her heart still. "Did I?" she answered too sharply. "But is that not his name?"

"So it is." There was nothing of the laughing rogue in him now, just a grim, almost lethal seriousness. "But who told you?"

She hesitated a heartbeat too long. "I . . . why, my brother, I believe," she lied.

His black gaze cut through her, keen and quick as a carving knife. "Are you quite sure of that, my lady?"

"I . . . yes, quite."

He held her eyes ruthlessly, and she dared not look away. "I see," he finally said, his voice dangerously soft. "Good day to you, then, Lady Phaedra. I thank you for your time."

He turned, and Phaedra felt her knees sag. She had the sudden sense of having badly misjudged something. Of having seen, perhaps, only what he wished her to see—an unsettling thought indeed. Just then, something to the left caught her eye, and she noticed the slight, dark figure standing on the pavement below. "Miss Armstrong!" she said in some surprise.

"Hullo, Phae." Zoë looked up at Mr. Talbot almost coquettishly. "And Avoncliffe!" she murmured. "Bleeding again, I see. But still alive."

The man doffed his hat. "Much to the disappointment of my enemies," he said, bowing. "Miss Armstrong, you are looking well."

"I ought to," said Zoë dryly. "I haven't anything else to do, have I? So, are you and Phae friends?"

Talbot turned back to Phaedra and winked. "I am not perfectly sure," he said, his mood light again. "Phae? *Are* we friends?"

Phaedra ignored him. "Mr. Talbot called to ask some questions on behalf of his father," she said, coming partway down the steps. "About what happened yesterday."

"Did you indeed?" said Zoë cryptically. "How interesting."

"Yes, but we're finished—for now." Talbot took his horse's reins from the approaching footman. "What are you about, Miss Armstrong? Some sort of mischief?"

"No, I've come to ask Phae to a card party," she said. "My cousins and I are having a few friends over Thursday evening. Nothing too exciting."

"Nonetheless, with you at the helm, it will be the social event of the season," Talbot teased.

Zoë's gaze shifted to Phaedra appraisingly, then back to Talbot. "Are you still living in that bolt-hole over in Long Acre, Avoncliffe?" Her voice was laden with boredom. "I shall ask Aunt Winnie to send you a card, though the wagers will run a bit dull for your taste."

"You are all generosity, Miss Armstrong," he said, laughing. "Yes, I am still living in my humble abode. Now, lovely ladies, much as it goes against my grain, I fear that I must leave you."

"Oh, what nonsense." Zoë went up the steps past him. "From what I hear, Talbot, you have a whole gaggle of lovelies awaiting your attentions."

His grin deepened, and then Talbot made another sweeping bow to Zoë. "Miss Armstrong, might I call upon you—and your aunt, of course—tomorrow?" he asked more seriously. "Would one o'clock be too early?"

Now at Phaedra's side, Zoë pressed the back of her hand to her forehead. "Lud, the scandalous Lord Avoncliffe calling upon me!" she declared. "Aunt Winnie is like to faint." She dropped the hand and the sarcasm. "Yes, come round if you must—but make it two. I shall try to be up."

"Two it shall be, then."

In the street, Talbot's mount was already beginning to wheel her hindquarters impatiently, her velvety black nostrils wide and puffing. It was awfully big and awfully black, Phaedra noticed, not for the first time. But then, there must be a hundred such horses in London, mustn't there? It had been so dark that long ago night, and she so frightened. She had not worn her spectacles, and he—well, he had been utterly foxed. But she had heard a name. Not Talbot, though. And not Avoncliffe. She wracked her brain, but nothing came.

And it scarcely mattered. The horse wheeled to the right, and Talbot went with her, swinging himself up into the saddle effortlessly. He lifted his hat one last time, and in a bolting clatter of hooves, he was gone.

Chapter 4

I will upon all hazards well believe
Thou art my friend that know'st my tongue so well.

"Oh, my!" said Zoë, following Phaedra back to the parlor. "Lord Avoncliffe! Delicious to look at, is he not?"

"Is he?" said Phaedra vaguely. "I did not notice."

"What a liar you are, Phae!" Zoë slid out of her cloak without invitation. "I say, I hope you don't mind my sneaking over to see you," she continued. "It's dull as ditchwater across the way, and I wondered how you were after yesterday."

"Oh, no, I'm very glad to see you," said Phaedra honestly. On impulse, she gave Zoë a swift hug. "My mother and sister are out, though."

"Excellent," said Zoë, her eyes glittering. "Then we can talk—about Avoncliffe, I mean. He's far more exciting than any old murder."

"Is he?" Phaedra smiled, smoothing her skirts as she offered a seat. "But you seemed perfectly bored to see him."

Zoë flopped across the settee. "Well, I have a reputation to maintain," she said, draping one hand limply off the back. "The dead-bored debutante, perishing of ennui. And after three seasons, it's pretty near the truth." Suddenly she sat up straight again. "By the way, why was his cravat all bloody?"

Phaedra explained, keeping her voice as nonchalant as possible.

"Oh, Lud, that sounds like Avoncliffe!" Zoë rolled her big brown eyes. "He has frightfully rough edges—something ladies of the *ton* seem simply mad for."

"He did seem more brawn than brain," Phaedra answered. "How well do you know him?"

Zoë had begun to play with one end of her cashmere shawl. "Oh, well enough to know he's a scoundrel," she said. "I met him, I daresay, through my cousins. They run with a raffish sort of crowd. Which is not to say Avoncliffe is never seen in good company—he is occasionally, but just long enough to get what he wants."

"A womanizer, of course." Phaedra had begun to chew pensively at her thumbnail. She really did wish the man had not kept calling her *pretty* in that deep, rumbling voice of his.

"A womanizer, and perfectly brazen about it." Then Zoë hesitated as if a thought had just popped into her head. "I do hope, Phae, you did not see him alone?"

Phaedra jerked her thumbnail away. "He was bleeding," she protested. "I had the door open the whole time."

"Oh." Zoë pondered it. "Well, I hope he minded his manners. He's a very bad man, that one, but Aunt Winnie says he's a frightfully good kisser."

Phaedra lifted both brows. "And she would know?"

Zoë cut her a sly glance. "You'd have to ask Aunt Winnie," she said. "She might well. I do know there was a frightful row over him at a masque in Belgravia last season. Lady Holding and Mrs. Butler nearly scratched each other's eyes out in the ladies' retiring room. Avoncliffe is hotly in demand, if you know what I mean."

Good Lord. Phaedra felt suddenly out of place again, as if Zoë knew the secrets to the universe, and she was still hopelessly naïve. Zoë cut a glance at the door, then turned round again. "They say he's part Gitano—a sort of Gypsy—and part Sicilian," she continued in a conspiratorial whisper. "And Aunt Winnie says his mother was a flamenco dancer. Do you know what that is?"

Phaedra felt her eyes widen. "*Lord Hauxton* married a flamenco dancer? So Talbot's what? Spanish *and* Sicilian?"

"And God only knows what else." Zoë lifted a shoulder lightly. "Of course one does wonder if it's true," she admitted. "But I don't care. My mother was a dancer, too—and a bit of a mongrel. Whatever he is, I think I should rather like him to kiss *me*. All that black hair and warm skin—he looks so deliciously wicked."

Once again Phaedra felt her face flood with heat.

Zoë was looking at her strangely. "What?" she said innocently. Then she hesitated again, eyes widening. "Oh, no!" she breathed. "Phae, he *didn't*—?"

Phaedra's blush deepened. "Oh, my word!" said Zoë, sliding forward on the settee. "*Did* he kiss you? Why, the gall of that man! You are not the sort of girl a man like that kisses."

For an instant, Phaedra turned her face away, shame washing over her. *Zoë couldn't see it.* The ugly truth was, she was exactly that sort. She was wrong, somehow—dark inside—and some men sensed it. Some could see what she tried so hard to hide. The raging emotion that threatened to consume her. But Tristan Talbot—he seemed different, somehow. His kiss, at least, had not been lascivious, precisely. More . . . *playful.* "No, we are different, Zoë, you and I," she whispered.

But Zoë had cut her gaze away, her chin dropping. "Yes, you are the kind of girl a man marries," she said, her voice uncharacteristically quiet. "I am the kind they try to kiss in a dark corner."

"Oh," said Phaedra softly. Zoë, it seemed, was the naïve one here.

Zoë shrugged away the moment. "So, if I am to be kissed, Avoncliffe looks like a good bet." She looked up again and smiled. "But there! You kissed him first, Phae. Just do be careful, please? I think he really is a decent sort, but he can be perfectly dangerous."

"It wasn't really even a kiss, Zoë," Phaedra confessed. "It was a just *peck.* The merest little thing. Besides, I really mustn't see him again."

Zoë laughed. "Oh, I think I see intrigue in your eyes!" she said. "Have you any experience with men?" When Phaedra did not answer, and merely stared down at her clasped hands, Zoë leapt from her chair. "Come on, let's go for a walk in Hyde Park. I want to show you something."

Phaedra suddenly welcomed the offer. Perhaps fresh air would rid her head of Tristan Talbot's intriguing scent.

She sent a servant scurrying off for her cloak and bonnet, and in short order, she and Zoë were going back down the front steps, Agnes trailing dutifully behind.

While they walked, Zoë talked of her many seasons in Town, and of her father's increasing frustration that she was not wed. At the end of it, she sighed. "What of you, Phae?" she asked. "Does your family not press you?"

Phaedra shook her head. "They do not," she said quietly. Then, after a time, she continued. "Zoë, have you ever been in love?"

Zoë hesitated. "I thought I was," she finally said. "But he became haughty and high-handed and, like a bad case of the 'flu, I got over it. What of you, Phae?"

"I was in love once," Phaedra confessed. "Desperately. Foolishly. But I was young and it . . . it did not end well."

Sympathy sketched across Zoë's face. "Oh, Phae, I am so sorry," she said, catching Phaedra's hand and squeezing it hard. "What happened?"

Phaedra could not bear to tell the whole of it. "He died," she said simply.

"Oh." Zoë's voice was quiet. "Oh, my poor dear. Do you miss him still?"

Somehow, Phaedra lifted her face to the sun. "No," she answered, drawing in the warmth. "No, but I cannot yet bear to speak of it. Not . . . all of it. Forgive me?"

"What is there to forgive between friends?" Zoë flashed a weak smile, and hooked her arm through Phaedra's. "Even new ones such as us?"

"Thank you, Zoë."

They walked on in silence, arm in arm now. The warmth of the day was just beginning to wane, and the

scent of spring was in the air. Along the street, an open
carriage sped past, a barouche filled with elegant ladies
and gentlemen. The horses' hooves clopped briskly as they
flew, requiring one of the ladies to seize hold of her very
fetching pink straw bonnet. They were dressed for spring,
Phaedra realized, glancing down at her drab skirts. The
season was truly upon them, and for the first time, Phaedra wondered if she had made the right choices with her
life. People like Zoë Armstrong and Tristan Talbot seemed
so full of life, and happy with what they were. So certain
of their own emotions. Why wasn't it thus for her?

They reached the park, and Zoë followed the edge of
the Serpentine Pond, idly chattering. At Hyde Park
Bridge, however, all pretense of seriousness vanished. Zoë
plunged into the shrubbery, her eyes alight, dragging Phaedra by the arm. "Come, let's hide in here."

Phaedra cast Agnes a staying glance, and followed. Zoë
was up to some sort of wickedness. Deep within the shadows sat a bench. Zoë drew Phaedra down beside her, extracted a cheroot case from her skirts, and thumbed open
the lid. "Look what I have!"

"Zoë!" Phaedra sniffed it as Zoë drew it beneath her
nose. "Do *ladies* smoke those?"

"Why shouldn't we?" Zoë stuck it in her mouth and
struck a vesta on the bench.

"My word! Where did you get it?"

"From my cousin," she said round the cheroot. "Lord
Robert Rowland."

Phaedra knew she should have been scandalized, but
the emotion seemed beyond her. In the last two days, she'd

seen a man murdered, kissed a handsome scoundrel, and befriended a little gamine as wild as Phaedra was proper. Now she found herself merely wondering what a cheroot tasted like. "Lud, Zoë, but you are a corrupting influence," she muttered.

"I am, aren't I?" Puffing on the cheroot until her eyes watered, Zoë settled back onto the bench with a little cough. "Now," she said. "I simply *must* hear all about Avoncliffe's kiss. Precisely how did he go about it? And did he steal it? Surely he must have done?"

"He stole it." Phaedra felt suddenly lighthearted, rather like a schoolgirl. "I was handing him his hat. I didn't know what to do."

"Not to worry!" Zoë waved her cheroot airily. "I shall advise you."

"You are very kind, I'm sure," said Phaedra, "but as I said, I don't mean to see him again."

"But he might turn up at my card party," Zoë complained. "Then where would you be? No, you'd best let me help you. Next time it mightn't be just a peck. You'll want to be prepared."

"Well, I certainly shan't kiss him again, Zoë."

Zoë tossed her a disparaging glance, and passed Phaedra the cheroot. "Have you any notion, Phae, how the ladies of the *ton* vie for his attentions?" she whispered. "Believe me, there's scarcely a female in London who wouldn't like have Tristan Talbot's tongue in—" Here, she had the good grace to stop and blush. "Oh, I do apologize. I have been eavesdropping on Aunt Winnie too often."

"Yes, and you just said he shouldn't have kissed me at

all," Phaedra reminded her, still pinching the smoking cheroot.

"Try it," Zoë encouraged, "but don't inhale!"

Phaedra took a tentative puff, then blew out the bitter smoke on a cough. The truth was, she was embarrassed by her response to Talbot's kiss. She understood, logically, that women threw themselves at men like him. And she understood too well that men—most men—would take what they could, and never feel a modicum of guilt. Perhaps she was no better. The rush of emotions Tristan Talbot had reawakened in her today were about as welcome as a case of smallpox—and about as useful. She passed the cheroot back to Zoë, and looked away.

"You will come to my card party, will you not?" Zoë pressed. "Oh, do say you will."

Abruptly, Phaedra turned to face her. "There is something you should understand about me," she said quietly. "I—I am not like you, Zoë. I am not much accustomed to society."

Zoë looked at her in some surprise, then blew out a plume of curling white smoke. "Phae, you are hardly young," she said. "No, don't scowl at me—you are just a little older than me, I know—but what I'm saying is, surely you must have been to balls and dinner parties?"

Phaedra shrugged. "A bit, yes, but I never really . . . came out," she admitted. "I mean, there was no ball. No sparkling white dress. I just . . . it just wasn't what I wanted. I do go about in society sometimes. To musicales and literary readings, mostly."

"Literary readings?' Zoë drew back, aghast. "You poor, poor girl."

"It's what I want," she said again. "I like to read. I enjoy music."

"You poor, poor girl," Zoë repeated. "You have a vast deal of catching up to do. You are missing the exciting bits."

"What, the pretty, dimwitted scoundrels like Talbot? Or whatever his name is?"

"With a face like that," said Zoë, flicking the ash off her cheroot, "who cares if he's possessed of a brilliant mind? But listen to me, my dear. That one is a little dangerous. Do not mistake good humor for stupidity. Now, about the season—"

"It scarcely matters, for I do not care for the whirl of society," Phae interjected, kicking a small stone near her toe. "I do not go to balls and parties. I am not interested in marriage."

Zoë looked at her incredulously. "Lud, who mentioned marriage?"

"Is that not what the season is for?"

"Not to me!" Zoë laughed. "I've done everything I can think of to avoid marriage. Just ask Papa. No, going about in society is to meet people, you gudgeon."

"To . . . meet people?"

"Yes, and to laugh and be gay," Zoë added. "And to torment the men just a little, perhaps?" Here, Zoë paused to bat her long black lashes. "I mean to enjoy life, my dear. I suggest you do the same. One can always say *no* to a marriage proposal. I've done it half a dozen times."

"Oh."

Phaedra sat in silence for a time as Zoë took one last puff, then knocked the ash from her cheroot and restored it to her case. "Phaedra, listen to me," said Zoë, fleetingly solemn. "You mustn't let an old tragedy blight the present. Get out in the world. Have some fun."

Phaedra considered it. Socializing just for the pleasure of it? Flirting with men to torment them? *That* sounded dangerous. Fleetingly, she wished to return home; to retreat into the safety of her parlor and her books. She desperately feared another kiss from Tristan Talbot. She did not like the sensations his mouth sent shivering through her body. That awful swell of something churning and thwarted inside her. It brought back the shame, and reminded her yet again that she was not all that a lady should be.

Suddenly, Zoë leaned nearer. "Honestly, Phae, you could just *slay* men with those brilliant blue eyes of yours," she said, her voice low. "Just think of it—you could break a heart or two just for sport."

"Zoë, I . . . I cannot."

"Pish!" said Zoë. "They deserve it—most men, anyway. The nice ones, well, just avoid them. That way, no one gets hurt."

But people *did* get hurt. Hurt in ways no one could foresee, or ever repair. Phaedra knew that firsthand. Nonetheless, she contemplated Zoë's words as they strolled back through Mayfair. The truth was, despite her fears and failures—or perhaps because of them—there was a part of her that had begun to long for a little excitement. Just now, however, she had more pressing concerns. But perhaps . . . perhaps she should accede to Stefan's wishes. Perhaps she should buy those new gowns after all. She was no longer sure. She did not trust herself enough to choose—not even such a small, foolish thing as a new dress.

Half an hour later, Phaedra said good-bye to her new friend, leaving her at her front door across the street. Zoë waved good-bye, her smile sunny as ever.

Inside, Stabler took Phaedra's cloak and hat, and informed her that her mother and sister had retired to rest before dressing for dinner. The evidence of their afternoon's activity still sat by the front stairs—a tower of bandboxes and what looked like four bolts of fabric carefully wrapped in brown paper.

"She wished me to remind you they are to dine with Lady Henslow and her daughter," Stabler explained. "Your mother begs you will reconsider joining them."

"Thank you, but I cannot," said Phaedra hastily. "I mean—I have some reading to do. Urgent reading. Indeed, I do not wish to be further disturbed this evening."

"Of course, miss." The footman gave a slight bow. "I shall inform her ladyship."

"Thank you, Stabler." Phaedra felt suddenly swamped with fatigue. "I shall be in the parlor."

Phaedra returned to stand behind the chair in which Talbot had sat, its back still turned to the bay window. Was it her imagination, or did his warm, clean scent still linger there?

Agnes followed her to the doorway, then hesitated. For the first time, Phaedra noticed her unease. She turned to fully look at her. "What is it, Agnes?"

The maid's hands were clasped rigidly before her. "I did not get a chance to tell you, miss," she said quietly. "I had a letter in the afternoon post."

Phaedra's hand clenched the back of the chair. "From your great-aunt?"

"Just so, miss. I'm sorry. There was no news at all of Millie."

"Nothing?" But Phaedra saw the answering sadness in Agnes's eyes.

The maid shook her head, and let her chin fall. "No, miss," she answered. "Nary a word."

"What of Priscilla?" she asked hollowly.

"Aunt Kessie says Priss is a handful." Agnes's eyes had brightened. "But she cut another tooth. And she does not ask for her mother quite so often now."

"Oh, Agnes," said Phaedra sorrowfully. "I'm not at all sure that is a good thing. And your aunt is too old for this."

Phaedra left the window and sank into one of the worn brown armchairs. Her walk with Zoë Armstrong had been a pleasant diversion. But here, alone in the parlor, real life had already begun to intrude, and the full weight of their trouble was sinking back in upon her. In her mind's eye, she could still see little Priscilla, her plump hands fisted, her blue eyes pooling with tears. It wrenched at her heart to think of a child—any child—motherless. Priss was too young to understand why or where her mother had gone. Phaedra didn't understand it, either. It was the ultimate mistake—the ultimate sin—to abandon one's child. It was, perhaps, unforgivable.

"Are you going up to Soho tonight, miss?" Agnes's words cut into her consciousness.

Phaedra looked away, blinking back the hot press of tears. "Yes, though I don't know what good it will do," she answered. "I shall go as soon as it gets dark. If anyone should knock on my door—"

"Yes, miss," Agnes interrupted. "I'll make a lump with the pillows, and tell them you've a headache."

Phaedra bit her lip nervously. Yes, Agnes knew exactly what to do, she reassured herself. They had been at this for weeks now. So long, in fact, that she really was feeling quite desperate.

Phaedra clenched her hands so tightly her short nails dug into her palms. Damn it, it was just like Tony to be away from home at such a time. As usual, he had created a crisis, and left someone else to deal with it. Usually the job of salvaging Tony and his political career from impending ruination fell to Stefan. But Phaedra did not dare dump this tragedy in Stefan's lap. The last contretemps he had extricated Tony from had nearly ruined the both of them—and at a time when Stefan had at last met the woman of his dreams. Now he had a child to love and another on the way. He was finally happy.

No, there was no possible way she could allow this to fall on Stefan's ears. Besides, he might well throttle Tony this time. Slowly she rose from the chair. "I am going upstairs to try and get some sleep," she said to Agnes. "Wake me when it is dark, will you? And bring me your cloak and another dress—your dark blue, I think, fits me best."

Still wringing her hands, Agnes bobbed. "I will, miss," she said quietly. "And thank you."

The woman at the desk slammed another drawer, this time so hard a figurine fell from the adjacent shelf, shattering. The door sprang open at once, and the pale, broad-shouldered man who entered bowed, then stared down at the shards of fine Bohemian porcelain.

"Madame, what has happened?"

Her hand shaking with rage, Madame Vostrikova yanked open the topmost drawer and stabbed a finger at it. "The sphere, Lavrin." She spoke in staccato Russian. "What has become of the sphere? Tell me, for God's sake, that you have it."

His eyes widening, the man hastened behind the broad mahogany desk, and began to rip open the drawers for himself.

"You waste your time, Lavrin," she said, staring down at the back of his head. "And what is worse, you waste mine."

Lavrin opened the bottom drawer and stood, horrified. "It is gone!"

"My God, yes, it is gone!" Madame rolled her eyes. "This is Gorsky's work—that faithless bastard!"

"But Madame—" Lavrin folded his hands and stepped back, just out of her striking distance. "Madame, his rooms were searched."

She turned on him, quivering with rage. "Then search them again!" she said hoarsely, stabbing a finger at the ceiling. "Rip up the floorboards if you must."

Lavrin winced. "Madame, it will not be found there, I tell you," he insisted. "Perhaps he . . . he took it elsewhere?"

"Don't be a fool, Lavrin," she retorted. "He didn't know anyone. And after the boy was sent north, Gorsky was always followed and he spoke to no one."

"Perhaps, Madame, he took it with him that morning?"

"It would have been found." She shook her head, her ice-blond hair catching the sunlight. "When they searched him, it would have been found. It would have been brought to me."

Lavrin puffed out his cheeks. "*Da*," he said hesitantly, "if there was time."

She whirled on him, incredulous. "*If* there was time?" she said. "Do you mean to suggest, Lavrin, that I hired an assassin who did not take time to search the body for incrimination?"

Lavrin lifted both hands, palms up. "I do not know it for certain, Madame," he said. "But yes, it is possible."

Madame thrust a bejeweled finger in his face. "Then you will find him," she said to him. "You will find him, Lavrin, and you will ask him. And if this bumbling fool has allowed my sphere to be lost—*then you will kill him.*"

"Yes, Madame," he whispered.

She rammed the bottom shut with her shoe, causing Lavrin to jump. "And what of those girls?" she snapped. "Have we their names yet? Something? Anything?"

Lavrin drew back another inch. "Our source at Bow Street says they saw nothing," he said soothingly. "Even the papers contained no mention."

"So they are from influential families," said Madame pensively. "Their names have been hushed up."

"Or they saw nothing," Lavrin said again.

At that Madame sneered and slammed the top draw shut with a resounding crack. "My dear Lavrin," she answered sourly. "After a dozen years in this business, can you still be so very naïve?"

That night, a light fog rolled in off the Thames, settling over London like a gossamer shawl—albeit a shawl which stank of low tide and was tinged with coal smoke. Phaedra drew her chair as near to the window of her rented room in Soho as she dared, and peered through the fly-specked glass at the town house across the street.

All the windows were lit, some more brightly than others, as they had been every night she'd sat in this squalid little chamber. And yet she saw nothing. Save for the occasional messenger or servant, no one came. No one went. Indeed, she sourly considered, for such an infamous whorehouse, business seemed remarkably slow. Frustrated, Phaedra drew a handkerchief from her pocket, and scrubbed at the dirty glass as if the effort might reveal something of the house's secrets. A sudden knock at the door jolted her upright.

"Yes?" She was annoyed to hear her voice waver.

"Thompson?" The rough female voice was not especially warm. " 'Tis Tuesday, dearie."

Phaedra rose from her rickety wooden chair. "Aye?"

"If yer means to stay on, there's the rent to be paid," the voice reminded her.

Phaedra snatched the worn leather purse Agnes had lent her, and threw open the door. Mrs. Wooten, the lodging house owner, squinted at her through the gloom, a stub of a tallow candle held high. "One shilling three pence," she said, extending a knobby hand. "If yer stayin'?"

"Aye, another week, mum, if you please," said Phaedra, trying to sound like Agnes as she pressed the coins into Mrs. Wooten's palm.

The old woman fingered them for a moment, then, apparently satisfied, dropped them into her pocket. "That'll do nicely, dearie," she said, glancing up. "Yer found work, I hope?"

Phaedra set the purse away. "Aye, in a millinery," she lied. "In Piccadilly. The pay isn't much—but I can afford to stay on here."

"Odd hours for a milliner, in'it?" Mrs. Wooten remarked.

But the old woman looked disinterested, and Phaedra did not explain. Mrs. Wooten had made it plain when the impoverished widow Mrs. Thompson had let the room weeks ago that she wanted only the rent—paid in full, once a week—and cared little enough where the money had come from.

"Mrs. Wooten," said Phaedra as the woman turned to go, "I was just wondering . . ."

"Wot?" Despite the gloom, suspicion glinted in her eye.

Phaedra motioned toward the window. "That fine, big house across the way," she remarked. "Who lives there?"

"Now why would yer be arskin'?"

Phaedra shrugged. "The windows are all lit up late into the night," she answered. "Yet no one comes or goes. So I just wondered at it."

"Curiosity kilt the cat, din'it?" said the old woman sagely. "I'd stop wondering, if I were you. The doings wot goes on there is none o' my business, and none o' yours, if you're sharp."

"I see." Phaedra stepped back from the door. "Well, thank you, Mrs. Wooten. And good night to you."

Unexpectedly, the old woman's face softened. "If yer makin' a living on your back, lovie, it's naught ter me," she said quietly. "But yer don't wants ter do it there, awright? Keep ter the streets. 'Tis a good deal safer."

"Oh." Phaedra pressed her hand to her chest. "Thank you, Mrs. Wooten. I did not realize."

The woman's expression further relented. "Don't know much about the place, meself," she admitted. "But I knows a lot o' fine carriages come and go—through the back lane, dearie. Not the front. And a lot of pretty girls gets dragged out o' that house and put in them carriages—and some of 'em don't want ter go and don't never come back. So keep ter the streets, awright?"

The back lane. The carriages went through the back. What an idiot she had been!

Phaedra tried to look contrite. "Thank you, Mrs. Wooten, for warning me."

She shut the door, and turned to survey the narrow, tawdry room. She had wasted precious time confined in this dark garret, a chamber so low and so small it would not have held her mother's wardrobe. She returned to the window and craned her head as far to the left as she dared. Even without her spectacles, she could make out the street corner, and the shadow, perhaps, of the back lane beyond.

On impulse, she snatched Agnes's cloak, put out the lamp, and went out and down the steps. Shivering against the damp, she crossed the street, darting around a hackney cab and into the narrower side street almost opposite her window. For a time, the cobbles shone in the faint gaslight. Soon, however, soaring walls loomed up on her left and right, oppressively close, shutting out the air and what little light there had been. It was this—the sense of being entombed by brick and mortar—she most hated about London.

Phaedra turned left into the darkness, moving gingerly along the back lane. She discerned the rear of Mr. Gorsky's brothel by drawing her hand along the garden wall, counting off the gates as she went. Through the faint light which spilled from the windows, she could see the yard behind was long and narrow, without garden embellishments of any sort. The gate stood open and Phaedra could smell the privy just inside it.

Just then, the back door swung wide. A stout woman wearing a white smock came out of the house swinging an old-fashioned lantern in one hand, and a bucket in the other. She trudged down the path, hung the lamp on a peg, and stepped up into the privy to empty her bucket. Phaedra crept round the gatepost, keeping just to the shadow's edge.

"I beg your pardon," she said as the woman came out.

The servant whirled about, eyes wide. The privy door slammed behind her.

"I beg your pardon," Phaedra repeated. "I . . . I was looking for work. As a servant, I mean. In the house."

The woman just shook her head.

"Might there be a place vacant?" Phaedra pressed. "Or someone I might speak with?"

The woman's hand went fleetingly to the collar of her dress. Then she snatched her lamp from the peg, and darted back up the path again, leaving the bucket behind.

Phaedra's shoulders sagged as the door thumped shut and darkness fell over the garden. The woman was even less helpful than Gorsky had been. Indeed, she had been perfectly terrified to speak. Perhaps Gorsky should have been so terrified . . .

Phaedra shuddered. She was increasingly certain the dead Russian had been watching her, perhaps looking for an opportunity to speak with her alone. But why? The day she had so boldly—and foolishly—dropped the knocker at his brothel's front door, the man had denied any knowledge of a flame-haired Hampshire servant girl who might be working within the house. Indeed, it was as if Millie had come to London, entered the house, then vanished from the face of the earth.

Perhaps she had.

No, thought Phaedra, jerking herself up short. She would not give up. Millie might be a naïve country girl, but she had grit. She was a survivor. Phaedra had to get inside that house somehow. It was the only possible way to find her. But perhaps, as Mrs. Wooten had warned, Millie had been one of the unfortunates who had gone out the back way, and not come back in again.

At that dreadful thought, Phaedra shuddered again, and backed slowly into the alley. A hard, unyielding presence caught her up short. Her scream was muffled by a hand slapped firmly over her mouth. A strong arm lashed round her waist, dragging her into the pitch black of the opposite wall. Her voice muffled, Phaedra flailed desperately.

"Shush, don't scream," rumbled a warm, husky voice. "I mean you no harm."

Phaedra fought like a wildcat then, throwing back an elbow while doing her best to stomp upon his toes. The man chuckled deeply in her ear and swung her around, forcing her chest against the brick. "Hold still, for God's sake." The rumbling voice was gentle and—had she not been too panicked to realize it—oddly familiar. "Just listen."

"No! Let me go!" Phaedra shouted, but the words were muffled against his hand.

With a grunt, the fiend shoved a long, hard-muscled leg between hers, pinning her. Phaedra's palms were flat against the damp brick. She could feel the broad wall of his chest against her back, and the cuff of his boot scrubbing her inner thigh. The heat of his body pressed against her, searing her length. Angrily, she thrashed again, then somehow got her mouth open and bit down hard. Leather gloves saved him from the worst of it, and he did nothing but chuckle again.

"Why, you little vixen!"

"Fiend!" she cried into the leather. "Help! Help!"

"Stop shouting and I'll remove my hand," he offered. "Just tell me what you know about that house. That's all I want. Just information. I heard you speaking with that servant."

His mouth was warm against her ear, stirring the loose strands of hair at her temple. The scent of hot, aggravated male surrounded her; a hint of bergamot and male perspiration. A familiar, enticing scent.

Oh, Lord. Surely not? Against her better judgment, Phaedra stopped struggling. His weight sagged against her as the tension left his body. "Very good," he said quietly, "I shall remove my hand. Be so good as to tell me what you know about that house."

"N-n-noffink," Phaedra croaked, trying to mimic a Cockney accent. "Just arskin' for a bit o' scullery work, I was."

"Scullery work, eh?" Phaedra realized in some embarrassment that his other hand all but grasped her left breast. "Now why do I not quite believe that?"

"Believe wot yer please."

His mouth was still at her ear, his nose almost buried in her hair, and Phaedra's fear was melting into something more treacherous. He drew a deep breath. "By God, you don't smell like any scullery maid I ever met."

"Filled your 'ands wiv a few, 'ave you, gov?"

Throwing back his head, her assailant laughed richly. And that was it. Phaedra was certain.

Please, please, please, she silently prayed. *Don't let him guess.* "Let go!" she protested, wiggling more desperately. "Let go! I tol' you wot I knows."

"Let go?" he murmured. "That's a hard task, love, with a handful of ripe breast and that plump little arse of yours wiggling against my nether regions."

Phaedra went instantly rigid.

His lips skated down the turn of her neck. Phaedra shivered. "Are you sure, my dear?" he murmured. "There's something about you I can't quite—"

"Let me go!" she interjected. *"Now."*

"Ah, well," he murmured, his grip relaxing. "The lady demurs. Another time, perhaps?"

She shifted to slip away, but made the mistake of casting a wary glance at him, as if she might see through the pitch black night. He must have felt her turn and laughed again, catching her mouth with his. It began teasingly, almost innocently. But in an instant, it shifted, his lips moving hungrily over hers, his hand coming up to fully grasp her breast.

Almost against her will, Phaedra opened beneath him, eliciting a deep groan from him as he thrust inside. This was no stolen peck behind the parlor door. Their tongues tangled and stroked, causing a heat to well up from Phaedra's belly, all the way to her throat. His palm rolled over her breast, cradling it as his erection began to swell in earnest against her backside. He made a soft sound of pleasure in the back of his throat, then fleetingly lifted his mouth as if to speak.

Phaedra seized her chance. She jerked from his grasp and bolted—not from him, but from herself—running down the alley and into the side street as fast as her legs could go. And all while she knew that he was allowing her to escape. Oh, yes. With those long, hard-muscled legs of his, had Tristan Talbot wished to catch a woman, she would never have stood a chance.

Chapter 5

※❦※

Speak, cousin; or, if you cannot,
stop his mouth with a kiss,
and let not him speak neither.

"Eliza says that to catch a proper husband, one must master watercolors." Snaring her lower lip between her pearl-white teeth, Lady Phoebe Northampton leaned forward to dab at her canvas horizon with her brush. "There!" she said, leaning back again. "The perfect fluffy cloud, is it not, Miss Armstrong?"

"The whole thing is perfect," said Zoë appreciatively. "With that kind of talent, you shall doubtless land yourself a duke before the season is out, Lady Phoebe."

Phoebe laughed, her cheeks blushing prettily. She had always been able to blush on cue, her sister noted—unlike Phaedra, who seemed to blush over the most seemingly insignificant things, and at the worst possible moments.

They sat in the back garden of Tony's house, the late afternoon having turned shockingly warm and sunny. Zoë Armstrong had provided a bright spot in Phaedra's day by dropping by again unexpectedly—this time to hand deliver the invitation to her card party, and to make the acquaintance of Phaedra's mother and sister.

Now, a full hour after her arrival, the Dowager Lady Nash was still looking at the card. "Well, I cannot think what's best, Miss Armstrong," she chirped. "Phoebe and I are engaged to dine with friends. To permit Phaedra to come alone as you suggest . . . oh, I just do not think . . . ."

Zoë Armstrong slid forward on her garden chair and looked at Lady Nash plaintively. "But it is quite informal, ma'am," she wheedled. "Just a silly group of young people to play a few hands of cards. And we are just across the street. Wait—I have an idea."

"What?" asked Phaedra suspiciously.

She, too, was torn. Such frivolous entertainments were not for her. But there was something in Zoë Armstrong's attitude—her rather refreshing view of life—which struck Phaedra as liberating. Infectious. Something that made Phaedra wonder if perhaps she had made a mistake in letting life overlook her. Perhaps marriage and a so-called normal existence were not life's only options. Oh, she had long told herself that. But Zoë Armstrong seemed to live her conviction—and to get away with it.

She returned her attention to Zoë, whose bright smile still shone upon her mother. "The three of you must come to call beforehand, Lady Nash," she suggested. "We shall have a cup of tea. Afterward, Aunt Winnie will keep a watchful eye on Lady Phaedra. She is the most frightful dragon, I do assure you. Nothing untoward will escape her notice." Then, with mischief in her eye, Zoë turned to Phaedra and winked.

Phoebe laid down her brush with a clatter. "Oh, let her go, Mamma," she said, turning from her easel. "Phae needs to get out of the house before she turns into a piece of furniture—a footstool, most likely."

Suddenly, Phaedra jerked to her feet. She was rather alarmed to find herself almost excited by the prospect of Zoë's card party, an excitement which had more to do with Zoë's guest list than was strictly wise. Fleetingly, she closed her eyes, still able to feel the strength of Talbot's long, lean body pressed to hers. The searing heat of his hand on her breast. Dear God. She must be quite mad.

"I do not know, Zoë," she murmured, her hand settling lightly over her abdomen. "I . . . I haven't anything to wear."

"Wear my new pink silk," Phoebe suggested, snapping shut her paint box. "It's too long for me anyway, and too low, Mamma says." This last was added with a disparaging glance at Lady Nash.

"You are a debutante, Phoebe," her mother protested. "And the neckline is far too daring. I can't think where my mind was to have let you order it."

Phoebe shrugged and stood. "Then Phae might as well have it," she said equivocally. "I've a dozen more anyway. Come upstairs with us, Miss Armstrong. You must see if it will do."

"No," said Phaedra two minutes later in Phoebe's bed-chamber. "No, this isn't right for me. I prefer gray. Or brown."

"Oh, I *love* it." Zoë whispered the words almost reverently.

Of course Zoë loved it. Her wardrobe was dashing.

Zoë was dashing. Phaedra was not. And yet, when she looked down at the shimmering pink silk draped across her arm, Phaedra longed for a bit of adventure. The pale fabric looked almost opalescent against her ivory skin, and the high waist was encircled by a wide satin ribbon in a daring shade of green.

"You must have it," her sister declared. "You can wear the pink sapphire necklace Nash gave you for your twenty-first. It is to die for, Phae, and you've never even had it out of the box."

"No," she repeated, letting it slide onto the bed in a crush of fabric. "I . . . I cannot. My figure—it is too ample. This is too revealing."

"Nonsense!" declared Zoë, snatching it up again. "Phae, it is perfect! You will be quite the most striking lady present."

Phaedra looked at her in confusion. "Why are you doing this, Zoë?" she asked quietly.

Still clutching the gown, Zoë folded her arms across her chest, and let her gaze trail down Phaedra's white chemise. "Because I have decided, Phae, that you are to be my project this season," she said musingly. "You are going to save me from expiring of my terminal ennui."

"Ah, is that it?" said Phaedra dryly.

"No, not all of it," Zoë admitted. Then she hesitated. "Phae, are your breasts bound under that shift?"

Phaedra colored furiously. "They just need smoothing out, that's all."

Phoebe giggled. "She thinks they are too large, but they're the same as mine."

Zoë shook her head and made a *tsk* sound. "What nonsense," she said. "Unwrap that frightful rag at once. Now, listen. I have a tidbit of fascinating news to share."

"Indeed?" Phaedra eyed her suspiciously. "Of what sort?"

"The *very* fascinating sort." Zoë fanned her face with her empty hand as if overheated. "The wicked Lord Avoncliffe sent his acceptance this morning. It seems *something* about my silly little party has intrigued him. Now will you please try on the dress? And the necklace. What about those spectacles? Must you absolutely wear them?"

"Only for reading, but she won't admit it," said Phoebe, leaping from the window seat from which she'd been observing. "Now who is Lord Avoncliffe, Phae? How did you meet him?"

"He is no one," said Phaedra. "And yes, I need my spectacles."

"Oh, he's someone," Phoebe sang, "and I'm going to tell Mamma."

Zoë looked down her nose. "Really, Lady Phoebe," she murmured, her tone as haughty as a duchess. "I should have thought you more grown up than that. After all, what is a season in Town without its little intrigues?"

Phoebe hesitated. "Oh, well . . . yes, I daresay." She flashed Zoë a conciliatory smile. "And Phae only wears the glasses to make herself appear smarter than the rest of us."

Phaedra surveyed them both with steady eyes. "That is not hard to do when you both are so very silly," she said. "And there is no intrigue. Lord Avoncliffe is a handsome gentleman who thinks far too well of himself. Moreover, I can't think why it matters what I wear."

"Because we all wish to see something besides gray with that marvelous hair of yours," Zoë urged.

It was on the tip of Phaedra's tongue to refuse her, and to do so with the tart-tongued gracelessness she generally reserved for people who meddled in her business—in other words, Mamma and Phoebe. But she said nothing. It had been a long time since Phaedra had had a friend near her own age—one who could match her in wit and intellect—so she was loath to disappoint Zoë.

Moreover, there was a second, more troublesome reason for her hesitation. Phaedra turned her face to the shaft of afternoon sun which spilt through the window and looked at the garden beyond. The feel of Tristan Talbot's full, soft lips upon hers was not yet a distant memory. And last night—the taut, barely-leashed strength in him. His spicy-clean scent teasing at her nostrils and the warmth of his mouth near her ear. Phaedra closed her eyes as the dreamy, seductive listlessness began to melt through her again.

Oh, foolish, foolish girl! Had she not learnt her lesson long ago?

Apparently not.

Apparently, she had not changed at all. Her passions, it seemed—those foolish fantasies and that dark, unseemly hunger—still lurked just below the detached demeanor she had so carefully crafted these last few years. Phaedra's will was little more than a façade, and one which was destined to crack, it would now appear, at the merest blow. A kiss. A tiny, teasing kiss from a scoundrel who would likely never wish to kiss her again. And yet this knowledge—this shameful certainty—could not stop her from yearning to be an utter fool.

"Phae, please," Zoë gently pressed. "Take Phoebe's dress. We are friends now, are we not?"

Phaedra turned back, draped the dress carefully across her arm, then lifted her gaze to Zoë and Phoebe. "Thank you both, then," she said quietly. "I shall take it."

For the third time in as many days, Tristan Talbot found himself rigging out as a proper gentleman, then digging through his old jewelry case. Uglow watched wordlessly as Tristan again slid the heavy signet ring onto his finger, then helped him into his coat.

Tristan looked down as his hand slid from the sleeve. The chunk of gold seemed to weigh down his hand much as he was weighed down by duty, and by the hope that this time, in some small way, he would not fail his father.

As much as he hated to admit it, there was a part of him that felt challenged for the first time in a long while. There was the vaguest sense of purpose stirring inside the void which constituted his conscience, rather like an acorn rolling about in an empty ale keg. And yet there it was, clattering round and round, the sound not entirely unwelcome.

"Shall I 'ave the gig brought round, sir?" Uglow's deep voice sounded as if it had risen from a tomb—a tomb in Whitechapel, of course.

"Just my stick, old boy," said Tristan, giving his cuffs one last tug. "I think I shall walk."

Perhaps, he considered as he set off, the spring air would clear his head. His morning had been spent with his father again, and with chasing ghosts, or so it felt.

In the past several days, he had had meetings with both

the young ladies who'd witnessed the murder—the former of which had been almost disconcertingly memorable, if not useful. For her part, Zoë Armstrong had wanted only to tease, and to talk of Lady Phaedra, a topic Tristan would as soon have avoided.

Following that, he'd interviewed three separate members of the Metropolitan Police. His nights had been spent lurking about Madame Vostrikova's and discovering all he could about her notorious establishment. All of it had been to no avail, unless one counted the sweetly chaste kiss he'd stolen from Lady Phaedra behind her parlor door. He still had a dead Russian on his hands, and no one knew anything. No one had seen or heard anything. Even worse, perhaps, no one cared.

No one save his father. And his reasons were not precisely altruistic.

Perhaps Lord de Vendenheim, Peel's man in the Home Office, cared? Tristan was about to find out.

The walk to the Travellers' Club was less than a mile beneath high, blue skies. Gossamer clouds scuttled across Westminster, whilst beneath the sun's glory, everyday London went about its business. Tristan set a steady pace along the choked streets, his rarely used walking stick in hand.

The Travellers' Club was not a stodgy sort of establishment in the style of Brooks's or White's Club. It was a place for adventurers and men who had seen a little of the world. A great many foreigners belonged, thus the club boasted one of the best libraries in London, along with newspapers in half a dozen languages. The food was decent, the coffee notoriously strong, and the billiards tables level. Cards, of course, were played all night. It was perhaps the one small slice of London society in which Tristan did not feel out of place, and though he rarely visited, they never failed to remember him.

In Pall Mall, he entered the cool, shadowy depths of the club's entrance hall and handed the stick over to the elderly porter who greeted him.

"My lord." The servant bowed.

"How do you do, Fleming?" Tristan passed him his hat. "I'm looking for a chap named de Vendenheim. Can't say as I know him."

Fleming motioned toward the morning room. "The vicomte is alone at a table by the windows, my lord," he said. "A very tall, very dark man. You cannot miss him."

Tristan thanked him and went in. Fleming was right. De Vendenheim was a man one noticed. He was taller, even, than Tristan himself, and almost as dark. Observing Tristan's approach, he snapped shut his newspaper and came at once to his feet, unfolding himself with an elegant grace.

He was not, however, an especially elegant man upon closer inspection. His clothing, Tristan noted with approval, was of good quality but hardly fashionable. His long, olive face had a cast as foreign as Tristan's, with hard cheekbones accented by a pair of dark, hooded eyes which looked deeply cynical. The newspaper, too, was foreign. Italian, Tristan thought, glancing at it.

He extended his hand. "Good afternoon, de Vendenheim," he said. "Thank you for coming."

"Had I any choice, given who your father is?" The words were not accusatory, merely blunt.

Tristan's smile was muted. "No more choice than I, I daresay, when he bade me look into this wretched business," he answered, sweeping his hand toward a table. "Shall we sit, sir? Perhaps have some coffee?"

De Vendenheim's eyes were grim. "At least it's strong here."

Tristan sent one of the servants off to fetch a pot, then sat, stretching out his booted legs. "Owing to my father's health," he began, "I had little choice but to accept his request to help him in this matter. I should like you to understand that. Though what, precisely, I'm to do thus far escapes me."

De Vendenheim was studying his face. "I'm given to understand you worked reconnaissance for a time in Greece," he remarked. "I daresay Hauxton thinks you have something to offer."

Tristan laughed, but it was cold and flat. "I was a mercenary," he corrected. "I made war for sport—or helped to make it—because I was young and idealistic, and it seemed like an exciting life."

Something bleak and knowing passed over de Vendenheim's visage. "Ah, I see," he finally said. "And did you find it so?"

Tristan looked away. "For a time, I suppose," he said. "War always sounds exhilarating to those who have not seen it firsthand. It always sounds . . . so bloody noble."

"And instead it is merely bloody." De Vendenheim's mouth twisted. "In that, sir, we do agree. I have most assuredly seen it firsthand, and do not care to do so again."

Tristan surveyed his tight countenance. "Napoleon," he guessed. "You are from the Continent, I collect."

"Alsace, amongst other places," he said, sorrow softening his hard black eyes. "But there is little left of the Alsace that I remember."

The moment was weighted by a shared understanding, and with a poignancy Tristan had not felt in a long time. Sharply, he cleared his throat. "Look here, de Vendenheim, I don't mean to cause any trouble for you fellows at the Home Office. I think I can manage my father. But part of the problem is that he's sick—or more honestly, he's dying. And for a man with his sense of duty, the powerlessness which the end brings is almost more than he can bear."

"I'm sorry. I did not know." De Vendenheim seemed to relax, his shoulders rolling almost imperceptibly forward. "Well, go on. What did you wish to ask?"

Tristan relaxed into his chair as the servant returned with a silver tray. "I've already spoken to the Metropolitan Police and the two young ladies who witnessed the death," he said, observing as the servant tipped the pot and lifted it high, filling the cups expertly. "If you'll just tell me what you've learnt of this dead chap, I'll be on my way."

De Vendenheim took his cup, then mechanically repeated much of what Tristan already knew. Gorsky was a Russian who had been in England for many years. He lived in a flat in the rear of one of Vostrikova's houses, had no family, and was widely believed a homosexual which, given his profession, made a perverse sort of sense.

"Yes, I've managed to learn a bit about Mr. Gorsky's brothel myself," said Tristan. "I gather the sort of clientele they attract prefer not to be seen entering the front door."

A ghost of a smile touched his lips. "They are also not

the sort of clients who will welcome your father's interference," he said. "The house caters to the kind of perversions most men would rather keep secret."

"Like what?" asked Tristan flatly.

De Vendenheim turned his hand palm up, a gesture of resignation. "Flagellation," he admitted. "Sodomy. Bondage of all types. Young girls—and more recently, boys, too. Unimaginable cruelty, in some cases."

Tristan knew all this, of course, but he'd wished to have de Vendenheim confirm it. Nonetheless, hearing it recited aloud made him wince.

De Vendenheim shrugged. "It is not for me to judge the depravity of other men's sexual appetites," he said, "so long as no one unwilling is involved. But the madam who owns the brothel is said to be able to procure anything on a whim—anything needed to tempt the jaded palates of her wealthy customers. And that has the stench of *un*willingness about it."

Tristan sipped at his coffee. "I saw two fine unmarked carriages pull through the back lane whilst I watched the place last night," said he pensively.

"While you *watched*?" Anger sketched across his face. "I hope to God you weren't seen."

Tristan lifted a steady gaze. "My dear fellow," he said quietly, "there's not a chance in hell."

De Vendenheim looked at him for a moment, then nodded tightly as if acknowledging his opponent's skill. "I trust you were not, then."

"The carriages stopped but an instant," said Tristan, resuming his tale. "Both times, women were bundled out the back door and into the carriages. One of them appeared hunched forward beneath her cloak, and there was something . . . something in her posture." He set the coffee down again and looked at de Vendenheim very directly. "I wondered, frankly, if she were bound."

De Vendenheim's jaw hardened. "I do not doubt it," he gritted. "I fear a dead man in the Strand will be the least of this foul business before all's said and done."

"What do you know of the proprietress?"

De Vendenheim appeared to sneer. "Her name is Vostrikova," he said quietly. "Lilya Vostrikova. I've tried like the devil to find her, but they claim she's away at her country house in Bordeaux."

Tristan returned his gaze to de Vendenheim. "My father tells me Madame Vostrikova was once thought to be a spy," he said, "and that she came to London with Czartoryski, the Russian statesman."

"Yes, but he's a Pole," said de Vendenheim meaningfully. "And just now, trouble is brewing in Poland and Russia is not happy. Czartoryski is stuck in the middle of it."

Tristan had eyed an unusual knot in the woodwork of the tabletop, and was absently circling it with his fingertip. "Trouble is always brewing in Europe," he said noncommittally. "Which reminds me—do you not find it interesting that this dead man somehow found his way to one of the very few people in London who has a connection to Russia?"

De Vendenheim lifted his angular black brows. "Kemble, do you mean?" he murmured. "Certainly he has business associates there, and knows a little of the language. But what does that suggest?"

Tristan's finger stopped in midmotion. "Actually, I meant Lady Phaedra Northampton."

"Lady *Phaedra*?"

"Indeed." Tristan watched him steadily. "Do you know her?"

"I do," he said stiffly. "The lady is a paragon of virtue."

"But her half brother, Lord Nash, is Russian, is he not?"

"I . . . why, yes," de Vendenheim admitted. "In part."

Tristan could sense the man's hesitance. "Wasn't Nash mixed up in that French scandal over gun running to the Greek revolutionaries a year or two back?" he pressed. "I daresay *that* got Russia's attention."

A deathly silence fell across the table. The man's face had gone black as murder. "I should like to know, Lord Avoncliffe, just who you have been speaking with," said de Vendenheim icily. "This is not a topic to be bandied about in club rooms."

"Oh, I am not *bandying* it," said Tristan, his voice equally cold. "I am stating it as a fact. I know he was in Paris. I know he spent weeks meeting with the French authorities. And I know, Lord de Vendenheim, that a great deal of Greek money changed hands in that misbegotten deal."

"And *I* wish to know who told you all this so that I can relieve him of his employment." De Vendenheim looked as if he were about to pound his fist upon the table. "This is a serious business, you fool."

Tristan leaned very slowly into him. "I fear you forget yourself, my lord." His voice was lethally soft. "And you forget that I have contacts—close contacts—all over the

Hellenic Peninsula. Indeed, I have watched their sons and their brothers die in the mud and the blood of Greece. I do not need some insignificant English bureaucrat whispering drawing room tittle-tattle in my ear."

De Vendenheim drew back, his gaze lowering. "Your pardon," he said stiffly. "Again, I forget your past."

Tristan inclined his head. De Vendenheim realized he had misjudged his adversary. People often did that, he had noticed. It was his appearance, perhaps—he had been cursed with boyish good looks. Or perhaps it was his mongrel lineage, or his less-than-serious attitude about life.

Whatever the cause, Tristan was often thought something less than brilliant, and indeed, he was often perfectly stupid, but not in the way people generally believed. *Esse quam videri.* That was his motto.

"Are you going to answer my question, de Vendenheim?" he asked calmly.

"As you wish." The man glowered across the table. "Lord Nash is part Russian, but he has no contact with the government and scarcely any family. A couple of elderly cousins, both of whom have one foot in the grave. You may trust we looked into it. Yes, he did go to Paris, but as . . . as a sort of an emissary of the Government. If you do not believe me, you may ask Mr. Peel. Or your father, perhaps."

He was lying. Tristan realized it at once. And yet not wholly lying, either. Tristan watched him warily for a moment, judging his next move. "Very well," he finally said. "You believe the two young ladies were just innocent bystanders?"

"I do."

"And your associate, Mr. Kemble?" asked Tristan. "He was innocent, too?"

De Vendenheim gave a bark of laughter. "God, no," he said. "Kemble wasn't even born innocent. But in this matter . . . yes, I believe him above suspicion."

Tristan smiled, and pushed away his coffee cup. He wasn't sure he believed it. "Well, it would seem Mr. Gorsky had the remarkable misfortune to be simply in the wrong alley, leaning on the wrong door, at the wrong time," he said, rising. "Rather a bad streak, if you ask me. But you, however, are in luck."

De Vendenheim sounded unimpressed. "How is that, sir?"

Tristan extracted his pocket watch. "I am about to be late to a card game," he said, looking at it. "A very important card game."

He looked up to see that de Vendenheim had pinned him with a hooded *why-am-I-not-surprised* stare.

Tristan tucked his watch away, bade his companion good evening, and headed toward the door, whistling. Behind him, de Vendenheim snapped his newspaper. "By the way, Talbot," he said, just as Tristan's foot touched the threshold. "We pulled a dead man out of the river last night."

Tristan turned. "Is that something new?"

De Vendenheim shrugged. "This one was," he answered. "The River Police found a note in his pocket written in Russian—and a very nasty slash across his throat."

Aunt Winnie, the Dowager Lady Nash soon learned, was Mrs. Weyden, a rather merry widow who was not, as it happened, anyone's aunt, but rather an old family friend of Lord and Lady Rannoch. The marquess was a hard-edged, rather unsociable Scot with more money than Croesus and enough temper to match. Lady Rannoch had given him two children with a third on the way, and had brought two young siblings and an orphaned cousin into the marriage.

In addition, Mrs. Weyden had two sons whom Zoë Armstrong also accounted as relations. And somewhere in the picture, Zoë had explained, was an elderly uncle, Sir Hugh, upon whom she doted. Zoë had grown up with a large, rather raucous family, something Phaedra rather envied.

Lady Nash, of course, had begun to dither over the entire business by early evening. "Dear, dear!" she clucked as they started down the steps. "Mrs. Weyden is said to be a little *outré*, Phaedra. And Miss Armstrong—well, there is the unfortunate mystery of her parentage. Indeed, this mightn't be quite the thing."

"It is too late, Mamma," Phoebe warned, lifting her hems and stepping onto the pavement. "Besides, Miss Armstrong's father *is* a marquess. And if Lord Rannoch trusts Mrs. Weyden to chaperone his daughter, she must be quite nice."

"It is too late," Phaedra agreed, almost wishing it were not. "Besides, the whole affair will be a dead bore, I am sure."

This was madness, she thought as Lady Nash dropped the knocker. Not the fact that she was attending a simple card party. Phaedra was not a complete recluse. No, the madness was this dangerous, wholly irrational sense of euphoria. An almost girlish giddiness which seemed to lift her from her slippers. Moreover, an evening spent in frivolity was an evening *not* spent looking for Millie. Phaedra had not fully considered that before accepting Zoë's invitation.

Mr. Talbot likely would not turn up, but if he did, perhaps she might learn something from him pertaining to Gorsky? And that might help find Millie. The thought consoled her, but only slightly.

They were politely received into a small but fashionable parlor by Mrs. Weyden. The room was decorated in shades of deep red and yellow, not in the French fashion, but in a darker, heavier style which Phaedra thought might be Dutch. A bombé commode chest with an ornately carved cornice and ball feet dominated one wall, while bowls of flowers seemed to be everywhere. It was a room which was at once foreign and pleasantly inviting.

Zoë made a pretty curtsy to Lady Nash, and thanked her again for allowing Phaedra to keep her company for the evening. Tonight Zoë wore shimmering gold, a confection of lace and ruching which was cut square across the neckline, with full sleeves to the elbow. She looked especially small and dark—like a porcelain doll—and utterly charming.

After exchanging half an hour of pleasantries, Lady Nash and Phoebe floated out the door, and as so often was the case, Phaedra was forgotten. Phaedra did not mind. Being forgotten about, she had learned, allowed one a measure of freedom. Sometimes a dangerous measure.

Zoë drew Phaedra into the withdrawing room where the card tables had been set up. Servants were already scurrying in and out with trays of crystal and platters of refreshments, and one of the housemaids was mixing lemon juice into a massive silver punch bowl. She was eyeing the arrangement almost gleefully. "I have a notion, Phae," she whispered. "If the cards are too dull, we shall roll back the rugs and waltz! You do dance, do you not?"

Phaedra smiled lamely. "A little, but very ill," she said. "Country dances, mostly."

"Oh, a country dance won't do." Zoë was drifting about the room, nibbling at the various refreshments. "Avoncliffe will wish you to waltz with him—especially in that dress."

"Zoë, pray do not be silly." Phaedra shifted uncomfortably.

Zoë spun around, a sliver of cucumber pinched delicately between her fingers. "Oh, he will," she said confidently. "Besides, I think the waltz should be the only dance allowed. Avoncliffe is famous for it, by the way. Yes, he will certainly ask you. Indeed, I believe he might be bewitched by you, Phae."

Phaedra rolled her eyes. "Oh, he's nothing but a handsome fribble, Zoë," she chided. "You cannot believe him serious."

"Oh, I don't know." Zoë closed the distance between them. "When he came to call on me yesterday, he asked a score of questions about you."

"About *me*—?"

A mischievous smile curled Zoë's mouth. "Of course I dared not mention any of it in front of your mother and your sister."

"What sort of questions?"

Zoë cast her eyes upward as if pondering it. "Let's see, he asked how long I'd known you," she answered. "How did the two of us come to be shopping together. That sort of thing. Oh—and Lord Nash. He seemed most interested in the fact that Nash was your half-brother."

Phaedra hesitated. "What can my brother have to do with anything?"

"I couldn't say." Zoë shrugged. "By the way, is it true Lord Nash is Russian? I did not know."

Phaedra instantly stiffened. "Stefan's mother was related to the Russian royal family on one side," she acknowledged. "But her father was Montenegrin. Stefan was born there. It is his home—after England, of course."

"Oh, then that's not quite the same thing, is it?" Zoë snapped off one end of the cucumber between her flawless white teeth.

But Phaedra's mind was working furiously. What bearing could Stefan's background possibly have on the Foreign Office's investigation? Surely Talbot did not think Stefan was involved? Good Lord. Nothing could be further from the truth. Horror flooded through Phaedra—horror that swiftly turned to irritation. By God, she would not have Talbot dragging this mess to Stefan's doorstep. That was precisely what she had striven to avoid. What she *had* to avoid.

A quarter hour later, the drawing room was swimming with guests, most of whom were soon drinking champagne, and all of whom seemed to know one another well. It was a shockingly boisterous crowd, and certainly not drawn from the highest echelons of the *ton*.

Phaedra wanted, inexplicably, to see Tristan Talbot again. Perhaps if she did, she could convince herself that she had been right about him all along; that he was just a handsome ne'er-do-well of no special significance. And that the kisses they had shared had meant nothing. Still, there was a raw, unrestrained sensuality in him that called to the deepest, most hidden places in her soul, to those feelings she wasn't sure she wished ever to feel again.

Mrs. Weyden had returned to stand by the door and greet everyone—not with a smile or a curtsy, but by kissing both their cheeks in a most familiar way. Zoë lifted one shoulder. "She lived a long while in Flanders," she whispered by way of explanation. "I think they must kiss like the French there."

To her acute discomfort, Phaedra sensed it the moment Tristan Talbot entered the room. It was not a sort of raised-hackles awareness—though perhaps it should have been—but more of a shimmering, disconcerting warmth. She was standing by the piano with a glass of lemonade, chatting with one of Mrs. Weyden's sons, when a faint stillness settled over the room, as if all eyes had turned toward the door.

Phaedra, too, turned. The awareness sharpened, piercing and acute. Their gazes met, and Talbot's hand—engaged in passing his elegant, gold-knobbed stick to the footman—froze. A look passed between them; something swift. Heated. A bolt of raw desire shot through Phaedra, utterly unexpected.

And then the moment passed. He cut his glittering gaze away. The murmur of the crowd resumed, if indeed it had ever paused. By the fireplace, someone laughed. Crystal tinkled on a tray. Talbot bowed elegantly over Mrs. Weyden's hand, then lifted it to his lips, making her titter almost nervously.

Phaedra felt instantly shaken. *Heated, indeed!*

Dear God, what a goose she was. Had she no moral compass at all? To feel such lust for a man one hardly knew and didn't especially like. Her mother was doubtless right. Lust was a wayward, shameful emotion, something true ladies did not feel. Brothels like Mr. Gorsky's existed for a reason. Gentlemen, Lady Nash had once said, might need to taste a little sin from time to time, but they did not wish to come home and converse with it over the dinner table. No man would ever wish to wed a woman who could scarce control her own passions.

But despite all this well-remembered advice, Phaedra could not suppress a surreptitious glance in Talbot's direction. He was striding across the room on his long, muscular legs to greet Zoë. Indeed, he had scarcely seen Phaedra at all.

Somehow, she turned back to Augustus Weyden and brightened her smile. "You were telling me, Mr. Weyden, of your life in Ghent," she said. "How often are you there?"

"Half the year, thereabouts," he answered, setting a light hand under her elbow. "It is something of a Mecca for painters, and we are a family of artists, you know." He paused to gesture across the room with his wineglass. "Come, Lady Phaedra, I see my brother has just arrived."

Phaedra passed the next hour going mechanically through the motions of making idle conversation, offering her hand to those gentlemen whom she did not know, and curtsying when appropriate. Her manners, she knew, were flawless. Lady Nash's flightiness notwithstanding, she understood what society demanded of a marquess's daughter, and had ruthlessly instilled it in both of hers. But all the while, she watched Talbot.

The man drew people like bees to a field of clover, she noted peevishly. The older women, a trio of Mrs. Weyden's friends, hovered about him for a time, flirting and fanning a little too furiously. When he gave them no encouragement beyond his beaming, sideways grin, they drifted away one by one, their void filled by a knot of fashionable young men. They surrounded Talbot like a litter of fawning puppies, almost tumbling over one another in their efforts to angle for his attention.

Mr. Popularity, she thought a little sourly. Yet another thing she and Talbot would never have in common.

A raconteur of noted skill, apparently, Talbot was soon holding up both hands, palms out, and laughing until he at last gave in to their pleadings for some sort of story. The small crowd was soon near stitches as the tale—something to do with runaway horses, a pack of foxhounds, and a half-naked magistrate—built to its crescendo. From time to time, his booming, good-natured laughter would ring out, and Phaedra would be unable to stop herself from turning to look once again.

It should be against the law, really, for a man to be so unnaturally handsome.

But was there any harm in looking? All the other females in the room were; the young ones surreptitiously, the older ladies almost avariciously. Talbot's skin was like warm honey, his hair a dark mass of unruly waves which would have looked unfashionable and far too long on any other man.

Above his sinfully full lips, his cheeks were smooth and lean, giving over to high, perfect cheekbones, putting Phaedra in mind of some sleek, sensuous Sicilian prince— not that she'd ever seen such a creature. His jaw was a hard angle, and a pair of thick, inky eyebrows rose to an arch near their ends, almost as an afterthought.

Only his nose saved him from perfection. Hawkish and arrogant, it was Lord Hauxton's, beyond question. Had anyone questioned Talbot's paternity, that nose could have hammered a nail in the coffin of doubt. Somehow, Phaedra managed to turn away and distract herself by chatting with another of Zoë's friends, a Miss Miranda Reesdale, a rather plump, pretty lady who seemed amiable enough. Nonetheless, she was almost relieved when Zoë called for the card playing to commence.

Suddenly, Phaedra felt a warm, heavy hand settle lightly at the small of her back.

"Is it too much to hope, Phae, that we might pair off?" someone murmured in her ear.

Phaedra turned to look over her shoulder. "I beg your pardon?" she managed, forcing herself to ignore the surge of heat against her spine.

Tristan Talbot grinned down at her, sending more warmth instantly to her cheeks—and to some other places as well. "The two of us," he said again. "Might we partner?"

But she was looking at him in stupefaction, somehow distracted by his thick, black eyelashes, which were impossibly long, and by his mouth as it moved to form the words. *A harlot's mouth,* she thought. Full, beautifully sculpted lips that settled over you like butterfly wings. And oh, how she wanted it.

But he had a lean, hard warrior's body to go with that lush mouth, she reminded herself, and the insidious ability to seem far more benign than he was. She must be careful. She must not gaze too long upon that mouth, and let her mind wander. And yet, that plump, sensuous swell in the middle of his bottom lip was so—

"Lady Phaedra?" he repeated. "Have you a partner for whist?"

The card game. "I . . . no, th-thank you," she stuttered. "I am engaged to play with Mr. Upjohn."

Talbot's hand did not move, but instead made a warm— and entirely inappropriate—little circle at the small of her back. "Lucky devil," he remarked, his gaze drifting over her face. "Ah, well. Another time, perhaps?"

Another time, perhaps. The same words he'd spoken just two nights past, his body pressed to hers in the alleyway. The words he probably spoke to every winsome woman who turned him down. If any of them did.

Suddenly, a flash of certainty struck. Yes. That long-ago night in the tavern . . . She was quite certain now, though it had been dark, and he had been battered and bloodied. Drunk, too—and yet oddly chivalrous. Was she forever destined to keep bumping into the infernal man in dark, dangerous places—and, in truth, be thoroughly charmed by him? Still, she could ill afford to turn to mush now. "Pray take your flirtations elsewhere, Mr. Talbot," she said coolly. "You have no rapt audience here."

The irrepressible smile deepened. "Ah, perhaps not," he

acknowledged. "But even a big dumb ox likes a challenge now and again."

"Kindly take your hand from my spine before someone notices." Her voice was quiet and a little unsteady. "Really, Mr. Talbot. Or Lord Avoncliffe. Or whoever you are. I am not a challenge to you. I am not . . . anything to you."

"You are a most remarkably beautiful woman to me," he countered. "That pink gown, by the way, is simply stunning, and the greenish ribbon is a dashing touch."

"Thank you," she said stiffly.

"But I think I like you best in gray, and with your spectacles sliding down your nose." He leaned into her, and dropped his voice. "You look so very stern and disapproving. Like a repressed governess looking for a wayward pupil to punish."

Phaedra's eyes widened. "I beg your pardon?"

"I could volunteer," he murmured, his grin widening—if such a thing were possible.

Her eyebrows snapped together. "Volunteer for what?"

He gave a speciously innocent shrug. "I cannot say," he admitted. "It is very hard for a wayward pupil to choose his own punishment. There are so many to consider."

"I could slap your face," she suggested tartly.

"That wasn't the part I had in mind," he answered.

"Nonetheless, it strikes me as ideal," she answered. "Really, Mr. Talbot. I am a lady. I am not supposed to have an earthly clue what you are talking about. Kindly allow me to at least feign innocence, and go ply your naughty wares with one of those ladies who looks eager to buy them."

He lifted his perfect, angular eyebrows. "I can be

cheaply had," he offered, eyes sparkling. Then he sighed. "You are perfectly right, I know. I should pretend. But you are no green miss, Phae—I don't know how I know that, but I do—and you're no fool, either."

No green miss.

He could not know the blow he had struck her, however true his words might have been. Talbot saw. They all saw—once they got close enough. It was why he had dared to kiss her to begin with.

Good God. Her imagination was running wild. Phaedra drew in a steadying breath. "You presume to know me very well, sir, upon one short meeting."

"Ah, but it was one short, *memorable* meeting," he countered. "In fact, not one instant of it has escaped me. Tell me, Lady Phaedra, why do you not have a husband at your age?—not that I'm offering, mind—it would never do. Still, a man does wonder."

Phaedra set her head to one side and studied him for a moment. "Does it never occur to anyone of your sex, I wonder, that perhaps there are women who simply do not wish the annoyance of a husband?"

His eyes widened in surprise, then just as quickly fell again. "Explanation accepted," he said swiftly. "Which rather clears the decks for me, since I find you so charming to flirt with."

Phaedra let her gaze fall to the floor. "Flirting can be a dangerous business, Mr. Talbot," she said. "Not for you, perhaps. But for me. Now kindly excuse me."

And on that, she walked away, abandoning him to the now-empty corner. Her hands, however, were shaking. That cursed, inevitable question. Even from the likes of

Talbot, whose morals certainly left no room to suspect hers. And flirting? Good heavens, she did not flirt.

The other guests were now milling around the card tables as Zoë organized who was to sit where. Phaedra and Mr. Upjohn were seated with Miss Reesdale, who, Phaedra learned, was betrothed to Mr. Upjohn's elder brother, who was not present tonight. She was partnered instead by another of Zoë's distant relations, Lord Robert Rowland, a young man known vaguely to Phaedra as something of a scoundrel—and the source of Zoë's illicit cheroots.

Like Tristan Talbot, Lord Robert was too handsome for his own good. He flirted outrageously with both she and Miss Reesdale, and kept leaning just a little too near them, his voice a little too solicitous. Phaedra found herself able to ignore him. *He was just a handsome man.* A boy, really. He would not weaken her will or her knees or any other part of her body simply by sharing a card table with her, and engaging in a little harmless flirtation. He was not Tristan Talbot, who—Phaedra was beginning to suspect—ran deep and still and dark beneath his patina of aimless charm. Perhaps that was why Talbot drew her. *Tempted* her. It was an unsettling thought indeed.

The four of them played whist, but in a rather desultory fashion, and for stakes which were, of course, almost laughably low to the gentlemen. It hardly mattered. Miss Reesdale wished to gossip, and to talk about her wedding, a topic which the gentlemen warmed to with surprising grace.

Phaedra tried not to envy Miss Reesdale her excitement. A wedding, after all, was thought to be the high point of a woman's life. Well, second only, perhaps, to the birth of her children—and Miss Reesdale's marriage would doubtless be blessed with children. She would grow old with a husband whom she likely would respect, possibly even adore. She would have her own home, and be permitted a measure of freedom which society allowed only to married women.

But there were other things in life, Phaedra consoled herself. And for the most part, she already had a household to run. Tony's wife was in exile. At Stefan's seat in Hampshire, his wife Xanthia was present but perhaps two or three months a year, and was happy to leave the running of things to others. Phaedra lived a life of luxury under her elder brother's gentle protection. Her close and loving family involved her—so much as she would allow—in everything they did. Few spinsters had it so well. And yet it was not enough.

Whose fault, however, was that? This loneliness—this awful aching emptiness she sometimes felt—would never be filled. Never be quieted.

Her surging guilt was interrupted by the heat of someone's gaze. She turned only slightly, and gave a careful, sidelong glance. From across the room, Tristan Talbot was watching her, his eyes flashing with dark fire, and he assuredly was not grinning. Indeed, he looked nothing like himself.

"Lady Phaedra?" A cool hand touched her wrist.

She turned back to see Miss Reesdale blinking at her.

"Yes, I beg your pardon," said Phaedra a little breathlessly.

"Currants or plums?" she asked, her eyes wide. "For the bride cake?"

Phaedra managed a smile. "Oh, plums," she said with certainty. "I attended eight weddings last year, and everyone had currants."

"Did they indeed?" Miss Reesdale's fine eyebrows drew together. "Well, one wouldn't wish to be ordinary."

"For my part, Miss Reesdale, I *adore* plums," said Lord Robert, covering her hand with his as his gaze swept down her purple gown. "The plumper and the sweeter the better."

"Robin," said Upjohn warningly, "don't make me call you out." He grinned good-naturedly, tossed down a ten of clubs, and shoved the hand to his left. "If you keep flirting with my sister-to-be, I shall feel duty bound to kill you."

"What?" demanded Lord Robert. "What did I say?"

"Oh, don't come the innocent with me," said Upjohn. "Even Avoncliffe over there has been eyeing you disapprovingly—and he is the master of scoundrels."

Miss Reesdale was giggling now, and blushing prettily. Phaedra turned to Lord Robert and smiled dryly. "It would appear, Lord Robert, that your reputation precedes you," she said. "Miss Reesdale, I believe the trick was yours?"

"Oh," said Miss Reesdale vaguely. "Oh, dear. I have forgotten—what is trumps?"

"Hearts, my dear," said Lord Robert, winking at her. "How could it be otherwise with two such beauties at the table?"

Finally Miss Reesdale tossed down a card.

"Your cousin is a lovely girl," Phaedra remarked to Lord Robert as the play went round again. "It has been my great pleasure to make her acquaintance."

"Who?" Lord Robert looked up from his hand. "Oh, Powder Keg! Yes, she's cracking good fun."

Phaedra's brow furrowed. "Powder Keg?"

Mr. Upjohn leaned nearer. "Robin's brother nicknamed Miss Armstrong that when she was twelve," he said conspiratorially, "and it stuck."

"Aye, and the truest things are said in jest," declared Lord Robert, laying down a trump and sweeping up the hand. "Zoë's positively explosive."

"Speaking of that—" Mr. Upjohn paused to rummage through his coat pocket. "Who d'you like for the pigeon this season, Robin? I've got ten guineas on Sir Edgar Haverfield."

"Sir Edgar?" Lord Robert blew out his cheeks and pondered it. "No, he can't be such a fool as all that. Not two years running."

Upjohn lifted one shoulder and extracted a small leather folio from his coat. "I'm writing it in the book," he declared. "Wager against me at your peril."

"I beg your pardon," twittered Miss Reesdale. "What are you gentlemen wagering *on*?"

"Hearts." Lord Robert declared, tossing down the king of spades.

"But that's a spade," Miss Reesdale protested.

"Heart*break*," Lord Robert clarified. "Specifically, whose heart Zoë will shatter this season."

"It's become an annual ritual," Upjohn chimed in.

"When all was said and done, I pocketed forty pounds on Sir Edgar last year."

To her shock, Phaedra found herself laughing with the three of them, then she considered the plight of the ill-fated Sir Edgar. "Lord Robert," she said, lightly touching his coat sleeve, "really, I think we ought not encourage this."

But when she looked up again, Tristan Talbot was still watching her, his visage dark as a thundercloud. His roguish smile had vanished. Phaedra drew her hand away, and dropped her gaze to her cards.

From across the room, Tristan observed the card games unfolding in Mrs. Weyden's drawing room. In the end, her guests had tallied up to an odd number, so Tristan had politely—and happily—bowed himself out of the game. He had not come, after all, to play cards.

Indeed, he wasn't perfectly sure why he had come. Pondering it made him twist a little uncomfortably in his chair. Mrs. Weyden leaned across the tea table solicitously. "More claret, Avoncliffe?" she asked, holding out the decanter.

Tristan nodded, though he'd been drinking it steadily this last hour or better. "Thank you," he said. "You keep a fine cellar, Mrs. Weyden."

He watched halfheartedly as she poured, the ruby red liquid swirling thickly into the bowl of his glass. They lingered by the fire now; he, his hostess, and one of her admirers, Sir Bertram Peck, a jovial chap whom Tristan knew from the racing circuit. Taking his glass, Tristan rose to stretch his legs, pacing nearer to the fire which danced in the grate. He felt restless, impatient for something he could not quite put his finger on. It was a novel frustration for him. Indeed, since leaving the battlefields of Greece, Tristan could count on one hand the times he'd felt such chafing dissatisfaction.

Sir Bertram had one hand draped across the settee on which he reclined, his glass lifted in the other as he regaled their hostess. "Yes, last year's Derby left me plump in the pocket, I don't mind saying," he was bragging. "So this year I did it, Winnie. I bought that colt I'd been looking at, the one I mentioned last week?"

"Yes, yes, Hot Pursuit!" Mrs. Weyden looked rapt. "One could never forget that name."

Sir Bertram slapped his thigh. "A good one, ain't it?" he agreed. "Anyway, he's three now, so I'll have him at the Guineas next month. You should come up with us to Newmarket, old thing—you, too, Avoncliffe."

Tristan, however, was again observing the card players over the rim of his wineglass—four of them in particular—and was compelled to stir himself to attention. "I thank you, Sir Bertram," he said, propping one foot on the brass fender. "But just now my father's health precludes it."

"Quite so, quite so!" said Sir Bertram with gruff sympathy. "Completely understand, old chap. Next year, perhaps?"

Tristan smiled and gave a little bow. "Nothing would give me more pleasure, sir."

But that was a lie, he realized, returning his gaze to the cards. Pulling the pins from Lady Phaedra Northampton's hair, he was increasingly certain, would be vastly more pleasurable than any horse race he'd ever seen—and he'd had some bloody good fun on the circuit in his day.

In his day? Tristan shuddered. God, those sounded like his father's words. Like a man who was cresting the hill of middle age and getting ready to peer down that slippery slope into the fog of the other side. Perhaps it was the fact that he'd recently turned thirty. Or perhaps his father's impending death was troubling him a great deal more than he comprehended.

Was that why he couldn't get his mind off Lady Phaedra? If he was going to look about for a serious flirtation, why not that saucy minx, Zoë Armstrong? She was rich and beautiful, and though some might sneer at her bloodlines, he certainly did not. But he wasn't looking—had never looked—and never really intended to. But there was something . . . something in the turn of Phaedra's face. The sweet, soft line of her cheek. Something deeply feminine which made his heart bottom out. Desire shot to his loins, hot and sweet. Tristan jerked to a halt and drew a deep breath.

Steady on, old boy, he told himself.

But Lady Phaedra had turned her face just so that afternoon in her parlor when she'd dashed behind the door to fetch his hat. His reaction then, whilst cloaked in frivolity, had been irrepressible—and a little dangerous. He had no wish to end up wed to Lady Phaedra Northampton.

But he certainly would like to bed her. All that tightly bound emotion and tightly bound hair were just waiting, he was sure, for some man to set them loose. And that dusky voice. Those *breasts*. Good Lord. Enough to fill a man's hands and then some. How on earth had he missed those the first time round? Perhaps because he'd been distracted by her wide, intelligent eyes. That was surely a first.

Oh, he wasn't serious. He kept to the riper fruit on the low hanging branches, and God knew it was falling in his lap. Ladies who would swiftly invite him to their beds—if not, perhaps, their drawing rooms. Still, he found himself thinking of the Northampton chit at least a dozen times a day. And strangely, every element of his investigation of this murder in the Strand seemed to lead back to her in some small, subtle way. Was he just going a little mad? Or was something deep inside his mind trying to tell him something?

Perhaps he was becoming mildly obsessed by her. Certainly he was obsessed by this wild-goose chase his father had set him off on. He wondered if his father had known that this would happen. Hauxton was a cagey devil, one who understood the darker side of man better than most. He sensed what drove people. What frightened people. It was a part of what made him such a grand and imperious statesman.

Just then Zoë Armstrong approached, bearing down upon her aunt. "Aunt Winnie, we've grown tired of cards," she said in a wheedling voice. "May we not dance? Mrs. Hankle has volunteered to play the pianoforte."

There was no question, of course, of denying Zoë. Across the room, the gentlemen were already drawing back the chairs, and Lady Phaedra was helping Upjohn throw open the four French windows which gave onto the terrace. Indeed, she was looking into the darkened gardens beyond it almost longingly. Inwardly, Tristan grinned. Perhaps opportunity beckoned. And he'd never been a man to pass *that* up.

Chapter 6

Dance on the sands, and yet no footing seen:
Love is a spirit all compact of fire.

With its crackling fire and tasteful brocade furnishings, Madame Vostrikova's parlor was an oasis of elegance in a sea of sin. Reaching across the narrow table, Lavrin moved his pawn forward two spaces and set it down with a quiet *click*.

"The man they call de Vendenheim is asking questions again, Madame," he murmured, straightening up. "It seems Mr. Peel is taking an interest in our little contretemps."

In the shimmering lamplight, Madame Vostrikova sipped pensively at her wine. "You are wise to warn me, Lavrin," she murmured. "The Home Office, of course, oversees the actions of the police. We will watch carefully, and hope it is no more than that."

"And if it is?"

She surveyed him across the table, her eyes hooded in the lamplight. "Then you will persuade them to lose interest," she said coolly. "Do you comprehend me?"

"*Da*, Madame." Lavrin watched her long, thin hand hover over the board. It little mattered, he knew, which piece she chose. He would fight the good fight, but in the end, he would lose—deliberately, if need be. He was not such a fool as Gorsky had been to tempt Madame's viciousness. Certainly he would not lose his wits—or his life—over a pretty piece of flesh, be it male or female.

Madame slid her bishop diagonally left, capturing the space. "You are quiet, Lavrin," she murmured. "You disagree with my strategy?"

Lavrin lifted one shoulder. "De Vendenheim knows the owner of the shop where Gorsky was found," he answered. "Coincidence, I hope. I theorize that Gorsky knew he was being followed and slipped into the alley to hide. Still, you are wise to be cautious."

Madame Vostrikova considered it. "Gorsky spoke to no one before he died, and he carried nothing on his person," she said. "Your assassin confirmed this, did he not?"

Yes, with a knife to his throat, thought Lavrin. But why risk Madame's wrath? "He was quite sure of it," he answered.

"Still, it bears watching." Her dark gaze flashed. "It is your move, Lavrin, is it not?"

Lavrin chose his next piece—and his next words—with care. "De Vendenheim was seen at the Travellers' Club this afternoon taking coffee with Hauxton's heir," he murmured, flicking a quick glance up at her. "Of course, they are both members, so it likely means nothing, but I mention it, in case—"

"In case I was thinking of having *your* throat slit?" A smile twitched at Madame's mouth. "On that point, my dear Lavrin, I think we needn't worry. Lord Hauxton's son is too busy with the organ between his legs to have much use for the one behind his eyes, *da?*"

Lavrin smiled faintly. "You have Hauxton's assistant now in your pocket?"

"Soon, Lavrin, soon." Madame's gaze darkened. "Nebbett is bringing us some fascinating letters. And in return, I shall give him the young girl whom you found in Calais."

"The girl who was chosen for Lord Cotting?"

"Cotting caught sight of the other redhead," said Madame, lifting one shoulder. "The tavern maid. Besides, the French girl is a beauty—not worth wasting on Cotting, for he knows nothing useful after all. He is—what is the term?—a bag of wind?"

Lavrin chuckled. "A disappointment, yes," he admitted. "But the French girl, she's a fighter."

Madame laughed. "Oh, my friend, have you so little faith in me?" she said. "I had her gagged, then ordered Hettie to rip out her nest with a hot sugar wax. The little bitch is smooth as an egg now, and looks no more than twelve. Can you imagine what a fiend like Nebbett will do for a taste of that?"

Lavrin jumped his knight over a pawn and took the space. "I hope, Lilya, that she does not prove more trouble than she is worth."

"If I get what I want from Nebbett, the inconvenience will little matter." Her eyes were drifting over the board, keen as a hawk's. "A pity Hauxton himself did not possess such tastes. What a juicy little plum he would have made for my pudding."

"There is always the son," Lavrin suggested. "He is, I believe, what the English call a wastrel."

"And therefore utterly useless," said Vostrikova. "Unless he means to step into his father's shoes?"

"There have been rumblings of envy at the Foreign Office," Lavrin answered, moving carelessly. "There are rumors Hauxton wishes him to join the Foreign Office in some secret capacity."

"Indeed?" Madame's mouth curled into a sinister smile as she lifted her next piece. "Then perhaps, Lavrin, I shall wish to reconsider my strategy? That one, most assuredly, can be led around by his cock."

Then Vostrikova set her queen back down. And in that instant, Lavrin realized that—as so often happened when one dealt with the devil—his end was to come swiftly.

"Ah, Lavrin, my friend," she said quietly. "I believe that I have you in check again."

Phaedra set her palms flat against the sturdy wooden column which supported Mrs. Weyden's pergola, then let her spine settle back against it. Forcing her shoulders to relax, Phaedra drew in the scent of spring—blossoming trees and freshly turned earth—while she watched the garden shadows dance to the sway of the lanterns behind her.

Mrs. Weyden's drawing room had grown unbearably hot, and despite the chill of the evening, Phaedra had seized the first moment to escape the stifling air—and the awkward expectations. She was in no mood for the lively exertions of a country dance, and the waltz ... well, she simply did not dance the waltz, though that was precisely what Zoë had ordered the pianist to strike up.

This one was a light, lovely piece. Schubert, she thought. Fleetingly, Phaedra closed her eyes and allowed herself the pleasure of mentally swaying to the soft, tinkling notes which drifted through the drawing room doors.

"I must confess," said the quiet voice through the gloom, "that I did not much care for the way Lord Robert Rowland kept ogling your bodice tonight."

Eyes flying open, Phaedra gasped.

Tristan Talbot surveyed her from the opposite column, his arms thrown casually over one another, his long legs crossed at the ankles, the picture of perfect masculine repose. How long he had been relaxing there—still as death itself, apparently—was anyone's guess.

"Really, Mr. Talbot." Phaedra's whisper was sharp. "Must you lurk about like that, frightening people?"

"I beg your pardon," he murmured, coming away from the column to pace toward her. "I did not mean to startle you."

"Don't be ridiculous," she returned. "You meant precisely that. Otherwise you would have made your presence known when I came out here five minutes ago."

"I beg your pardon," he said again, his voice a soothing rumble. "But I was not here five minutes ago."

"What nonsense," she said tartly. "You could not possibly have walked past me."

"Could I not?" he murmured. "Perhaps, then, it was magic?"

But distressed by his earlier comment—and her reaction to it—Phaedra had grown wary. "Indeed, I think I should go inside."

"Wait." He caught her gently, his broad, long-fingered hand surprisingly warm upon her arm. "I am sorry, Phae. Have I really upset you?"

He had, but she was not about to tell him so. The problem was not with him, but with her—with her deep, perplexing attraction to him. She was beginning to wish to see beyond the lighthearted façade to those still and dark waters she sometimes glimpsed within. But what if she were just being foolish again? What if the façade was all there was? She had been mistaken before—and let her heart make irreparable misjudgments.

Inside the drawing room behind her, the music fell away. The dancers parted amidst light applause and laughter. "I merely wish to be alone," she finally said, turning to go.

"Not if you go in there, you don't," he said, drawing her incrementally nearer. "It's turned into rather a madhouse."

Phaedra glanced over her shoulder to see that indeed, the crowd appeared to have swollen, and that couples were now crowding the floor as they attempted to square up for a quadrille. She returned her gaze to Talbot and saw nothing but kindness in his face. But handsome men, she knew, were not to be trusted. She shook him off, and stepped back. "Very well," she retorted. "Let us remain, sir. There was something I wished to say to you."

Talbot stood very near her now, his eyes assessing as they drifted over her face, and then perhaps lower. "My, my," he said dryly. "We really aren't flirting anymore, are we?"

"No, we are not." Phaedra tilted her head, attempting

to catch his gaze. "Up, up, if you please, Mr. Talbot! Kindly look at me, not my bosom. You and Lord Robert are scoundrels cut from the same cloth, I fear."

His head did jerk up then, his eyes wide with shock. But the lazy grin soon slid back into place. "I can scarce deny the truth," he agreed. "I take exception to him, I suppose, because I've a pretty fair notion what the cad is thinking—and after all, Phae, I did see you first."

The words were seductive. Possessive. They flowed over her, warm as molten honey. "You have no claim to me, sir," she managed. "Nor am I fool enough to believe you wish one. Now, let us concern ourselves with the trouble at hand. I demand to know why you have been asking questions about my elder brother."

With a nonchalance she sensed was feigned, Talbot scrubbed the toe of his evening slipper across a mossy vein in the flagstone. "Oh, just curious, I daresay," he answered. "The coincidence, you see, struck me."

"What coincidence?" she demanded.

Talbot rocked back onto his heels, his gaze focused somewhere in the depths of the garden. "Well, this dead chap—Gorsky—he was Russian, you know."

Something cold washed through Phaedra's veins. "So you have said."

"Actually, my dear, *you* said it." Talbot's gaze snapped to hers, dark and penetrating, with a speed which left her breathless. "And your brother—he is part Russian, is he not?"

"A quarter, perhaps," Phaedra retorted. "But he knows nothing of Russia—hasn't been there for twenty years or more. Nash is decent man, Talbot. A good brother, and a good patriot. *You leave him out of your tawdry pokings-about.* Do you hear me?"

Talbot was watching her assessingly, like a lion in the sun wondering if he should bestir himself to take down his prey. She had said too much, she realized. And too angrily. Suddenly, he shifted his shoulders as if restless, and crossed his arms over his broad chest. "Do you know, Phae," he said quietly, "I rather admire you—and envy your brother. No one in my family ever looked out for me. The whole lot of 'em likely couldn't stir up a teaspoon of indignation on my behalf."

She opened her mouth to rail at him, then abruptly shut it when his words sunk in. There was a look deep in Talbot's eyes that was suddenly all too solemn. All too tender. Was that what his life was like? No familial devotion? No one to count on? That, she could not imagine. She was reminded of her wish to see beyond his beautiful façade—but every glimpse seemed to shake her.

Good heavens, she thought, glancing away. She really did not need this just now. Not desire and compassion and—yes, a bit of admiration for the man. "Just leave Nash alone, Talbot." Her voice had softened. "He does not deserve the trouble you would cause. Please believe he had nothing to do with this mess."

"You seem awfully certain of that," he murmured. "And perhaps that's one of the reasons, Phae, I keep getting the oddest notion there's something you aren't telling me."

"I don't have to listen to this," she returned, her voice low and tremulous. "And I certainly don't have to tell you anything."

She spun about to go, but again, Talbot caught her arm.

This time his grip was unrelenting as he jerked her to him. His eyes bore down on her, narrow and dark. "Can you not accept, Phaedra, that *I* am not your enemy?" his voice suddenly edged with emotion. "That I wish only to help you? To protect you from whatever it is that you fear?"

"To *protect* me?" Her eyes searched his face, wondering if he spoke the truth. "Is that what you are trying to do?"

He had the good grace to drop his gaze. "I begin to fear so."

For an instant they stood there, toe-to-toe, his fingers digging into her arm, their breath coming harder than was wise. Suddenly, something like surrender—but not surrender at all—softened his visage, and Talbot cursed softly. Then his lips came down upon hers.

It was a kiss almost artless in its simplicity, his lips opening hungrily over hers. Phaedra wanted, suddenly, to believe him. To lean on him, and be enveloped in his arms and in his strength. Something like a groan escaped her lips. Against her will, her palms skated up the front of his coat, then her fingers curled into the soft black wool of his lapels. In an instant, Talbot had one hand at the back of her head, and an arm banded about her waist. He drew her to him in a crush of pink silk, then, somehow, Phaedra's spine was against the pergola column again. His mouth was insistent, driving her head back. Relentless.

His lips molded over hers again and again, seductive and irresistible. And when his tongue teased lightly across her lips, Phaedra melted against him, a liquescent cascade of womanhood pooling at Talbot's feet. She opened without the merest hint of protest, inviting his tongue to slide silkily along hers, then responding in kind. The house, the music, the twenty-odd people just beyond the terrace; all of it spun away. For long, mindless moments, they deepened the contact, his fingers plunging into her hair as his tongue plundered her mouth, claiming her as his.

His leg was between hers now, his groin throbbing urgently against her thigh. Dimly, Phaedra recognized the hard bulge for what it was—for what it meant—and yet she urged herself against it. The kiss was endless. Drugging. Phaedra swam in sensation and yearning, aching desire. A dream—a fevered, sleep-tossed fantasy of Talbot naked in her bed—came to her, vivid as the morning's sun. And then somehow, his lips were torn from hers, and Phaedra was left swaying in his embrace, blinking her eyes as if dazed. Talbot cursed again, and drew away.

"Good God," he uttered. "I must be mad." The words were spoken beneath his breath, with a vehemence she would never have expected. She looked up at him, muted and a little disoriented.

Then the glower relented. "My dear, you are on the verge of ruination here," he murmured, letting his hand drop. "And I am on the verge of losing my notoriously unreliable self-control. Where is that sharp tongue of yours, Lady Phaedra, when I really deserve it?"

The sounds of the night returned to her, and the tinkle of Mrs. Weyden's pianoforte again wafted from the drawing room. The *chink* of crystal, and the trill of distant laughter. All of it brought her back to what she'd just done. "I do beg your pardon," she whispered, taking a step back. "You must think that I am . . ."

He gave a rueful smile. "What I think, my dear, is that it is I who should beg pardon," he answered. "And the only thing I am imagining is how beautiful you would be with your clothes off and that glorious chestnut hair down about your waist—a fantasy neither of us can afford just now."

Phaedra's blush deepened.

Suddenly, he grabbed her hand, and pulled her toward a towering tree in the center of the garden. In the full glow of one of the lanterns, a pair of swings hung from a tree. Talbot urged her to sit down, then took the opposite swing, setting some distance between them.

"Well, that was not easy to do." His eyes flicked over her as if checking for damage. "But at least we are in view of the French windows now. No harm, I pray, was done."

But great harm had been done, Phaedra acknowledged. Tristan Talbot had kissed her again, lessening her precious control, and inside she still trembled. He had awakened the thing within her—that tempestuous creature she did not know and could scarce restrain. And with him it was worse—far worse—than ever. Phaedra looked away, and blinked her eyes rapidly.

When she turned around, he was looking at her quite intently. "Now," he said softly, "our little indiscretion aside, Phae, don't you think you'd best confide in me?"

For an instant, Phaedra thought he was asking for a different sort of confession altogether. "Confide in you?"

Though he looked incongruous in the swing, Talbot had begun to move with that languid, catlike grace which laced his every motion. "About Gorsky," he clarified, pushing absently back and forth with one heel. "You need to tell me everything you know, Phae. It might be important to the government, but more troubling to me is that *you* could be in danger."

Phaedra felt her resolve weakening. "I don't know anything about Mr. Gorsky." She forced out the words. "The man fell dead at my feet whilst I was minding my own business."

"Liar," said Talbot. His voice was soft but certain.

"How dare you!" Phaedra moved as if to leap from the swing, but he stopped her.

"Phae, you knew his name," said Tristan, his voice gently accusing. "You *knew* his name."

Suddenly, she understood. "I—I explained that," she protested. "My brother mentioned it."

Tristan shook his head. "No, love, he didn't," he answered. "Lord Nash couldn't have known it. Not unless he was somehow involved. I checked with my father. Gorsky's name had been provided to no one outside the Foreign Office."

Phaedra closed her eyes, and let the horror wash over her. She was caught out in a lie of her own doing. Caught out with no way to explain it—and no way to keep Stefan out of it—unless she dared tell Talbot the truth. The notion should have been absurd. And yet she found herself considering it.

Suddenly, a group of young people burst onto the terrace. Phaedra realized the music had stopped abruptly. "No more quadrilles!" commanded Zoë, in the lead. "Another waltz, if you please, Mrs. Hankle, and we shall dance it here, beneath the stars with room to spare."

At that, Zoë lifted her arms heavenward, and went

spinning across the terrace. Lord Robert Rowland seized her hand, and spun her back again, yanking her unceremoniously into his arms. Zoë fell backward in the crook of his elbow, Lord Robert lowering her almost to the floor. Everyone laughed, and the music began. The couples spilled across the terrace and onto the grass.

Talbot twisted his swing around, and made a gallant gesture of extending his hand. "My lady, might I have the pleasure?"

Phaedra shook her head. "Thank you, no."

Talbot unfolded himself from the swing and stood towering over her. He offered both his hands. "Come, Phae," he ordered. "We'll raise fewer eyebrows if we blend into the crowd."

Still, she hesitated.

"You do not waltz?" he gently prodded.

Lamely, she lifted one shoulder. "Not in a very long while," she confessed. "And never in public."

"In the schoolroom, then?"

"Yes. Something like that."

His smile returned, fainter and less flirtatious now, deepening the ever-present dimple to the right side of his mouth. "Then there is no time like the present, my dear," he said, the words rumbling softly in his chest. "Come, put yourself in the hands of a master."

And so she did. Because it seemed easier to dance than to answer his questions. Because she had not waltzed in an age, and she yearned to feel the music moving through her. And because his body looked warm and solid, his arms open and inviting. Knowing all this, and fearing it, too, Phaedra set her hand to his broad shoulder, and allowed him to draw her close. Too close.

With a smile, he took her hand in his, and swept her under the pergola. But instead of daintily clasping it as was traditionally done, he entwined his fingers through hers, palm to palm, as if to hold her captive. Effortlessly, Talbot twirled her away from the pergola and toward the other dancers. His hand was heavy at her waist, but his steps were light and sure. His familiar heat and scent surrounded her like a comforting, sensual embrace.

He brushed his lips over the shell of her ear. "You are perfect, Phae," he whispered against her ear. "Weightless. Lovely. Someone should waltz you round the drawing room every day of your life."

"How silly you are, Mr. Talbot," she managed.

The sounds of the music rose and fell, their bodies moving as one to the rhythm. Though she was tall, against him she felt perfectly matched. He led her expertly. Fluidly. And when Talbot spun her into an especially sweeping turn, something inside Phaedra seemed to lift, and become buoyant just beneath her heart. It felt like . . . joy, which was odd when, mere moments earlier, she had felt an instant of terror.

But there was no terror in Talbot's arms. And no lack of strength or skill. His lithe body was like quicksilver flowing over the smoothest of glass. They wove unerringly through and around the other dancers now, flashes of light and color spinning round Phaedra in an effortless whirl. Awed, she lowered her gaze to the simple diamond pin in the folds of his cravat, marveling at his command of his body—and of hers. She felt buoyant, as if she might trip over her own two feet, and something in Talbot's elegant step would have carried her gracefully forward.

His lips brushed her ear again. "However much we may quarrel, Phae," Talbot whispered, "our bodies seem to know one another perfectly—and perhaps *that* is what we should most worry about?"

She should have laughed. Or rebuked him. But it was a giddy, oddly magical moment. Even the moon had come out, peeping over the rooftops of Mayfair. Everyone twirling about them was smiling and gay. And no one else, Phaedra noticed, was cutting much of a dash. Instead they were laughing and moving in a most relaxed and companionable way. Most were also watching Talbot; some in admiration, others with envy. A few, however, were otherwise occupied. Lord Robert Rowland had twirled Zoë beneath the shadowy, vine-laden pergola, and looked very much as if he meant to steal a kiss.

Talbot, too, noticed it. He tipped back his head and laughed, the corners of his eyes crinkling most attractively. They stood so near, she could feel the laughter rumble deep in his chest. "Rowland never gives up, does he?" he murmured against her ear. "Before the night's out, that impudent pup will have kissed every female here—save one, I hope."

Phaedra opened her mouth to speak, but at that instant, Talbot looked down at her, and something in their gazes caught. That stab of desire sliced through her again, sudden and piercing. She could not catch her breath. His eyes held hers, deep, unknowable pools which commanded her and left her trembling. As he spun her around, it was as if her feet left the grass, borne upward by some magnetic force which drew her to him. There was nothing of the lighthearted rogue in him now, just the searing warmth of his body pressed improperly near, and the sense that he held her in some sort of thrall.

Phaedra wanted to demand what sensual spell he had cast, but words would not come. There was only the heavy heat of his grip on her waist. The glittering emotion in his eyes, which in this moment verged on ruthlessness. And suddenly, something more consuming. The slow burn of longing, more fierce than anything she'd ever felt. The rush of need for something desirable yet dangerous.

The weakening of her resolve frightened her, and left her angry with herself—and unfairly, with him. Somehow, she forced her face into a dispassionate mask. "You are quite the dancer, Mr. Talbot," she managed. "Zoë said you were famous for your skill in the ballroom."

Talbot's gaze darkened. "Yes, a gift from my mother, I daresay," he murmured, drawing her fully against him. "But I have other skills, my dear, which are equally honed—and for which I am equally renowned."

"Why, Mr. Talbot, I do believe you are bragging again," she murmured, drawing a little away from him. "But you needn't. Your reputation precedes you."

"My reputation for what?" A smile quirked his mouth. "Hedonism?"

She managed to hold his gaze. "Yes, actually."

The strange look in his eyes intensified. "You kiss like a hedonist," he murmured, drawing her into the next turn. "And what is the harm in it?" he continued when she stiffened in his arms. "Passion, Phae, can be a beautiful thing.

I enjoy women. They enjoy me. I am not breaking hearts
for sport, or corrupting innocence."

Phaedra felt suddenly unsteady on her feet. "Blithe
words, sir," she answered. "Nonetheless, there is a darkness
in you—a hint of bitterness which I am not sure you mean
others to see. So, not a total hedonist, I think?"

His mouth twisted, and his eyes flashed. "You have a
vivid imagination, my lady," he answered. "Let us not become too serious in our flirtations, *hmm?*"

"I do not flirt," she said.

"And I do not bare my soul," he returned. "It would be
a dashed dull business anyway."

She felt a flash of irritation, but at that moment, something brushed her arm. Talbot spun her smoothly to a
halt. Mrs. Weyden stood at the edge of the terrace, a hint
of chagrin in her eyes.

"I do beg your pardon, Lady Phaedra," she said beneath
the music. "But your mother and sister have come."

Phaedra dropped her arms and stepped back. Talbot
did likewise, but his hands slid away with a reluctance she
did not think was feigned.

Beyond Mrs. Weyden's shoulder, Phaedra could see her
mother and Phoebe inside the drawing room, clutching
their reticules and looking at them quite pointedly, burning curiosity writ plain across their faces.

"Oh, Lord," Phaedra muttered.

"Phae." Talbot seized her arm. "Introduce me." His
voice was low and surprisingly rough.

Phaedra stepped away. "I . . . I cannot."

Some nameless emotion flared in his gaze. "Cannot or

will not?" he asked, ignoring Mrs. Weyden's presence. "Which is it, Phaedra?"

"Not now," she hissed.

"Or *not ever?*" he suggested, his dark eyes taking on a vaguely bitter cast. "Fine. But this is not over, Phae."

With one last wary glance, Mrs. Weyden drew away, and hastened toward the drawing room.

Phaedra felt a rush of panic. "There is no *this*, Talbot," she whispered. "Are you quite mad?"

His lips thinned. "By God, you just kissed me as if there was a *this*."

She forgot that the other dancers were still whirling about them. That her mother and sister still watched, eyes agog.

"Let us not become too serious in our flirtations, my lord," she retorted. "Must you force me to admit I am not immune to your charms? Fine, you have done so. But women like me don't mean anything to you. Pray do not pretend they do. We have nothing further to discuss."

He still held her arm. "There is still the matter of a dead man in the Strand," he gritted, that cold, penetrating look back in his eyes. "Do not even think of toying with me, my lady. Or you will rue the day."

Phaedra's eyes widened. She could hear her own heartbeat pounding in her ears now. "I . . . I cannot believe you serious."

"Believe it," he snapped, releasing her. "Send word of a time and place to meet me—or *I will come to you*. In Brook Street, no less. In front of your fine family."

This time it was she who grabbed his arm. "Wait just

one moment, sir," she hissed, anger surging. "Do not dare put words into my mouth. I have already invited you into my home, and gladly. But neither I nor my brother nor anyone in my *fine family* knows anything of this business in the Strand."

"Madam, you are a liar," he said, his voice cold and quiet. "*You* are involved. And for your own safety, you had best tell me why."

She pursed her lips for a moment, then spun on her heel and walked away.

"Phae." Behind her, his voice had softened only a little. "I *will* find out."

Phaedra drew in her breath roughly. But when she glanced over her shoulder, Tristan Talbot was striding toward the shadows of the pergola.

Lady Nash hastened to meet her at the French doors. "Who was that?" she demanded, her voice sharp. "Who were you quarreling with?"

Phaedra looked round again. Talbot had melted into the gloom. It was as if he'd never been there at all. "No one," she said quietly, turning back around. "He is no one. Come, Mamma. I think it's time we went home."

Chapter 7

❦

*Things without all remedy
Should be without regard; what's done is done.*

The mansion in Cavendish Square lay in shadows, the streetlamp near it having gone out again, as it had long been wont to do. Tristan went up the polished white steps, and let himself in with the key he had never returned—and, to his father's credit, had never been asked to return.

That thought only served to increase his restlessness; that chafing dissatisfaction which had followed him from Mrs. Weyden's and into the night. He rolled his shoulders beneath the wool of his coat, then pushed the door open on silent hinges.

Inside the grand vaulted entrance hall, all was silent. Sconces flickered along the walls, casting faint shadows up the massive marble staircase. As with his visit to Mrs. Weyden's, Tristan wasn't sure why he was here. Nonetheless, he stripped off his gloves, set down his hat, then went upstairs, helping himself to a candlestick as he went.

He found Pemberton propped in a chair by his father's bed, his hands folded over his belly, his chin sunk deep in the folds of his cravat. Tristan touched the butler lightly on his hand, and when he roused, set a finger to his lips.

Pemberton's eyes blinked against the candlelight, his expression one of unconcealed surprise. "Lord Avoncliffe," he murmured, rising awkwardly. "Good evening, sir."

"Go to bed, Pem," Tristan whispered, inclining his head toward the door. "I shall sit with him the night."

Pemberton blinked again. "My lord, are you sure?"

"Quite," said Tristan. "Go. Get some rest."

"We are taking shifts," said the butler. "One of the footmen will relieve you at three."

Tristan shook his head. "He needn't bother, thank you." He already knew he would not sleep this night. He was feeling guilty for the cold words he'd spoken to Lady Phaedra, but lust and frustration were fraying at his temper. Infernal woman.

Pemberton bowed, and went to the sideboard. Tristan sank into the still warm chair, and looked at his father's frail form barely distinguishable beneath the bedcovers. The butler returned with a galleried silver tray set with a flagon of port and a decanter of cognac. One of Lord Hauxton's Venetian crystal glasses sat alongside them. He placed the tray on Hauxton's bed table, bowed again, and left the room as quietly as Tristan had entered.

Tristan took up the decanter, and poured a dram of the heavy amber liquid into the glass. It was going to be a bloody long night, he thought, tossing off the brandy in one swallow.

What in God's name had he been thinking this evening? To have flirted with Lady Phaedra Northampton as if she were some practiced courtesan? And flirtation hadn't been the half of it. He had actually felt a stab of jealousy tonight. It was unheard of. When it came to women, he was a man who cut his losses so fast the strings were still flapping in the breeze as he walked away. And then on the heels of jealousy, the anger. The utter certainty that Phaedra was a liar. *Good God.* It made him remember why he no longer did this for a living.

Tristan blocked that thought from his mind, and savored the burn of alcohol as it trailed down his throat. His eyes went again to the man in the bed. Hauxton's nightshirt was fastened neatly at the throat, his nightcap securely in place. His thin, long-fingered hands lay upon the coverlet in smooth, perfect symmetry. Even in repose—even as he waited for death—Hauxton was the perfect English gentleman.

Tristan set down the glass, and laid his own hand alongside his father's, almost laughing aloud when he realized how nearly identical they were. Not just the thinness, or the length, but the short nails, a little flatter than most, with faint vertical ridges. The broad palms, and the thumbs which turned at the very same angle. But where his father's hands had been pale even at his most vigorous, Tristan's were brown as a sepoy's.

Tristan's eyes trailed back up to his father's sandy hair, now swept with white, and then to the nose. Ah, the famous Talbot nose, sharp and arrogant. Like the fingers, it attested to their kinship more plainly than any birth record could have done. As a child, he had not failed to notice how his father's relations remarked upon the nose and sighed with relief as age brought it burgeoning forth in all its Talbot glory. Even then, he had known that the sighs meant something—something which left him acutely uncomfortable and a little angry. Now he understood what he had been too naïve to grasp at the age of twelve. They had not believed him Hauxton's child.

They had certainly not wished his misbegotten blood to mingle with their bluer, more perfect hue, but they had feared even more a total imposter in their midst. How in God's name had his mother survived the suspicion? That cold, quiet condescension which, even now, could cut him to the quick?

In truth, he supposed, she had not. She had left England when he was but a child, and died within the year. Tristan could still remember the shouted quarrels and the slamming doors. The deep, wracking sobs, and his mother sitting by his bed, her face bloodless, her eyes limpid with grief, a handkerchief clutched in one tremulous hand as she stroked him with the other.

He could still hear his father's parting words, too, shouted over the dinner table that night, loud enough to carry up the stairs. "Go, then, damn you!" Hauxton had cried. "You faithless bitch! But for this marriage, I would have been Prime Minister by now—and *you*, Carlotta—by God, *you were not worth it!*"

This last had been followed by the shattering of crystal. His mother's doing, no doubt. The only display of emotion Hauxton ever allowed himself was the rarely raised voice. And at dawn, the carriages had come. Tristan could still see the trunks being carried down by the footmen in solemn procession, their white gloves and white wigs stark against the dark leather and wood as they bore them on their shoulders. He did not know who he had been angrier with, his father for letting her go, or his mother for leaving. But there had been no question of Tristan's going with her. The heir to an earldom could not be raised abroad. Certainly he could not be raised by a horde of near-landless mongrels—at least that's how it would have appeared to the English aristocracy.

Just then he was recalled to the present by his father, who stirred restlessly on the bed. His eyes fluttered opened, and he stared at Tristan, blindly at first, and then with a lucidity which was surprising.

"Tristan," he muttered, lifting his head. "You have come home."

It was not home, but Tristan had not the heart to correct him.

"Indeed, sir," he answered, laying his hand over his father's fingers, which had begun to pick almost nervously at the coverlet. "Now go back to sleep. You'll need your strength on the morrow. After all, someone must run the country."

His father's faint smile held an unmistakable irony. "I fear I must soon give my little portion of it over into someone else's hands," he answered. "You . . . you had something to tell me? Something about the Russian, perhaps?"

Tristan patted his hand. "No, sir," he answered. "I have learnt little, and it will wait."

With that, his father nodded, his nightcap scrubbing the linen pillowslip, then drifted off again, leaving Tristan alone with his thoughts. He poured another tumbler of the cognac, halfway to the brim this time, then fell back into the deep armchair, cradling the glass against his waistcoat.

He had made a fool of himself with Lady Phaedra tonight—and even worse, he had made her angry. Oh, the business about Gorsky and her brother, that he did not regret. There was something strange going on, and his twitching cock aside, he would get to the bottom of it. But kissing her again—and kissing her as one might a light-skirt, not a virginal young lady—deeply. Possessively. It was madness. Which only emphasized the paradox.

He did not kiss virginal young ladies.

Like most men of his ilk, he avoided them like the plague. Even had his intentions been honorable—which they weren't—Tristan had no interest in tutoring an un-tried female in the ways of passion. Which emphasized the second paradox. Lady Phaedra did not kiss like an un-tried female. She had not panicked. Had not backhanded him as he deserved. Indeed, the woman had gone toe-to-toe with him and scarcely blushed when it was done. Only later had she become outraged. Only when he had pressed her for an introduction to her family.

She had refused. And he—perhaps unfairly—had leapt to an ill conclusion. He had let his temper snap. It had been a long time since a beautiful woman had shaken him so thoroughly. Made him behave so stupidly. Really, what had he been thinking from the neck up? Had he thought to court her? The lady said she did not want a husband—and by God, he believed her. It was not just a frivolous protestation to whet the challenge in a man.

But she was not immune to his touch. Indeed, Tristan had felt a passion in her which even still left him reeling. Repressed sensuality simmered just beneath the surface of her every move. Her every glance. Could no one else see it? He hoped not. Prayed not.

In a day or two, he would approach her again. There was nothing else for it. But this time, he must persuade the truth from her with logic. He thought that tonight, perhaps, he very nearly had. In the garden earlier, he had seen something—something like resignation and perhaps even relief in her eyes. The wish to unburden her soul. It was a look he well knew from his time in Greece, and took no joy in. Then Miss Armstrong had burst onto the scene, and the moment had been lost.

Tristan sipped pensively at the brandy, then set it down again. He had lost the taste for it. Instead, the taste of Lady Phaedra was still on his lips, and the warmth of her hand yet lingered in his. If he closed his eyes, he could still feel the strains of the music, and her body swaying as one with his.

God's truth, but this was very odd.

Perhaps he needed that brandy after all. He picked it up, and slowly sipped it down.

In his sleep, his father's breath hitched a little alarmingly. Tristan looked at him, and again felt that strange, utterly submerging wave of grief wash over him. In a few weeks—days, perhaps—the great Lord Hauxton would be dead. And whatever chasm lay between them would never be breached. All the unspoken words, all those small, seething resentments. Tristan's deeply entrenched sense of having failed at the one thing he had been born to do. Yes, all of it would still remain. There was no grave deep enough to bury all of that.

Was that why he had come here tonight? To mourn what could have been? Should have been? To wallow in his anger and mull over the missed opportunities—opportunities, perhaps, to put things right? Or had it even been within his power to do so? He could not change who he was, or the color of his skin. He could not alter his father's choice to make an improvident marriage, then resent himself for his own weakness in having done so.

And why tonight, of all nights, had he come here? What was it about Lady Phaedra Northampton that had the power to drive him to the one place no one would have expected? *Home.* Or what there was of it. His elbow propped on the chair arm, Tristan bent his head and pinched hard at the bridge of his nose. The swell of grief rose up, and he found himself clenching his jaw against the pain. He wanted to laugh bitterly at himself and at his own folly. But was it tonight's folly? Or the folly of the last twenty years?

Somewhere in the depths of the house, a clock struck two. As he had learned to do in the army, he forced his mind to empty and his body to relax. Slowly, the stillness of the great house settled over Tristan, but little peace came with it. It was going to be a long night. Just he and his dying father—and the lingering warmth of Lady Phaedra's lush body pressed to his.

Phaedra arrived home, still trembling inside with emotion, to find Agnes waiting in her bedchamber, a basket of crewelwork on her lap. She set it aside, and came at once toward the door.

"Good evening, miss."

"Good evening, Agnes," said Phaedra, setting aside her reticule. "You needn't have waited up."

"What, and leave you to take that great pile of hair down by yourself?" Agnes chided. "You aren't accustomed to anything so fancy. Do sit down, miss, and let me brush it out."

"Thank you, Agnes." Phaedra tossed aside her shawl and sank down onto the stool at the small, giltwood dressing table. She watched in silence as Agnes pulled the pins from her hair, her mind running back over the events of the evening, particularly the end of the evening.

She was very angry at Tristan Talbot, and more than a little unsure how to manage him. And Phaedra was—as her brothers so often remarked—a managing sort of female. Talbot, however, was not amenable to management. What was worse, all his flirting, dancing, kissing, and jumping to conclusions had left her head in a whirl. One instant he was naught but a handsome rogue, and the next . . . dear Lord. His eyes had the look burning coals. Piercing. Accusing. Tempting. Damn him.

She must have cursed aloud.

"Did you see him, then, miss?" Another pin rang out as Agnes tossed it into the crystal dish on the dressing table. "Did you winkle anything out of him?"

No, thought Phaedra dryly. *I thought it made more sense to let him kiss me silly.*

But what she said was, "I'm sorry, Agnes. I did see him, but I did not much advance our cause. Never fear, however. I mean to see him again tomorrow—if, that is, you can help me?"

Agnes looked up and caught her gaze in the mirror, the brush stilling. "Anything, miss. You have only to ask it."

Phaedra thought through her hastily made plan one last time. It would do, she thought. Talbot might be a little dangerous, but there was honor in him, she believed. Pray God she was not wrong. Her track record on that score was dismal, it was true, but she must learn to trust herself again. She hoped Talbot would not let her down.

"I must get a note to Mr. Talbot in the morning," she said when Agnes put the brush down. She rose and went to her writing desk by the windows. Sitting, she extracted a sheet of foolscap from the drawer, and lifted the lid from her inkpot.

Agnes had followed her. "And you wish me to take it to him?" she suggested.

"Yes, and tell no one," said Phaedra. "Should my mother discover—"

Agnes laid a hand on her shoulder. "She won't, miss," said the maid softly. "I'd die first."

Phaedra nodded, and bent her head to the task. "Mr. Talbot lives in Long Acre," she explained, scratching out the note. "I don't know where, precisely. You'll have to ask about. Can you do that?"

Agnes swiftly nodded. "For little Priss, my lady? Aye, I'd run down the devil himself."

"That's about what it amounts to," said Phaedra, fanning the ink. "So start with the vintners. Then go on to the tobacconists, the chop houses, and—oh, yes—the gunsmiths. I won't ask you to enter the brothels or the gaming hells until all hope is lost."

"Aye, a man of large appetites, is he?" said Agnes, grinning. " 'Tis to be expected, I daresay, from a fellow such as that one."

"My thoughts exactly," said Phaedra dryly, folding the sheet of foolscap.

Agnes lifted one shoulder, and snatched up the note. "Aye, well, from the little glimpse I caught of 'im, a girl could do worse."

Phaedra was silent for a moment. "We must hope, then, Agnes, that Talbot is as much a man as you think him," she finally said. "I believe I am going to have to bring him into our confidence. I am going to have to tell him about Millie—and about Tony, too, I fear."

At that, Agnes paled. "Oh, lawks, miss," she said. "Mr. Hayden-Worth will be frightfully angry."

Phaedra's lips thinned to a tight line. "Well, perhaps Mr. Hayden-Worth should have thought of that before leaving others to tidy up his messes," she replied. "Or before he set about easing his frustrations with a poor tavern girl he'd no business bedding, come to that."

Agnes hung her head. "Oh, you don't know Millie, miss," she answered. "Ever so determined, she was, to have him. And so sure of herself, too. It's why she run off to London, you know. She said if Mr. Hayden-Worth didn't want to keep 'er up, some other fine gentleman would."

"Yes, because Tony put grand ideas in her head," Phaedra gritted. "And now it is Priscilla who must pay the price. Her mother has vanished, and her father is an ocean away—not that he would be of any help, mind. So that beautiful child—*our niece*—is left all but an orphan."

Agnes wrung her hands. "Perhaps—" she awkwardly

began, "—oh, perhaps we ought to tell his lordship of all this, miss?"

Phaedra's head jerked up. "Stefan?" she said sharply. "No, Agnes. No, that really would not be wise. You must trust me on this."

Phaedra was not about to tell Agnes the truth. That Stefan would likely throttle Tony. That not long past, Stefan had been required to pay off Tony's blackmailers for an entirely different sort of sexual indiscretion, then bribe the French *commissaire de police* to free Tony's wife from smuggling charges. Those escapades had cost Stefan a bloody fortune, and all of it had been hushed up by the Government at great political cost.

Tony's meteoric career in the Commons had been saved yet again. But Stefan was now at the end of his tether when it came to Tony and his bollixed-up relationships. And Phaedra—well, like everyone, she still loved Tony. One could not help it. For all his indiscreet behavior, he was a good man. And a brilliant politician who, despite his own confused proclivities, had England's best interests at heart.

Once he obtained a divorce from Jenny—once Tony could settle down in some sort of permanent, loving relationship—Phaedra prayed he would be able to lead a happy, relatively normal life. She just had to keep Stefan from killing him first. A sharp *pop* of cinders in the hearth bestirred her to the present, and to Agnes's fretful gaze. "No," she said again, her voice quiet in the gloom. "No, Agnes. There can be no question of Lord Nash's knowing. We are stuck, I fear, with Mr. Talbot."

Agnes looked unconvinced. "But what can he do, miss, that we can't?"

Phaedra lifted her gaze to the maid's. "He can get me into that house, Agnes," she said softly. "And once I am inside, I *will* find Millie."

"Oh, miss," said Agnes. "That sounds frightfully dangerous."

"And another thing, Agnes." Phaedra's voice was pensive. "I wish you to bring down one of Tony's best evening suits. You must pin it up on me, then take it to a tailor—not his usual fellow, mind. I shall want a hat and gloves, too. Oh—and that wig Jenny used to have. The one she wore as Puck to the Midsummer Ball? Can you find it?"

"Oh, I don't like the sound of this." Agnes wrung her hands again. "But yes, miss. I'll do my best."

But Phaedra was trying not to think of the danger. And she was trying not to think of the small shiver of excitement which ran down her back when she considered the prospect of being alone—completely and utterly alone—with Tristan Talbot.

"Will there be anything else, miss?" Agnes asked.

Phaedra looked at her blankly for an instant. "Oh, yes," she answered. "One of my yellow garters has gone missing. Have you seen it, by chance?"

"I put one in the mending last week," she said. "One of the little roses had torn away."

"Yes, I recall." Phaedra furrowed her brow. "Oh, well. It will turn up, I daresay." A mislaid garter was the least of her worries. Abruptly, she excused Agnes for the night, left the desk, and crossed the room to her bed. When the door clicked shut, Phaedra knelt to say her evening prayers. But her usual prayer of thanks did not come. Instead, she simply set her forehead against the turned-down sheets, and prayed for strength.

God forbid anyone should know the dreams that tormented her each night, she thought, climbing wearily into the bed. And God curse the day Talbot had walked into her life with his long legs and seductive smile to awaken all her feverish fantasies—then magnify them tenfold.

At precisely seven sharp, Lord Hauxton's valet came in to strop the earl's razor. On his heels came a housemaid to draw the drapes and sweep the grate. A footman followed as if precisely timed, bearing a breakfast tray containing exactly what it had contained for the last forty years: one soft boiled egg, tea, a rasher of bacon, and two slices of toast.

Roused by all the precision marching, Tristan rose and shook off the remnants of sleep, a little disconcerted to realize he had actually drifted off.

Soon Hauxton was hoisted up in the bed, shaved, dressed in a fresh nightshirt, and given a fork which he then used to push his food impotently about the plate. Tristan paced back and forth by the windows, explaining what little he had managed to discover.

"And you are quite sure, Tristan, that de Vendenheim was lying to you?" his father asked when Tristan had finished his tale. "About Lord Nash's involvement in those arms shipments?"

Tristan turned to face his father. "He was not completely honest. That is the best I can say of him."

Hauxton surveyed him, one eye narrowed. "Quite so," he murmured. "God knows you have your faults, Tristan. But you have a solid grasp of human nature." It was as close to a compliment as his father ever came.

"What was he lying about?" Tristan demanded.

"Nash was involved in the scandal, but the guilt lay with his stepbrother's wife," said his father. "Peel helped Nash cover it up to spare the family. His stepbrother, you know, is quite an up-and-comer in the Commons."

"Yes, Anthony Hayden-Worth," said Tristan, pacing toward the bed. "He was ahead of me at Eton. What happened to the wife?"

Again, Hauxton smiled, this time a little sourly. "Nash exiled her to America," he said, pushing his breakfast tray away. "Her father owns Carlow Arms Manufacturing in Connecticut."

"Carlow?" He gave a low whistle.

"Yes, the temptation of easy money, I collect, was too great for Mrs. Hayden-Worth and her father," said Hauxton. "They got in bed with some duplicitous French diplomats running guns to the Greeks."

Tristan gave a low whistle. "So that's who it was!"

"But Nash was innocent, and his brother was . . . well, merely foolish for having let his wife run wild. It cost Nash a small fortune in bribes to extricate her."

Tristan caught his thumbs in the waist of his trousers and stared pensively at the frail form in the bed. "And you are sure?" he asked. "Nash is clean in this Gorsky business?"

Hauxton nodded. "Quite sure."

And there went his theory regarding Lady Phaedra. The

thought should have made him happy. And it did. But underneath it all was the realization that he'd called her a liar to her face. That she had been telling him the truth about her brother. None of them were involved. And he had no further excuse to see her again.

But that was probably a good thing. Sharply, he cleared his throat. "I have been thinking, sir," he said. "I have a plan."

Hauxton paused in the middle of sipping at his tea. "Go on."

Tristan studied the swirling pattern of his father's Oriental carpet. "I wish you to tell a lie," he finally said. "A very public lie. I wish you to put it about that I am to help manage your tasks in the Foreign Office until you are well again."

"I think, Tristan, that you would be perfectly capable of doing that someday, would you but set your mind to it," he answered. "I do not think, however, I will be getting well again."

"I know we both fear that, sir," Tristan answered. "As to the work, you know my feelings in that regard. But what I wish you to say is that I am your go-between until you can return to the office. I wish people to believe that I have access to all of your files and all of your staff. That I am—and have been for some time—wholly in your confidence."

Hauxton was looking at him quizzically. "Yes, I see," he murmured. "And this will achieve . . . what?"

"I have been compiling a list, sir," said Tristan. "A list of all the known clients of Madame Vostrikova. I've had but limited success."

"As I said, it is a business which is conducted with the utmost discretion," said Hauxton. "I wonder you've managed to find anyone at all."

"I have been watching the house at all hours," Tristan admitted. "And asking around. Calling in a few favors and notes-of-hand. Oh, and I bribed a scullery maid. I've come up with about a dozen names."

His father looked impressed. "Yes, and all very affluent, I do not doubt," he said. "That sort of vice comes dear."

"Oddly enough, not everyone on the list is wealthy," he answered, beginning to pace back and forth across the carpet. "What they are is *powerful*—in one way or another. High-ranking military officers. Active members of Parliament. Government bureaucrats—all gentlemen, of course, but some of rather modest means."

Hauxton was leaning attentively forward. "Yes? Go on."

Tristan turned to face his father. "Did you know Madame Vostrikova requires a . . . a sort of business contract with her clients?"

Slowly, Hauxton shook his head.

"She requires them to state what services they are seeking, and set forth an agreed upon price," said Tristan. "Sometimes this contract stipulates a particular person whose services are being engaged, a time frame, and if the time frame is lengthy, it might provide for an annuity for the woman—"

"—or man?" his father interjected.

Tristan shrugged. "It's possible."

His father looked perplexed. "Men have been known to draw up contracts and annuities for their mistresses," he muttered. "But the other—surely no one would be so imprudent?"

"When it comes to sexual appetites, there is nothing so imprudent as a man with a stiff cock," Tristan remarked. "They will do incredibly foolish, remarkably shortsighted things to get a particular itch scratched, and worry about the cost to them afterward."

Hauxton lost what little color remained. His face went suddenly stark, and the trembling in his hands visibly worsened. Tristan lifted his gaze to the earl's, and understanding struck like a blow. His father, he realized, was thinking of his own marriage. Of his desperation to have that delicate, desirable thing which society and its strictures had placed just beyond his reach.

Well, he had taken it anyway. And they had all paid a price.

Sharply, Tristan cleared his throat. "Some sexual perversions can be almost addictive," he continued. "I've heard that Madame will allow you to sample the wares perhaps once, just enough to give you a taste of whatever depravity you desire. And then—if you let her—she will enslave you to it."

"In writing?"

Tristan shook his head. "That is the rumor," he answered. "Though it is hard for me to credit it."

"Dear God." Hauxton's hands drew into knobby fists. "Have you the list?"

Tristan extracted a scrap of paper from his coat pocket and passed it to his father.

His faded eyes ran down the names. "Dear God," he said again. "Are you sure?"

"Not remotely," said Tristan, going to the lamp by his father's bed. He took the note, lifted the glass, then touched it to the flame. He dropped it, smoldering, onto this father's breakfast tray.

Hauxton watched it burn. "Yes," he said when the paper had turned into a curl of black ash. "Yes, I daresay that was for the best."

A moment later, the door again opened. The black crows began flocking in, bringing with them their file boxes and their campaign desks, and alighting about the room in preparation for the day's activities. Tristan took the opportunity to make his bow to his father and flee, thanking God that he was not one of them.

He walked the mile back to Long Acre at a brisk clip, hoping to clear his head. For once, he had done what his father asked, and remarkably, Hauxton had seemed pleased with what he had thus far accomplished. In the past, Tristan had never given a damn whether his father was pleased or not. But today . . . yes, today he had almost begun to care. Then his father had shattered whatever nascent sense of camaraderie that had existed between them.

Nonetheless, Tristan had done his duty, and would continue to do so. Now if he could just expunge that vision of his father's face from his memory. That pale, stark look of recognition, and of regret. For if a man regretted his marriage, well, did he not also regret his children?

Hauxton did. On occasion, he'd even said so. When Tristan had pushed him beyond the range of bearing with his pranks and poor marks. His running away to become a mercenary. And later, with the choices he had made in leading his life. Many a truth was said in jest, or so the old saying went. Tristan had always believed the same could be said of rage.

"A woman came round looking for you, sir," said Uglow when he arrived home.

"A woman, eh?" he said as Uglow lifted the coat from his shoulders and set it aside for brushing. "Buxom and pretty, I hope?"

"Aye, a proper looker," Uglow agreed. "But all business, if yer knows wot I mean."

Something in Tristan's chest leapt. "Was she indeed?" he said, unbuttoning his waistcoat. "With chestnut hair, by any chance? And spectacles?"

Uglow looked at him oddly, the deep furrow returning to his brow. "Reddish-yellow hair," he said. "Left yer a letter."

Tristan's heart settled back into place and his brain kicked in. Lady Phaedra would never be so scandalous as to call upon a gentleman in his bachelor quarters. And he had no business hoping she had done so.

"On yer desk," Uglow grunted, pointing.

Tristan followed Uglow's finger, then hastened across the room, his waistcoat flapping open. The note was sealed in red wax, but the impression was perfectly ordinary. Roughly, he slit it open.

You wished me to name a time and place:
Tomorrow night. Half past nine.
The house opposite Gorsky's.
Ask for Mrs. Thompson.

Mrs. Thompson? Who the hell was Mrs. Thompson?

Then his parting words last night came back to him. Tristan whistled softly through his teeth. The note was written in a fine, tight copperplate with a sharp nib and nary a drip in sight. The foolscap was the heavy, ivory sort. The expensive sort. He knew who the note was from as surely as if he'd watched her write it out.

The house opposite Gorsky's. She meant across from Vostrikova's brothel, of course. A sudden chill settled over him, and with it came a strange frisson of excitement.

Good Lord. His gut had not been wrong after all.

Which only begged one question. What on earth was Phaedra Northampton up to?

Chapter 8

Stars, hide your fires,
Let not light see my black and deep desires.

The following afternoon a heavy dampness swept up from the Channel, creeping across Surrey and Sussex to swathe London in a murky brume. Tristan pulled on his oldest boots and the worn leather overcoat which had served him well during his years on the Continent, then set out on foot just as dusk approached. He had long ago learned the power of reconnaissance, and the importance of never walking into a situation one did not control.

Soho, being filled with dens of iniquity of one ilk or another, was well known to Tristan. He pulled down his hat brim, turned up his collar, and strolled past Madame Vostrikova's as dark settled in. The damp clung to his skin like a cool, wet froth, settling over his face and seemingly into his lungs. At the top of the street, a crested coach turned from the alley and went spinning through a puddle, throwing up filth which spattered across his boots.

Tristan looked down and cursed. On days like this, he almost—almost—missed Greece. But the spray of water, he reminded himself, was better than the spray of blood. Particularly one's own. Or that of an innocent, and God knew there were always plenty of innocents.

The house he watched stood three floors high, plus cellar and garret, and was tucked between a rather disreputable-looking coffeehouse and a shuttered linen draper's. At half past seven, someone lit a lamp on the first floor, but no one came or went through the front. Tristan crossed the street and ducked into the coffeehouse just as the drizzle turned to a dull roar that bounced off the pavement and rattled the downspouts.

"I'm looking for lodging," he said over the din, addressing the boy who'd brought his coffee. "What do you know of the house next door?"

The lad eyed him up and down. "I knows it ain't for the likes of you."

Apparently his old coat was not quite battered enough. "A bit dodgy, eh?" Tristan smiled. "Not a nunnery, is it?"

The boy shrugged and took the coin Tristan offered. "No, but not quite a doss house, neither," he said. "There's a girl or two works out o' there, though. Ask at the public house on Greek Street."

"The Pillars of Hercules?" Tristan knew it well.

"Aye, tell 'em you want ter see Cross-eyed Polly," the lad suggested. "She'll know 'oo's workin' tonight."

Tristan knew Polly, too. He rather liked her eyes. But he did not require a tankard of ale or anything Polly's friends might be selling. Tristan finished his coffee, then went around to the alleyway. The rain was coming down hard now. Grateful for his hat and coat, he made his way to the rear of the house, finding it as unremarkable as the front, save for the piles of old barrels and trash which had accumulated between the house and the privy.

A ditch ran along the garden wall, fetid and murky in the feeble light. Tristan stepped gingerly over it, almost tripped over a hissing cat, then picked his way through the rubbish to the kitchen windows. Through the rain that dribbled off his hat, he could see a girl sitting at a rough-hewn table, peeling potatoes. Otherwise nothing stirred.

It was a deceptive sort of calm. He was being drawn into something he could not control. His father had cast a lure; a lure he had known Tristan would be unable to resist. And now a piece of the puzzle lay inside that house—something tangled up in his own obsession over Phaedra Northampton—but in what shape or form, he did not know. He was inexplicably afraid for her.

Tristan rose from the window, took the knife from the cuff of his boot, and slipped it into the depths of his coat pocket. Then he went back to the front and dropped the knocker. A pockmarked crone in a faded smock answered the door, and a frightful smell—something like unwashed bodies simmering in stewed cabbage—assailed his nostrils.

"Good evening," he said, raising his voice over the rain. "I'm looking for Mrs. Thompson."

The woman eyed him up and down a little nastily. "Aye, no doubt," she muttered. "A milliner's assistant, indeed!"

Tristan looked down his impressive Talbot nose, mimicking his father's most imperious glare. "Mrs. Thompson," he said again. "If you please."

"Mind yer boots, then," she grumbled, gesturing toward a frayed rug. "Follow me—and be quiet about your business, sir. I run a respectable lodging 'ouse."

Deeply curious now, he shook the worst of rain from his coat and followed the woman up the twisting staircase until they could go no farther. A narrow door sat at the top of the steps. She rapped on it with the back of her gnarled hand. "Thompson!" she wheezed. "Yer got a caller."

The door creaked slowly open to reveal a nearly dark room. A woman in a white cap stood just inside, her form draped in shadow. "Aye?"

Tristan strained to see through the gloom, but the woman moved and sounded nothing like Phaedra. A frisson of apprehension ran down his spine. Who else, he wondered, might lurk there in the dark? His hand went to the knife, taking a firm grip on the hilt.

The crone leaned across the threshold. "If yer meanin' to entertain gents up here, Thompson, I'm to get 'alf," she said, her voice like gravel. "I said as much when yer took the room."

"Very well," said the woman in the shadows. "I shall settle with you later."

"Aye, that you will," said the crone. Shooting Tristan one last glower, she descended the steps.

Tristan did not wait, but pushed his way inside and shoved the door shut. One hand still on the knife, he yanked the woman to him and spun her about, his arm hooked over her throat. Her worn white cap slid to the floor.

The woman gasped in outrage, but the scent of Phaedra's fragrance and clean hair was unmistakable. A rush of relief flooded him. He released her throat and grabbed her arm.

"What the devil do you think you're doing?" he demanded, hauling her toward the lamp's meager light. "Have you any notion the danger you might be in?"

Remarkably unshaken, Phaedra regarded him disdainfully, one hand at her throat. "Danger?" Her usual cultured voice had returned. "From what? Ruffians like you?"

He looked down into her flashing blue eyes, and he felt the unwanted stir of raw, almost angry lust. "Yes, by God, perhaps." Then, before he realized what he meant to do, he yanked her to him and kissed her hard, with his lips and with his tongue, far more roughly than he should have done. But instead of slapping him senseless, Phaedra turned her face into his, opening her mouth. Water trickled from his hair onto her face, but she rose to him, and gave back as good as she got.

It did not last. Somehow, she pushed away from him, but she was shaken. Hell, *he* was shaken. "That coat smells like a wet dog, Talbot," she managed, her voice unsteady. "And you are dripping on my floor."

"Aye?" He yanked off his sodden hat, angry with himself for wanting her. "It's raining torrents, in case you hadn't noticed."

"Fine, give it to me." She made an impatient motion with her hand. "You may as well stay."

"Oh, I'm staying." He slipped the knife back into the depths of his pocket and slid out of the coat. "Now," he said darkly, "explain to me what you're doing in this place."

Phaedra hung the sodden garment on a peg, then

yanked a chair from an old deal table which was wedged into the corner. "You asked to meet me, you will recall," she said. "I do not need your permission to be here."

"No, you need the palm of your brother's hand on your backside for pulling this dangerous ruse," he returned.

She planted one hand on the table and leaned into him. "It sounds as if you're in a mood to do the job for him, Talbot," she whispered. "And here I'd thought you were all blithe charm and aimless flirtation."

"Aye, well, the truth will out, won't it?" He spoke with cold certainty. "You are playing a treacherous game, here, Phae."

She tossed him a speaking glance, drew out the adjacent chair, and sat. Reluctantly, he followed suit, his gaze drifting about the room. His eyes having adjusted to the light, Tristan could see that the garret was small and narrow, the rain loud on the roof which lay just inches above their heads. The chamber held a hearth with a hob, an old oak cupboard, and—to his acute discomfort—an old barley-twist bed tucked under the rafters in the rear. Save for the rickety table and chairs they sat in, the low room was devoid of any decoration.

He returned his gaze to Phaedra. Her lips were faintly swollen from the roughness of his kiss. Frustrated, he tossed his hat onto the table, and plowed a hand through his damp hair. Good God, he did not need this; did not want the hot rush of desire which seemed to strike him every time he saw the girl. "All right," he said quietly. "Let's talk."

Phaedra reached for the lamp which sat on the table and turned up the wick. The flame cast dancing shadows across the planes of her face as she leaned over it, magnifying the length of her thick, feathery lashes and heightening her extraordinary cheekbones.

Tonight she had again eschewed her spectacles and twisted her hair into a tight, plain knot. She wore drab, loose clothing that clearly was not her own. With that habit of keeping her face turned slightly away from one's gaze, as if she wished to melt into her surroundings, she could have been a servant or even a shopgirl. She looked . . . anonymous. And he sensed she'd had years of practice at being anonymous, in one form or another.

"I let this garret a few weeks ago," she said. "Shortly after we came up from Hampshire."

His eyes never left her face. "Why?"

Phaedra drew back an inch. "I do not care for your tone, Talbot," she retorted. "Indeed, I liked you better as a frivolous scoundrel. I begin to wonder why I should I talk to you at all."

Because if she didn't, he was going to kidnap her this instant, and give her over into Nash's keeping—or, if he gave into his baser nature, something worse. Either way, she'd be safe—from everything save him. Somehow, Tristan held his tongue.

He turned one hand over, opening it. As if it had been planned, the hammer of the rain on the roof just above them relented to a dull rattle, and a calm settled over the room. "Phae, you should talk to me because I am on your side," he answered, forcing his tone to soften with the rain. "Because I care for you and your safety. This is a questionable neighborhood, and this place—" Here, he paused to cast his gaze about the tawdry garret. "God's truth, Phae, you don't belong in a place like this."

He watched in the flickering lamplight as something in her eyes softened. "It is perfectly wretched, isn't it?" she murmured. "And yet better than what a great many in London enjoy. But I chose it because it has the perfect vantage point. It overlooks Mr. Gorsky's front door."

Tristan's jaw hardened. "You have been watching him."

"Yes." She cut an assessing glance at him. "Or watching the house, I should say."

His hands fisting, Tristan closed his eyes and swallowed hard. "Good God," he whispered hollowly. "It was *you*. In the alleyway that night. When I . . . when I tried to—"

"—to tempt me into your bed?" she dryly suggested. "Or would there even have been a bed involved in the bargain? Alas, I was compelled to decline the honor. I'm sure, though, that you would have been all that legend suggests."

"Phaedra," he managed. "For God's sake. This is not funny. What if I had—"

"You wouldn't," she swiftly interjected. "Whatever else you may be, you are too much a gentleman for that."

"You don't know that," he warned her.

"Oh, but I do." She gave a swift, oddly muted smile. She was keeping, he sensed, some sort of secret from him. "Trust me, Talbot. I know the difference between a man who understands *no* and a man who presses his advantage unfairly."

He looked at her for a long moment, wondering what she meant as he studied the angles of her face in the lamplight. The high forehead and slightly sharp nose. The wide, intelligent eyes and the mouth which, strictly speaking, was too wide, and yet looked perfect on her face.

Yes, she had always been vaguely familiar to him. But why? Even that night in the alley, it had been as if he'd known her on some visceral level he could not quite explain. If he closed his eyes, only for an instant, he could still feel her round, perfect backside pressed against his swollen . . . ah, but as she said, what was there now to talk about? "I think," he said darkly, "that you'd best tell me what you know of Gorsky."

"Almost nothing," she swore, setting one hand flat upon the table as if it were the Bible. "You must believe me."

"Go on."

"I met him quite by accident," she continued. "I called there once, you see. At the house across the way. And . . . well, when I refused to leave—rather loudly, I might add—the girl who'd answered the door sent for him."

Somehow, Tristan hid his terror. He reached across the table and covered her hand with his. "Why would you go to such a place, Phae?" he asked. "Surely you comprehend the risk to your reputation?"

"I was looking for someone," she began. "And for a reason more important to me than my reputation."

"Who?"

She stared into the gloomy depths of the room. "A girl from our village in Hampshire," she whispered. "My maid Agnes's younger sister. Her name is Millie, and she worked in the village tavern. She's barely nineteen, you see, and she ran away to London just before Christmastime. To seek her fortune."

"Yes?" asked Tristan skeptically. "And how did she mean to do it?"

Phaedra dropped her gaze. "On her back, of course," she admitted. "Millie has this cloud of brilliant red hair— just a lovely, almost ethereal creature. And I think she imagined that—"

"That a rich man might be persuaded to keep her?" he interjected.

Phaedra nodded. "Yes, poor girl," she murmured. "She told her aunt that she was tired of being poor, and that she meant to make a fortune to support Priss, her daughter. But Millie is too young and to naïve to understand what she is giving up. *Her child*, Talbot. And if I could find her—oh, surely I could convince her what an unforgivable mistake that would be?"

"I don't know," he said honestly.

Phaedra hung her head. "I am sure, too, that Millie never considered when Priss was older, she would realize that . . . well, that her mother was a fallen woman."

Tristan was willing to bet she'd thought of it, and didn't give a bloody damn. He leaned back in his chair and tossed one booted ankle across his knee. "And this child," he prodded. "Has she a father?"

Phaedra stared into the lamplight for a long moment. "Must I say?" she asked. "Will you refuse to help me if I do not tell you?"

He was beginning to have a deep, uneasy suspicion as to why she'd summoned him here. "Phaedra, I can't help you even if you do," he answered. "You are in danger. One man is already dead. That house—those people over there—they are treacherous."

At that, Phaedra reached out, and set both her hands on his forearm. "Talbot, listen to me." Her words were low and hoarse. "You don't understand. *They have Millie.*"

"They have her?" His eyes searched her face. "Phae, how do you know?"

Phaedra released his arm and let her shoulders sag. Her every gesture spoke of a bone-deep weariness. It made Tristan wonder how long she'd been at this—worrying herself sick and skulking around all night, he did not doubt. He wished he could have saved her from it.

"Millie's letters home all came from this house," Phaedra whispered. "She had taken a room here from Mrs. Wooten. In one of her letters she told Agnes that she had found a place with a woman who lived across the street. This woman . . . she had promised to help Millie. And to—I don't know—to facilitate her entrée into whatever world one would call it."

"The demimonde," said Tristan. "At least that's what your Millie likely hoped. But what those people over there do, Phae—it is nothing like the simple arrangements gentlemen make with their high flyers. What they do—what they sell—are sexual perversions of the worst sort."

Phaedra let her head fall back against the upper slat of the rickety chair. "Oh, Lord," she breathed. "I just knew it was something dreadful. Millie's last letter came near Candlemas. And after that . . . nothing."

Tristan leaned into her. "Phaedra, you cannot be sure," he pressed. "If she went there, she may be gone already. She may have been given over to a man for his use, and taken away. That often happens in that house. Or, sadly, she may have come to a bad end."

He regretted his hard words the moment he saw her gaze soften. "Oh, Talbot," she whispered. "Oh, please do not say that. I could not bear to think of Priss motherless."

"Tristan," he said quietly. "Phae, I think at this point you should call me Tristan."

She laughed, but there was a faintly hysterical edge to it. "I should be calling you Avoncliffe," she said. "*That* is your name."

He took her hand in his, and this time he did not release it. "I would like you to call me Tristan, Phae, when we're alone—which, of course, we never should be. I shouldn't have come here, and now that I see you are alone, I ought to leave. If I were any sort of a gentleman, I would."

"You are concerned for me?" The edge was still in her voice. "Good God, with everything else we have to worry about. Please. Tristan. Just . . . stay. Help me think what to do."

He tightened his grip on her hand. "Phae, I'm staying, but I'm certainly not the sort of man your family would wish you to keep company with," he said. "I think we both know that's why you did not want me to meet your mother."

Her smile was wry in the lamplight. "Do have a care, sir, when you leap to your conclusions," she warned. "My mother long ago lost whatever discernment she possessed in regard to finding me a husband. You will do quite nicely, I can assure you."

His mouth curled into a smile. "Have you been so very difficult?" he murmured. "One can scarce imagine it."

"I know my own mind," she said.

"And you are not looking for a husband." He squeezed her hand once more, then let it go. "That is a shame. But God knows I am not looking for a wife. Look, Phae, let me see you safely home to Brook Street. I'm afraid I must insist."

"No," she said firmly. "Not until I've found Millie."

"We must accept that she may have vanished into the netherworld of London. Phae, it happens."

"No," Phaedra retorted, fisting both hands. "No, I cannot accept that. I won't. Priss is not even two years old, Tristan. She *needs* a mother."

The tone of her voice was determined. Almost ruthless. Tristan knew, then, what he was up against. A little roughly, he shoved back his chair and jerked to his feet to walk away. It was either that, or drag Phaedra over his knee for a spanking. Or into his lap for something worse. He began to pace the narrow chamber, dipping his head unthinkingly to avoid the low ceilings.

"You are dragging your hand through your hair again," she said from her chair. "What does that mean?"

That he was losing his mind. That he was questioning everything he'd ever wanted.

As to going home, Phaedra would not be persuaded. He already knew it. She wanted him to help her. And if he did not . . . well, God only knew what she might do. Bumble along on her own, no doubt, and get herself killed as Gorsky had done. The frightening thing was, in some ways, helping her did not seem so illogical. They both wanted the same thing. They wanted to know just what was going on inside that house.

"Tell me about Gorsky," he finally said, knowing he would regret it. "Tell me every word that passed between you."

And so she did. In the end she had, it seemed, made rather a scene at Vostrikova's, demanding her Millie be brought down and refusing to leave without her. But Gorsky had denied any knowledge of the girl, turning aside even Phaedra's most emotional pleas. Then Phaedra had resorted to threats—and made the mistake, perhaps, of invoking her elder brother's name.

"Of course I would never have gone to Stefan," she explained. "I daresay Gorsky knew it, too. He was enough of a predator to sense my desperation. There was a look, Tristan . . . this sort of dead yet watchful look in his eyes."

Tristan knew, strangely, just what she meant. He had seen such men on the battlefield; weary and without sentiment, from the years of enduring man's inhumanity to man. "He has seen so much degradation," Tristan murmured, "he likely did not care."

At that, Phaedra lifted a delicately arched eyebrow. "So I thought, at first," she said. "But at the end, there was perhaps a hint of . . . well, of *empathy* in his eyes. I had the oddest feeling he was considering helping me. Nonetheless, he did not relent."

Suddenly Tristan stopped pacing. She had just made a very good point. "Your threat, Phae, about Nash," he said a little sharply. "Why didn't you simply go to him to begin with? Why try to handle this tawdry business on your own?"

At that, Phaedra hesitated. "I . . . I cannot involve Stefan in this."

Tristan swiftly ran through the logic. "The child is his?" he asked. "The child is his, and he does not know? Or he doesn't wish his wife to know?"

"Oh, no!" said Phaedra sharply. "You must not think such a thing."

"Then the child is Mr. Hayden-Worth's," said Tristan more certainly. "And you didn't wish Lord Nash to know that his brother had seduced a young village girl."

Phaedra said nothing, but the blush of truth was upon her face. The notion made a certain amount of sense, too. Nash had already dealt with the expensive scandal Hayden-Worth's wife had caused the Government. Perhaps he was at the end of his tether when it came to his stepbrother?

On the other hand, Tristan had always heard that Hayden-Worth's sexual preferences ran in an altogether different direction. But then, he *had* taken a wife. Which might or might not mean a damned thing.

Phaedra was looking downcast. "If you could but see her, you would understand," she said, her voice laced with pain. "She is such a rosy-cheeked, pretty little thing— Priss, I mean. But she cried for a whole day and a whole night after Millie left. It . . . It breaks my heart. I would take her, Tristan, if I could. I would take her and raise her as my own—but I cannot."

Tristan sat back down again, and drew his chair closer.

"I confess, Phae, I don't care who your brother's been bedding," he said. "But this child—"

"She's my *niece*," Phaedra interjected. "She's my *blood*, Tristan. I have a duty to her, don't I? Even if her paternity is a secret?"

Little in a country village was secret. But he would permit Phaedra this one small fantasy. "And you are to be commended for wishing to do your duty," he said quietly, his mind still turning matters over. "Tell me, Phae, did you ever speak to Madame Vostrikova? Could she identify you?"

He prayed to God the answer was *no*.

Apparently, it was. Phaedra was looking at him blankly. "Who is Madame Vostrikova?"

Tristan hesitated. "The brothel's . . . er, owner, if you will," he said. "You did not know?"

Phaedra shook her head. "I didn't even know Gorsky till I rang the bell," she repeated. "But the day he died . . ." Her expression went suddenly stark.

Tristan leaned forward and took both her hands. "Yes?"

Phaedra sighed. "Tristan, I think Gorsky had been following me," she answered. "That day, I saw him hiding in the shadows on my way to Mr. Kemble's shop. But when he saw Agnes, he . . . well, he seemed simply to vanish."

"Indeed," Tristan murmured. "And then you went on to Mr. Kemble's?"

Phaedra nodded. "I had sketched Gorsky, you see. From memory. I'm not a bad hand with pencils, so I drew a passable likeness, and was taking my folio down to Mr. Kemble's to see if perhaps Gorsky was anyone he recognized. I thought . . . oh, I don't know. I thought Kemble might be able to help me somehow. He . . . knows people who know things, if you know what I mean."

Tristan did know, but another alarm bell was clanging in his head. "Phae," he said urgently, "this sketch. Did anyone else see it?"

"No." She shook her head. "No, not even Mr. Kemble. Zoë came in, you see, and we got distracted. Later, after Gorsky was stabbed, I took it home and I burnt it. It just seemed . . . safest. I knew he had died for a reason. I just sensed it."

"Good girl," said Tristan.

She lifted her gaze to his, her eyes wide and grieving. "Tristan, what in God's name is happening?" she asked. "Did I . . . did *I* cause that man to be killed?"

"You did not," said Tristan firmly. "His choice of a dangerous career working for an evil woman is what killed him. But what I should like to know is who did it."

She cut a swift, assessing glance at him. "I think you already have a theory."

He hesitated, uncertain how much to tell her. "It is said that he and Madame Vostrikova had a terrible row over something," Tristan said reluctantly. "Specifically . . . well, a young man."

"A young man?"

"Vostrikova had engaged a young lad to work for her," he answered. "A very pretty young man. God only knows how she got him. Kidnapped him or drugged him or just enslaved him with money or perhaps with something worse."

"Oh," said Phaedra softly. She had begun to toy with a button on the front of her smock. "Yes. I . . . I think perhaps I comprehend."

Tristan almost hoped she did not, but he plunged ahead. "Gorsky, it is said, developed an attachment to the lad," he continued. "I really should rather not explain it further, Phae, if you do not mind. Suffice it to say Gorsky began to take objection to Vostrikova's use of the boy, and—"

"Boy?" Phaedra's head jerked up. "I thought you said he was a young man?"

The lad had been fourteen, or so Tristan had been told, and Vostrikova had leased him out to a peer with a penchant for pretty boys and a seat in faraway Lancashire. It had taken twenty pounds and a passage to Jamaica to get the scullery maid to tell him that much, and she hadn't known the man's name.

But Tristan wasn't sure how to explain such vile things to Phaedra. Still, if the man was a government nabob— and Vostrikova ensnared no other kind—then he would be found sooner rather than later. Lancashire just wasn't that large a place.

"He was a young man," said Tristan quietly. "And Vostrikova sent him away. That's all I can say. But it was the root, I begin to think, of a falling-out between Vostrikova and her henchman."

"What happened to the boy?" She had defaulted, Tristan noticed, to the more diminutive term. Yet again he realized Phaedra was not naïve. She understood the world could be a wicked place.

"I saw de Vendenheim this morning in Whitehall," said Tristan. "I gave him what information I had. They are looking for the lad. He will find him."

"So he will." Phaedra relaxed into her chair. "He's perfectly ruthless when right is on his side—and sometimes even when it isn't. No one keeps secrets from de Vendenheim."

Her remark brought home to him yet again the importance of getting Phaedra out of this mess. He simply prayed she was still beyond Vostrikova's notice, and that Gorsky's murder while following her was just a crime of opportunity. Everything he had learned thus far suggested as much. But Gorsky, he suspected, had been looking for a private moment in which to approach Phaedra.

Perhaps he had wished to unburden himself. Or, more likely, he'd wished to see Vostrikova punished for sending the object of his affection away. And Phaedra had the right connections for that: two prominent brothers, one rich and powerful, the other politically influential—and both of them untainted, so far as Tristan could discover, by any association with Vostrikova.

One word to them of the blackmail, treason, and outright enslavement which went on under her roof, and the infamous madam might never have seen the outside of a prison cell again. Yes, Gorsky, he suspected, had been looking to strike a bargain with Phaedra.

"You have been very brave, Phae, in trying to find your Millie," he said quietly. "And it was very clever of you, taking this room."

"Little good it's done," she answered. "As we now know, most everyone comes and goes through the rear."

"Yes, well, they have the sort of clients with much to hide," said Tristan. "As you have probably guessed, Madame Vostrikova is running a very particular sort of brothel."

In the candlelight, a lovely shade of pink graced her cheeks. "Indeed, I collect the place is thought quite dangerous," she answered. "People will tell Mrs. Thompson things they won't so willingly share with Lady Phaedra."

"There are some wicked goings-on in that house, it's true," he acknowledged.

Her gaze drifted up him, and to his shock, there was a heated flicker of sensual assessment in her eyes. "Anything you haven't done?"

"Oh, a thing or two, I daresay," he answered, wishing to the devil his cock didn't rouse every time she came within three feet of him. "My appetites, Phae, are pretty conventional by comparison to that crowd."

"What do you think of them?" she asked quietly. "These men, I mean, who wish to engage in such things? Are they . . . evil? Or merely depraved?"

Tristan shrugged. "So long as those men aren't hurting anyone—well, anyone who doesn't wish to be hurt—then it's no one's business, I daresay. But Vostrikova doesn't stop at that."

She looked away, color flaming up her cheeks. "What about women, Tristan?" she whispered. "Are there women who enjoy wickedness? And if they do, aren't they just like those men? If they . . . if they just can't stop thinking about it, are they—I don't know—wrong, somehow? Do they tempt men to be bad?"

"Some, perhaps," he agreed, not entirely certain what

she was asking. "Yes, there are women who are sirens of a sort, I suppose."

Her eyes flashed with an emotion he'd never seen before. "I'm tired of being ignorant," she rasped. "I don't know what's happened to Millie. And I don't understand anything. Everyone walks dainty circles around me, and I'm sick to death of it."

He lifted her hand from his arm, but did not release it. "My dear, we're treading dangerous ground," he replied. "Come, let me take you home."

"Please don't think me ungrateful," she retorted, turning a little away from him. "But I mean to play this role until I know what's happened to Millie. And in some ways, Tristan, being Mrs. Thompson has its advantages."

"What do you mean?"

She lifted one shoulder. "This place might be a hovel, but I may do as I please here," she answered. "People believe me an impoverished, lower-class widow, not some virginal, pampered princess who might faint if she learnt anything of the real world—the world beyond Temple Bar and Covent Garden. The world of Mr. Gorsky and those poor women who must work there. There is beauty, Tristan, in truth, even when it is an ugly truth."

He thought he understood, strangely, what she meant. A woman like Phaedra—especially when unwed—lived in a gilded cage. A beautiful existence, but a cage nonetheless.

She rose, and he followed suit. Her chin was up, her shoulders straight but delicate, and the sudden, fierce longing to protect her surged inside him again. But it wasn't what she wanted, he knew. Moreover, the notion doubtless would pass, as did most of his more honorable impulses. God knew he was no guardian angel. Nonetheless, he lifted his hand, and set the back of his fingers to her cheek. It was warm and soft, like the rest of her body, he did not doubt. "Let me, Phae," he ordered. "Let me deal with this Millie business for you."

Her eyes flashed. "No, I mean to see this through," she said. "I won't be mollycoddled, Tristan. Not by any man."

"By God, Phae, I am not *any man*," he said darkly, gripping her upper arm. "I weigh thirteen stone and stand better than six feet. I have a knife in my pocket and a pistol in my boot, both of which I am extraordinarily skilled in using. I've been shot, stabbed, and beaten half to death so often it doesn't much bother me. Furthermore, I have the full faith and authorization of the Crown behind me. But aye, I'm a just man."

"Well, when you put it that way, you sound such a tempting package." She cut a curious glance at him. "We will work together, Tristan. It mayn't be what you want, but that is my offer."

He jerked her closer, his frustration deepening. "You aren't in a position to offer me anything, my dear," he gritted. "Certainly not what I *want*."

She looked at him boldly then, her body mere inches from his. "What *do* you want, then, Tristan?" she murmured, her voice low and throaty. "Just say it. I am, after all, Mrs. Thompson tonight."

"What the devil does that mean?"

She lowered her lashes seductively. "I am . . . anonymous," she answered. "I am, one might argue, that same woman you met in the alleyway. The one you invited to your bed."

"I'll show you want I want, then." The words came out low and rough. He kissed her again, this time more sensuously. Phaedra made a soft sound in the back of her throat, then reached up to curl one hand behind his head, to avoid the wound she had so carefully stitched. Slowly, he thrust inside her mouth, tasting her deeply and languidly, half waiting for her to shove him away. The intimacy of the kiss—what he suggested—was unmistakable.

But she did not push him away. Instead she slid her tongue sinuously along his, making him shudder with barely tethered restraint. Eventually, her mouth slid from his, skimming lightly along his jaw. "Another time, perhaps," she whispered, her lips moving up to brush his ear. "Those were your words to me in the alley that night. Did you mean it? I've seen how they all look at you, fanning and whispering."

"Careful what you wish for, love," he rasped.

"It's wrong, I know." She sounded breathless. A little frightened of herself. "My mother says . . ."

He ran this thumb across her cheek. "What?"

Phaedra's eyes closed, her lashes like dark lace across her skin, and something inside him tore. "Mamma says a real lady shouldn't feel lust," she whispered. "But you know things, don't you? About pleasing women, I mean?"

He made a sound of disbelief. "If real ladies do not feel lust, Phae, why are they forever handing me their cards?" His opposite hand came up to cradle her face, and he was shocked to see it tremble. "Your mother is wrong, Phae. Passion is beautiful. Normal. *Necessary.*"

"I am tempted, Tristan," she murmured, the second hand joining the first, flat against his chest as she leaned into him. "Can you live up to your lofty reputation?"

He didn't like her choice of words, but he'd earned his notoriety, he supposed. And now he was treading in dark water, for there was something about her that called to what was left of the gentleman in him, and made him think of foolish, fanciful things. Alone, in this cocoon of quiet intimacy, with the seductive rumble of the rain just inches above their heads, and that old spindle bed tempting him, Phaedra was beginning to make a frightening amount of sense.

Desire had been simmering in his loins since the moment he'd entered this room, growling and snarling at the chit. His mask was down—that jovial, devil-may-care façade he reserved for the rest of the world—with her, it no longer worked. And he wasn't sure he wished it to.

Phaedra turned her face into the curve of his hand. "Tristan," she whispered against it, her tongue lightly brushing his palm. "Can you make me stop . . . aching?"

So be it.

Tristan let his fingers slide into the fine, soft hair at Phaedra's temples, and felt his breath shudder from his lungs. "A month, then," he whispered. "Give me one month, Phae, to deal with Vostrikova. And I promise you, I will discover what happened to Millie. Will you do that? Will you trust me?"

She licked her lips, and cut her eyes away. "Yes," she said softly. "I . . . I shall try."

Still cradling her face in his hands, he bent his head and took her mouth roughly. If his kiss beneath the pergola had been too bold, this one was an outright pillage. He drove her head back, surging inside with long, deep strokes which left no doubt of his body's intention. To take. To thrust. To taste until he was sated.

Perhaps he hoped, somewhere deep in his mind, that she would turn tail and bolt down the stairs. If so, he was to be disappointed. Phaedra's mouth molded hungrily to his, her body rising until her breasts were flat against his chest. It was as if she melted into him, her hands sliding around his waist, then up, to the heavy muscles of his upper back.

Her every motion was seduction itself, but without guile, without the calculation he'd come to expect of his lovers. She did not mean to tempt him. She simply did, answering his lust with her own. Later he realized he should have questioned her grasp of what was about to happen, but in those first heated moments it was beyond him.

She said no more, but instead slid her hands beneath his coat, pushing it off his shoulders. Tristan let it go. Her fingers tugged at the hem of his shirt, drawing it from his trousers, and he gave one last thought to ordering her to stop. It didn't last. She set her palms to the bare skin of his ribs and he shivered, then drew her back into his arms for another kiss.

Only a cad would do this to an innocent, he told himself. But Phaedra kept touching him—touching him in a way that was not at all innocent—and driving him past the point of control. He was not perfectly sure who undressed who. He remembered only her hands on his bare flesh, and her breasts rising and falling beneath the thin lawn of her shift. And his fingers fulfilling his fantasy—pulling the pins from her hair as he watched it spill down in heavy, chestnut waves. Stripped to the waist, he pulled her to the bed and drew her between his legs. "I shouldn't," he murmured, his mouth going to her collarbone.

He kissed her there longingly as she stood before him, then untied her shift and pushed the fabric off one shoulder. To his surprise, her breasts were bound with a strip of cotton wrapped twice around. He tugged it loose and they sprang free like large, ripe fruit, their tips already taut and erect, begging for his mouth. His lips captured one through the fabric, and she cried out, her hands spearing into his hair as she stilled his head.

"*Tristan*," she murmured.

Lazily, he circled her nipple with his tongue, his hand going to the other breast, weighing it, then lightly thumbing the nipple until she arched into his palm with another thready cry of pleasure.

His head swam with the scent of her hair. He fisted his hand in her hem and dragged it almost savagely to her waist. His cock was shoving at the fabric of his trousers now. He untied her drawers and felt the soft linen breeze down her legs. Tristan forced himself to resist the urge to free his straining weight; to pull her into his lap and thrust up and inside her on one triumphant stroke. It would not do; not for a woman of no experience.

Instead he found the swell of her firm buttock and filled his hand, squeezing it. Good God, he wanted to take her like this, he realized. On her belly. On her knees. On top of him. Any way he could have her. But not yet. Not yet.

When she moaned against his mouth, he stood and lifted her greedily to him. In response, she pulled her lips from his, her eyes glassy, her breath rough. Without speaking, Phaedra set her hands to work at the buttons of his trousers, almost tearing them free in her awkward eagerness.

He was a man who ordinarily took his time with such things, but he shucked his trousers and boots in a fevered rush. Dimly he realized they were approaching a point of no return. Phaedra did not mean to stop him. He knew that this was inevitable. Knew he was going to lie her down on that shabby little bed, thrust himself deep inside her, and make her his forever. The realization frightened him. Awed him. And did not slow him down one whit.

When he turned to face her, his erection heavy and jutting through his drawers, Phaedra's eyes widened. But undeterred, she came into his arms, setting her warm palms against his chest, this time stroking her fingers down the hair which dusted his chest and ran down his belly. "I want you," she murmured, as if convincing herself. "I want this, Tristan."

When she touched him lower with her light, clever fingers, he gasped. "Minx," he said again. "You're going to have me. Get on the bed."

With one last glance at his jutting manhood, Phaedra did as he asked, settling onto it almost girlishly, one leg tucked beneath her. Dimly he recalled that, no matter how passionate she might be, she was untutored. He followed her to the bed, his drawers hanging low on his hips, dipping his head beneath the low, peaked rafters. He bent over her to kiss her again, hotly and openmouthed, twining his tongue sinuously in a seductive dance of need.

When they came apart gasping, he slowly drew the shift over her head. Phaedra lifted her arms and bent her head slightly as the fabric slid away, a vision of beautiful, feminine surrender. Only then, when the linen had drifted to the floor and Phaedra sat naked before him did he fully comprehend the beauty of her body.

His eyes swept over her as his mouth went dry. Phaedra was made for sin, with wide hips, lush, slightly pendulous breasts, and legs almost as long as his own. Legs which went on forever—until they didn't. And there lay her glory, a nest of dark gold curls which invited a man's tongue—and some of his other appendages—to linger. "Phae, you are made for this," he whispered. "Those gray gowns—yes, I can see why you had to wear them."

She lifted her gaze to him and said nothing, but merely raised her arms as if to draw him to her. Tristan did not need another invitation. Pure longing and a raw, pulsing need hammered in his head and throbbed in his rod with every beat of his heart.

He set one knee to the bed and crawled over her, pushing her onto the mattress as he went. When her head lay back against the bolster, her brown-gold hair fanned out like a pheasant's wings, he kissed her again, his arms braced over her head. Beneath him she squirmed, then her body arched to his like a magnet drawn to north, brushing her curls against this heated cock. With one hand, he pushed her down again. "You wanted me to live up to my reputation," he whispered, his tongue stroking along the shell of her ear. "Lie back, sweet, and let me make you grateful."

"Yes . . . all right."

Without explanation, he slid down the bed and pushed her thighs wide. He shifted his weight between her legs, ignoring the insistent throb between his own. Phaedra sucked in her breath when he set his lips to her belly, and shivered when he thrust his tongue into her navel, languidly circling.

She gasped again when he spread her flesh wide with his fingers. He set his mouth where his fingers had been, and she shuddered beneath him. Lightly, teasingly, he stroked his tongue through her open flesh, and Phaedra whimpered softly, then cried out his name.

"Shush, shush," he whispered. "Hold tight."

Her nails dug into the tattered coverlet, her hips arching. Then Tristan plunged his tongue deep into the silken folds of her womanhood, lightly licking at the silken pearl of her arousal. Phaedra's trembling deepened, and one hand lashed out to grasp his shoulder.

Softly, he laughed. "Relax, my sweet," he murmured. "Relax and let it take you."

"I—I thought you would come inside me," she whispered uncertainly. "I think . . . that this could be more dangerous."

"Oh?" he murmured, just before stroking her again. "In what way?"

He flicked a quick glance up to see that her head had rolled back against the bolster. "Addictive," she whispered into the low rafters, quivering again. "Utterly . . . enslaving. Oh, God. I fear I will dream of this."

"Oh, that is the very idea, love," he said. "I would gladly have you as my slave and bend you to my will."

And bend her over the bed. And over his knee. And perhaps, he considered, *given that fine, plump arse of hers, over the kitchen table.* One look at her lush, ripe body and a man's mind began to run hot and mad.

Ah, but his turn was next, he consoled himself. Tristan dipped his head and lapped at her with light, teasing strokes until she shook and the bed began to shake with her. Phaedra's fingers went to the head of the bed, seizing at the spindles of the old oak headboard and entwining her hands through them as if she might cut off her own blood. As if she feared being cast out to sea on the waves of her own passion.

"Hold me," she whispered, wrenching at the spindles. "I can't—*oh*. Hold me."

Tristan watched her writhe, awestruck as her hunger deepened, almost exploding himself. Passion possessed her—left her gasping—and yet Phaedra could not reach it. On impulse, he spread his upper arms across her legs and held her immobile, fully exposed to his mouth. It seemed to be just what she wanted. It drove her near the edge.

She cried out softly at first, and then her panting rose to a breathy, urgent rhythm as he suckled her little nub. Then her head went back one last time on a silent, open cry. She shuddered, and shuddered again, and then was spent.

When Phaedra again lay limply, her hands above her head relaxing and her fingers slowly curling into her palms, Tristan crawled back up the bed, biting back his own burning need. Steeling himself for what was to come. *He could still stop*, he dimly reminded himself.

A better man than himself would have. But Phaedra lay beneath him, her heavy breasts still tipped with tautly budded nipples, her eyes somnolent with pleasure, her legs open to take him, and Tristan knew he hadn't the strength. He had committed himself to the inevitable. To her. He knelt over her, and drew his hand up through the warm folds of her flesh, then probed deeper with his fingers. One finger and then a second slipped inside as Phaedra watched him. She was ready and slick with her own need, her womanly passage open for their joining. Their union as man and woman. Lover and beloved.

There was no point in postponing the inevitable, for like any sort of pain, keen and quick was best. Tristan took himself in hand and probed gently. As if she were made for him, he slipped easily inside. Phaedra moaned, but not in pain, her eyelashes dropping shut. Tristan, too, closed his eyes, drew back, and thrust deep.

And there was . . . nothing. Nothing but warm, feminine flesh enfolding him. Welcoming him. Drawing him deep as if drawing him home. Tentatively, he rocked himself back and forth inside her.

Well. This he had not expected.

Phaedra touched him lightly, a little uncertainly, her hands settling over his shoulders. He opened his eyes and smiled down at her. He began to move back and forth, and it was like turning up the wick on a lamp. Heat and flame sprung at once to her eyes. "Yes," she said, holding his gaze. "Ohh! Tristan. Like that."

There was no hesitation, and no pain. Just a clear blue

sea of pleasure ahead of him, stretching to infinity. Tristan set a rhythm of deep, perfect thrusts, sliding their bodies together even as he reined back his own eagerness. He knew without asking that Phaedra would reach the stars with him. Already her need was growing. She drew her knees up, and moved restlessly beneath him as their bodies slickened and slid and moved as one, making the old bed creak.

"Yes," she said again, closing her eyes and licking her lips. "Oh, God."

It had been a long time since Tristan had seen a woman lose herself so deeply and so quickly. Phaedra's need was a palpable thing, and it served only to ratchet his own desire to a feverish pitch. And yet it challenged him. Drove him. On impulse, he picked up her knee and hitched it over his shoulder, deepening his thrust.

Phaedra opened her eyes, and looked at him hungrily then lifted her other leg and followed suit. "Oh, yes," she murmured, hooking it over his shoulder. "Like that, Tris. *Ohh—!*"

He dragged her fully against him, both hands grasping the slender turn of her waist, driving himself home again and again as he ruthlessly stilled her to his thrusts. Phaedra took him deep, her face a mask of welling passion.

For long moments he loved her, until the rain had stopped and the streets beyond the little garret grew still. Until he was panting, perspiration trickling down his throat, dripping onto her pale, perfect breasts. Again and again he thrust, rocking into her, driving them into an upward, feverish spiral. The ropes of the old bed were groaning in protest even as Phaedra's sobbing heightened.

She was on the edge, and he was about to explode. And still there was no end.

Good God, he thought. *She was going to kill him.* She was supposed to be an untutored virgin, and he the indefatigable Lothario. *And she was going to kill him.*

Phaedra had both wrists twisted almost painfully through the wooden spindles of the bed now as she writhed and sobbed beneath him, seeking her release. And suddenly, it dawned on him that what she craved—whether she understood it or not—was to be controlled. To be restrained in some way. Her own passion was almost beyond her. The raw eroticism of the notion shocked him.

Her knees tightened over his shoulders, dragging her feminine heat to his groin, increasing the friction of their bodies, and still she could not find her edge. Abruptly, he stopped, and bent over her to kiss her, fumbling at the edge of the bed.

Her eyes flew open and she looked at him beseechingly, her gaze moving over his face. "Tristan?" she whispered uncertainly.

"Give me your hand." The words came out thick and husky.

Obediently she disentangled it from the spindles. Already her thumb had turned faintly blue. He encircled her wrist with his cravat, once, and then again for good measure, lashing it tight. He held it up for her to see.

"Is this what you need, Phae?" he rasped.

She opened her mouth soundlessly. "I don't know what I need," she whimpered. "I just want and want—and for what, I don't know." She turned her face away and closed her eyes.

"Give me the other hand," he said more gently.

Willingly, she did so. He bound both wrists together, tightly but not so tight as to lessen the blood flow, then shoved them high above her head. Deftly, he lashed both hands to the spindles until he was sure she could not escape.

"Pull hard against it," he ordered.

She did so, her eyes widening, her throat working up and down. It was understood. She was his to command now.

"Does it hurt?" he asked.

She shook her head, her thick hair scrubbing the bolster. "Not . . . not in a bad way."

He set his hands to either side of her face and kissed her deeply with his lips and with his tongue—and perhaps even with a little bit of his heart. "There," he said when he was done. "You're bound to me, love."

She looked at him unblinkingly, her eyes still soft with need. "Yes," she whispered eagerly. "Yes, Tristan."

He gave the knots a hard yank. "See, Phae?" he whispered. "You can't get free. No matter how hard you fight it, you can't get free of me. Now let yourself go, love. Come to me."

She nodded, and swallowed again. Still hard enough to hammer nails, Tristan thrust inside her, tentatively at first. Phaedra closed her eyes, drew down on the knot, and gave a hum of pleasure. He picked up the rhythm, driving inside her, thrusting over and over, gliding against Phaedra's sweet, perfect center.

Her warm, sleek skin tightened and pulled around his cock, milking the pleasure from his flesh. And when he thought he would surely, surely go mad from the pain and the pleasure, Phaedra began to writhe and to sob in earnest. She rose high against him again and again, tears streaming from the corners of her eyes.

The secret to Phaedra was simple. She needed someone—or something—to control her. *It was*, he *thought, the damnedest thing he'd ever seen.* And probably the most erotic.

"Tristan, Tristan, yes," she chanted. "Oh, yes. Oh."

He strained and strained for that last sweet stroke, and when they came together, it was in a blinding, white-hot fury that seized his every muscle and every nerve, shattering him into a thousand shards of light, each of them a piece of her. Each of them a piece of his heart.

When he returned to the mortal world, he was bent over her, his hands planted to either side of her shoulders, and drenched in sweat. Phaedra's hands were still bound tight to the bed, her knees still hooked over his shoulders. He bowed his head and let their foreheads touch.

It had been life altering. And there was nothing more to be said.

Gently, he lifted her leg and shifted to her side, then unfastened the knot which bound her. Phaedra did not open her eyes until he was done. Then she watched as the cravat slithered off the bed, and licked her love-swollen lips uncertainly. "You can say it now," she whispered. "The earth won't split and swallow us whole."

Tristan drew one finger down her cheek and smiled into her eyes. "Say what, Phae? That you are beautiful and passionate?"

She swallowed hard and held his gaze, and even then, he could sense what it cost her. "No. That I wasn't a virgin."

"Were you not?" he murmured, plucking a thick curl of her hair and twining it round his finger. "Can't say as I ever had a virgin myself. But then, it really isn't any of my business, is it?"

She shifted her gaze away, and looked at her wrists, which still bore the faint lines of his cravat. "You must think me disgraceful," she murmured. "That I am . . . terribly wrong, somehow. The way I'm made, I mean. And your cravat—I never dreamt such a thing . . ."

"But you liked it, aye?" He trailed a fingertip down her breastbone, and dropped his voice to a more serious tone. "Phae, love, there's nothing wrong with you. It's just bed play. Many people find that erotic."

"Do they?" She cast him a dubious glance. "I wish I understood. My body is so . . . hungry. And my mind is so . . . not my own. Not . . . when I'm like that."

He reclined on one elbow and looked down at her. "You have no idea, do you?" he murmured. "Such passion is a gift, Phae. You would be a treasure to any man whose bed you graced."

Gently, she chaffed her wrist. "You do not find me . . . strange?"

"I don't find you anything but charming," he murmured, rolling forward just far enough to kiss her nose. "Well, and bullheaded, of course. You just haven't learned to leash your own desire. To trust yourself. You are so passionate, Phae, but so caught up in thinking it's wrong—

when it isn't. It's beautiful. Natural. And all that confusion . . . it just overwhelms you. Give yourself time, love. Give yourself time to learn to govern your own body."

Her soft gaze searched his face. "And what if . . . what if I cannot?"

He winked at her. "Then I daresay I shall just have to keep doing it for you," he said, laughing. "Oh, what a bloody shame that would be!"

She fell silent for a time as if pondering it. Tristan rolled to one side, then flopped flat on his back to let the cool of the room settle over him. Beside him, Phaedra shifted onto her left side, a few inches away. When the silence began to feel heavy and a little expectant, he rolled back again. "Phae." He dipped his head and kissed the turn of her neck as he held her. "Do you want to talk? About . . . anything else?"

She shook her head. "No," she murmured. "Let's not spoil it."

Once again it came home to him how very different she was from any other woman he had known. He opened his mouth to press the issue, then closed it again. Instead, he shut his eyes and drew in the scent of warm, spent woman, and felt that unfamiliar instinct—that surging wish to protect her—tug at him again. He had done it. He had committed . . . to *something*, surely?

Steady on, old boy, said the devilish imp on his shoulder. *And keep your mouth shut. You don't owe her a bloody thing.*

It was true, perhaps, Tristan realized. The heat of lust had given way to the languor of enervation, and his cooler, more rational mind was beginning to function again. Phaedra had not been a virgin. He had not—well, taken anything from her save his own pleasure. He had not irreparably damaged her in any way.

No, someone else had done that. And he wanted—suddenly and fiercely—to kill them. But *why?* Why wasn't he thanking his lucky stars? He had leapt into this mess believing himself some sort of martyr, ready to do the right thing—and that fact by itself was damning. But now to learn his martyrdom was not needed . . .

He should have been relieved. And he was, he supposed. Yet beneath it lay an odd sort of anger. Not with Phaedra, no. He was not yet so sunk in self-absorption as to believe he could hold her to a higher standard than himself. So she wasn't a virgin. There had been someone—perhaps more than one someone—before him. And there he was, back to those paradoxes again. For never had he met a woman more innocent, more artless, and more wholly unaware of her own charms than this one. Certainly he'd never met one so deeply, innately passionate. None of it—nothing about this whole blasted night—made sense to him.

But there was no resolving the matter just now. There was still the shadow of Gorsky's death lingering over them, and the business of the house across the street. He still needed to somehow convince her to leave matters to him. Oh, she'd promised him a month, but she'd lied through her teeth, perhaps unconsciously, but a lie all the same. Just now, however, he hadn't the energy for that sort of fight. So he kissed the round of her shoulder, and drifted off with Phaedra in his arms.

Chapter 9

※

Jesters do oft prove prophets.

That night, Phaedra dreamed of Priss, and of Hampshire in the spring. They lay on blankets in Brierwood's bottom, just a slow, lazy walk from the village. Even in sleep, Phaedra could hear the rhythmic *swoosh-swoosh-swoosh* of the mill in the distance, and feel the faint rumble of the millstones deep in the alluvial earth.

Priss sat on her round bottom, her fat baby legs crooked out beneath her, a white-brimmed bonnet shading her cheeks from the sun as she played with a fistful of daisies.

"No, Priss, like this." Agnes sat up on the blanket to show her how to make a small bouquet. "Not squishing from your fingers all higgledy-piggledy. Then we tie it up with ribbon."

Her blue eyes wide beneath the white bonnet, Priss stuck out her bow lip, and watched intently as Agnes looped the ribbon around.

Priss gurgled with laughter and flailed one hand. "Like *dis*," she said, rolling over to half crawl onto Phaedra. She laid her fist on Phaedra's chest and opened it, depositing her flowers in a tangle of green and gold. "For you," she said proudly. "Dis for you, Phae."

Phaedra looked up into the child's round face and felt a flood of maternal affection, and a deep, lingering sadness she could not explain. "Thank you, Priss," she said. "It is the most beautiful bouquet I ever received."

But Priss faded away and for a fleeting instant, became another, more distant memory. It was all mixed up together. In her head and in her heart. And when she blinked her eyes, Phaedra was looking not at the child that haunted her, but at Tristan Talbot.

He was waiting. Waiting for her to explain. She opened her mouth, but no sound came out.

"Phae?" he said quietly.

"I tried," she finally whispered. "Oh, Tristan, I tried."

Tristan set his hand to her feverish cheek. "To do what, Phae?"

Phaedra swallowed uncertainly. "I . . . I don't know," she murmured. "I wanted to save her."

"The child?" His touch was tender. "You were saying something about a child."

"Was I?" she rasped, awake now. "I—I don't want to think about that now."

The rain had cleared to an ethereally brilliant night, the full moon centered in the narrow attic window. Tristan loomed beside her in the darkness, propped on one elbow, steadily watching her with eyes which once were dancing, but tonight were remarkably solemn.

"Make me," she whispered. "Make me not think about it." And when she lifted her arms to him, he turned her onto her back and mounted her, entering on one swift thrust.

In the silence of the room he rode her, capturing her wrists in his strong, long-fingered hands and forcing them high above her head. Pinning her to the bed. Impaling her. Driving her again to that exquisite, perfect height. Sweat slicked his body, the sinewy tendons of his arms and the layered muscles of his chest glowing in the lamplight. She came not in a whirling firestorm, but in a quiet, shuddering release. This time, however, Tristan jerked himself from her body, spilling his seed onto her stomach as he cried out on a silent shout, his head going back, the tendons of his neck straining.

Then Tristan fell against her, and again Phaedra drowsed, not entirely certain if any of it had been real, or just another of her feverish dreams. She wasn't sure how long she slept entwined in Tristan's arms, but when next she began to rouse, it was in a cold sweat, with a vision of Gorsky's disembodied face swimming in the gloom before her.

Not Gorsky's cold visage as he had turned her away at the door in Soho, nor Gorsky's bent head as he lurked in the shadows of the tobacconist's. No, it was Gorsky's mask of death. The glassy, wide-eyed stare of a man who had seen his end coming; seen, perhaps, the very face of his killer. He had fallen face-first in a heap at Phaedra's feet, one hand outstretched as if pleading . . .

As if pleading.

Through the fog of sleep, Phaedra tried to recall. Yes, his hand had been outstretched . . .

She must have cried out in the darkness.

"Phae?" Tristan's voice cut through the haze. "Phae, what is it?"

Phaedra opened her eyes and looked at Tristan. Was she sleeping? Or awake? The rain had picked up again, thundering on the roof above the bed. She was awake. "His hand," she murmured. "Gorsky's hand. He . . . he was reaching out to me. He was clutching something."

"Clutching something?" Tristan muttered, dragging a shock of wavy black hair off his forehead.

Phaedra set a hand to her heart, and jerked upright. "There was something in his hand," she said

"Phae, what are you talking about?"

"Something tumbled from his hand—and it sounded . . . I don't know. Wooden, almost? And it rolled. Yes, it rolled across the floor."

"Wooden?" he asked. "Are we talking about Gorsky?"

"My God." Phaedra's hand lashed out, catching his wrist. "What time is it?"

Tristan glanced at the window. Even through the rain, he sensed the full moon was fading. "Late, blast it," he said. "Dawn can't be more than an hour away."

Phaedra leapt from the bed, and snatched something from the floor. "My God," she said again, dragging her shift over her head. "We must hurry."

Propped on one elbow, he reached out for her hand. "Wait, Phae." And then he asked the one question—that simple but telling question—the one he'd never asked of any woman. "When will I see you again?"

Caught in midmotion of snatching her stocking from the floor, Phaedra went perfectly still. For a long moment, she said nothing, as if she did not trust herself to speak.

"At nine o'clock," she finally said. "That's when Kemble opens. Number Eight, in the Strand."

He sat up, snared her wrist, and pulled her between his bare legs. "The Strand?" he said, setting his hands on her slender waist. "What about . . . well, what about *us*, Phae?"

"Us?" she echoed hollowly.

Tristan, of course, wished to snatch back the phrase as soon as it left his mouth. If he'd had a ha'penny for every time a woman had said that to him . . . ah, well. The shoe was on the other foot—at least this morning—and to his surprise, it pinched a little.

Phaedra's eyes softened, and an emotion which might have been regret sketched over her face. "Tristan, there is no us," she said in her quiet, husky voice.

There is no us. Well. No expectations here, then. And he couldn't afford to bed her again anyway. Women like Phaedra you married—or you left them alone. Which meant another clean getaway for the infamous Tristan Talbot. He forced himself to smile up at her.

"As you wish, love," he said, releasing her hand. "Nine o'clock it is."

"Un balai! Un balai!" Mr. Kemble was on his knees in his workroom floor, his snug, elegant arse stuck high in the air as he peered beneath a row of cabinets. "Jean-Claude! *Dépêche-toi!"*

Tristan watched as Kemble's lean, dark-haired assistant leapt from the floor and went rushing toward a closet tucked beneath the stairs. He returned with a broom, and knelt to tentatively offer it.

"*Merci,*" grunted Mr. Kemble, snatching it.

Kemble, of course, had been surprised to see Phaedra and her maid awaiting him when he came down to unlock the shop at nine. He had been even more surprised to see Tristan, and had surveyed him up and down with open suspicion.

The vague awkwardness between Tristan and Phaedra had likely been palpable to those around them. Tristan had felt it the moment he joined her on the pavement outside Kemble's door. Her unwillingness to quite hold his gaze. The stiff formality in her language which could not be wholly explained by the very public place in which they stood. Regret and uncertainty seemed to linger in the air between them.

Or perhaps it was only Tristan who felt that press of unspoken questions. That diffident uncertainty of an awkward morning after. They were lovers who did not yet fully know one another—and likely never would. The thought left Tristan strangely melancholy.

But Phaedra's focus now was on finding the object she was so certain Gorsky had dropped. She was watching Kemble ply his broom, her expression chagrinned. "I can't think why I didn't remember this sooner," she said for the tenth time. "But there was just so much blood . . ."

"You were in shock, as any rational person would have been," said Tristan, observing as Kemble eased the broom beneath the last piece, a massive chinoiserie armoire, and drew it gingerly across its width.

Kemble flicked an irritated glance up at Tristan. "Anything?"

Tristan glanced down at the side legs of the armoire. "Dust balls," he said.

Kemble hissed through his teeth. "Try to make yourself useful," he snapped. "Look behind the blasted thing. Perhaps I pushed it through."

Tristan strode round the wardrobe and leaned as far back as he could. "Well, it's dark behind there—"

"No, seriously?" Kemble acerbically interjected.

"—but I think I see something far to the right."

Phaedra, too, had knelt on the floor now, and was trying to look under it. "Perhaps it's stuck?" she said unhelpfully. "Perhaps if we moved it?"

"What, and get a hernia?" said Kemble, horrified. "One's trousers would never fit smoothly again."

Tristan stood to the left of the offending furniture. With a grunt, he braced his hands at both the front and the back, gave it a good shove, then lifted and pivoted it forward on its right rear leg with a horrendous scraping sound. A dusty, cavernous space opened up behind it.

Kemble's broom clattered to the floor. "Good God," he said, scrambling to his feet. "All that brawn is good for something after all."

Jean-Claude, Tristan noticed, was eyeing him with a newfound appreciation.

At least someone was. Phaedra was too busy attempting to squeeze behind the armoire. "I am the smallest," she said, her voice muffled behind the wood. "So if I can just wedge in here—"

"Shall I simply heft it up again?" asked Tristan dryly. "After all, I live to serve you, my lady."

The barb sailed over her head. "Oh, look!" she said brightly. "Here it is!"

She backed out of the space, a cobweb caught in her

hair, and held out her hand. A wooden sphere slightly smaller than a cricket ball rested on her palm. Tristan and Kemble stepped nearer, studying it.

"I haven't a clue what that might be," Kemble admitted.

Tristan was somewhat surprised to hear it, given the contents of Kemble's shop. Every oddity in the world seemed to rest upon his shelves or hang upon his walls. But the ball was indeed a curiosity. It was made of a golden, lacquered wood and cut with little squares rather like a spherical chessboard. Each of the squares was inlaid with a tiny letter in a darker wood.

"It looks Cyrillic," said Phaedra.

"Yes, Russian, I believe," Kemble said, poking at the ball.

He was likely right, Tristan realized. Each square contained a letter of a Cyrillic-style alphabet.

Kemble took the ball, and turned it over and over. "I can read a little Russian," he said. "But this doesn't actually *say* anything so far as I can see."

Tristan held out his hand. "May I?"

"By all means." Kemble dropped the ball into his palm.

Experimentally, Tristan pressed with his pinkie finger on one of the squares. The wood gave with a little *snick*, and the wooden bar slid through to protrude on the other side.

"Interesting," said Kemble. "Press another."

He did so, but the ball seemed locked. Tristan returned the original letter to its place by pressing on the opposite end of the bar. The letter clicked back into place, and the ball was smooth again. He pushed another, and again, the bar slid through.

"It is a puzzle ball," said Mr. Kemble thoughtfully. "I've seen such things from Eastern Europe, but never in this shape. And certainly never this complicated."

"I think you're right," said Tristan pensively. "I saw a similar device once on a dead Turk—a spy, actually. But square in shape, and far more rudimentary."

"What does it do?" asked Phaedra.

Tristan shook his head. "I think, if one presses the right letters in the right series, the thing will open to reveal a secret," he said. "A gem or a *billet-doux*. Something like that."

"What series of letters?" asked Kemble sharply.

"That can be decided, I daresay, only when the ball is open," said Tristan. "Or perhaps by the woodcarver who made it."

"So we cannot open it?" Phaedra sounded crushed.

Kemble lifted his gaze to Tristan's. "I think we ought not try," he said quietly. "We'd be better served by taking this straight to de Vendenheim. The boys in the Home Office can have a look."

"Quite right," said Tristan, turning the thing over in his hand. "And the sooner the better. Shall I do the honors?"

Kemble tossed a well-manicured hand. "Oh, God, yes," he said. "I avoid Whitehall at all cost."

Phaedra's shoulders fell. As he tucked the ball into his coat pocket, Tristan regarded her quietly. He did not like the look of dejection in her eyes. He knew what she was thinking. Gently, he set his hand on her arm, and drew her a little away. Mr. Kemble and his clerk returned to one of their worktables, and discreetly occupied themselves by poking about in a pile of old silver.

Tristan caught her keen blue gaze with his own. "Phae, remember that month we discussed?" A look of guilt sketched across her face. "You cannot go with me, my dear," he continued. "It was brilliant of you to remember this. But you cannot go. Your brother will hear of it."

Fleetingly, she hesitated. "And you promise to let me know what you discover?"

Tristan watched her warily. "Is that an invitation to call upon you?"

Phaedra snared her lip between her teeth. "I suppose it is," she finally answered. "In fact, my Mamma and sister and I would be pleased, Mr. Talbot, if you could take tea with us this afternoon."

"Thank you," said Tristan solemnly. "I shall try to be there."

In the Strand, traffic was picking up with carriages rattling up and down the street, and pedestrians pushing past him on the pavement. Tristan retrieved Callidora from the lad he'd paid to hold her. After running a judicious eye over the horse, Tristan fed her a lump of sugar from his pocket, then threw himself into the saddle and reined her round for the journey deeper into Westminster.

In the end, however, Tristan's journey was of little use. He arrived in Whitehall at half past ten, only to be told that his quarry was out, and that he should come back that afternoon. Frustrated, tired, and with his emotions oddly raw, Tristan turned round and went up to Cavendish Square to check on Hauxton whilst he cooled his heels. It was quite possibly the stupidest thing he could have done.

Pemberton let him in with the news that his father was perhaps a little stronger, and had taken a bit of his breakfast. Tristan went upstairs to find that the black crows had flapped off in search of tea, leaving a measure of quiet, if not the peace that went along with it.

On being presented with the puzzle ball, and the story behind it, his father offered his usual stiff compliments on Tristan's good work, turning the ball over and over in his hands. "And who did you say found this?" he asked after a time.

Tristan cleared his throat a little sharply. "Lady Phaedra Northampton."

"Yes, the one who witnessed the murder," said his father, laying the wooden ball aside. "What manner of female is she, this Lady Phaedra?"

"Why, she is a woman of great intelligence and refinement," said Tristan stiffly.

"But a girl of some years?" said his father. "Not, I collect, a chit from the schoolroom?"

"No, sir," Tristan agreed. "She is, I should guess, not above four-and-twenty."

"Is she a beauty?" asked his father.

Tristan started at the question. "I believe she is generally thought quite plain," he answered, "but only to those who have not looked closely."

His father lifted his graying eyebrows. "Yes, I see," he murmured. "And you have been paying her a marked amount of attention, I believe? I trust you will recall, Tristan, that she is an innocent, unwed girl of impeccable breeding, and not your usual fare. Indeed, I hope you are not engaging in a flirtation merely in order to further this investigation."

The accusation stung. "What, you want your murder solved *and* tied up with a pretty pink ribbon?" he asked a little snidely. "Since when do you give a damn, sir, if I flirt with a woman?"

Hauxton removed the silver spectacles from his nose, and sighed. "I had harbored some faint hope, I suppose, that it was more than just a flirtation," he said wearily. "But indeed, your life is none of my business, Tristan. You have made that abundantly clear these many years."

Tristan jerked from his chair, and strode to the windows which looked out over the square. *My father is ill,* he reminded himself. But Hauxton's barbed questions stung more than they should have, and his ugly assumptions hurt far more than usual. The fact that his warning was not wholly uncalled for only made matters worse. Phaedra was not the sort of woman a decent man dallied with, but that was precisely what he was doing, wasn't it?

"I am scarcely good enough, sir, for my own family," he finally said, his voice less steady than he would have wished. "I can assure you I'll never be good enough for the Northamptons."

A heavy silence settled over the room, broken only by the rhythmic *clop-clop-clop* of a lone rider in the square below, and by his father's labored breathing. And Tristan waited, counting off the strikes of the horse's shoes. Waited for the apology that never came. Waited for his father tell him to go to hell and get out for good. Waited for *any-*

thing save this bloody damned impasse which seemed to loom eternally between them.

Of course, when his father finally spoke, it was the latter. "The circumstances of your birth were regrettable, Tristan," he acknowledged, "and I know the Talbot line has not always been as welcoming to you as they might have been. I am sorry for it."

Tristan whirled on him, incredulous. "Not as *welcoming*?" he echoed. "My own grandmother could scarce bear to look upon me. To this day, your cousins barely acknowledge my existence, whilst your brother sat 'til his dying day perched like a vulture over the doorstep, hoping to God I'd perish at the hand of a murderous Turk or some irate, unhinged cuckold."

"Yes," said his father dryly, "and you tried your best to oblige him."

Tristan shook his head. "And you call the circumstances of my birth regrettable," he continued. "My mother, sir, was not *regrettable*. Not to me."

Hauxton folded his hands one across the other atop his bedsheet. "You are my son, Tristan," he said quietly. "And I have tried to make the best of that. I wish only that you had done the same."

You are my son. He always spoke the words as if they were a curse to be borne.

Tristan left the windows and snatched up the wooden puzzle. "I should leave you now, sir," he said tightly. "You need your rest."

Hauxton took up his spectacles again. "By the way, Tristan, I have done as you asked," he calmly replied. "You are now, ostensibly, assistant to the Under-Secretary of

State for Foreign Affairs with a staff and full access to the very highest state secrets. It's been put about that you've been serving unofficially here since my illness."

"Yes, the word's out already," said Tristan mordantly. "I just came up from Whitehall where I had to poke people's eyeballs back into their heads right and left."

The sarcasm escaped Hauxton. "What, then, is your next step?"

"To get inside that house," said Tristan. "I am acquainted with a few of her patrons. Amongst them, I've subtly suggested I might possess, shall we say, certain unnatural itches that might require scratching."

"And what will this accomplish?" asked his father. "You may but pique Vostrikova's curiosity and get your throat slit."

Tristan shrugged. "Either that, or I'll get bound, gagged, and caned by a pair of buxom blondes in black corsets."

Hauxton's lip curled with distaste. "Your comments strike me as deliberately obscene."

"What strikes me, sir," Tristan retorted, "is that doing your dirty work is rather like making haggis. You might take a bite when it's finished, but by God, you don't want to know how the job got done."

"Tristan, you don't—"

"No, *you* don't understand," Tristan interjected. "You have sent me on a vile errand, sir. To do it I must consort with people whom even I consider offensive—and that's saying something. And I'll quite likely be required to engage in behaviors that are dangerous and disgusting. But you want to know what Vostrikova is up to, and there is only one way to find out. To get invited inside."

Hauxton waved his hand weakly. "Fine, just brief de Vendenheim," he managed. "Then just . . . finish the job, Tristan."

His hand already on the door, Tristan hesitated. Yes, by God, he meant to finish it, for he had the bit between his teeth now. Just as his father, devil take him, had known he would. Besides, he had to unleash his roiling, thwarted emotions on someone. It might as well be Madame Vostrikova. "I have given you my word, sir," he answered with a tight nod. "And I shall keep it. Good day to you."

He went back down the elegant spiral staircase, cursing himself and cursing his father. He wondered how the devil Hauxton had got wind of his flirtation with Lady Phaedra so quickly.

There was only one way, of course. Hauxton had set spies on his spy. Cursing one last time beneath his breath, Tristan restored the wooden ball to his pocket, and let the front door slam behind him.

Phaedra arrived home at midmorning, enervated yet on edge, only to find Zoë Armstrong on the doorstep, her hand poised to drop the knocker. Her maid stood dutifully on the middle step, something frothy draped across her arm. On seeing Phaedra's approach, she lightly touched her mistress's elbow.

"Phae!" Zoë turned round, and came back down the steps. "What luck!"

"Hello, Zoë." Phaedra tried to brighten her smile. "You're up early."

Zoë pulled a long face. "Papa insisted on having breakfast with me," she said on a sigh. "It was time to have The Talk."

Phae opened the door and they went in together. "What sort of talk?" she asked, handing their cloaks to Stabler.

Zoë took the dress from her maid's arm, and looked around conspiratorially. "Let's go up to your room," she said. "I wish you to see my new ball gown—and I want to hear all about Avoncliffe."

After inviting Zoë's maid to go belowstairs for a cup of tea, Phaedra went up the steps, Zoë chatting amiably behind her. "Now The Talk, you must understand, is an annual ritual," she said. "We have it just before every season commences, with Papa looking all solemn and proper—as if *he* wasn't once the worst rakehell in Christendom—and telling me how I must mend my ways."

Phaedra closed her door and motioned Zoë to a chair by the windows. She was glad, she decided, for the distraction. Zoë's effervescence was the perfect antidote for her blue mood, and it would keep her from dwelling on the night of passion she'd just spent in Tristan Talbot's arms—those long, strong, beautifully sculpted arms which she'd been trying desperately not to think about since bounding out of bed this morning.

Indeed, it had taken all her strength not to beg Tristan to linger into the wee hours of dawn and make love to her yet again. She had wanted, shockingly, to forget about Millie and Gorsky and duty and obligation—and to think only of herself and this beautiful man who, at least last night, had seemingly understood her better than she understood herself. Only when Phaedra had grasped the turn her mind was taking this morning did the alarm bells go off in her head and send her all but bolting from the room.

She forced her attention to her guest. "So the talk is about . . . what, exactly?"

Zoë had flung the gown onto Phaedra's bed, and flopped into the chair with a huff. "Oh, the talk is all about decorum and discretion and delicacy," she answered with an airy gesture of her fingers. "It is about the importance of my behaving myself, making a good impression, and finding myself a suitable husband."

"Then I begin to see why it is necessary to repeat this talk." Phaedra managed to grin at her. "You are failing on two of those counts rather miserably, my dear."

Zoë rolled her eyes. "And you are supposed to be my friend," she said. "Hurry, Phae, and look at my dress. Then let's go out to gossip and shop."

"Shopping again?" asked Phaedra.

"Phoebe said you might choose patterns and fabrics for new gowns this morning," Zoë explained. "And I mean to go along, else you'll have that frightful rag wrapped round your dumplings again, and your bodices yanked up to here." Zoë chopped a hand dramatically across her throat.

"I beg your pardon?" Phaedra picked up the dress and cut a curious, sidelong glance at her. "My *dumplings*? Remind me again, Zoë, why we struck up this strange friendship."

Zoë grinned. "It is because I am the anti-Phaedra," she said. "You are drawn to me because I am exactly what you try not to be."

"Indeed?" Phaedra fluffed out the hem of Zoë's dress, amazed at the layers of ruffles. "So I am the opposite of you?"

Zoë laughed. "Yes, we are extremes, both of us," she said. "And deep in our hearts, perhaps, we hope we will rub off on one another. Deep in our hearts, perhaps, I should like to be a bit good like you, and you should like to be a bit bad like me."

But Zoë had no idea how bad Phaedra longed to be. There was a sensual, twisting hunger inside Phaedra that frightened her, a thing she could never wish on her younger friend. She thought of Tristan's neckcloth bound about her wrists and shivered.

"Zoë, you are perfectly silly," she said. Then swiftly, she changed the subject. "This gown is utterly gorgeous, by the way. Try it on."

Zoë leapt at once to her feet, and Phaedra began to undo her buttons. It really was an odd sort of friendship, she mused, but in some inexplicable way, Phaedra longed for Zoë's company. Zoë was refreshing—and a little dangerous. And like Phaedra, she did not suffer fools. Though Zoë might pretend otherwise, she was smart as a whip.

They had been meeting at least once a day for tea, or to shop and gossip, and in the process, Zoë had made Phaedra feel almost girlish again. Between Phoebe and Zoë, she had somehow been persuaded to take up Stefan's offer of an opulent new wardrobe. And Phaedra was beginning to look forward to it. Indeed, with Zoë, Phaedra felt more herself—the self, perhaps, that she could have been had her life turned out a little differently.

At last the new gown was pulled over Zoë's sleek, dark

hair, spilling to the floor in a cascade of ruby-colored silk. "Breathtaking," said Phaedra, doing up the back. "What is it for?"

"Lady Kirton's charity ball," said Zoë on an unladylike yawn. "It's the big season opener this year. Have you a card for it?"

"I daresay," she answered. "Mamma usually goes."

"Then my nefarious plan proceeds apace," said Zoë, turning round. "This year *you* shall go, too."

"Oh, I think not." Phaedra busied herself neatening the ruffles of Zoë's new gown.

"Lord Robert and Mr. Upjohn will be there," Zoë wheedled in her singsong voice. "Perhaps even Avoncliffe will turn up. Which reminds me, Phae—where the devil were you last night?"

Phaedra's hand stilled, and she looked up again. "I beg your pardon?"

Zoë tucked her head and grinned. "Last night," she said. "I came round about one and threw rocks at your window."

"Zoë!" Phaedra rose from the floor. "Why?"

Zoë lifted one narrow shoulder. "Well, I went to the musicale at Mrs. Hendrick's and it was just frightful," she complained. "So Aunt Winnie claimed a headache and we left. But I got home and I was bored and I knew, of course, that you'd be up reading, so when the rain let up, I slipped out with a fresh cheroot and came to get you."

"Zoë!" With a muted smile, Phaedra turned her and began to unfasten the buttons. "You will make me scandalous before the season's out."

Zoë's grin deepened. "What's scandalous, if you ask

me, is that you weren't home," she answered, winking over her shoulder. "Especially when I know for a fact your mamma and your sister were at Mrs. Hendrick's."

Phae said nothing.

"So——?" asked Zoë.

"So what?" Phaedra looked down at her work.

"*Who* were you with?" Zoë was still trying to catch Phaedra's eyes.

"How do you know I was with anyone?" she finally answered.

"If you'd been home, Phae, you'd have already complained that you didn't hear any rocks," said Zoë, wiggling the red dress down her hips. "But you *haven't* said that."

"I didn't hear any rocks."

"Too late!" Zoë's grin deepened. "Besides, I cracked a pane of glass, I think. It made a frightful noise—and no one could have slept through that."

Phaedra felt her face flame. "Shush, Zoë," she begged. "I *cannot* be caught."

"As wicked as that, was it?" Zoë feigned a look of contrition, and tossed the dress aside. "You'd better tell me, Phae. If anyone thought they saw you—well, I can at least be your alibi."

"Oh, thank you, Zoë!" Phae collapsed onto the bed beside the heap of red silk. She really wished she could talk to someone, but not even to Zoë could she tell the whole truth.

"I went for a walk," she finally said. "To . . . To meet Mr. Talbot—Avoncliffe—if you must know."

"Oh, Lud!" Zoë slapped her hands to her cheeks. "I knew it. I just *knew* it. He's smitten, Phae. Everyone noticed how he singled you out the other night. But, oh, Phae, have a care with that one!"

"It isn't what you think," Phaedra lied. "I just needed his help with something."

"Yes, a lot of women do, I've heard." Zoë giggled. "And he's known to be quite obliging."

"Zoë!" Phaedra's shoulders fell. "Really!"

"Yes, *really!*" Zoë's tone was low and vaguely appreciative. "I begin to wonder, Phae, if you are the anti-Zoë after all. Did he kiss you again?"

Phaedra's blush deepened, and she turned to the window. Perhaps she shouldn't have told Zoë of that first kiss. But she had—in one of those whispered, girlish confessionals which Phaedra had always thought herself above— because, for the first time in her life, she *really* needed a friend.

"He *did* kiss you," said Zoë, following her across the room. "But was it a kiss, Phae. Or was it a *kiss?*"

Phaedra lifted her gaze to the glass, and looked at Zoë's watery reflection. "It was a *kiss,*" she whispered. "Oh, Zoë. It was . . . very much a kiss."

"Oh, Lord." Zoë's eyes were like saucers. "Avoncliffe is either the greatest cad that ever breathed—or for once, he's deadly serious. Either, I daresay, is possible."

"What on earth do you mean?"

Zoë shrugged. "Well, I've never thought Avoncliffe a bad sort," she mused. "He's . . . well, he's not a *rake,* if you know what I mean. He's a scoundrel. And there's a difference."

Phaedra closed her eyes, willing the vision Zoë's words

conjured to go away. A rake, a scoundrel—what was the difference to her if she fell for him?

"But he's a good sort of scoundrel, I collect." Zoë was clearly pondering aloud. "I've never heard of him trifling with virgins. Have you quite a large dowry, Phae?"

"Yes, as it happens," said Phaedra. "Not that I mean to use it."

Zoë ignored her. "No, that's not it," she mused, shaking her head. "Avoncliffe needn't marry you for your money."

"*Marry* me?" Phaedra turned from the window.

Zoë looked at her as if she were a silly child. "Phae, if you keep sneaking out to kiss Avoncliffe, eventually, you *will* get caught," she warned. "Even I know that. And then Lord Nash will demand he do the right thing. And Avoncliffe might just do it, especially if it spares you a scandal."

Phaedra leaned back against the window frame and crossed her arms over her chest. "Even if you're right about him, Zoë, *I* won't do it," she said, regarding her friend solemnly. "You forget that."

"Oh, you'll marry him," said Zoë knowingly. "Depend upon it. For they will assail you with all sorts of talk about family honor and scandal and how you will ruin Phoebe's marriage prospects, and blah, blah, blah, and you will surrender, Phae. You will cave in like a house of cards."

"But you don't cave in."

"That's because I'm selfish," said Zoë, sitting back down on the bed. "You aren't like that, Phae. You'll do it."

Phaedra stood silent for a moment, half afraid that Zoë was right.

Zoë tilted her head to one side. "Surely, Phae, you've not fallen in love?"

Phaedra just clasped her hands. "Oh, Zoë, surely I have not? This is just . . . infatuation. Isn't it?"

Zoë shrugged, and brightened her smile. "Well, it mightn't be so bad," she said cheerfully. "As a husband, Avoncliffe's hand wouldn't be a heavy one, and at least you'd have him in your bed. A definite advantage, that. Besides, he needs an heir. He'll have to marry eventually."

That brought Phaedra's foolish fantasies up short. "I think *you* should have to get married," she said mordantly. "I think you should marry Lord Robert Rowland, instead of just sneaking off into the dark with him."

"Marry Robin?" Zoë laughed uproariously. "Now *that* will never happen. Besides, the woman who takes him on will have naught but hell to pay. Surely, Phae, even I do not deserve *that?"*

But Phaedra couldn't hold her gaze. Zoë's words were a stark reminder of the risks she was running, and of the fact that she was scarcely a suitable bride for anyone. As the firstborn son of an earl, Tristan would inherit uncountable wealth, and with it the hopes and dreams and weighty expectations of three hundred years of history. And he would be required to bear a son in turn. He would be required to take a wife who was fertile. Fondness or affection or even love would likely not enter into it.

No, even if a man were willing to take a tarnished bride, he could never take a woman who might never give him children. Life simply did not work that way.

"I'm sorry, Zoë. I oughtn't tease you about Lord Robert." Phaedra had gone to her desk, and absently picked up her letter-knife. "And I'm afraid I cannot go shopping today. I must stay in."

"Oh, I don't care a fig about teasing," she answered. "But why can we not go order your new gowns?"

Phaedra turned from the desk with a twisted smile. "We're stripping the rugs and draperies upstairs for spring cleaning," she said quietly. "And then—well, Mr. Talbot is coming to tea with Mamma and me, if you must know."

Zoë's eyes widened as her grin returned. "Oh, Lud! Sounds like a case of honorable intentions to me. Truly, Phae! After last night, why—what if he *offers* for you?"

Phaedra tried to shake her head. But the hot press of tears had risen behind her eyes, and she felt suddenly as if a welled-up dam were about to burst. Her lips trembled, and she felt her face begin to crumple.

Zoë sprang off the bed at once, her eyes going soft. "Oh, Phae!" she said, circling an arm around her shoulders. "My dear, what is wrong? What did he do? That cad! I shall kill him with my bare hands!"

Phaedra bit her lip, and shook her head. "It's not Tristan. Not . . . like that, I mean."

Zoë drew her back to the bed, and urged her to sit. "Then what, Phae?" she whispered. "Did something happen last night?"

"No," Phaedra whispered. "Not last night."

"Oh, my poor Phae!" Zoë extracted a lace handkerchief and began to blot Phaedra's cheeks. "Oh, please, my dear, do not cry. Whatever is wrong, why, we shall fix it."

To see Zoë suddenly so solemn and so affected was the last straw. And as Phaedra's tears spilt out, the words went with them. "Oh, Zoë, you are a dear, but no one can fix this! And it happened a long time ago. I had an illness, you see, and afterward, the doctors told me . . . they told me I was likely barren. That I likely couldn't have children. Now do you understand?"

"Oh, Phaedra! Truly?" Sorrow welled in Zoë's eyes.

Phaedra let her head fall against Zoë's shoulder. "I don't think about it often," she whispered, blinking hard. "I *don't*. Really. But then I met *him*. And I don't want to marry him, Zoë. Truly, I don't. And he doesn't want me. But it's just that . . . it's just that . . ."

"It's just that if you *did* want him," Zoë whispered, drawing a warm, heavy hand down Phaedra's hair, "you wouldn't have him, would you? You would do the honorable thing."

"I would do *nothing*," Phaedra said, snuffling against Zoë's shoulder. "That's what I always do. I keep to myself, Zoë. Because it is too hard to explain something so personal, then watch disappointment dawn in a man's eyes. To see the pity there, and then watch him draw away. I could not bear it."

"No, nor could I." Zoë said nothing further for a long moment. Instead, she simply stroked Phaedra's hair. "I am so sorry, Phae," she finally murmured. "So very sorry. Someday, perhaps, you will find a man to whom such things won't matter? But regardless, you may always depend, of course, upon my confidence—and my friendship."

"Thank you, Zoë."

And there was really nothing more to be said. They sat there together on the bed, clutching one another in a tight embrace, until the slanting sun left the window to rise high above the roofs of Mayfair. Then Phaedra kissed her new friend's cheek, and walked her to the door, all the while thinking of the afternoon that was to come, of the tea which she had to get through, and of the heart she must somehow preserve, whole and intact.

When Tristan returned to Whitehall that afternoon, he was escorted up by a harried, black-coated civil servant who looked very much like one of Hauxton's crows, to find Lord de Vendenheim in a small office at the top of the stairs. To his shock, a great black dog the size of small pony lay flopped out before the desk, his massive jowls drooling faintly on the carpet. Upon seeing Tristan, the hellhound licked his chops, then—apparently judging him too sinewy for a decent meal—drifted off to sleep again.

"Good Lord," Tristan muttered, stepping lightly past him.

It took less than ten minutes to brief de Vendenheim on the progress of his investigation. Then Tristan extracted Phaedra's prize. Unfortunately, de Vendenheim knew less about the sphere than either Tristan or Kemble. The vicomte stood by the window which overlooked the river and street below, turning the ball over in his fingers. "And it fell from Gorsky's hand, you say?"

"Yes, Lady Phaedra saw it," Tristan answered. "She recalled it suddenly late last night."

De Vendenheim's head jerked up, his eyes sharp. "Late last night?"

Tristan hesitated. "Or so she said."

De Vendenheim returned his focus to the wooden sphere. "We have experts, of course, in the Cyrillic languages," he said musingly. "But I don't know how long it will take to find one."

"Blast," Tristan muttered. "Time is of the essence."

"And you think I don't know that?" de Vendenheim snapped. "But what I don't know is whether or not this blasted chunk of wood says anything. Perhaps the letters are random? Or perhaps it's Cicero's lost *Consolatio*? How the hell would I know?"

Tristan ignored his outburst. The vicomte's frustration was understandable. "All we really need just now," he mused, "is someone who reads Russian fluently."

De Vendenheim lifted his gaze to Tristan's, and his eyes lit with understanding. "Exactly!" he said. He retrieved his coat from behind the door. "Lucifer!" he said to the dog. *"Vieni qui!"*

"Where do we go?" asked Tristan.

The vicomte was already throwing on a sweeping black cloak. "To Mayfair," he said, shoving the ball into his coat pocket. "To one of the few Englishmen who can read Russian like his mother tongue—and perhaps the only one whom I trust."

Understanding washed over Tristan like a cold bucket of water. But there was nothing for it now. De Vendenheim was half out the door, the massive dog on his heels. Tristan hastened after them. He had wondered, vaguely, what Phaedra's powerful elder brother was like. Apparently, he was going to find out.

"By the way, I hear you've gone to work in the Foreign Office." De Vendenheim flicked him an appraising glance as they went down the steps. "Is it true?"

"Utter balderdash," said Tristan quietly. "Still, it may bring me to Vostrikova's notice."

De Vendenheim glanced at him again. "Then be careful, Talbot."

Lord and Lady Nash lived in a town house so vast it seemed at first impression to span half of Park Lane. *"Sta' fermo!"* said the vicomte, looking down at the dog. The great beast flopped down upon the top step, settling his head onto his paws with a sigh that shuddered his jowls.

Tristan and de Vendenheim were whisked into an elegant chamber overlooking Hyde Park which the footman called "the gold parlor," but which would have constituted two withdrawing rooms in most London homes. The room positively dripped with gilt, and its walls were hung with champagne-colored silk; a chamber which spoke of elegance and of calm. Yet they had scarcely been seated when a clamor arose in the hall beyond the parlor's gilt doors. The happy shrieks of a child, a barking dog, and above it, a woman's voice cautioning quiet. Eventually, the racket settled down, and the woman's voice could be heard in the parlor.

"Is he indeed?" she said, her heels clicking across the marble.

A lovely, dark-haired lady appeared at the door, a child propped on her hip, and a small, barking spaniel at her heels, nominally leashed by a red ribbon. It was Lady Nash, Tristan decided, judging by her attire. A footman brought up the rear, one suspicious eye upon the dog, a creature so small he would scarce have made a snack for the beast out front.

"Max!" The lady hastened in, somehow managing to embrace de Vendenheim despite her encumbrances. The vicomte, Tristan judged, was a good deal closer to Lord and Lady Nash than he had disclosed.

De Vendenheim presented Tristan as Mr. Talbot, and some inscrutable emotion flared in the lady's eyes. "But you are also Lord Avoncliffe, are you not?" said the marchioness, her keen gaze sweeping over him. "At long last, I have the pleasure."

"I'm generally known as Talbot," said Tristan, wondering at her words. Still, he made her his most elegant bow—and his best bows were very elegant indeed. Unfortunately, the tiny spaniel—a feathery black-and-white concoction—chose that moment to launch himself at Tristan, somehow ending in his arms, his tongue making quick work of Tristan's face.

More gleeful shrieking ensued as Lady Nash attempted to claw the dog away. De Vendenheim bent to catch the dog's ribbon, which Lady Nash dropped. Somehow, amidst a vast deal of apologizing and brushing at Tristan's coat, she managed to pass the squealing child to de Vendenheim, capture the dog, and thrust him at the footman.

"This is Chin-Chin," she said, roughly tousling the dog's ears. "He is my brother's dog, a wicked creature whom my son begs to have visit. I should have let Lucifer eat him."

His nose aloft, the unfortunate Vernon toted the barking creature away. The child followed them with his bereft gaze, then stuck a consoling thumb into his mouth.

"Do sit, gentlemen, please." The lady took the child from the vicomte, and relaxed onto a brocade divan.

"Young Luke is growing apace," remarked de Venden- heim as she bounced the babe on her knee. "You have been out enjoying the weather today, I collect?"

Lady Nash laughed. "No, indeed, we've just come from Wapping." She turned to Tristan and smiled. "My family has some shipping interests, Mr. Talbot. Luke has his own nursery above our counting house, and a lovely nurse looks after him whilst I work."

Whilst she worked? How very odd. And if he did not miss his guess, the nursery was about to become a little more crowded. Lady Nash looked like a pale, vibrant madonna, with lively eyes and luxurious dark hair. Pre- cisely the sort of woman he would ordinarily have made note of, just in case disillusionment should strike her marriage, or a case of ennui should overcome her better judgment.

Today, however, he watched her clinically, wondering at the sort of man her husband was. Wondering if she was a good sister to Phaedra, and what manner of family they constituted. A close-knit one, perhaps. The lady still dan- dled the child on her knee, and there was neither a nurse nor a governess in sight.

"Well, I shall leave you," she finally said after they had passed a few moments in pleasant conversation. "Nash should be down shortly. Mr. Talbot, it was a pleasure. I'm frightfully sorry about Chin-Chin."

Tristan came swiftly to his feet as she rose. "The pleasure was mine, my lady," he said. "I rather like dogs."

"Well, not at the expense of a good coat, perhaps." She smiled musingly, shot him one last lingering look, then hitched the child onto her hip and left.

From his chair, Tristan could see the sweeping staircase, and the tall, dark man who was swiftly descending it. He met Lady Nash at the foot, embraced her openly, then kissed the boy on the cheek.

Lord Nash, most assuredly. The gentleman came into the room, his presence instantly commanding. He stood perhaps an inch taller than Tristan, and just a little less lean. His dark eyes swept over the room, and Tristan had the oddest impression he took in everything at once.

The man shook de Vendenheim's hand, and turned his piercing gaze on Tristan. His clothing was stark, dark, and extremely expensive. His eyes were set at a slightly exotic angle, his hair swept off a high, aristocratic forehead in a style which, like Tristan's, was too long and too dark to be strictly fashionable.

"Talbot." Lord Nash bowed stiffly at the neck. "Pleased to meet you at last."

There it was again, thought Tristan. That faintly expectant remark which suggested . . . *something*. Tristan's hackles went up like a wolf scenting an enemy, and he felt his posture stiffen. But Nash turned his attention to the vicomte at once, and listened attentively to his story about the wooden sphere. Tristan, it seemed, was forgotten.

"Why have I heard nothing from Phaedra of this sphere business?" he demanded when de Vendenheim was done.

"I believe she recalled it just last night," said the vicomte.

"Last night?" His head swiveled like a hawk's, his gaze again nailing Tristan. "Is that correct, Talbot?"

Good God. He lifted his hands. "That's what she said, sir."

"She summoned you to meet her at Kemble's?"

Ah, thought Tristan, there was the slippery slope Lord Nash was inviting him to slide down. "Someone sent word round, I collect," he said breezily. "I was abed myself."

Nash held his gaze for a long moment, then looked down to study the sphere, turning it lightly in his hand. "These are nothing but letters arranged more or less in alphabetical order," he said after a time. "There is no secret message here."

"Have you seen such things before?" asked the vicomte.

Nash shook his head. "This inlay, however, is some of the finest I've seen," he said pensively. "It might be Hungarian, or even Italian."

"Or Polish?" Tristan suggested.

Nash looked at him strangely. "Possibly."

De Vendenheim made a tight, frustrated fist. "I wish to the devil we knew how to open it."

"I don't think opening it is the issue," said Tristan.

The two men looked at him blankly. Tristan shrugged. "There's more than one way to skin a cat," he suggested. "You gentlemen must merely decide whether you wish to have the sphere, or whether you wish to have what is inside."

De Vendenheim and Nash exchanged glances. "By God, I want what's inside," said the vicomte. "I don't give a twopenny damn for the beauty of the thing."

Tristan took the sphere from Nash, slid one of the wooden bars all the way through, strode to a spot beyond the opulent Oriental carpet, and set it on the marble floor. He flicked a quick glance at the two men. "You are quite sure?"

De Vendenheim looked at him dubiously. "Quite certain," he answered. "But short of a hacksaw—"

His words were cut off by the splintering of wood.

Tristan set his boot heel back down, and stood looking over what was left of the sphere. "Simple physics," he said.

"Look." De Vendenheim went down on one knee by the shards of wood. "A scrap of paper." Carefully, he pulled apart the mangled bars of wood and plucked the tiny fold of foolscap from it.

Nash still sat in his chair, his fingers thoughtfully steepled as the vicomte unfolded the scrap. "May I translate for you, old fellow?" he said when de Vendenheim did not speak.

"No," said the vicomte hollowly. "No, that won't be necessary."

Tristan was watching the vicomte. "You look a tad pale, de Vendenheim," he said. "Might I have a look?"

The vicomte cast him a dark glance, then with obvious reluctance, passed the paper over. It was nothing but a list of names. The first was unknown to Tristan, but the next were vaguely familiar. *The black crows.* Three of them, anyway. He glanced at de Vendenheim. "You recognize these men?"

The vicomte hesitated. "All work within the Government, yes. This ball was how the Russians let her know whom they wished her to turn."

"Or Vostrikova's way of telling *them* whom she had already turned." Tristan extended the paper to Lord Nash, who held up both hands, palms out.

"I am well out of this, gentlemen," he said quietly. "I do not work for His Majesty in any capacity save for my service in the Lords."

"As you wish," said de Vendenheim, taking the paper.

Nash stood and rang for a servant. "Vernon," he said when the footman appeared, "kindly sweep up that mess, and wrap the pieces for Lord de Vendenheim."

De Vendenheim tucked the paper away. "Well, I must be off. Be so good as to have that broken wood sent down to my office, won't you, Nash?"

"Certainly, old chap," he said, his voice oddly quiet. Nash turned his glittering gaze upon Tristan. "Talbot, if you would be so kind as to stay? I should like a word."

De Vendenheim cast him an almost sympathetic look, and hastened from the room. Nash's suppressed emotion was now all but palpable. It was wrath, Tristan thought. The knowledge, strangely, did not frighten him. He had taken on bigger fellows than Nash and come out on top. If Nash wished to throw down a gauntlet, Tristan would simply have to pick it up.

He sat, and lifted one eyebrow inquiringly.

Lord Nash regarded the man who sat opposite him with a measure of icy disdain. Talbot was a handsome devil, he'd give him that. Personable and more clever, too, than he'd been given to understand. But there were many handsome, clever, personable men in the world, and bloody few of them—to borrow de Vendenheim's apt phrase—worth a twopenny damn. It remained to be seen, so far as Nash was concerned, to which side of the bar Talbot fell.

"You are aware, Talbot, that Lady Phaedra Northampton is my sister?" he said quietly. "That I am, in fact, her guardian?"

"I am aware, yes," he answered.

"Then kindly explain to me, sir, whose idea it was for you to meet surreptitiously with her? It was inappropriate, and you know it."

Despite his olive skin, Talbot seemed to lose a little of his color. "Surreptitious, sir?" he repeated. "I wasn't aware you'd learnt of it."

"No," said Nash dryly. "I daresay you were not. But servants talk, Talbot. And in this case, I also pay their salaries. A fact you would be prudent to remember."

"You are speaking of Brook Street, then?" Talbot's shoulders appeared to sag with relief. "I meant Lady Phaedra no harm, I assure you."

Nash jerked to his feet. "Yes, Brook Street," he said, pacing across the room. "What else would I mean?"

Talbot smiled faintly. "I wasn't certain," he answered, standing at once with Nash. "I also had the pleasure of seeing your sister at a card party."

"Indeed," said Nash. "A party at which you were seen whispering in her ear, and waltzing with her—and far too closely—or so the Dowager Lady Nash has informed me."

Talbot's gaze swept almost disdainfully down him. "Lady Phaedra is not permitted to waltz, sir?" he asked brusquely. "What a pity. She dances beautifully—when she can be persuaded. And I think, sir, if you'll forgive my saying so, that she has spent entirely too much time *not* dancing."

Lord Nash regarded his quarry for a long, silent moment. "Have you any notion, Talbot, how long it had been since my sister put on a beautiful gown and spent an evening in frivolous pursuits?"

"Too long, I'd say," Talbot snapped.

"Precisely," said Lord Nash. "And now that she has done so, it leads me to wonder why."

"I have no idea, sir."

Nash felt the muscle in his jaw twitch. "No, I thought perhaps you did not." He carefully considered his next words. "You are known to me, Talbot, only by your reputation—and of late, there has been nothing in it to recommend you."

"How kind of you to concern yourself," he said coolly.

The marquess ignored the sarcasm. "But," he continued, "I am aware, too, of your past exploits on the battlefield. Whatever you lack in brains, you apparently make up for in ballocks. That, at least, says something about you."

"Could you kindly come to your point, sir?" Talbot's voice was cold. "We have a murderer on the loose, you'll recall. And witless, well-hung ox that I am, I still harbor some faint hope of helping catch the bastard."

Talbot had a point. Moreover, it had been but a year or two since Nash had had this same discussion with his wife's brother—but then it had been he on the receiving end of the interrogation, and not without reason. He sensed, however, that Talbot, for all his blithe manner, was not a man to be pushed. There was a dark shimmer of dangerous waters beneath all that nonchalance, and though Talbot had spent the last several years as a skirt-chasing wastrel, his near-suicidal exploits in the revolution were the stuff of legend, as was his sudden departure from Greece after the bloody Siege of Tripolitsa—an atrocity in which the Greeks had massacred every Jew and Turk within the city walls, slowly torturing even the women and children.

Talbot, apparently, was amongst the many who had quickly turned their backs on the once-romanticized Greek cause—and Nash thought more of him for having done so. And he had to admit that, from the carefully veiled look he thought he'd glimpsed in Talbot's eyes, combined with Edwina's twittering, he had begun to think it possible that there might be *something* between this man and Phaedra. And despite his grave misgivings, he found himself loath to crush it out.

He was spared these few moments to temper his words since Vernon had returned with the broom and a small box. *Ashes to ashes, and dust to dust,* thought Nash as the footman swept. Nothing—not even solid wood or stone-cold hearts—lasted forever.

He turned his attention back to Talbot as soon as Vernon left the room. "Our discussion is finished, sir," he said quietly. "Go and find de Vendenheim, then catch your killer. Just don't—" His voice caught embarrassingly, and Nash was compelled to look away.

"Just don't what?" asked Talbot softly.

Nash swallowed hard, cleared his throat, and returned his gaze to his unexpected guest. "For God's sake, do not hurt my sister, Talbot," he answered. "She has been hurt so very much already. If you wish only to trifle with a pretty female, I beg you, go and find another. Phaedra does not deserve it."

Talbot regarded him steadily. "I think, sir, that your sister is a very strong woman," he finally said. "Stronger, I believe, than you give her credit."

But Nash just shook his head. "Now that, Talbot, simply proves how little you know her," he said. "Behind her carefully crafted façade is in truth a woman as fragile as spun glass."

Talbot was looking into the depths of the room as if mulling over Nash's words. "I must confess, Nash, that I do not see her that way."

"Few people do," said Nash. "And that is why, sir, I will be very, very slow to give her over into another man's hands. Do you understand me?"

Talbot looked deeply perplexed, and deeply unhappy. He lowered his eyes, and gave a faint bow of his head. "I believe, my lord, that we have reached an understanding."

"I hope, for your sake, sir, that we have," said Nash stiffly. "For if my sister should ever be hurt at your hand, you will not live to tell the tale."

Talbot looked unafraid. "I shan't do anything to hurt Phaedra, sir." His voice was strong and confident. "In that regard, your threat is unnecessary." And with that, Talbot bowed again, and quit the room, his gait long and utterly relaxed.

Her arms crossed beneath her face, the girl lay naked, prostrate upon the narrow cot, a shaft of afternoon sunlight cutting across the welts which striped her buttocks. The old woman who leaned over her made a *tut-tutting* sound, and dabbed again at the worst of the lashes, a swollen ridge of flesh already purpling beneath the skin.

At the sting of the cloth, the girl started, hissing through her teeth.

"Lie still, Flora, or she'll be in 'ere," the old woman whispered. "On yer like a hawk, that one, and a'pecking at yer eyes."

"It in't my fault!" the girl cried into her arms. "A right bastard, 'e is—and stark starin' mad, Hettie. I . . . I couldn't bear it."

Too late, the door burst open. A tall, lean form towered on the threshold, her ice-blond hair contrasting sharply with the black bombazine of her gown. The girl sobbed, and turned her face to the wall.

"What's happened here?" Madame Vostrikova stabbed her finger at the girl, her ruby ring catching the shaft of sunlight, sending shards of blood-red fire through the room. "Why is Flora not upstairs earning her keep?"

The old woman set down her basin and cloth, hesitating.

"By God, I asked a question." Madame swished into the narrow room, her hand raised to strike.

The old woman flinched. "Lord Horrowood sent 'er back down, ma'am. Flora took ill on 'im."

"Took *ill*?" Madame's voice was shrill. "If that little bitch has disgraced me, she had best pray it's fatal."

"She fainted, that's all," said the old woman. "Horrowood was taking 'is pleasure, and, 'e got too rough, Madame. Plain as that. These wounds are like ter turn putrid. She'll not sit for a week and then some."

Madame strolled slowly to the table, then, with a swift snatch of her hand, seized the girl up by her mass of rich, red-gold curls. The girl's eyes shied round like a frightened colt as Madame bent over her.

"Now you listen, you little cunt, and you listen well," she whispered. "I need Lord Horrowood, and you are getting paid to deliver him, do you hear me?"

"In't like I din't try, mum," said the girl on a gasping shudder. "I did try, I swear ter Gawd. But the whip—'e wanted the big one, mum—and I . . . I couldn't take it."

"Why you craven little guttersnipe." Madame shoved her face-first into the table. "I dragged you out of Whitechapel, dressed you, fed you, and put a roof over your head—and this is the thanks I get?"

"I'm sorry," cried the girl, her voice muffled by the cot. "I'll go. Just . . . let me go back, awright? I'd rather be a threepenny uprighter back in Brick Lane."

Madame laughed richly. "Oh, that's as much a fantasy as Horrowood's," she answered. "Now get up, get dressed, and get back to work or the lashes he striped across your bottom will pale in comparison to the next you'll wear— for they'll be laid at *my* hands."

"Ye—" The girl's voice hitched on a sob. "Yes, Madame."

The melancholy *tick-tock, tick-tock* of the longcase clock accentuated the stillness of the Dowager Lady Nash's drawing room, and cast a sense of impending doom across an otherwise tranquil scene. To quell her impatience, Phaedra sat up perfectly straight in her chair and began to rearrange the pleats of her skirt.

"Just think of it!" The dowager twitched a little nervously at the lace of her fichu. "A gentleman paying a call upon Phaedra!"

Phoebe leaned forward and plucked another lemon biscuit from the tray which had been brought in early at her wheedling. "Well, I don't know if one can call Avoncliffe a gentleman," she said, studying it. "But he's certainly handsome enough."

Phaedra snatched the tidbit from her sister's hand. "Must you eat all the best biscuits, Phee, before he even gets here?" she complained. "And Lord Avoncliffe is every inch a gentleman. His appearance, however, is of no consequence to me."

Phoebe eyed her warily. "Well, it certainly would be to me."

"He is unaccountably *dark*," said the dowager a little uneasily, "and I hear he keeps very low company. And Mrs. Hendrick claims that Lady Hauxton was part Gypsy. But still . . ."

But still, Phaedra mentally filled in the blanks, *his father is rich, and my daughter is desperate.*

She did not say the words aloud. Instead, she smiled dotingly. "His breeding is exceptional, Mamma, but it needn't concern you," she answered. "He is merely grateful for my help to his father and wishes to call and thank me. I am sure the thought of courting never crossed his mind."

Lady Nash looked unconvinced. "I thought you said you meant to invite him to walk in the garden?"

Phaedra hesitated. She did indeed need a moment alone with Tristan in order to discover what he'd learned from de Vendenheim, and to reassure him that last night had not meant . . . well, anything either of them needed to worry about.

From the very first she had assumed that last night was something of an anomaly, a thing of beauty to be seized fleetingly, like a firefly, and then released into the night. Tristan, however, had surprised her. His parting words had suggested that perhaps he wished to see her again. Indeed, he had acted a little wounded, but perhaps that had been nothing but his male pride stinging a little at her hesitance. Doubtless he was accustomed to females flinging themselves at his feet.

But what either of them wanted or expected scarcely mattered now. Zoë's wild ramblings had brought home to Phaedra the very real risk of continuing to see him again alone.

For Priss's sake—and for Millie's—Phaedra would insist he keep her apprised of his success in investigating Gorsky's death. They had made a bargain. For one month, she would stay out of his way—God knew she'd accomplished nothing on her own—but she must insist that Tristan call upon her from time to time. And if her mother and Phoebe wished to read something more into it, it was a price she would have to pay. To ensure Priss's happiness, it would be worth enduring Phoebe's teasing and her mother's expectations.

Tick-tock, tick-tock.

The clock, Phaedra decided, was getting louder.

"I vow, Mamma, how much longer must we wait?"

Phoebe's sharp voice cut into the silence. "Can we not at least have the teapot brought in?"

Lady Nash flicked a glance at the clock. "Oh, not yet, my sweet, for—"

Her words were cut off by the butler's entry. He came forward bearing a silver salver, a calling card placed squarely in the center of it. It was the third which had arrived this afternoon, but to her disconcertion, Phaedra's heart leapt with hope again.

The butler bowed to the dowager. "The Duchess of Reyferry, madam," he intoned, "accompanied by her niece, Lady Anne Jenkins-Smythe."

Phoebe's eyes widened. "Oh, Lud! And I wore my second-best muslin!"

Lady Nash's hand quivered over the card, then abruptly she snatched it back. "No, Winston," she said hastily. "We are not in."

"*Not in* to the Duchess of Reyferry?" Phoebe seized her mother's chair arm. "Mamma, are you quite mad?"

Lady Nash pursed her lips and shook her head. "I'm sorry, Phoebe," she said. "As I said, I wish us to give Lord Avoncliffe our full attention."

"But I long for a card to her ball!" Phoebe's lip came out. "Really, Mamma, the others were nobodies, but you must see *her*. This is my big chance."

Lady Nash leaned forward, and tucked a wayward curl behind Phoebe's ear. "We must think of Phaedra, my pet," she said consolingly. "She hasn't the opportunities you have."

Winston bowed again, and left.

Phoebe fell back into her chair.

Tick-tock, tick-tock.

The clock struck the hour—an unfashionably late hour for callers. Phoebe scowled across the tea table, then leaned forward to snatch the lemon biscuit again.

"He isn't coming, I tell you," she said, looking venomously at her sister. Then she bit into the morsel with her sharp, white teeth.

The clock went on in the cavernous silence.

And she was right. No one came.

Tristan lingered in Grosvenor Square, one elbow propped on the iron railing as Callidora knabbled and tugged at what little grass her velvety lips could reach through the bars. The afternoon was all but gone, he thought, his gaze focused down Brook Street.

He was cold, he realized, letting his boot slip from the fence's stone footings. His fingers which clutched Callidora's reins were growing stiff from immobility. Or perhaps from being clenched in wracking uncertainty.

Good God. He was not a man who suffered uncertainty. There was nothing to mourn, or to rail against, for Nash had taken nothing from him that had ever been his to claim. So why, then, did he still stand here, gazing like a mooncalf at her front door and wondering about what could have been? What was this dark, welling emptiness? He felt, strangely, as he had felt watching his mother's trunks go down the steps.

Had Phaedra waited for him, he wondered? Had she even noticed he had not come?

He had watched through the early afternoon as society's *crème de la crème* paid their incongruously named morning calls. Three fine carriages had drawn up at the Northamptons' door, their well-dressed occupants descending and going up the steps only to be turned away and sent back down again.

Tristan snorted and drew a hand down Callidora's sleek, black neck. If the occupants of those crested carriages were being turned away, he had even less hope, perhaps, than he had realized. But hope—or the lack of it—had little to do with why he still stood in the middle of Mayfair with the wind whipping through his hair and Callidora wanting her dinner. He was accustomed to being less than welcome. No, he lingered here, his hands going numb and his heart heavy, because he knew, deep down, that Nash was right. And his father was right. Even if they would throw open that door to him, he had no business pursuing Phaedra.

Oh, he didn't fear Nash. He feared hurting a girl who didn't deserve it. Even if his heart were pure, his life was unsettled. His mission quite possibly dangerous. Did he really want to involve her in this mess? Did he really want *her*? He was beginning to fear he did. Still, some would say he was a rogue and a rotter to his very core, and incapable of being what Phaedra deserved or needed.

And it might not matter. Phaedra had made it plain: she did not wish to be bound by marriage. Initially, he'd thought that suited him. But now he was wondering *why* she resisted, and the fact that he was so curious was a dangerous sign.

A woman as fragile as spun glass.

Nash was right on that point, too, Tristan thought, watching as a tow-haired housemaid came out to sweep the Northamptons' doorstep. Tristan, however, hadn't recognized that frailty for what it was until someone thrust it in his face. Perhaps, as Phaedra had once accused, his gaze had not traveled much beyond her breasts.

That was a shame. Especially when there was no denying the fact that an unmistakable melancholy lingered in her eyes if one but looked for it. No woman made the cold, hard choices Phaedra had made—not without a damned good reason. She had been terribly hurt, her brother said. And it took no great leap of logic to figure out what had happened. Someone had promised her undying love, gained her family's trust, then taken what he wanted from her and left, possibly breaking her heart in the process.

Tristan wondered if the bastard was still alive to tell the tale. Not likely, he judged, based on what he'd seen of the Marquess of Nash. That was as well, he supposed. Tristan would have been tempted to do the job himself. Not out of possessiveness, or even misplaced male pride—no, he had no right to those things. He would have done it because of what it stripped from her. Opportunity. Love. Hope—hope for something a little better than a clandestine tumble with London's most arrant womanizer.

But so far as fleeting physical affection went, Tristan might be the best she could do now, and the realization scarcely warmed the cockles of his heart. In fact, for the first time in his life, he was almost ashamed of what he had let himself become. A lady's last resort. A whore, even.

He watched emotionlessly as a lamp flared to life behind a second floor window. A bedchamber, most likely. Perhaps even Phaedra's. Fleetingly he closed his eyes and watched her undress again. In his mind, he could see her peeling away the muslin gown she doubtless wore, and then the shift which lay beneath it. Unwinding that coil of magnificent chestnut hair which hung nearly to her waist. Lord, if ever a woman had been made for a man's embrace—for a man's worship—it was she.

Just then, the clock at St. George's struck the hour, the sound low and mournful beneath leaden skies. Tristan pulled out his pocket watch and cursed. He was late for a meeting at a coffeehouse in St. James, where he was pursuing a friendship with an old school chum—and a client of Vostrikova's. Tonight they would laugh, and talk of women, then go on to dine, or perhaps visit a gaming hell or two. And with a little luck, the conversation might turn to the topic of where a man might go to slake his less salubrious desires.

On impulse, he extracted the band of ruched lace and yellow silk from his coat, and looked at it, so innocent and dainty in the broad palm of his hand. The little rose still dangled by its loose thread, tenacious as his foolish infatuation. He'd stolen it the day she stitched up his head, and he still wasn't sure why. On impulse, he looped it over one of the iron fence posts as if to leave it. Then abruptly, he changed his mind and shoved it back into the depths of his pocket.

With a soft *whuff* of her velvety nostrils, Callidora cropped one last mouthful of spring grass, then cut a baleful glance up at him. Tristan drew her head up, and slicked his hand down her neck one more time. "Come on, old girl," he said, shoving his boot into his stirrup. "There's nothing more for us here."

Chapter 10

❧

O but they say the tongues of dying men
Enforce attention like deep harmony.

Phaedra endured the next weeks with a measure of sto-
icism, biting back her impatience and hurt. When tempestuous, wicked dreams woke her in the dead of night,
she got up and sluiced her face in cold water, then forced
herself to read a chapter of *Pilgrim's Progress*. She tried not
to think of Tristan Talbot, and of the tea that never was.

Her mother, however, glossed it over for days after, pat-
ting Phaedra on the arm as if she were a child again, and
declaring that Phaedra could do far better anyway. It was
a cold comfort.

On the morning of Lady Kirton's charity ball, two
weeks after that fateful night in Tristan's arms, she awoke
bent double with cramping pain. By the feeble light of
dawn, she climbed down from the bed with a heavy heart,
and went to the washstand only to have her secret fears
confirmed. The blood between her legs lay bright red upon
the facecloth, damning evidence of the void within. Phaedra fell to her knees, sudden sobs wracking her body.

It made no sense. Oh, she *knew* it made no sense! She should have been thanking God above for her good fortune at having been saved, this once, from her own stupidity. Her wicked, wayward passions. Except that it wasn't good fortune at all. It was a tragedy all over again—a smaller tragedy, yes—but it was heartbreak all the same.

Somehow Phaedra dragged herself up, and through the tears, made a fold of white linen, then crawled back into bed to bury her face in the pillow. Awash in misery and self-pity, for once she let herself give in to it. She cried as she had not cried since girlhood.

She had wanted Tristan's child.

She had wanted it for days, deep in her heart, even though she'd known it was all but impossible. Indeed, she had barely dared hope—not in her conscious mind. Not until she'd seen the blood. What, precisely, she would have done about a child so far as Tristan was concerned she hardly knew. And it scarcely mattered. She could have raised a child alone. She was *sure* of it now. And the scandal—her mother's wailing, Stefan's disappointment, even Phoebe's blighted chances—none of it would have mattered to Phaedra could she but have the opportunity to hold her own child in her arms.

Oh, it was wrong, and it was selfish, and she would not have given a damn. She was sick of being Phaedra the Good. Phaedra the Dutiful. But she was not to have that chance. Indeed, she was scarcely able to have her cry and sleep long enough for the blotches to leave her face before Phoebe came twirling into the bedroom, bursting with conversation about the gown she was to wear to Lady

Kirton's, and the flowers and fawning she expected to receive the following day.

"Gentlemen would send you flowers, too, Phaedra," her mother twittered over breakfast, "would you but apply yourself."

But there was little need for Phaedra to apply herself to anything, Phoebe declared, when Zoë Armstrong was doing everything for her.

There was some truth to Phoebe's barb. During those early weeks, Zoë took her vow to make Phaedra her season's project quite seriously. Dresses and fripperies arrived almost daily, both frothy and flounced, in shades from shimmering sky blue to deepest emerald, and invitations which in the past would have been summarily rejected were accepted at Zoë's cajoling—and sometimes her berating.

So as the season opened in earnest, Phaedra went out. The eyeglasses did not. She danced a little, flirted not at all, and as the days passed, watched a bit of the worry fall from her brother's face even as she looked in vain for Tristan around every corner. Under Zoë's tutelage—heavy handed though it was—Phaedra learned to bare her ample décolletage if not proudly, then at least without embarrassment, and to flutter her fan a bit. And she realized, too, that she need no longer fear being seduced by every handsome man who cut an assessing glance her way.

Oh, her old defenses were still firmly in place, though their shape and substance had altered. Gone was her armor of gray wool and linen binding. And in their place was the dawning knowledge that her voluptuousness was not a sin, and that the passion she'd once feared ungovernable now craved but one outlet—not that it brought her much comfort to know she was half in love with a scoundrel. A scoundrel who did not keep his appointments and likely wasn't going to keep his promises, either.

And through all of this, Phaedra tried to consider the possibility that Millie simply might not be coming back. That Priss might have to grow up with neither mother nor father, and that Phaedra must somehow make it right from a distance. Rationally, she understood that she was fighting not Priscilla's fight, but another fight lost long ago. In her heart, however, she believed none of this.

But she did believe, strange as it seemed, in Tristan. She had promised him a month, and she trusted that he was keeping his bargain. He might not be communicating with her as he'd promised, and had doubtless grown tired of flirting with her, but he was a good deal more apt to find Millie than she. But when two weeks turned to three, and she had heard not a word from the man, even this slender reed of hope began to slip her grasp and Phaedra grew exasperated.

It was the day of Lord and Lady Blaine's long-promised ball when Zoë next accompanied Phaedra to Bond Street. Phoebe was laid low by a case of the sniffles—or a case of having danced until three in the morning, depending upon how one looked at it—and Phaedra was called upon to go down for the final fitting of her sister's gown.

"Oh, do remember, Phae, to slouch, or the hem won't be quite right!" Phoebe pleaded, waving a handkerchief from her bed. "That cat Eliza will tell everyone at Brierwood if I go dressed like a rustic."

"And buy yourself a little something, my dear—a new

hat, perhaps?" her mother called out from her chair by the bed. "Miss Armstrong, do help her pick something out. Your taste is always *comme il faut*."

"Oh, and my yellow slippers!" cried Phoebe. "For Aunt Henslow's garden party on Saturday. Pick them up, Phae, won't you?"

"Very well," said Phaedra. She dragged Zoë toward the door to make her escape before the shopping list lengthened.

"I wish you were coming to the Blaines' ball tonight," she said to Zoë as they strolled along Brook Street, their maids following dutifully behind.

"I do, too," said Zoë morosely. "But I have to be here." She gestured toward an elegant double-fronted town house which Phaedra had often passed.

Phaedra turned to study it. "Isn't that the Countess of Kildermore's house? Lord Robert's mother?"

"No, it belongs to her eldest son, the Marquess of Mercer now," she said darkly. "I go there with Papa every year. To a birthday party for the countess."

"What, you do not wish to go?" Phaedra crooked her head to look at Zoë.

"I don't know what I want." Zoë was uncharacteristically quiet. "At least, Phae, you know that much. In a perfect world, you'd want Avoncliffe—not that he deserves you, mind, given this disappearing act of his."

Phaedra cut a sharp, sidelong glance at her. They had had this argument a dozen times already, and Phaedra had grown tired of pretending Zoë was wrong. "I miss him," she quietly admitted. "I miss his wicked grin and that warm, dark skin. Those little crinkles at the corners of his eyes. Oh, he's a shameless cad, I know. But I miss him so much. Zoë, am I an utter gudgeon?"

"Yes," said Zoë glumly. "And I think, perhaps, that I am, too."

In Bond Street, however, Zoë shook off her doldrums by impelling Phaedra to buy a new straw bonnet with a wide blue ribbon which, Zoë swore, perfectly matched her eyes. Then they picked up the shoes and visited the modiste, who made the final tucks in Phoebe's gown and promised to deliver it later that afternoon.

"Now, let's go have an ice," Zoë said as they stepped out of the shop.

"One of these days, Zoë, you are going to turn into an ice," Phaedra warned. "*And* get fat."

But Zoë did not snap back with her usual biting retort. Phaedra glanced over to see that her friend's gaze had darkened warily. "Well, well," she murmured aside. "I see Avoncliffe is back to his old tricks."

With a sinking sensation, Phaedra looked farther down the pavement to see Tristan coming up the street, his head thrown back in laughter, his beautiful eyes twinkling. In the crook of one elbow he carried two bandboxes, and on his arm was a beautiful, dark-haired woman of perhaps something less than forty, her ardent gaze fixed firmly on his face.

"The devil," Zoë muttered. Then she lifted her hand, and waved merrily. "Avoncliffe! Oh, Avoncliffe! How do you do?"

Phaedra realized it the instant he spotted them. His gait hitched, and she could almost feel his hesitance. But left with no alternative, Tristan drew up beside them on the pavement. The light, however, faded at once from his eyes, and his companion's mouth turned into a faint pout.

"Good morning, Miss Armstrong," he said, bowing. "Lady Phaedra. How do you do?"

"Quite well," said Phaedra, surprised at the jealousy which stirred in her breast.

"Do you ladies know my friend, Mrs. Nebbett?" he asked.

"Oh, you know us silly debutantes, Avoncliffe," said Zoë lightly. "We scarcely know anyone over thirty. Ma'am, how do you do?"

Mrs. Nebbett's eyes flared at the subtle dig. Swiftly, Tristan made the introductions. Zoë and Phaedra curtsied, as did Mrs. Nebbett, but her smile was stiff and perfunctory. Clearly, she had better things to do, thought Phaedra maliciously.

"Mrs. Nebbett's husband works for my father," Tristan remarked conversationally.

"Indeed?" said Zoë. "I collect Mr. Nebbett is not a fan of shopping?"

"Mr. Nebbett's hours have become intolerable of late," the lady returned. "Today I needed help with my packages, and Avoncliffe kindly offered his arm."

"Ah, well, sometimes one's work must suffer in a good cause," said Tristan cheerfully. "And a beautiful lady is always a good cause—at least that's always been my philosophy."

Zoë was eyeing him up and down. "Yes, I hear you've become gainfully employed yourself, Avoncliffe," she remarked. "Civilization as we know it has just altered, has it not?"

Still clinging to his arm, Mrs. Nebbett looked vaguely affronted. "Indeed, Lord Avoncliffe is now an assistant to the Under-Secretary of State for Foreign Affairs." She cut a doting glance up at him, setting her dark ringlets to bouncing. "It is a *very* important post—dealing with the highest state secrets."

Zoë widened her eyes. "And here I was imagining him shoveling out grates and sharpening pencils."

Tristan laughed. "Oh, I am just pitching in a bit whilst Father is laid low," he remarked, tucking his companion's hand more snuggly over his arm. "And what better way to help than to squire Mrs. Nebbett up and down Bond Street?"

"Yes, after all, every man has his field of expertise," said Zoë a little snidely.

Just then, a bewigged servant approached, attired in a red coat and gray velvet knee breeches—a livery Phaedra did not recognize. He bowed to Tristan, and glanced round at the ladies apologetically. "My lord, forgive me," he said. "Pemberton asked me to tell you that you are needed in Cavendish Square most urgently. A matter of state business, he told me to say."

"Well, duty calls!" said Zoë brightly. Then she waved a cheery good-bye, and seized Phaedra by the arm. "Have a lovely day, both of you—and, oh, Mrs. Nebbett! Watson's is having a sale on their jacquard silks just two doors down. You really mustn't miss it."

"Jacquard silks?"

"Yes, they cast the light upward so beautifully." Zoë's eyes widened ingenuously. "My aunt declares they can take five years off one's complexion."

For an instant, Mrs. Nebbett could only stare after them, her mouth hanging slightly open.

"Zoë, that was rude," hissed Phaedra as they walked away.

Zoë's gaze narrowed. "Well, don't you just want to scratch her eyes out?"

When Phaedra said nothing, Zoë yanked her arm, turning her around to face her. "Well, don't you, Phae?" she demanded. "Come, admit it. You'd like to smack that simpering smile off her face—or at least I hope you would."

"Zoë!"

"No, listen to me," said Zoë hotly. "I know you're in love with him, Phae—and it was his doing, not yours. After all, he has kissed you. *More than once.* And you are not the kind of girl a man so lightly kisses. Even if you're barren as the bloody desert, you deserve something a little better than a sudden disappearance, and that cat in your face."

But Phaedra was, apparently, exactly that sort of girl. Tristan had clearly forgotten her, and he had been none too pleased to see her again, either. That much had been painfully apparent.

"She used to be his paramour, by the way," Zoë added spitefully. "When he first came back from the war, she sunk her claws in and made a frightful fool of herself. He cannot possibly want her again."

"Zoë," she said wearily, "what is your point?"

"My point is, if you want him, Phae, go after him."

"What? Now?"

"No, not *now*," said Zoë impatiently. "You must think

of another way—but punish him first, Phae. Make him suffer. Break his heart. A man will never respect a woman who cannot bring him to heel."

"I don't know how," she confessed.

Zoë caught her by her shoulder. "Tease him," she whispered against Phaedra's ear. "You are the cat, *ma chère*. He is the mouse. You must bring him to *your* claws."

Tease him? Phaedra scarcely knew how to begin.

Zoë's ice forgotten, they walked back to Brook Street in silence, Phaedra pondering what Zoë had said. It was true. *She was in love with Tristan.* There was no halfway to it. And it had not taken Zoë's outburst to make her realize it, either. No, the mere vision of that woman's hand on Tristan's arm had brought it home to her more acutely than anything else could have done, for she had felt not just jealousy, but a hot, righteous anger, and on its heels, that deep and lingering sadness again.

But a woman could not hold a man to an unspoken promise, or to a fantasy. Still, Tristan Talbot had spoken one promise aloud to her. He had sworn to search for Millie, and made a vow to keep her apprised of his progress. And to that promise, at the very least, she could hold him accountable.

It took Tristan all of ten minutes to send Mrs. Nebbett back to Whitehall in the company of his father's footman, and make his way up to Cavendish Square. He had not needed the footman to tell him what the matter was. And in that moment, he hadn't given a damn about Mrs. Nebbett or what information he might pry out of her. He cared only about seeing his father.

He burst into the shadowy great hall to find Mrs. Wight, the housekeeper, quietly sobbing at Pemberton's side. The butler himself looked pale and rather shaken.

"You've come, sir," he said, stepping forward. "Thank God. I sent for you at once, but it took Simpkin a while."

Tristan's jaw was set grimly. "How bad, Pem?"

"Quite, sir." Pemberton started toward the stairs. "His lordship has been asking for you all morning," he continued as they hastened up. "Well, until perhaps an hour ago. Dr. Glockner is with him now. I think, though, that it won't be long."

Tristan felt hollow. Cold and still inside. "But he rallied yesterday, Pemberton," he muttered. "What the devil happened?"

"Dr. Glockner says that is often the way with the mortally ill," said Pemberton. "They have one last good day, and then . . ." He lifted a hand impotently.

Tristan nodded, and pushed open the door to his father's bedchamber—the same heavy oak door he'd been going in and out of, sometimes twice a day, for almost a month now. Indeed, throughout the whole of his life, Tristan couldn't remember ever having spent so much time in his father's company. There had always been his father's duty to the Crown. Always—*always*—that had come first.

And the fact was, it had been nothing but the same duty which had caused Hauxton to call his son to his bedside these last weeks, Tristan realized, looking down at his father's ashen, emotionless face. And nothing but duty which had prompted him to answer. They needn't delude themselves. He did not regret, this once, doing his father's bidding. Indeed, the challenge of it had awakened something long dormant—a grim sort of determination—inside him. But the sad truth of it did not escape him.

He leaned over the bed, and picked up his father's hand, which was already cold and limp to the touch. He flicked a quick glance at the physician, who had respectfully backed away.

"No." The doctor formed the word softly, and shook his head. "But it won't be long . . . my lord."

Tristan ignored the belated honor. He pulled his usual chair to the edge of the bed and sat, feeling—perhaps for the first time in his life—old and worn. Seeing Phae again had damn near broken his heart, and driven home to him an unfathomable truth. Was he now to have a second loss to be endured on its heels?

As if it had been agreed upon, Pemberton drew the physician from the room and quietly closed the door.

The physician, he realized, was right. Already Tristan could hear the faintest hint of what he knew would become a death rattle in the back of Hauxton's throat. God knew it was a sound a man never forgot. After the fall of Tripolitsa, soldiers' bodies had lain so thick upon the ground, one could scarce enter the city walls without trodding upon the dead and dying. The sounds of death drawing nigh had rasped from the mounds of bodies, a ghastly testament to the barbarity of their end. And then the worst—the systematic slaughter of the women and children—had begun.

The truth was, wars were made by men like Hauxton. And yet Tristan was grateful his father was to have the comfort of dying in his own bed, never knowing what war truly was. He looked down to see that every emotion had fallen from Hauxton's face, and that his pallid skin now lay smooth, unfurrowed by worry. But it was, apparently, something of an illusion.

Tristan laid his hand over his father's, clasping it between his own. "I am here, sir," he said quietly. "If you need me, I am here."

To his surprise, his father's eyes flickered open, but his gaze was unfocused. Unseeing. "Tristan."

Gently, Tristan squeezed his hand. "Are you in pain, sir?" he asked. "Do you need your laudanum?"

"No." Hauxton's mouth tried to turn up in a sneer. "Just tell . . ." he finally managed. "What . . . news?"

Work. Always, it was work. But what else was there to speak of? It was the only thing he and Hauxton shared. The only thing they had discussed since his father's lecture about Phaedra—a lifetime ago, it seemed. And so Tristan began this bedside chat as he had every conversation he and Hauxton had shared these last many weeks.

"I dined with James Ridler again last night as planned, sir," he reported. "I now have an open invitation to visit Vostrikova's brothel and—as Ridler put it—sample the wares. As soon as you're feeling more the thing, I'll—"

"*No.* Mustn't . . . wait." The words were a thready rasp with a hitching breath between. "What . . . else?"

Tristan was reluctant to continue. "I spent much of the morning with Mrs. Nebbett as we'd planned," he finally said. "It seems her husband's finances took an upward turn last month—a card game at White's, or so he told her. And I confirmed that Nebbett has indeed been bringing home diplomatic correspondence. No doubt he is sharing it with Vostrikova."

"Corres . . ." Hauxton managed. His eyes fell half closed. "Wha . . . sort?"

"Really, sir. This *must* wait." Damn it, was even his father's dying breath to be devoted to England?

"What . . . *sort?*" Hauxton rasped, his voice barely audible.

Tristan closed his eyes, and swallowed hard. "Letters from Whitehall to our man in Warsaw, from what I found hidden in his desk," he answered. "The Russians are trying to ascertain if England will hold firm to their side should war break out."

"Damned . . . conniving . . . bastard." A shudder ran through his feeble body. "*Trusted . . .* Nebbett."

And suddenly Tristan realized why his father had involved him. Hauxton had suspected, with his unfailing political instinct, that traitors lurked within his midst. So he had called Tristan—the one person he knew who was well outside his circle. It was a cold comfort now, as he watched his father lay dying, to know he was little more than the instrument of the man's revenge. That he was a mercenary still; a mercenary bought not with money, but by the immutable need for his father's approval.

Hauxton tried to speak, but the words just gurgled in the back of his throat.

"*Stop*, sir." Tristan squeezed his father's hand more firmly. "This is not necessary. You need to rest."

Hauxton drew a deep, rattling breath. "You . . . stop it," he whispered, squeezing Tristan's hand. "*Promise . . . stop her. All of them.*"

"Yes, sir." Tristan hung his head. "I will do my best, sir."

And with that, his father's hand relaxed and went limp within Tristan's grasp.

The rattle in his throat deepened. Hauxton's eyes were still half open. His legs as leaden as his heart, Tristan went to the door and allowed Pemberton and the physician to return. There was a flurry of activity as the doctor threw open his satchel and extracted his stethoscope, whilst Pemberton unfastened Hauxton's nightshirt.

Glockner set the wooden tube to Hauxton's chest and listened. "It is very faint," he reported. "He shan't last the night. I'm sorry, my lord."

So Tristan sat back down in the chair, joining in the long, dark vigil. Sometime around midnight, the rattle became a quiet gurgle. Then Hauxton's breathing began to hitch in long, expectant pauses. At three in the morning, he drew what would be his last. Tristan got up and waited, leaning over the bed in prayer, willing his father to live.

Breathe again, he begged. *Just one more time.*

Just one more chance. Yes, that, really, was what he begged for. Even after all these years, he wanted one more chance with his father—to do what, he did not know. But Hauxton did not breathe again.

"I am sorry." The doctor laid a heavy hand on Tristan's shoulder. Pemberton withdrew a handkerchief, and softly blew his nose.

Tristan reached across the bed, drew down his father's eyelids, then fastened the throat of his nightshirt. He gave his father, insofar as it was possible, a small measure of dignity in death.

He turned to the butler. "I must go now," he said quietly. "But you must do one more thing for him, Pemberton."

"Yes, my lord. You have only to ask."

Tristan looked back and forth between the two men. "Allow no one into the house," he said. "Say nothing of his death yet, particularly to anyone at the Foreign Office. Just tell them he is too ill, and they cannot come in on my orders. Trust me, this is what he would have wanted."

"Very well," said the butler uncertainly.

Tristan laid a hand on the butler's sleeve. "There was one last task my father bade me finish, Pemberton," he said quietly. "But I need time. And it will go far easier if no one knows he is dead."

"Yes, my lord." Pemberton's voice was more certain this time. "I shall arrange for the undertaker to come here, and have your father laid out in the state drawing room."

"Thank you, Pemberton," he said, noticing that the butler was looking at him with extreme deference.

Suddenly Tristan realized why. This—the servants, the house, the duty, all the burdens his father had borne— they were now his to bear. It was nothing he'd ever wished for. But whatever the cost, he would at least see this miserable business finished first. He would let his father rest in peace, his will carried out.

In the end, perhaps, that was all that mattered. In the end, he supposed, that's what families were for.

Phaedra rose early the following morning and girded her loins for the trouble she knew was to come. Saturday was the day of Lord and Lady Henslow's annual picnic at their

Thames-side estate in Richmond, and to call it a gala affair was a true injustice. This being Phoebe's come-out season, she and Lady Nash were to travel down early to prepare for the festivities. Phaedra, however, was not.

"I can't think *why* you must be so stubborn, Phaedra," her mother complained over breakfast. "Most young ladies would kill for an invitation. My elder sister will think you no longer hold her in any affection whatsoever."

Phaedra looked down at her plate a little guiltily. She did love Aunt Henslow—and dearly. But her aunt understood Phaedra's reluctance to move about in society. And sometimes, if Phaedra were honest, it was just a little hard to bear her aunt's company. "I have never gone to Aunt Henslow's picnic, Mamma," she said quietly. "And I don't mean to start. Besides, I think we might turn out all the second floor bedchambers for cleaning whilst you're away. Pray do not quarrel with me."

Her mother, of course, did quarrel. She railed, complained, and finally, wheedled, until at last there was a series of loud bumps in the corridor beyond, and two footmen came past the door bearing a huge traveling trunk high on their shoulders. Her mother sprang up to implore them not to drop it, lest the locks spring and all her finery tumble down the front steps into Brook Street.

Phaedra took the opportunity to get up and poke about on the sideboard, though she ate little. In truth, she had no appetite, and had scarcely slept. A tangle of dreams had tormented her night; sweet dreams of Priss in her arms, and dreams of Tristan all caught up with them, in ways which made no sense at all. Twice she'd awoken in a tangle of sheets, feverish and yearning, the feel of his hands warming her body, the scent of him teasing at her nostrils.

How could one both welcome and dread seeing him again? Was this really about Priss now? Or was she, as she had said to Zoë, an utter gudgeon, chasing after a rogue she'd foolishly fallen for? Her mind in a whirl, Phaedra was barely able to wait until the trunk had been loaded into the family's traveling coach, and her mother and sister handed up inside.

"Do try, my dear, to keep your nails clean and the smut stains from your face," said Lady Nash, leaning down to have her cheek kissed. "We will have Lady Huston's soiree to attend on Tuesday."

As soon as the carriage had vanished, Phaedra went belowstairs and shocked the staff by giving most of them two days off, then hastened up to her bedchamber and rang for Agnes. "They are gone," she said when Agnes came in. "Now pin up my hair—as tight as is humanly possible."

"Oh, miss," said Agnes quietly. "Oh, I *do* hope you know what you're doing."

Phaedra hoped so, too.

According to Agnes, Tristan Talbot lived in a first-floor maisonette, its entrance wedged between a secondhand bookseller and a shop stuffed full of dusty, dubious-looking crockery. Ordinarily a bookshop would have caught Phaedra's notice, but she hastened to the next door with scarcely a passing glance, and dropped the knocker hard.

"In for a penny, in for a pound," she reminded herself. But her shield of righteous indignation had begun to tar-

nish during her march across Covent Garden, and she was beginning to fear this intrusion was just a little less about helping Priss than was wise.

Too late. Phaedra could hear heavy footfalls coming down the stairs. A great beast of a creature opened the door, his slablike forehead deeply creased as if he could not quite make out the slight young gentleman standing upon his master's doorstep.

Phaedra, however, knew him at once. Still, the reminder hit her a little sideways, and left her knees shaking more than they already were. Though the taproom at the Three Shovels had been desperately dark that long-ago night, the man's width, breadth, and utterly bald pate gave him away. Somehow, Phaedra found the presence of mind to hand him a card.

"Mr. Hayden-Worth to see Avoncliffe," she said, dropping her voice an octave. Surely the man would not know Tony was three inches taller and a good deal older?

As she stripped off her gloves, the brute scowled down at the card which his massive thumb almost obscured. "The master's still abed," he said flatly.

Phaedra pushed past him and into the tiny entranceway. "Yes, afternoon comes frightfully early, doesn't it?" she said dryly, handing him her hat and her walking stick. "Kindly get him up. My business is urgent."

The scowl deepened, if such a thing were possible. Phaedra got the impression they didn't get a great many callers, for though the foyer held a decent mahogany table with a well-scrubbed lamp and a fine Chinese bowl, there was no salver for receiving cards. Tony's card still pinched between his massive fingers, the servant led her up the stairs into a long, narrow sitting room hung with hand-colored prints—mostly hunting scenes—then vanished through an interior door between two overstuffed book-cases which stretched to the ceiling.

Phaedra gazed about the room, drawing in the scent of musty books and some exotic blend of tobacco, the smell sweet and oddly seductive. An old leather sofa stretched across most of the back wall, the table before it worn with the evidence of boot heels flung thoughtlessly upon it. A faded Turkish carpet covered the floor, and a stout Jaco-bean desk, cluttered and black with age, sat between the windows which overlooked Long Acre.

Here and there Phaedra noted various *bibelots*: an or-nate Persian platter of etched silver, a wicked-looking scimitar glittering upon the wall, an ancient telescope, the wood worn smooth, the brass warm with age—all of it from Tristan's travels, no doubt. It was every inch a man's room, she thought, looking about it with mild approval.

Though Phaedra could still hear the rumble of an oc-casional carriage in the street below, the house lay silent, and she began to wonder if Tristan had simply gone out the back to avoid her. It little mattered; she'd run him to ground eventually. Impatient, she crossed the room to the bookcases, and let her eyes run over the shelves. It was a remarkably eclectic assortment of history, philosophy, old racing sheets, their corners dog-eared, and even the occa-sional novel. To calm her nerves, Phaedra reached for one.

"I don't know who you hope to fool in that rig," rasped someone behind her.

Phaedra dropped the book, and spun round. "*Must* you keep doing that?"

In the narrow room, he seemed suddenly larger—and angrier—than she remembered. With his dark shadow of beard and flashing black eyes, Tristan looked like the devil himself. He stood in his shirtsleeves and stocking feet, his cuffs rolled up to reveal a pair of dark, well-muscled forearms dusted with dark hair, and his tousled hair made it plain he'd just risen from his bed.

He regarded her through slitted eyes. "What's this about, Phae?"

"You are late, Talbot," she said, keeping her voice low.

"Late?" He had begun to jerk down his cuffs. "For what?"

"For tea," she snapped, pushing past him toward the narrow sofa. "By about three weeks."

Tristan's manservant returned, a garment of flowing red silk draped over his arm, and looking as if he didn't quite know what to make of her. At least someone was fooled.

"Uglow, a word?" Tristan took the garment—a dressing gown—and spoke quietly as he drew it on over his open shirt. The servant nodded and vanished. An instant later, a door slammed in the rear and heavy steps went trundling down a flight of stairs.

Tristan turned his glower back to her. "Your pardon, Phaedra," he said, his voice laced with barely suppressed rage. "But I am not accustomed to receiving ladies in my shirtsleeves."

Phaedra let her gaze run down the red silk. "Oh, I've seen you in somewhat less formal attire, Talbot," she said. "Or had you forgotten?"

"I've forgotten nothing," he snapped. "And you'd best have a very good reason for turning up here like this."

His words stung, and she realized in some humiliation she'd hoped for a different sort of welcome. But she turned to hold his gaze directly. "Oh," she said quietly, "I have a very good reason."

Some nameless emotion sketched across his face then. Joy? Terror? In two strides, he had crossed the room to seize her by the upper arms. "Phae, *good God*—?"

The fervency of his words shocked her, and she staggered back a step. It was just a fleeting, subtle glance, his eyes falling to her belly so quickly most women would not have noticed. But Phaedra did. And suddenly, she knew.

"Oh," she whispered, her brow knotting. "Tristan, no. Not that." He held her gaze bleakly for a long moment, and there was a silent pleading in his eyes. For what, she did not know. "No," she said again. "Really, you cannot possibly have feared—"

"Three weeks, you said." He was still holding her gaze, watchful and intense. Suddenly, his ruthless grip relaxed. "No," he whispered, putting her away in a swirl of red silk. "No, you wouldn't know, would you?"

She followed him across the room. "Listen to me," she said. "I *do* know. You needn't worry."

"How can I not?" He turned again, his eyes bleak, his emotions clearly frayed—all most uncharacteristic. "I worry for you—that you might have been seen coming here. And worried about that, yes." Again, he flicked a quick glance down. "I am not a total cad, Phae."

"And I'm concerned with the child who *is*, not the child

who will never be." She set a hand on his arm, the shimmering red silk soft against her fingers. "Tristan, I . . . I cannot have children. I am barren, or likely so. Please put it from your mind."

He looked at her again with that deep, penetrating gaze of his. "Barren?" he echoed. "How can you know?"

Phaedra cut her eyes away, toward the door through which the servant had vanished. "It is a long story," she answered. "I had a fever once, and some . . . complications. That's all. It happens, you know."

"No, it doesn't." His voice was firm. "Not like that. And it doesn't explain—"

"Why I've dressed up in my brother's clothes and come to call?" Her mouth twitched. "Is it really that obvious?"

He hesitated. "Well, you're good with voices, and the walk's about right," he grimly admitted. "All in all, a damned good ruse, but if you're not carrying my child, you'd better have a damned good reason to go with it."

"Why, I never ceased to be amazed how quickly an indolent scoundrel can turn into a judgmental tyrant," said Phaedra, releasing his arm. "What is *your* reason for *your* behavior, Tristan? I have heard nothing from you in all these weeks. We had an arrangement, sir. You promised to keep me informed."

He paced across the room. "Oh, no," he said warningly. "You'll not turn this around on me, my girl."

"So you make a habit of that, do you?" she snapped. "Kissing a woman senseless, then bending her to your will so that *you* get the bargain you want?"

He spun around, the red silk whipping round his ankles

again. "We had no bargain," he gritted, stabbing a finger in her direction. "I promised you nothing. And trust me, Phae, if you were bent to my will, you'd be bent over that sofa right about now."

"Oh, now *there's* a fantasy," she retorted. "You said we would work together to find Millie."

"No, my dear, *you* said that." He had returned to stand before her, tall and whipcord lean, his lips drawn thin with implacability. "Think back carefully, Phae. I may be a scoundrel, but I don't make women promises I cannot keep."

She started to turn away. "Tristan, you swore—"

"No, I said I'd find out what happened to her," he interjected, grabbing Phaedra hard by the shoulders. "And I asked you to stay out of harm's way. Is that really so difficult? Do you really trust me so little?"

"*La*, sir, I don't know," she said speciously, laying a finger to her cheek. "Let's see, you spent yesterday—and likely last night—tending to your Mrs. Nebbett. One can only infer what you spent the other twenty days doing."

"No, I spent *yesterday* wheedling information out of Mrs. Nebbett," he said, his voice rising to a near shout. "And I spent last night praying by my father's deathbed. And I do not need you, Phae, to come here now to tell me how to do my job—"

"Tristan, I—"

"And I don't need *you*," he shouted over her, "scaring the bloody hell out of me because I have to worry what dangerous ruse you'll pull next. Whether yours will be the next dead body they pull out of the river with a slit throat. Do you understand me, Phae?" He jerked her hard for emphasis, but Phaedra was still stuck on the word *deathbed.*

She raised an unsteady hand to her forehead, only to feel the stiff, foreign curls of Jenny's wig brush her hand. It all seemed so ludicrous now; so suddenly unimportant. "I beg your pardon," she managed to whisper. "Your father . . . he . . . he is gone?"

"He is gone." The words were flat. Almost emotionless.

She looked up to see Tristan's eyes swimming with unshed tears. The full import of it struck her. "Oh, my God." She set her palms to the lapels of his dressing gown. "Oh, Tristan, I am so sorry. I did not know."

The room went perfectly still for a long, awful moment. "No one knows," he finally rasped.

"No one?"

"The doctor. The household." He released his grip on her shoulders, and shrugged. "It must be kept quiet for a time."

She drew back, meaning to ask him why. But the raw pain in his eyes stripped away every question. Every shred of anger. "I am so sorry," she said again. "You must have loved him very much. And he you."

He shook his head once, but it was a slight, uncertain movement. "I thought I loved him not at all," he managed. "And that he loved me no better."

"Oh, Tristan, that cannot be true." Firmly, she set her hands to his lean, unshaven cheeks. "There is too much grief in your eyes for that. And your father, perhaps he was not a demonstrative man—so many of his ilk are not. But how could anyone, once they truly knew you, not love you?"

"Phae." He dragged a hand through his thick hair. "Phae. You are a fool for coming here."

"No," she said with quiet confidence. "I am not that. Not any longer."

And suddenly, it seemed the most natural thing on earth to kiss him—no, it seemed *necessary*. As necessary—and as inexplicable—as her need to come here today. Phaedra rose onto her tiptoes, and set her lips lightly to his, and it was as if time spun away. As if she stood again in the parlor in Brook Street, tucked behind the door with Tristan's mouth upon hers in a sweet, gentle kiss.

But this was a kiss of pure seduction. His tousled black waves fell forward as that beautiful harlot's mouth softened over hers. Molding to her lips in pliant, coaxing strokes. Sending that sweet, hot ribbon of need twisting through her. Drawing her fully into him.

Then just as abruptly, he lifted his mouth and left her staggering. "Go now," he said thickly. "I'll deal with your Millie, and send word, I swear. Go home, Phae."

Impulsively, she brushed the corner of his mouth with her lips. "Is that really what you wish?" she asked, her eyes dropping shut. "I think not."

"Go home, love," he rasped. "I'm so bloody tired and ill-tempered. I'm not myself, Phae."

She opened her eyes, and searched his face. His expression was stark, his eyes soft with grief. "I think that perhaps you are more real than I have ever seen you," she whispered. "At least you are angry. Sorrowful. Worried. At least you *care*."

His mouth lifted at one corner, a dry, humorless smile. "Aye, as I said—not myself."

She shook her head. "That man who laughs all the time and cares for naught," she said. "That charming knave on Mrs. Nebbett's arm. Tristan, tell me, is that really you? I . . . I need to know."

He closed his eyes wearily, as if he feared what message she might read there.

Acting on instinct, Phaedra slid her palms up the red silk of his gown, then kissed him again, twining her hands behind his neck. It was to have been a kiss of compassion, and of reassurance. But there was a hard edge to him today, something brittle and desperate. And when he drew his tongue hungrily across the seam of her lips, she opened. Something inside him snapped—like a burning lamp sent crashing to the floor in a cascade of flame as he thrust inside. Heat washed through Phaedra, welled up and surged through her every vein. She could feel it in him, too; that same helplessness as his mouth moved over hers. The sense of inevitability, and of rightness.

His lashes still wet with tears, his face twisted with grief, Tristan held her to him. She responded, opening fully, giving willingly whatever he needed to take. He slanted his mouth over hers, the sensuous swell of that bottom lip dragging faintly over her own, his unshaven cheeks raking her. His arms came fully around her, powerful and warm as he lifted her to him. With each breath, she drew him deeper inside herself, luxuriating in the clean scent of plain soap and warm male skin. Phaedra felt herself relaxing into the supple strength of his body, as if the lee of his broad chest might shelter her.

"Phaedra," he whispered.

She felt weak, without will or good sense, unable to

pull her mouth from the soft temptation of his lips. Her heart cried out for him; it was no longer just her body. She kissed him again, more boldly, and let her hands slide beneath the red silk. Her palms stroked down the hard slabs of muscle at his back to the curve of his spine, and lower still, pulling him into her. Offering what comfort she could.

He accepted, thrusting deep, his tongue parrying with hers, his hands roaming over her, heavy and seductive. She could hear her own heartbeat now. She knew what was going to happen, and welcomed it. Whatever he needed— whatever they were together—it was right in this moment.

Somewhere by the sofa, he shoved the coat from her shoulders, still kissing her desperately. Her neckcloth followed, a trail of white across the opulence of the Oriental carpet. In the swirling heat and madness, Phaedra hitched up against something, and a pile of magazines cascaded to the floor. *The bookcase.*

Unthinkingly, her hands went to the close of his trousers, slipping loose the buttons. A snatch of some long-ago eulogy sketched through her mind. *Even in death there is life.*

These past weeks, *she* had felt alive. Alive for the first time in more years than she could bear to count. Back from the dead of a shuttered and hopeless life. She wanted to drink it in—the pleasure and even the pain—all of life's richness she had so long denied herself.

Her waistcoat slid away, allowing her shirt to fall open down her throat. Tony's trousers slithered to her hips. Somehow, she stepped out of one leg, and hitched the knee about Tristan's waist. He tore his mouth from hers, then on a soft curse, turned her, and swept his arm across the desk. The Persian platter went clanging to the floor in a cascade of quills, paper, and ink pots.

Roughly, he lifted her, perching her on the edge of the desk heedless of the windows to either side. The wood was cool against the flushed heat of her bottom. Tristan fumbled at the fall of his trousers, pushing down the snarl of linen drawers. His manhood sprang free, swollen and jutting, far more intimidating in the light of day. Uncertainly, Phaedra slid one hand down the hot, silken length of it, causing him to moan. Emboldened, she drew him near. Tristan entered roughly, on one hard stroke, burying himself deep and letting his head fall back.

"I'm sorry, Phae," he choked. "Oh, God."

"Don't be sorry." Her lips brushed down his cheek.

He thrust, and thrust again, each stroke deep and shuddering, lifting her off the wood, the desk and even the prints hanging above it shaking at the impact. Phaedra clung to him as if clinging to sanity, taking his kisses deep and returning them in full measure.

"I'm sorry, I'm sorry," he said thickly.

Then Tristan thrust one last time, coming inside her on a low, inhuman groan. The rush of his seed surged into her in a hot, satisfying flood. And in a minute—three, perhaps—the storm was over. She fell against him in a tangle of limbs and linen shirts, their breath coming in deep, heaving gasps.

"*Phae*," he rasped. "Oh, God. Tell me you wanted that."

"I wanted that," she whispered, her nose buried against his damp neck.

His arms wrapped around her, Tristan responded by pulling her off the desk.

Phaedra wound both legs round his waist as he carried her through the door into the depths of the house. Halfway down the darkened passageway, her second shoe fell off, and she lost the last leg of her trousers. Tristan turned into a shadowy room—his bedchamber, she realized, for the cool, still air was redolent with his scent. They collapsed onto the bed, their bodies still joined, the roping beneath creaking in protest.

Hesitantly, he lifted his hand and tucked a bit of her hair beneath the cap of Jenny's old wig. "Well, that was utterly humiliating," he murmured, his eyes roaming over her face. "A world record, I daresay, of the worst sort."

She kissed him again, settling her mouth softly to his cheek. "Sometimes it's best to just take what one needs at the moment," she whispered. "Sometimes, Tristan, that's what lovers are for."

"And what about you?" he asked. "Do your needs count for nothing?"

She smiled, a muted Madonna-like smile. "You needn't play Lothario for me," she murmured. "I did not give myself to you so that I might get something in return."

"Did you not?" he asked lightly, one hand cupping her face. "Why, then?"

She glanced away, hesitating. "Because I care for you far more than I might wish, I daresay," she finally answered. "If the guilt is more than you can live with, make it up to me."

"Phae." The word was soft; almost as soft as the kiss which followed. "I oughtn't be—"

She laid a finger to his lips. Her anger—and his—had burnt down to ash. "Do not speak to me, Tristan, of *ought*," she said quietly. "I know what I want. Who I am. I have been changed by this. By you. Oh, my dear, I'm not naïve. I know exactly what we are doing. And exactly how far it should go."

"How far?" he rasped.

She looked away.

"Phae." His voice sounded pleading. "What do you want of me?"

"Just . . . this," she replied. "Must we speak of it now, and ruin it? Your father is dead, Tristan. Mourn him however you must—or simply celebrate being alive. Nothing else matters just now."

It wasn't quite the answer Tristan had hoped for, strangely. His heart still thudding, he let his eyes roam over Phaedra. He was glad—selfishly, disconcertingly glad—she had come. And God knew he hadn't honor enough to send her away again.

Lingeringly, he let himself savor her every aspect, taking in her strangely seductive contrasts. The cropped brown hair which only accentuated the feminine turn of her neck. Her fine-boned wrists encircled by deep, white cuffs. The starched, masculine shirt, and beneath it, the tantalizing swell of womanly breasts that rose with her roughened breath, threatening to burst from her linen binding.

In the dreams which had begun to torment him nightly, Phaedra wore only the most feminine of fabrics; layers of lace and virginal white silk. Frothy, ephemeral garments which slithered inch by inch down her body as he painstakingly unfastened each button. Row upon row of tight, tiny, impossible buttons, as if Morpheus meant merely to tempt him. To deny him what he burned for. Night after night, she came to his bed, her smile knowing, her eyes unreadable. And never were the buttons fully undone. He would awake shaking, in a sweat; purity and salvation always just beyond his reach.

Perhaps it was what he deserved. But Phaedra was here, in his bed now, and his desire for her was but barely slaked. With a hand which trembled, Tristan folded back the opening of her shirt, exposing the creamy swells of her cleavage to his gaze, mesmerized by the contrast of his dark fingers against her pale skin.

The vision was not enough. He lifted her gently, drew the shirt from her body, then closed his eyes and bent over her, setting his cheek to hers.

"I need you to say it, Tristan," she whispered, her breath stirring against his ear.

"Say what, love?"

"Tell me you are glad that I am here."

He gave a dark, sensual laugh. "You shouldn't be here at all."

"I think we are well past *shouldn't* by now."

He closed his eyes, and inhaled deeply of her scent. Of lavender and warm, sensuous woman. She was right. Things between them had changed inexorably, shifted and altered into something more undeniable, for good or for ill. Keeping his distance from her would not change that now. It probably wouldn't even keep her from getting hurt. "I thank God you are here, Phae," he finally admitted.

She sighed beneath him and began to twist free of the linen binding. Tristan rolled onto one elbow and stripped off what remained of his clothing. When he looked down at her again, he could see some nameless emotion flickering in her eyes. Desire, yes, and something more. A hint of uncertainty, perhaps?

He wanted to laugh bitterly. Any woman who considered throwing her lot in with his ought well to feel a healthy dose of doubt. And suddenly, he wanted to strip that doubt away. For once in his life, he wanted to be worthy of something better and greater than himself. And when Phaedra parted her lips, and looked at him, he kissed her gently, cupping her face with one hand as his tongue lightly explored her mouth.

She tasted sultry and a little tart, like wild strawberries warmed by the sun. Her heavy breasts lay fully exposed now, a shaft of midday light cutting through the sheer draperies to cast her in a faint, warm glow. Cupping one breast in his hand, Tristan bent his head and touched his tongue lightly to her nipple, making her shudder beside him. "They are too large," she whispered self-consciously.

He laughed deep in his throat and lifted his head to look at her. "You have the silliest, most endearing notions," he said, smiling down at her.

She cut an uncertain glance away. "I always wished for a pair of pert little teacup breasts," she said. "Not something . . . not something that made me look as if I were made for sin—a body made merely to tempt men to wickedness."

He flicked an appreciative glance over them. "You are made for adoration, Phae," he corrected. "A lush beauty in the full flower of womanhood. What could be more pure and perfect than that?"

She shot him a chiding glance. "You are only saying that to get what you want."

At that, he threw back his head and laughed. "I already got what I wanted," he corrected. "Now I am merely lingering, worshipful."

Her hand slid down to grasp the hardening rod of his erection. "What a frightful liar you are," she whispered, her soft blue gaze catching his.

He closed his eyes again, the breath shuddering from his body on a low, hungry growl. "I am a liar," he admitted. "I want to make love to you, Phae—and your perfect breasts. Slowly. Exquisitely."

And in that moment, it mattered not at all that, despite her fears, he might leave her with child, or that her brother might kill him for it. It mattered only that he knew what brought her satisfaction. That he knew the sounds of her need, and the scent of her body. He knew how she liked to be taken—with control and yes, a little domination. And he knew the unalloyed pleasure of spending himself inside her.

Slowly, he touched her, circling one taut nipple with the tip of his finger until she sighed with pleasure. But his hands still trembled imperceptibly with each stroke, and with the knowledge that he had been given—at least for today—a precious gift.

Phaedra's hands came up to cradle his face, drawing his mouth to her breast as her bare foot slid up the length of his leg. Deftly, she curled her limb around his, like a cat seeking the pleasure of a stroke. Somewhere amidst the pleasured sighs, Tristan pushed the mop of curls away and unwound her real hair, the glorious golden brown coils spilling down her shoulders and over her breasts. The tangle of clothing was kicked off the bed and the covers shoved fully down. The expanse of white sheeting was his canvas, and she was to be his masterwork.

Tristan let his hands and his mouth roam over her until her soft gasps of pleasure filled the cool stillness of the room. Her breasts, her belly, her long, beautifully sculpted thighs. He let his hand run up the length of her leg from ankle to the crease of her joining. He let his tongue toy with the sweet, hard nub between her legs, but only enough to make her arch with pleasure.

"Tristan," she rasped when he licked his way up, and plunged his tongue into her navel. "Tristan, *wait.*"

There was an urgency in her voice which made him lift his head.

Her long, brown lashes fluttered almost shut, and the tip of her tongue came out to toy with one corner of her mouth.

He drew himself up and lay down alongside her. "What is it, love?" he murmured, nuzzling her left breast. "Shall I stop? Go faster?"

She shook her head.

He drew a finger down the smooth white length of her breastbone. "Come, Phae," he whispered against her throat. "We are lovers now. Tell me. Let me please you."

She turned her head away, her throat working up and down. "I want what you did in the garret," she whispered. "I want . . . I don't know how to explain it."

He shifted the weight of his body atop her, bracketed

her face in both hands, and kissed her long and deep. "You wish to be fully beneath me?" he said when she was breathless. "You wish . . . something more?"

Her eyes still closed, she nodded. "Sometimes it feels . . . like too much," she said. "Too *good*. As if I cannot trust myself to . . . to . . . I do not know. I . . . I don't understand myself."

Something dark and knowing surged inside him. "You want me to possess you," he murmured huskily. "To control you."

"Yes." The word was a hungry whisper. "I wish you to—"

"I think I know what you wish," he whispered.

A sigh of relief escaped her. "I am . . . wrong, somehow," she whispered. "But this—this will be our secret, Tristan. Yes?"

"You are not *wrong*," he said. "You are a deeply sensual woman, Phae, but for some reason, you don't trust yourself. So, for now, you want a strong lover who dominates. And there is no shame in that, so long as it is done gently and with . . . with deep affection."

She looked at him in confusion.

"Phae, in time you can learn to master your own desires," he said. "Or do you wish me to master you? I will, love—gently—but only if that's what you want."

When she did not answer, he rose from the bed and went to the lowboy by the windows. When he returned, he laid a coil of soft rope across her belly, then stretched himself back out along her length. What is that?" she asked without looking at it.

"A *kinbaku* rope from the Far East." He picked up one

frayed end and teased lightly at her nipple. "This one is made of silk, and very soft. It is used to heighten sensual pleasure, if a person is so inclined."

Her face flushed with pink. "I cannot believe you own such a thing," she sputtered. "You are more wicked, I daresay, than even Zoë knows."

Tristan laughed, and did not tell her the truth—that the silk rope was a recent acquisition, bought in the East End in a moment of reckless melancholy. He had not thought ever to use it, and wasn't perfectly sure he should do so now.

But Phaedra had twisted the other end of the white rope about her wrist and was looking at it, transfixed. "How do you use it?"

"Oh, I think you have some idea, my sweet," he murmured. "I can simply tie your hands to the bed, and mount you."

"Oh, my," she said huskily.

"Or I can tie your legs open."

"*Oh,*" she breathed.

"Or I can bind this round your breasts and then to your wrists," he suggested. "That, I daresay, might keep my naughty girl in her place?"

"Yes." Her eyes flew open, her gaze clear and hungry. "*That.*"

Dear God. Tristan swallowed hard. But he had bought the rope, and offered it to her. "Sit up," he said, his voice roughening.

He wrapped the rope twice beneath her breasts, knotted it to one side of her spine, then twice above her breasts until the rope pressed down tight upon her pale mounds.

Carefully, he worked the rope through her cleavage. Good God, it was a beautiful, highly erotic sight.

"Lie down," he rasped.

A smile flirted at the corner of her mouth. "My, you are getting tyrannical already," she murmured.

"I must admit, my dear," he said darkly, "that the notion of finally having you obey me is rather intoxicating." He drew the silk up her throat, and stretched her arms high, binding them together in gentle coils from her lower wrist to above her thumbs. He knotted the rope to the bed and sat back on his haunches surveying his handiwork.

Not a bad job for an amateur, he thought.

Phaedra's eyes widened as she tested the knot. *"Oh,"* she said softly as her breasts lifted against the strain.

Tristan let his gaze drift over the ropes which pressed into the plump mounds and felt raw lust surge. God, he was very much afraid a man could get used to this. The eroticism of having Phaedra—bossy, meddlesome female that she was—fully bound and immobile beneath him was dizzying. But as he bent over her and kissed her deeply, he realized that the real eroticism came not from the control, but from the trust—the trust which Phaedra so willingly offered him. It grieved him to wonder how long she'd felt such shame, unable to unburden herself to a lover who would not judge. How lonely her life must have been. Perhaps he understood more than she might guess.

And in that moment of stark, clean realization, as their mouths sought solace in one another, it was as if something inside him broke under the pressure of craving her. Dear God, he was in too deep to ever get out of this, and suddenly weary of his life spent pleasuring other women.

Tired of rising from their beds so cheerfully apathetic, often unable to recall their names or even why he had wanted them in the first place.

Whatever she needed, Tristan burned to drive Phaedra mad with pleasure. To enslave her with it, and bind her to him forever. He nudged her legs wide with his knee and braced himself over her on one arm. He took her mouth again, more roughly, and drew his fingertips through the damp, feminine heat between her thighs. The dew slicked his fingers, and sent desire shafting through him, red-hot and searing. His cock throbbed insistently. To tamp down his impatience, he shifted his weight lower, and settled one arm across her thigh.

Slowly he slipped two fingers inside her as she watched beneath heavy eyes. Phaedra's passage tightened, pulling him into her; drawing him deeper into the sensual haze. He wanted to lose himself. To thrust his flesh into hers and claim her once again. Instead, he kissed her there, then held her gaze as his tongue teased deeper.

She gasped, the ropes drawing taut, then relaxing again. Something passed between them; a look of acceptance and surrender. "I have you under my control, Phae," he whispered. "There is no escape unless you beg for it."

No escape unless you beg.

Phaedra heard the words and shivered. The ropes which bound her pressed into her flesh, tight but not painful, yet confining all the same. Binding her to his touch. Laying her out like a feast for his eyes and for his body. She felt the weight of Tristan's erection throb against the tender skin of her inner leg, and gave herself up to the torment.

Using his thumb, he opened her more fully, and set the other hand on her inner thigh, gently urging her wider. His tongue stroked into her warmth, sin and sensation washing over her. It was decadence unimaginable. When she struggled, and tried to shift away, he laughed and nipped gently at the tender flesh of her belly. "Mind what you do," he growled. "You are under my control, remember?"

Oh, she remembered. And it frightened her a little.

His tongue stroked deeper, the stubble of his beard rough against her skin. Beneath the pressure of the rope, Phaedra's nipples had hardened to pebbles. He was drowning her in desire and that swirling hot madness. He stroked again, this time sliding one finger inside her, and Phaedra's hips bucked off the mattress.

In response, he licked lightly at the very center of her madness. Enslaving her with his mouth and his hands and his rope, until at last the rush of sensation swamped her. She cried out, pleading, and then was lost in him. The waves crashed in, dragged her down into a world of drugging, lethargic pleasure.

When she resurfaced in the present, limp and trembling, Tristan was braced over her, the tan, sculpted muscles of his arms taut, his eyes dark with desire. She licked her lips uncertainly. "Untie me?"

Slowly, he shook his head. "I don't think so, love." The words rasped from his throat. "Not unless you beg me."

With a tentative smile, Phaedra let her eyes rake down Tristan. His was a warrior's body; lean and hard, with scars across his arm and his hip—God's perfection marred by man's inhumanity. And he was all the more beautiful for it. She let her eyes feast on fine shoulders as wide as her thighs, and the sleek turn of his waist. Between the two points there lay nothing but honey-colored muscle layered over strong ribs and dusted with a hint of dark, curling hair which winnowed away to nothing at his navel. And below that, *oh* … .

Phaedra was shocked to feel the return of desire. She lifted her hips in invitation. "I'm not begging," she whispered. "Not for that, at any rate."

With his knee, he nudged her leg wider, then he set his hand to her mound. "Have you any idea, Phae, how beautiful you are?" His black Gypsy eyes enthralled her, shook her just a little. "Have you any notion how desperately I want you?"

She managed a feeble grin. "You probably say that to all the girls you tie up," she whispered.

He looked at her blankly, his eyes still dark with need. "I have no idea," he muttered. "Right now I can't even remember ever making love to anyone else."

With that, he drew one hand down his cock and closed his eyes, as if savoring the moment. Then he settled himself over her and thrust, his head going back as he buried himself inside her again.

He thrust inside her rhythmically, his arms rigid with muscle, his belly drawn taut. She could understand why women might fight over this. Tristan made love like he danced, with a raw, physical grace. Living life to the fullest, seeking pleasure only in the present. There was glorious, wild beauty in it—and a life lesson, too, she feared.

She let her head fall back into the softness of the bed, and rose to him, taking his strokes with equal abandon.

His scent—bergamot and soap and his own sensual warmth—teased her nostrils. She wanted desperately to please him, as he had pleased her. The afternoon light was strengthening now as the sun shifted over the roofs of Covent Garden. It shone over him, bathing his honeyed skin in a golden glow. With his dancer's grace, he deepened his rhythm, moving inside her with sweet, perfectly timed strokes.

She felt her hunger spiral higher, and gave herself up to him. Their skin was damp now, their bodies sliding wetly against one another. "Phae," he cried, his hair falling forward to shadow one eye.

Boldly, she rose to him, watching him in the fading light. That masculine beauty, the utter magnificence of his body, was her undoing. She cried out and felt the stars fall. Felt herself tumbling headlong into the unknown, Tristan's arms tight and strong about her.

Long moments later, she stirred to feel the weight of Tristan's leg thrown over hers. He lay facedown beside her, his lips pressed to the turn of her neck, one arm banded about her waist in a sweet, possessive gesture. She was his. Whether he knew it or not—whether it ever came to anything more than this—she was his. She was, headlong and hopelessly, in love.

His body spent and still shuddering within, Tristan sensed Phaedra stirring. Somehow, he found the strength to kiss her lightly below her ear. *"Ummm."*

"Oh, my." Beneath him, Phaedra exhaled on a shudder. "Tristan. That was . . ."

"Ummm," he moaned again. "Perfect."

"Yes, *perfect*," she sighed. "Let's do it again."

He lifted his head and looked at her through a shock of inky, disordered hair. "You cannot be serious."

Phaedra's face colored furiously.

She *was* serious. Well, he had never been one to resist a challenge. He laughed, and rolled onto his elbow. "Greedy puss!" he muttered. "You are insatiable."

She looked away. "Sometimes I'm afraid I might be," she said softly. "But you make this seem so beautiful. So . . . *normal.* Can you? Do it again?"

He reached over the edge of the bed and felt for the knife he always left inside his boot. Then he lifted the rope which stretched down her cleavage, unsheathed the blade with his teeth, and slipped the knife between her breasts. He jerked up, slicing the ropes cleanly.

In a moment, Phaedra had shaken her hands free of the remaining coils. He tossed the knife onto his bedside table with a clatter, and seized her wrists, turning them this way and that in a shaft of afternoon light. He looked down to see the embarrassment had faded from her cheeks. He bent to kiss her, gently and lingeringly.

"Now," he said when he had thoroughly ravished her mouth, "to answer your question—*yes.* I can do it again." Already he felt the faint stirring of lust. "But this time, Phae, we do it without the rope."

"Without the rope?"

"And with you on top."

Her eyes widened. "But I . . . I don't know—"

He cut her off by setting his hands to her waist. "Oh, I'll show you," he promised, rolling onto his back and taking her with him. "This time, Phae, you are in control—and for as long as it takes, love."

It took a while. She was sweetly slow and uncertain. Inexperienced as she was, Phaedra would take time to become comfortable in her own skin, he knew. And admittedly, he was not at his best. Perhaps his age was finally telling. Or perhaps it was the fact that he was spent—not just physically, but emotionally, by an exhausting mélange of grief and lust, and by the disconcerting realization of just how deep he was where Phaedra was concerned. But in that moment—in that perfect time and place—it scarcely mattered. His body was soon joined again to hers, and fleetingly, the world was his.

Chapter 11

❦

O, how this spring of love resembleth
The uncertain glory of an April day!

Long moments later, Tristan lay sated beside Phaedra, twining a lock of her chestnut hair round and round his finger, and pondering what he ought to do about his rapidly deepening feelings for the girl. Nothing yet, he thought, regrettably. There was too much hanging over them. His father's death, and this business with Vostrikova to finish. Her family's disapproval. Her obsession with this motherless child and missing tavern maid. And above all, the danger.

But when his gaze drifted over her face, sweetly softened in sleep, he felt his heart lurch.

Suddenly, the *thump* of the front door roused him. Tristan glanced at the clock. *Half past three.* Bloody hell. It was Uglow returning, most likely. He could hear heavy feet trundling around in the sitting room. A few moments later, the floor in the passageway creaked ominously.

Phaedra's eyes fluttered wide. Tristan set a swift finger

to her lips, and drew the bedcovers up. The footsteps continued, slow and heavy, stopping just outside the door. Instinctively, Tristan rolled to one side and snatched up his knife.

A slow, heavy knock sounded, a dirge upon the wood. "My lord?" Uglow's voice sounded strained. Unnatural.

Tristan dropped the knife. "Aye, what?" he said impatiently.

There was a long, pregnant pause, then the door opened just a crack to reveal the servant's broad back. "My lord," said Uglow solemnly. "I'm afraid I've got ter give me notice."

"What, this minute?" Tristan sat up in bed, and pinned the door with his dark gaze. "Are you mad?"

"I've been through it wiv you, sir, the thick and the thin," he said grimly. "Put up wiv yer wicked women and vile habits. Them murderous Turks trying ter slice me throat wiv their nasty, crooked knives. But even a chap like me draws the line at *this*."

Tony's trousers sailed through the air, landing on the bed with a *whuff*.

A horrible realization dawned.

"Uglow!" Tristan snatched up his silk robe from the floor. "Wait. No. It's not what you think."

Uglow hesitated, then slammed the door shut. "It's an unnatural act, sir, wot yer about wiv that lad," he said through the wood. "And I'll 'ave no part in it."

Beside him, Phaedra spurted with laughter, then clamped a hand over her mouth. Tristan shot her a dark look. "Wait, Uglow." He rolled out of bed, shoving his arms into the red silk robe. "And you—be quiet," he said, whirling around to Phaedra. "Not a peep till I return, do you hear me?"

She grinned, and drew the covers to her nose. "Oh, yes, my lord and master!" she said in her gentleman's voice, a little too loudly. "Please, oh, please don't tie me up and have your wicked way with me again!"

"Awright. That's it!" Uglow's heavy tread carried away from the door.

Tristan stabbed a finger in Phaedra's direction. "You. Will. Be. *Quiet.*"

Then he slammed the door behind him.

A quarter-hour later, with Uglow somewhat mollified, Tristan returned, the robe wrapped tight about his waist, to find fresh water in the basin, and a damp towel tossed over the wash stand. Phaedra was sitting up, her hair tidied, and wearing her brother's shirt.

"I am very angry with you," he said, slamming the door. "Your reputation could be in tatters right now."

She looked at him and grinned. "Nonsense," she said, "and you know it. By now you will have persuaded him that I am some insatiable, faithless wife out on a lark behind her husband's back."

Tristan felt his face heat. That was, in fact, precisely what he'd told Uglow. Not that Uglow quite believed it, for the old boy had a nose for trouble. But he did believe, at least, that Tristan was bedding a female, which was a damned good thing considering Uglow's prudish notions. Over the years, Tristan had come to depend upon the chap pretty thoroughly.

He shucked the robe, sluiced cold water down his face

with both hands, then hastily bathed. The intimacy of it—Phaedra in his bed, him striding about stark naked, and the two of them sniping at one another just a little—all of it felt perfectly natural. Comfortable. Seductively so.

She felt it, too, he sensed. Bedcovers pulled up to her chin, Phaedra watched him towel off his chest and groin with a warm, appreciative gaze, but with a casualness which suggested they did this every day of the week. Despite his frustration, it was an oddly comforting notion.

He tossed down the towel and returned to bed.

"Well, we are even, Tristan," she said, falling back into a pile of pillows. "I came here angry with you."

"Aye, you were." Tristan crawled between the sheets, weary. "I'm sorry for it, but I daresay it won't be the last time."

At that, she looked at him strangely. He lay back down, but she did not. Instead, she sat up, folding and refolding the hem of the coverlet, her brow in a faint knot.

Now, ordinarily, this was the point at which Tristan would deliberately drowse off to sleep, and hope his lover's gratitude would outweigh whatever she was about to scold him for. If that didn't work, he usually rolled out of bed and pled a forgotten engagement. But he was beginning to fear his running days might be coming to a precipitous end. Ah, well. There was nothing else for it. He rolled back to face her, and took her hand.

"What is it, Phae?" he murmured, planting a kiss atop her fingers.

She trembled on the verge of some uncertainty. Then finally, she spoke, blurting out the words. "Why did you not come to tea, Tristan?" she demanded, her low, warm voice uncharacteristically unsteady. "Was the prospect so very dreadful?"

For a moment, he weighed what to tell her. But they were beyond prevarication, he supposed. "I spent much of that afternoon with your brother," he admitted.

"Regarding the puzzle ball." Her voice was impatient. "Yes, I heard."

"And afterward, we . . . well, we spoke of you. He explained some things to me."

"What are you saying?" Phaedra looked at him, incredulous. "That Stefan warned you away from me?"

Tristan averted his eyes. "He warned me not to hurt you," he whispered. "And given who I am, it was not an unreasonable request."

Her lips had gone white with anger. "Oh, it wasn't a request, it was a *threat*," she said, her hands fisting in the coverlet she'd so neatly folded. "I know Stefan. I shall throttle him. I swear it."

"Phae, love, he was right." Gently, Tristan caught one hand, and smoothed out her fingers with this own. "I might hurt you. God knows I'd never wish to. But my life has hardly been one of sober rectitude. My reputation, as your brother so tactfully put, has little to recommend it. And now this business I must settle for my father—it might not end well."

Some of the anger went out of her then. "What do you mean to do?" she asked. "Tristan, what is going on? Your father is dead. And whatever you are about, it is far more than a murder investigation. Even *I* have figured out that much."

He kissed the back of her hand again, and drew her

back against him, cupping his body about hers. "I promised my father to see this through," he said, brushing his lips down her neck. "And I mean to do it. But you, Phae—much as it pains me, I think you should go home now. Before you're missed."

She cut a sidelong glance at him, as if measuring his reaction. "Oh, we still have some things to talk about, Tristan," she said. "Besides, Mamma and Phee have gone to Richmond, and I gave half the servants two days off—not that they'd dare question me. Agnes will make my excuses if trouble turns up."

He exhaled slowly, and considered it. He had little doubt she'd covered her tracks pretty thoroughly. "You must be mad, Phae," he said, brushing his lips over her cheek. "And I am weak. Too weak to do what's right, and send you packing."

She turned, and wiggled her rear against his groin, tucking herself spoonlike against him. "Please, let us just have this, Tristan," she whispered. "For a few more minutes, may we not just pretend?"

But pretend what? Inexplicably, he burned to know what was in her mind. How odd when, mere moments ago, he'd wished to avoid it.

But Phaedra did not say, and he had not the heart to ask. Instead, he circled one arm about her, and set the palm of his hand on the slight swell of her belly. It reminded him yet again of his reaction this afternoon upon seeing her. Of the foolish assumption he'd leapt to—and it had been, disconcertingly, a little more than an assumption. God help him, for one fleeting instant, he had felt *hope*.

He let his eyes roll heavenward at the thought. He had always been inordinately careful in that regard. And yet he had not been careful with her. Five times he'd made love to her, and only once had he taken even the slightest of precautions. If he wanted to bring down Lord Nash's wrath, and ruin Phaedra's life, he could scarce have chosen a better method.

Except that Phaedra believed herself barren. She had come to him an innocent, but not a virgin, so he had known there was a tragedy in it somewhere. But perhaps the tragedy was worse than he'd first imagined. He rolled up onto his elbow a little, and kissed the turn of her shoulder, his hand still stroking, wondering at what her life had been like, and feeling something pluck painfully at his heart.

Phaedra felt Tristan's hand circling her belly, and with it, the pendulous weight of unspoken words. She cut an uncertain glance up at him. "What is it?"

She was soon to wish she had not asked. He held her gaze watchfully for a long moment. "Phae, who was he?" he finally whispered. "Can you tell me?"

She knew, of course, what he asked. But just for an instant, she closed her eyes and let herself pretend she did not. But before she could speak, he did. "No." His voice was sharp. He fell back onto the mattress, striping away his warmth and comfort. "Christ, I'm sorry. Forget that. I have no right—and, today, of all days . . . I'm sorry, Phae."

She rolled over to look at him, her gaze drifting over his haunting brown eyes and that full, sensuous mouth. "I understand," she murmured. "You are curious about my first lover." But even as she spoke it, she hated the word. Even now it chilled her.

Tristan set the back of his hand to her cheek. "None of this matters to me, Phae," he said quietly. "I don't need to hear it."

She shot him a chiding glance. "Two lies, Tristan, one on the heels of the other," she murmured. "I know what you said earlier—in the sitting room—what you accused me of. But I trust you. I do. I might be a fool again . . . but I do not think so."

"What do you mean?"

But Phaedra had made up her mind. If Tristan wished to ruin her, he already possessed enough ammunition. "His name was Edward," she began, lying down on her shoulder to face him. "And I shan't tell you his last name, for it ceased to matter long ago."

He threaded a hand gently through the hair at her temple.

She plunged on. "I'm telling you not because you asked," she said, setting a finger to his lips. "But because I wish to. You said, Tristan, that I did not trust myself. Sexually, I mean. And I think that might be true."

"All right. Go on." He squeezed her hand.

Phaedra nodded, closed her eyes, and let herself remember. That year was fixed in her mind, as deep and as permanent as the etchings on a gravestone. "Edward came down to Brierwood for the summer," she began, as if she'd rehearsed it a thousand times. "He was an acquaintance of Tony's from Oxford. It was the year my father died."

"So you knew him?"

"No, but I found him fascinating," she admitted. "Of

course, I was, by all accounts, a strange girl. Bored, and too bookish, I daresay, for my own good. Edward and Tony talked so passionately of the things that interested me—of history and philosophy, and of politics—not fashion or furbelows like Mamma and Phee."

He smiled gently. "And so you fell in love?"

Had she? Phaedra was no longer sure. "I was infatuated with him, in the way foolish girls often are with beautiful blond men," she said. "I had read too much poetry, I daresay. And he . . . he flattered me with his attentions. Mamma and Tony thought it charming."

"Your mother hoped, perhaps, for a match between you?"

Again, she could not hold his gaze. "Mamma imagined he thought of me as a younger sister," she murmured. "Her attention was absorbed by Phoebe. Phoebe would not apply herself to her studies, and the governess despaired of her."

"And so you were the good girl?" said Tristan quietly. "The one who could be counted upon to do the right thing?"

"Yes."

"And then he broke off the courtship?" said Tristan, as if trying to make it easier for her. "I am so sorry, Phae. He was a fool, though it is a story old as time itself, I suppose."

"No, he did not break it, precisely." She closed her eyes. "Tony went back to London to stand for Commons, so Edward left. And I was too stupid to know what had happened. That I had conceived a child."

His hand reached out to touch her face uncertainly.

"Phae, Tony was two years ahead of me at school." She could hear realization dawning in his voice. "And he was standing for Commons? How . . . how old are you?"

She knew where this was going. Subtraction was no great task. "I shall be two-and-twenty next month," she answered.

A dark emotion sketched across his face. "Phae," he whispered. "Phae, how old were you then?"

She turned her head and gazed at the dressing table which sat by the window. "Fifteen," she whispered. "I had just turned fifteen."

Tristan sat up and turned toward her. "And he was a grown man," he said, brushing his knuckles down her cheek. "Oh, my poor girl."

A sour smile curved her mouth. "Edward was not a man," she said. "He was a reptile in a well-cut suit. But I was too sheltered to know it. I was so naïve, Tristan, I did not even grasp *what I had done* with him. What I had *given up.*"

"Phae." He smoothed both hands down her face, a cool, gentle caress, and she began to tremble. "Phae, love, did he force you?"

"No." She shook her head. "*I let him.* Because I loved him so much—or believed I did. Papa was gone, Stefan lived in London, and I . . . I just liked that someone paid attention to me."

"Christ," Tristan whispered.

But Phae pushed on. "That summer we read together in the gardens, and Mamma let him teach me to waltz, and I believed—oh, Tristan, I believed myself in heaven. He would even play battledore with me. Can you imagine? He . . . he began to kiss me when no one was looking. Then one night, he slipped into my room. He said that if I loved him, I must prove it. So I let him do what he wanted. More than once. And . . . I wanted it, too. Even then, I think I wanted it—or I wanted *him*, at least. That is not force, is it?"

"No," he gritted. "That is a lamb being left unprotected from a rapacious wolf. How old was that bastard?"

"Twenty-three," she confessed.

She could see the horror of it sickened him. He dragged a hand through his hair. "Your mother must have been heartsick."

Phaedra's hand lashed out, seizing his arm. "Mamma does not know," she whispered. "And no one, Tristan, must ever tell her. *Not ever.*"

Tristan looked at her incredulously. "What do you mean, *she does not know?*"

Phaedra searched for the right words to explain the emotional tangle that was her mother. "Mamma is a good person," she began. "But she is little more than a child herself, Tristan. She is just not terribly bright. I don't mean that to sound unkind, but her priorities are—well, though Stefan loves her, he calls her a pretty featherbrain."

"I am sorry," said Tristan stiffly. "But still, Phae, how could she *not* know?"

"Because I did not tell her," said Phaedra insistently. "I didn't even know the words to use. I was that ig-norant, Tristan. Finally, my governess noticed my figure rounding."

Tristan was still reeling with the ugliness of it. "Phae, I am so sorry." He had hoped, he supposed, the tale would take a less tragic turn, but he had known in his heart it would not. "What did she do?"

"Stefan was my guardian, and her employer," said Phaedra quietly. "She was terrified, of course. But she wrote to him with her fears. And Stefan knew there was no point in telling Mamma. She would have shattered quite utterly."

"You were but an innocent," Tristan whispered again, his gaze turned inward. "Far too young to be wed."

She flashed a withering smile. "By then I was five months gone," she said. "Those hideous empire waists . . . And there was no question of marriage. Edward had made off with a coal heiress from Northumberland—a girl richer, even, than I. Mamma read it to us from the *Times* over breakfast one morning, not knowing . . ."

The pain was still stark in her eyes. And given Lord Nash's reputation, Tristan could easily guess what happened next. "Did Nash kill him?"

Phaedra wrapped her arms around her chest. "Not quite," she whispered. "I begged him not to—not for Stefan's sake, but for Edward's. Because I still thought I loved him. Pathetic, isn't it?"

"Oh, Phae." Tristan lifted a hand and tucked a tendril of hair behind her ear. "My poor girl."

Phaedra managed a faint smile. "Stefan came straight down to Brierwood first, of course," she went on. "And announced I was to go abroad with my Aunt Henslow. She has always been more a mother to Mamma than a sister. So Aunt Henslow took me to France—a little holiday, Stefan told Mamma."

"What did they tell you?"

"That Aunt Henslow would . . . take care of things," she said. "Stefan left it to her—he was quite beyond himself with grief and rage, and wanted only to get his hands round Edward's throat. He said later—and I believe him—that he did not quite grasp what Aunt Henslow meant to do."

"What . . . did she do?"

Phaedra shrugged. "I thought, foolishly, that I would have the child," she said, "and that it would be . . . I don't know . . . taken somewhere safe? But when the doctor came to our flat in Paris, he said I was not quite six months along . . . and then he did something to me."

"Christ Jesus," he said again.

"And it did not go well." This time, her voice cracked pathetically, and her face with it. "I had a little girl, Tristan," she said through welling tears. "The loveliest, most beautiful little girl. They thought, you know, I was too addled to comprehend, that I would not remember seeing her."

"Phae, shush, shush," he cooed, dragging her into his arms.

"But I did see her, Tristan," she cried against his chest. "She was scarcely a babe at all, and she did not breathe, and so they took her away, and I do not know what became of her. *I do not know what became of her*, do you understand? She had fingers and ink-black hair, but she did not make a sound, and I kept thinking—*cry, cry, and they will have to give you to me!* But she just lay there in the doctor's hand, still as death. And then they just took her away."

"Oh, Phae." He rocked her, his lips pressed to her

hair, and tried not to cry with her. "Oh, my poor, poor girl."

"They still won't tell me where she is." Her voice was barely audible through the sobs now. "I know, of course, that she is dead. They caused her to come too soon. I know that now. But I didn't understand it then. I thought that every child should have its mother, or at least know that it was loved and wanted. I had believed someday we would be together. Instead, I fear, they buried her in some pauper's grave."

If that, thought Tristan grimly. Likely the child had been thrown out with the evening's rubbish. "I am sure, Phae, that they gave her a lovely service," he lied. "I am sure she is very much at peace."

"Do you think so?" But there was no hope in her voice. "I don't remember very much after that. I became deathly ill, and Aunt Henslow was terrified. When the fever finally broke, the doctor told us I was . . . damaged somehow. Scars, he said, from the infection. Aunt Henslow cried, and asked if I could still have children, and he said it was highly unlikely. That I should go home, and make a quiet life for myself. And so that's what I did. Until Millie ran away, and left Priss behind."

Tristan drew a hand down her hair, his chest tight with grief. This was what Nash had referred to; the thing which had left the anguish—and perhaps even that hint of rage—in his eyes. *Fragile as spun glass*, he had said. Dear God. Tristan was beginning to grasp the horrifying depth of this obsession Phae had with Priss, and with finding the child's missing mother.

"Phae, I hope we find Millie," he said softly. "But reuniting one mother and child . . . well, it won't reunite *you* with your daughter. I'm sorry. Tell me you understand that."

"I understand," she said, her voice rising. "I am not such a fool, Tristan, as all that. I understand my own motivations. My own *heart*."

"Why then?" he pleaded.

"Because Priss is my flesh and blood." Phaedra's voice was tremulous with emotion. "And because Millie does not understand the terrible price she will pay for what she has done. *I do.* She is too naïve, Tristan, to know how this will haunt her. She needs to be there for her child. To keep Priss safe. *She has that choice*, Tristan. The choice which was taken from me."

But she might not have a choice in this, either, Tristan considered. Millie quite likely knew exactly what she had done, and probably didn't care. On the other hand, there was a chance—a slight chance—that the girl was the naïve village innocent Phaedra so clearly believed her. In which case . . . dear God.

"What happened, Phae, to the man who abused you?" he asked. "What did Nash do?"

She flicked an uncertain glance up at him. "Thrashed him half to death with a horsewhip," she said. "But I'm not supposed to know."

"A horsewhipping was but half what he deserved," Tristan gritted.

Phaedra snuffled, and dashed her wrist across her eyes. "And then Stefan went down to Oxford, and thrashed Tony," she added. "He said Tony had brought a vile scourge into his home, and that Tony was as responsible as Edward for what happened to me."

"Well," said Tristan slowly, "I don't see a flaw in that logic."

But her eyes held a quiet grief now, the tears and the anger gone. "For better than a year, Tony kept his distance," she whispered. "Mamma knew, of course, that they had quarreled over something. She began to cry over it, heartsick, and finally Stefan relented. Not too long after that, Tony married Jenny. But that didn't work out so well, either."

Tristan was beginning to wonder if Tony hadn't got what he'd deserved. He remembered Mrs. Hayden-Worth vaguely, for she'd run with a fast, dangerous crowd. "So Edward lives in Northumberland with his rich bride and nothing worse than a few scars on his arse, savoring his wife's money," he said grimly. "God's truth, there is no justice in this world."

"A little, actually," she said. "When I was eighteen, Edward got caught in the schoolroom with his wife's niece. That rich father-in-law of his shot him through the heart—but it was hushed up."

Tristan felt his fists relax. "So how do you know?"

"Stefan told me." She gave a withering smile. "He thought it might make me feel better, I daresay. I don't know how he learnt of it, nor do I wish to."

Tristan rolled toward her and tucked one arm under his head, uncertain what next to say. His first instinct—to promise he'd kill the bastard who'd done this to her—was futile now. His second—to hold her in his arms and pledge her a lifetime of security and happiness—was just about as irrational.

He settled for simply holding her, tucking her spine to his chest, and wrapping his body protectively about hers. Quietly, he kissed her, just below the ear on that soft, perfect pulse-point that so often caught his gaze. "What will you do, love, when all this is over?" he asked, half afraid of her answer. "When your Millie is restored to you, and you can give up your Mrs. Thompson and your trousers and all your reluctant forays into society?"

Phaedra turned her head, and cast her gaze up to the ceiling. "Go home, I hope," she said. "Back to Brier-wood."

He gazed at her pensively for a time, then lifted his hand and stroked a finger over her face, memorizing the lines of it. "Lady Phaedra Northampton," he murmured, drawing his finger down to the tip of her nose. "I'm going to miss you when you're gone."

She laughed, a forced, light sound. "Oh, not for long, I daresay."

He picked up one of her long, chestnut curls and wrapped it round his index finger again. "What is it, Phae, that you miss so much? Why couldn't you linger in Town awhile? I should love nothing better, I think, than to go to one of those elegant society balls and waltz you round beneath your brother's nose."

She wriggled partway onto her side and looked at him. "I miss Priscilla," she said in a voice of quiet confession. "Oh, Tristan, she is the sweetest child ever. Fat, still, like a little cherub, you know? With pink apple cheeks and a little bow mouth and a laugh—sometimes an ear-splitting shriek, actually—that just warms your heart. Every day, Agnes and I walk to the village to play with her."

"I suppose I can understand that." His smile softened, and he drew her onto his shoulder. "Well, just rest in my arms for a little while, Phae, and dream of Priss. You will be back in Hampshire soon enough."

"Just for a little while?" she echoed, a hint of petulance in her tone.

He laughed. "A very little while," he corrected. "For I've got a hard night ahead. And you need to go home soon. Please."

Of course she ignored him, twisting around in his arms like a restless child. "Why, I have no plans for the evening," she murmured, her eyes searching his face. "What are yours?"

Tristan was instantly wary. "I'm going to Vostrikova's," he admitted. "I've managed to get myself invited to have a look round the place."

"No!" She sat halfway up in bed. "You've gained entry to that house?"

"And I haven't forgotten Millie," he hastily added. "I swear it."

But Phaedra's brow had knotted. "Tristan, what is going on? And don't take me for a fool. Stefan would tell me little about the puzzle ball. But I know this is no longer about a dead Russian in an alleyway—and I suspect it never was."

He toyed with the fraying hem of the coverlet, wondering how much to tell her. He wanted suddenly to unburden himself to her as she had done to him. To offer her at least a little trust, and, if he were honest, to deepen the circle of intimacy which surrounded them.

"No, it never was," he admitted. "Vostrikova is a Russian spy. Has been for years, we think."

Phaedra's eyes widened. "So that's why your father was involved," she whispered. "My word. A spy running a brothel catering to the Government's most powerful—that opens up a whole cesspit of intrigue, doesn't it?"

Tristan smiled at the analogy. "Vostrikova is an expert at exploiting men's weaknesses," he answered. "So I have acquired a few to tempt her."

"What is your plan, precisely?"

"To get in and get out quickly," he admitted. "Or as quickly as I can. Vostrikova has a suite of rooms in an adjoining house. That's where business gets done. The whole place is a rabbit warren, by the way. Not one house, but three, connected up and down, attics to cellars."

"So your aim is to get into her private office," said Phaedra musingly.

"Eventually, yes," he said. "Tonight, I hope."

"To search for what?"

"Correspondence," he said. "Encryption codes. A list of those men whose loyalty to the Crown has been compromised. And I mightn't have time to be subtle. As soon as I'm out, she'll probably know she's been had."

"You'll doubtless need to pick a lock or two," she murmured. "Can you?"

Inwardly, he sighed. Phaedra was quick—too quick for his comfort. "Your Mr. Kemble taught me," he answered. "A clever chap, that one."

Phaedra did not seem surprised by this revelation. Still, something was weighing on her. "Tristan, you do not owe me an answer to this," she finally began. "But I should just like to know . . ."

He cocked his head and studied her. "Yes?"

Her lashes swept down, a tentative, shy gesture. "What if you have to . . . to *do* something whilst you're there?"

He knew at once what she meant. And Phaedra was blushing three shades of pink. This, he had not wished to consider. Oh, when he'd begun this task, he'd assumed that participating in Vostrikova's debauchery would be unavoidable. But that was a sacrifice—a strange choice of words, admittedly—he was no longer willing to make.

"No," he said finally. "I've never availed myself of prostitutes, Phae, and I don't mean to start now."

Her shoulders relaxed, and she looked away. "In any case, you cannot do this alone," she said quietly. "It will be dangerous."

"I won't be alone," he said hastily. "De Vendenheim will have men stationed round back."

She nodded, remarkably cool and composed. "All right," she finally said. "So, who killed Gorsky? And why?"

He cast her an appraising glance. "Vostrikova had him killed," he admitted. "Then she had her assassin garroted. But de Vendenheim and I picked up the second killer three days ago, boarding a ship to Estonia, and he'll talk soon enough. No one else knows save Peel and . . . well, my father did."

"I'm impressed," she murmured. "But that does not explain *why* she did it."

"There is no honor among thieves, Phae," said Tristan, measuring his words. "Gorsky was her henchman, but when they fell out over the boy she'd sent away . . ."

"Revenge is always dangerous." She made a little shooing motion with her fingers. "And—?"

He lifted one shoulder. "Not long before their quarrel, you had dropped by, bandying about your brother's name, and threatening to bring the full force of the British government down on Gorsky's head, so perhaps he got creative," Tristan admitted. "After their quarrel, he likely saw a way to exact vengeance. Perhaps he'd been following you, wondering if it was safe to approach you."

"He wanted to speak to me," she whispered. "But he hadn't terribly good English."

"And that might be a part of it," Tristan admitted. "The man had no friends, for Vostrikova kept him on a short leash. Perhaps he meant to turn on her, and knew your brother spoke Russian? Or perhaps he merely wished to sell you information? We shall never know. He died before he could speak to you—and we hope Vostrikova knows none of this. Indeed, it is doubtful she does."

Phaedra had gone bloodless. "We?" She pressed a hand to her heart. "Tristan . . . who is *we?*"

This, too, he had hoped to avoid. "De Vendenheim," he confessed. "And me."

"You told him?" Her clutched fist went to her heart. "You told him I'd gone to that house?"

"Phae, what choice did I have?" He opened his hand, palm up. "The more we learned, the more likely it looked. At some point, I had to err on the side of your safely. I told him that you'd been there."

Her gaze was distant, her voice a whisper. "And he has not told my brother." Her knuckles were white now. "Not *yet*."

"No, and he won't." Tristan caught her hand. "He swore to me, Phae. But I could not leave you exposed. And I could not watch over you myself." *Not all the time*, he silently added.

But he had been watching her, far more often than he wished to admit. And if he had to observe her dash down her front steps in another seductive, low-cut ball gown with Zoë Armstrong laughing on her arm, he was beginning to think he might to have to cut off his own cock, or suffer the inconvenience of a perpetual third leg. The thought of her dancing in another's arms, perhaps meeting someone she might fall in love with . . . he had felt like the greenest lad, but he had burned nonetheless with jealousy.

But Phaedra was still pondering his words. "Exposed?" she asked. "What do you mean, *exposed*?"

"De Vendenheim set someone to keep an eye on you whilst we investigated," he admitted.

"*Spies*—? Surely you jest?"

"No, *guards*." Tristan looked at her chidingly. "Your Mr. Kemble, mostly, or one of his henchmen. Uglow once, though he's a hard one to hide. One of them is likely hanging about in Long Acre this minute, if they realized who you were when you left Mayfair."

"In Tony's kit?" She laughed. "Impossible."

Having seen her in disguise, Tristan agreed, but kept silent. There was no point in encouraging bad behavior. Still, she did look awfully fine in trousers . . .

"Besides, I went out through the garden," Phaedra continued, dragging the hair back off her face. "And I've never seen anyone observing me."

"Then they are doing their jobs," said Tristan firmly.

Her worried gaze searched his face. She grasped the seriousness of it, at least. "And you? What have you been doing?"

"I've spent the last weeks cultivating certain—shall we call them friendships?" he answered. "I have been drinking a little too much, and bragging a bit too loudly about my new Government post and my father's connections. And I have quietly compiled a list of Vostrikova's customers."

Phaedra's eyes widened. "To get you inside."

"That's the plan," he said grimly. "But it's been a near run thing. One does not precisely invite oneself; that would look too suspicious. Now, my dear, I've told you all I'm at liberty to say, and a good deal more. Dress, and I shall ring for Uglow to follow you home."

But Phaedra's brow was still furrowed, and her mind, he could see, was far away. "This is all very interesting," she murmured. "But how does any of it help us find Millie?"

Tristan looked down at her, his arms crossed over his chest. "*Us*, is it now?"

The afternoon sun swirled through the room in a kaleidoscope of fractured light, burnishing her hair and shooting it with gold. Fleetingly, he considered kissing her again to dissuade her from whatever she was about to say. It was useless, of course. She lifted her intelligent gaze to his. "If you found Millie, you could help her escape," she said, her voice perfectly calm. "But you do not know what she looks like."

"Describe her." He forced a tight smile. "Don't leave out a single detail."

She scowled. "I suppose she looks like half the prostitutes in London," she answered. "Young, pretty, and nubile—except that she has red hair. But even that won't narrow it down much."

Phaedra obviously hadn't met many of London's fair nightingales, not to mention the uprighters working the East End. "How tall is she?" Tristan persisted. "What color are her eyes?"

Phaedra looked at him askance. "They're prostitutes, Tristan," she said. "They won't be taking tea in the drawing room, and you can scarcely take time to go knocking on doors. You already said you may have to get in and get out quickly."

Tristan didn't deny it. And it wasn't that he didn't wish to help Phaedra, he did. He'd simply never believed Millie much of a victim. She hadn't been snatched from her own village, as so many of the younger girls were. Millie had gone looking for trouble. On the other hand, Vostrikova had been known to hold women captive, and even to sell them into what amounted to sexual slavery. The knowledge troubled him.

Phaedra leaned across the bed. "Tristan, this may end up like a kettle with its lid blown off," she said. "If this goes badly—if Vostrikova knows she's been compromised—we shan't get another chance. She'll be on the next boat bound for the Continent, and those girls will be scattered to the four winds or worse. And I will *never* forgive myself."

But *I will never forgive you* was what she meant. And she had a point. Tristan scrubbed a hand across the stubble of his beard and considered it. Good God, one prostitute in a house with perhaps two dozen, and a suite of rooms which would need a thorough pilfering . . .

Phaedra sensed his vacillation. "Please, Tristan." Her voice was low and tremulous now. "Perhaps Millie seems like a small concern to the Government, but to me *she is everything*. Priss needs a mother. Now, are you going to help me? Or must I go back to doing it on my own?"

He answered with icy certainty. "Out of the question."

"Tristan." She eyed him very deliberately. "Do not patronize me. You are not my master."

"There's always the silk rope." He eyed her grimly. "That seems to tame you down just a tad."

"You sliced it to bits with your knife," she retorted, setting her head at a stubborn angle. "More fool you. Now, about Millie?"

Slowly, he exhaled. "All right," he finally said. "I will find out what's happened to her. I swear it, Phae—and I don't promise what I cannot deliver."

"You need to *find* her," she gently pressed. "Or find out where she was taken. And to do it, you're going to need someone to go in with you. Someone who can poke about and ask questions whilst you slip downstairs."

He had known, of course, it would come to this. "I was invited alone," he said. "I'm not sure Vostrikova will welcome anyone else."

"Oh, I think she might." Phaedra was clearly thinking out loud now. "By now she will have heard your father is terribly ill."

"Aye, the doctor ordered his staff out on Wednesday,"

said Tristan grimly. "And today the house is shut up. To-morrow we'll have to announce it."

"But there's been a Lord Hauxton somewhere in the Foreign Office for the last century," Phaedra reminded him with a smile. "And then there is your infallible charm. That package will prove irresistible to Madame Vostrikova. She is a woman who lays long-term plans, I'll wager."

Tristan, of course, already knew all this. He was surprised, however, at how quickly Phaedra grasped it. "Very well, I shall take someone," he finally agreed. "One of de Vendenheim's chaps will have to do."

Phaedra smiled dotingly. "Thank you, Tristan," she said. "But none of them knows what Millie looks like. And I rather doubt, frankly, that they can pass for the sort of gentlemen Vostrikova entertains."

This time Tristan dragged both hands through his hair. He already knew where this was going. Fleetingly, he considered locking her in the house, and setting Uglow to watch her. But that made him little better, perhaps, than Vostrikova. And Phaedra was not a fool.

"Draw a sketch," he said hastily. "I'll fetch you paper and pencil now."

"I think that's risky." Gently, she took his hand in hers, lifted it to her lips, then, with a neat little jerk, snatched the gold signet ring from his pinkie finger.

"*Phae*—!"

With a sweet smile, she slid it onto the third finger of her right hand, then held it up in the shaft of afternoon light. "I always wanted to be a Talbot," she declared. "I think I shall be Harold, your first cousin."

He lifted both brows and shot her a dark look. "I quite loathe my family," he said. "And they loathe me."

"But you are about to inherit, my lord." She turned the ring this way and that, admiring the way it caught the sun. "All is generally forgiven in such cases."

He sighed. "Do I even have a cousin Harold?"

She tossed him a disdainful glance. "You dare to doubt Lady Phaedra's exhaustive knowledge of Debrett's?" she asked haughtily. "Harold is Uncle Tobias's eldest."

"Aye?" His glower deepened. "Go on."

"They live in Wiltshire, near your seat, and not far from Hampshire." She lowered the ring and smiled. "Unfortunately, they don't come up to Town very often. Still, young Harold is of an age where a lad might like to taste a little of the city's sin. And a doting elder cousin might oblige him."

His mouth twisted sourly. "No doubt."

"And if you should ever perish, God forbid, of one of those dread diseases the girls at Vostrikova's pass round," she said brightly, "young Harold—most conveniently— will become heir apparent. So I am sure Vostrikova would love to make his acquaintance, too."

Tristan sighed. The frightening thing was, Phaedra was quite probably capable of pulling it off. And he would much rather go in with her than without her. She was perfectly capable of thinking on her feet, and might well prove an asset. But if something went wrong, he'd kill himself. Assuming Phaedra's brother didn't get to him first.

"Phae, love, it's just not safe. And—God's truth, the debauchery—no lady should be subjected to such filth."

She lifted one shoulder in a casual, effortless motion. "Better I should go with you than on my own, as I did last time," she answered. "Besides, as you have already observed, I am hardly a demure innocent. I rather doubt that place will shock me."

"Love, this will go far beyond any bed games you and I might play," he cautioned. "But more importantly, what if I cannot protect you?"

"Tristan, you *can*," she pressed. "But you shan't need to. You'll be downstairs doing the dangerous work, and providing a distraction. I'll slip out the back to Kemble's men. Now, just listen. I have a plan, and it's a good one."

"I was afraid of that," he answered. "Does it include our hiring the services of a redhead for the night?"

Phaedra's eyes widened. "Oh, at the very least," she answered innocently. "Frankly, I'd suggest we hire two or three. This is a big night for Cousin Harold. I'm not sure he'll wish to share."

Chapter 12

I will wear my heart upon my sleeve
For daws to peck at.

Owing to the cloudless day and a stiff breeze, the stars made a rare appearance that evening, coming out to wink over London like a spattering of tiny jewels. But it took Phaedra another several hours of threats and outright begging to bend Tristan to her will, and another thirty minutes for her to twist her hair up snugly enough to permit the wig to be pulled back on.

When that was done to his satisfaction, Tristan made her practice her walk, her voice, her hand gestures, then he sat her back down and begged her again to give it all up.

But the truth was, she looked like a young English blueblood just down from Cambridge, all coltish legs and sullen disdain, projecting that quintessential air of aristocratic entitlement—a parody, perhaps, of her youngest brother at that age. And after all, it was his suit.

When she refused to capitulate to Tristan's final entreaties, as he'd known from the first she would, he sighed and rolled out the rough floor plan of Vostrikova's houses, sketched from what little information he'd managed to elicit from tradesmen and patrons. And through it all, he wished Millie the tavern maid to the devil.

This undertaking was not safe; he knew that. But he knew, too, the awful pain in her eyes, and the desperate need to make things right when something in your life had gone horribly wrong. That burning wish to expiate one's sins, real or imagined. It was a part of what had driven him from Greece as a young man. The carnage and the hopelessness, and the knowledge that he had not the power to repair it—nor even hinder it—no matter what he did. So Tristan had drowned his guilt in apathy. Numbed himself with licentious living. Phaedra, however, had chosen a different path.

Yes, in her heart, Phaedra believed that helping this child *would* change things; would somehow bring her life aright again. And if she felt, in even the smallest of ways, that this might atone in her heart for the child they had taken from her, who was he to say it would not? Yes, it was irrational. But the heart, he was beginning to understand, so often was.

Out of an abundance of caution, Tristan sent Phaedra out the front with instructions to go round the block and into the alley which skirted the rear of his house. They would make their way to Vostrikova's on foot, through the back lanes.

After counting off three minutes, impatient and on edge, he went down the back stairs and out into what passed for a garden. He saw her there, a lean, willowy form waiting by the gatepost, the feeble lamplight of the stable opposite casting a faint glow about her feet.

He picked his way through the dark, past the dustbins and outbuildings, silent and unseen. For a moment, he watched her, the passions and whispered secrets of the afternoon they had passed in each other's arms still sweet and heavy in his heart. And it occurred to him that this might be their last moment alone; if by some miracle Phaedra found her tavern maid tonight, she might hasten back to Hampshire.

He wanted, suddenly and desperately, to kiss her one last time. But when he reached out through the gloom to touch her, everything altered in an instant. Something lashed about his throat. A cord. *A garrote.* A vise-like arm whipped out of the dark. On a strangled cry, Tristan found himself hauled hard against something immobile, spun about, then hurled face-first into the weeds, a knee rammed hard against his spine.

"Tristan!" Phaedra's voice was harsh. "Stop! Unhand him!" He heard the sound of her kicking someone as he clawed at the choking garrote.

"Ouch! What?" His assailant's voice rasped in the gloom. "It's *Avoncliffe?*"

"Yes! Let him up!" Phaedra demanded.

"What the devil?" His assailant's knee relented and the garrote relaxed. Blood surging, Tristan forced his attacker off, rolled, and came up swinging. His fist whistled through the air, just an inch from Kemble's nose.

Phaedra thrust out a hand. "Wait! Stop!"

Tristan glared into the gloom, and spat out a curse. "Good God, man! Are you trying to kill me?"

Kemble bent, and in one smooth motion, picked up

Tristan's walking stick, tossing it to him. "If I were trying to kill you, my lord," he said quietly, "you would be dead now."

Tristan snatched the stick from midair, something in the man's voice sending a shiver down his spine. The mincing dandy was gone, and in his place was someone altogether more threatening. But Tristan was not easily intimidated. "Then what the hell *are* you doing?"

"Keeping her safe, you idiot." Kemble's gaze swept Phaedra as if she were a piece of his fine porcelain.

"Not from *me*, for God's sake!" Tristan bent down and snatched up his hat.

Kemble smiled and brushed a bit of grass from his sleeve. "Now, I wonder, Avoncliffe—would her brother share that view?" he mused. "Tell me, what have you naughty boys been up to all day?"

Heat flooded Tristan's face. He stabbed a finger toward Long Acre. "Have you been out there all afternoon?"

"*And* all night," said Kemble, tossing them a knowing glance. "Until about three minutes ago."

"You followed me." Phaedra sounded breathless.

"I did." Kemble was shooting his cuffs back into place. "And if Avoncliffe here had been the rear-attacking, stick-wielding assailant he looked to be, both of you would be kissing my boots for it right about now."

Tristan felt the fight go out of him then. "You are right, of course. I am sure my approach in the dark looked like something altogether different than it was."

"It looked rather as if you were about to press your attentions on an innocent, unmarried, gently-bred young lady," said Kemble. "Perhaps even lure her into your home—or your *bed*—for some sort of nefarious high jinks. Thank God I was *entirely* mistaken."

Tristan did not miss the acidity in his tone.

"Mr. Kemble, really!" Phaedra drew herself up very straight.

"I, however," Kemble continued, undeterred, "am willing to listen with an open mind." Here, he flashed a lupine smile at Phaedra. "My lady?"

"With all respect, Kemble," she said quietly, "it really isn't any of your business."

Tristan hitched Phaedra to his side. "You may congratulate me, Kemble," he said tightly. "This afternoon, Lady Phaedra made me the happiest man on earth—"

"Yes, that's what I was afraid of."

"—and generously consented to be my wife."

Lady Phaedra drew away in horror. "Good God. *Tristan.*"

Kemble sighed deeply. "Oh, spare me the theatrics, Avoncliffe." He extracted a silver snuff box, smooth as a cat in the dark, and languidly deposited a dainty pinch on the back of his hand. "I would not wish a wedding to you on my worst enemy. Just tell me what's going on here."

Phaedra sagged with relief, and something sharp pierced Tristan's heart. "I'm on my way to Vostrikova's as we'd planned," he snapped.

Kemble took his snuff, then looked up. "*And*—?" he said leadingly.

"And I'm going, too," said Phaedra, her chin rising.

Kemble flicked a dark glance at her. "I trust, my dear, that you know what you are about?" he murmured. "It is a vile, dangerous place. You're quick-witted enough, God knows. Still, your reasoning today, on any number of issues, quite escapes me."

Swiftly, Phaedra drew Kemble deeper into the shadows, and explained.

"Ah," said Kemble when she was done. "And who is the father of this child, I wonder."

"*Not*," said Phaedra darkly, "*Stefan*. And that is all I shall tell you, Kem."

Kemble was silent for a moment. "Well, well," he said quietly. "Mr. Hayden-Worth's tastes are more varied than I'd have guessed."

Phaedra actually cursed beneath her breath. "I *never* said the babe was his."

In the gloom, Kemble tossed his hand, once again the consummate dandy. "My dear girl, I am the soul of discretion," he answered. "Far be it for me to question what a man does after dark—or who he does it with. Now, how did you plan this joint assault on Vostrikova's bastion of perfidy?"

"Much as you and I discussed with de Vendenheim," said Tristan. Swiftly he explained what Phaedra would do. When he was done, he hesitated. "Do you think, Kemble, that she will be safe?"

Again, Kemble's quick glance flicked over her. "So long as she doesn't mind Vostrikova's muck on her shoes, yes," he answered, bending over to tug something from his boot. "Lady Phaedra is no one's fool."

Tristan exhaled with relief.

Until Kemble pressed the pistol into her hand.

In Soho, they were admitted through the rear, then escorted to the front of the house where Madame Vostrikova kept her private rooms. They were shown upstairs to a sitting room to find their hostess awaiting them on the landing. After a perfunctory introduction, her dark eyes looked Phaedra over, only the slightest flicker betraying her annoyance.

"Welcome," she said, "to my humble establishment." Then Madame Vostrikova linked her arm with Tristan's and strolled with them up the remaining stairs, fluttering her lashes like a thin, aging coquette.

The woman, Phaedra thought, was perfectly chilling. Ice-blond hair contrasted dramatically with the shimmering black silk of her gown, and she put one in mind of a straight razor, glistening with danger, ready to lay open one's throat at the slightest provocation.

She was, however, a flawless hostess with manners that would have done a countess proud. "Let me offer you a glass of my very best wine," she said, going at once to the sideboard. "It comes from my private vineyard in Bordeaux, and is reserved for only my most special guests."

"What an intriguing establishment you have created here, Madame." Phaedra watched as Tristan held his wineglass aloft with a studied languor, the pink liquid swirling above his long, thin fingers. As he had done since their arrival, he surveyed their hostess like a tomcat eyeing a bowl of cream, and wondering whether to trouble himself to lick it up.

Madame Vostrikova set down her crystal decanter, and turned from the sideboard. "I am delighted, my lord, at your interest."

"Interest is, perhaps, too mild a word," said Tristan. "Cousin Harold and I could not be better pleased. This wine, by the way, is excellent."

"*Spasiba*, my lord." Madame had settled into a chair opposite, studying them both from beneath hooded eyes. "You will find I offer my patrons only the very best of pleasures—both sensual and otherwise."

"They do say you are a woman of extraordinary discernment, Madame." Tristan's square, flawless teeth were white against his skin as he smiled over his glass. "What, precisely, do you call this?"

Madame Vostrikova preened just a trifle. "It is a claret, my lord," she answered. "But of a traditional sort—thus its pale color—scented with anise and cardamom. A far cry from that bland rubbish the French try to sell us nowadays."

Phaedra took another sip, her eyes running over the dark, elegant sitting room. The walls were hung with a deep blue silk, the furniture faintly Asiatic in style, and on the whole, it looked to have cost a small fortune. So far, nothing about Vostrikova's establishment resembled anything remotely like a brothel, or what Phaedra had imagined a brothel might look like.

"What do you think of my special claret, Mr. Talbot?" Madame Vostrikova asked.

Phaedra feigned a look of aristocratic boredom. "I like it well enough, thank you," she said, dropping her voice an octave, "but I should prefer something darker and more full-bodied—a redhead with large breasts, perhaps? That is, after all, what we came for."

Suddenly, Vostrikova's eyes sparkled with malice. "Indeed?"

Tristan severed the mood with a hearty laugh. "Ah, the impatience of youth, Madame," he said with a dismissive wave of his glass. "I fear Harold has not yet learnt to temper his appetites."

"Has he not?" said Vostrikova, eyeing Phaedra watchfully. "A wiser man might know how to savor that which is offered him."

"Precisely so." Tristan grinned. "Perhaps you have a young mistress who specializes in such disciplines? Someone who might teach the poor lad . . . well, shall we call it *patience*?"

The madam returned her languid gaze to Tristan's. "*Da*, my lord," the woman purred. "Anticipation is half the pleasure. But frankly, I did not expect Mr. Talbot. His visit is . . . most extraordinary."

"Ah, I understand completely, Madame!" Tristan set his wineglass on the elegant marquetry table by his chair, his every move speaking of blithe indolence. "Perhaps we should take up no more of your time."

For the first time, Madame's expression faltered a trifle. "Already, you must go?"

Tristan opened one hand. "It might be best," he said smoothly. "I have promised Harold here a night of debauchery, and I should hate him to be disappointed. After all, I have my reputation as the family sybarite to maintain."

Madame Vostrikova rose gracefully with Tristan. "You

will come again, I hope, my lord?" The word *alone* remained unspoken.

Phaedra shot Tristan a scornful glance. "Devil take you, Cuz," she uttered, jerking to her feet. "I thought you said this was a prime place for a bit of sport!"

Tristan ignored her, smiling seductively at their hostess. "I should like to call again, of course, Madame," he said, leaning very near. "Regrettably, my new duties in the Foreign Office grow more pressing by the day."

Her sharp, angular brows flew aloft. "How sorry I am to hear it."

Tristan threw back his head and laughed. "As am I, Madame," he said. "I begin to quite long for my old life as an utter wastrel. Instead, at my father's insistence, I shall be going abroad for a few weeks."

"But this is dreadful news!"

Tristan shrugged. "Alas, I must go," he complained. "Otherwise, Hauxton has threatened to cut off my allowance. I fear my father finds me a bit too indolent and self-absorbed for his taste."

"Ah, well," said Madame. "You will travel to someplace exciting, I hope?"

Tristan hesitated. "To Warsaw," he finally answered. "There is unrest in Poland, and my father wishes me to go there in his stead, and press Great Britain's interests with their government. Indeed, he has written down every word I am to say—as if I haven't a thought in my own head."

"Has he?" said Madame, her eyes gleaming. "Then I hope they are very clever words?"

Again Tristan laughed. "Madame, you are too kind," he

said. "I would not dare bore so great a courtesan as your-self with my father's dull state secrets. Come, Harold, fetch your stick and your hat. We have taken up quite enough of Madame's time."

Madame Vostrikova paused, frowning, her hand on the door. Tristan, Phaedra realized, had played her like a pro-fessional sharper, whilst looking like the witless, pretty face Phaedra had once believed him.

Phaedra struck a petulant pose by the door, throwing her arms across her chest. "I thought you were to show me a bit of fun, Cuz," she said to Tristan.

"I'll take you to Mother Lucy's, perhaps," said Tristan in a tone of mild exasperation. "Kindly do not make a scene, my boy." He turned and set his hand on the door-knob.

"Wait," said Madame Vostrikova.

Tristan dropped his hand and looked at her.

"It is a little irregular, my lord," she said with a quiet smile. "But after all, Mr. Talbot is your cousin and heir. And he is so young. One hates to disappoint the very young."

Tristan laughed jovially. "One hates to disappoint the old and jaded, too, Madame, I hope?" He smiled hugely. "Have you relented after all? Will you take us on tonight? I would account it a very great favor."

"And we want redheads," said Phaedra in a low, dark voice. "That's what Tris promised me, and by God, that's what I want. A pair of them—three, perhaps, if my cousin is feeling energetic."

Tristan widened his eyes. "Ah, the gauntlet has been

thrown down!" he said. He turned back to Vostrikova. "Madame, I suppose blood will tell. Can you accommodate our whims?"

Madame looked faintly pleased. "Just redheads, my lord?" she murmured. "Can I not offer you something . . . more exotic?"

Yes, thought Phaedra, *something more worthy of blackmail, perhaps?*

Tristan tilted his head toward Phaedra. "Soon, Madame," he said quietly. "For tonight—for the lad—just the women, I think?"

Vostrikova smiled. "I comprehend," she said. "My assistant Mademoiselle LaFoy will show you upstairs. I shall go and procure a pair of girls—*da*, Mr. Talbot, red-haired, if I can."

At the last instant, however, Tristan caught her wrist. "Your pardon, Madame," he said quietly, "but my cousin has a bit of a vicious streak in him. And I—well, I have some tastes I should as soon keep private. Your girls are . . . prepared for such things?"

Madame Vostrikova's mouth curled into something which might have been a smile, or might have been pure bloodlust. "Trust me, my lord," she said quietly. "You will not be disappointed."

"Well, *Harold*," said Tristan when the door was shut, "you very nearly managed to get us thrown out on our collective arses before we'd even had a good toss."

"Bugger off, Tris," said Phaedra. They had agreed to stay in character in case Vostrikova kept an ear to the door. Phaedra threw herself into one of the chairs, mimicking

Tony in one of his snits. "I've escaped Papa and his prudish notions for one night at least, and I mean to make the
most of it."

"Do you indeed?" murmured Tristan. "Uncle Tobias
must be so proud."

"Yes, and pour us some of that brandy, won't you?" said
Phaedra. "I should like something harder than that pink
rot."

Tristan eyed her a little nastily, but he poured a dram
and brought it to her. "You'll mind your manners, my boy,"
he said, pressing the glass into her hand. "Madame
Vostrikova has invited us here for a free taste. The next
time you'll pay—and dearly—for your buxom redhead."

Phaedra snorted, and sipped at the brandy. "Vostrikova
still has a fine pair of dumplings herself," she remarked.
"Old enough to be our mother, but still . . ."

Tristan almost spat out a mouthful of wine. "Dumplings?" he uttered after swallowing. "God's truth, Harold!
The words a lad learns at Cambridge nowadays."

Phaedra shrugged. After one last glower in her direction, Tristan began to pace, his pretense of indolence fading. Now that she knew him, Phaedra could sense the
tightly-coiled energy in his step, the restlessness which he
barely suppressed.

They fell into silence for a time, Tristan's footfalls heavy
and rhythmic on Vostrikova's Oriental carpet. To dispel
her own anxiety, Phaedra picked up one of the black books
which lay upon a side table. The volume was bound in
opulent, ornately tooled leather, with nothing but roman
numerals embossed in gilt on the spine. Curious, Phaedra
opened it, almost choking when she did so.

Tristan came at once to her side. "Oh, for pity's sake," he hissed. "Give me that!"

Eyes wide, Phaedra clutched it. "No, I think not," she murmured, her voice a little unsteady. She flipped through a few of the pages, which were little more than lavish, hand-colored prints, exquisitely detailed, and set with French captions, each drawing more vulgar than the last.

"Good Lord," Tristan said as the next page fell.

"Indeed," she murmured. "Look, Tris. Isn't this one intriguing?"

Tristan's hands were clutched tightly behind his back now. "Yes," he said tightly. "I daresay."

"What do you think she's doing on her knees like that?" Phaedra asked.

"I couldn't say," he gritted.

Phaedra looked up and grinned shamelessly. "Hazard a guess."

He bent lower. "Put the book away," he said quietly.

"Well, I think she's got his—er, his *cock*—in her mouth." Phaedra managed to maintain her gentleman's voice—and vocabulary. "I must remember that technique. I daresay it might prove useful someday."

"I daresay it might, *Harold*." Tristan's fingers, she noticed, were digging into the arm of her chair now.

"Ever tried it?" she asked lightly. "Perhaps you ought to have a go at it sometime."

"Good Lord," he choked, jerking upright.

Phaedra turned another page to find a similar drawing. This time the kneeling lady was servicing her lover orally as he reclined on a pile of pillows, whilst a second gentleman knelt behind her.

"My word!" This time, Phaedra's voice slipped a trifle. "That is . . . that is most remarkable."

Tristan was pinching the bridge of his nose now, as if the pain might distract him. "I believe," he said tightly, "that this is Madame's private pornography collection, Harold."

"And obviously meant to be shared," said Phaedra calmly. "That's why it is here, laid out upon the table, wouldn't you say? Now this second chap—the one on his knees behind her—where do you think his cock is?"

"*Harold*—!"

Phaedra pointed to the lady's ample buttocks which were tilted high in the air. "I ask, you see, because it appears to me to be stuck in her—"

Tristan seized the book from her lap at the very instant the door swung open. Phaedra jerked to her feet, and let the book go.

"*Bonsoir*, gentlemen." Another woman in black swept into the room, this one much younger. "I am Mademoiselle LaFoy."

"*Bonsoir, mademoiselle.*" Tristan bowed, and laid the book aside.

Phaedra tried not to gape, and sketched an awkward bow.

The woman wore a garment that was part evening gown and part corset. The corset half, however, did not quite cover her nipples, but instead thrust them up in a way which looked mortifyingly painful. Her inky hair was swept high and tight, her lips stained bloodred, and long drops of what looked like onyx swung from her ears. Her gaze fixed upon Phaedra, the woman did not walk so much as slither, drawing the length of a slender black riding crop through the opposite hand as she came.

"*Alors*, Madame tells me we have an insolent young man with us this evening," she said, her voice deep and throaty as she drew up in front of them. "Tell me, my lord, does your cousin need to be taught a lesson?"

Tristan's eyes glinted with humor. "Indeed, I'd rather enjoy a thorough caning of his buttocks right about now, how—"

"Tristan!" Phaedra almost squeaked out the word.

"—*However*," Tristan continued, "another day, perhaps? I have promised the lad his first orgy—well, just a little family affair, really."

At that, Phaedra elbowed him sharply.

"Ah—with redheads, of course," Tristan belatedly added.

Disappointment sketched across her face. "*Très bien*, my lord." Mademoiselle LaFoy inclined her head, and drew the crop through her hand one last time. "A pity. Now if you will follow me, gentlemen, I will take you upstairs."

They followed the young woman back into the corridor through which they had passed earlier, but this time turning up a flight of stairs and progressing deeper into the house. Every few yards they passed through a series of doors which existed, she explained, to afford maximum privacy to Madame's clients.

With a sinking sense of disappointment, Phaedra realized just how difficult her task was to be. All the individual chambers along the way appeared to be locked. She saw no salons, and no public rooms of any sort, just wide, elegant corridors decorated with small bookcases containing

more black leather books, and consoles topped with vulgar
objets d'art. Fine paintings lined the walls depicting all
manner of unnatural sex acts between puckish sprites,
goat-footed satyrs, and even marauding Romans. Phaedra
goggled at each as they passed, often to find herself hitched
up by the arm, and dragged onward by Tristan.

"You cater to a variety of tastes, do you not, *mademoiselle?*" asked Tristan lightly as they started up a second
flight of stairs. "You supply both males and females?"

"*Oui*, my lord," said Mademoiselle LaFoy. "And of any
age you wish. Shall I bring you a young—"

"No, no." Tristan waved his hand in obviation. "*Merci,
mademoiselle*. Given my new career, you must understand,
I can ill afford any rumors."

The woman drew herself up as if insulted. "My lord, I
remind you we specialize in discretion," she answered.
"You may contract with Madame for any sort of services
you wish with complete anonymity."

Tristan hesitated as if torn. The woman tossed a nasty
glance at Phaedra. Clearly they thought Cousin Harold a
hindrance to what might otherwise have been an evening
of true vice.

"Not tonight, I think," he finally answered. "But I am
intrigued, most certainly."

At the end of the passageway, the woman stopped,
tucked the crop beneath her arm, and unlocked a door, a
slab of solid oak some three inches thick. She pushed it
open to reveal a sitting room furnished in the same dark
elegance as the rest of the house. To the right through
double doors was the largest bed Phaedra had ever seen,
and to the left a smaller, darker room.

Mademoiselle LaFoy went to an armoire by the windows and opened it to reveal a set of deep drawers. Implements of black leather and burnished metal hung from hooks inside the doors. Though Phaedra recognized almost nothing, the effect was chilling. The woman turned to face them, her breasts jutting almost into Phaedra's face. "My lord, we supply a variety of implements to heighten the pleasure of your visit," she explained. "Our girls—and our boys—are well trained to tolerate them."

"Excellent," said Tristan. "And the door, I see, is quite thick. The walls, too, look double-plastered. I expect the sound does not carry?"

She smiled faintly. "It does not," she answered, waving a hand down the length of the armoire. "May I show you anything in particular? Or supply you with something more . . . exotic?"

Tristan made a pretense of opening the drawers. "No, I think this will do nicely," he answered. "What is in there?" He jerked his head toward the dark room.

Mademoiselle smiled faintly. "I shall leave you to discover that for yourself," she said. "Now, may I fetch you a late supper? Some refreshments, perhaps?"

"A bottle of brandy," said Tristan, "and some champagne."

The woman nodded, and withdrew, closing the door behind her.

Swiftly, Tristan began to move through the room, running his hands and his eyes over the walls, lifting the draperies, and even peering behind the artwork.

"What are you looking for?" asked Phaedra, following him.

"Peepholes," he answered. "Cubbyholes. Anything of that nature."

Phaedra moved to the opposite wall and began to search. "Do they use such things?"

"Most brothels do," he said, lifting a portrait of a lady pleasuring herself with some sort of implement. "But here, I think not." He let the painting drop. "I gather Madame focuses on the art of blackmail."

Phaedra finished her wall and moved toward the dark room.

"Don't!" Tristan cautioned.

But it was too late.

He caught her there, just inside the doorway, her eyes running over the walls. "My God," she whispered.

He jerked her arm roughly. "Come on, Phae," he said, forgetting their ruse. "You do not need to see this."

But as with so many of life's horrors, the room transfixed one's gaze, making it impossible to turn away. The only light came from a narrow, grated window near the ceiling, well beyond any human's reach. Chains and racks hung from bare walls like medieval torture devices. A narrow metal cot was bolted to one wall, and beneath the window sat a sort of padded wooden horse such as one might store a saddle upon, with iron manacles affixed to the wall above. The rest of it, she could not bear to contemplate.

At the sight of Phaedra's pallor, disgust dashed over Tristan like a bucket of ice water, cold and sickening. He drew her forcibly from the room, and pulled her into his arms. She dived into the embrace, and buried her head against his neck.

"Phae, I'm sorry," he murmured, setting a hand to the back of her head. "That room contains pure filth. Vostrikova specializes in it. She *addicts* men to it. Do you see now why I did not wish to bring you here?"

She lifted her head from his shoulder and stared into the depths of the narrow room, her eyes bleak. "Tristan, I know I like . . . the things you do to me. But that room—it just seems *vile*."

He forced her face back to his, and kissed her lightly on the nose. "Phae, what you enjoy is sex play," he explained. "You like a dominant partner, yes. But that room is for men—perhaps even a few women—who enjoy inflicting pain. Who are excited by the sexual humiliation of others. It is a far, far cry from the things we have done in bed together."

"I know." He felt her relax as she tilted her head toward the armoire. "What of the other things? Are they so wicked?"

He laughed. "Oh, a little, perhaps," he admitted. "There are some small but relatively harmless whips, and some manacles, but made of velvet, not metal. Some sex toys from France and the Orient. No one is apt to get hurt using any of those things."

Her eyes widened with curiosity. *"Velvet manacles?"* she whispered.

Tristan flashed a wicked grin. "I'll get you a pair," he answered. "But only if you promise to take turns."

"Take turns?"

"Well, it seems only fair," he answered, smiling down at her. "I think I should rather like to be chained to the bed and ridden to exhaustion."

She licked her lips uncertainly. "Have you . . . have you ever done that before?"

"I cannot recall," he lied, his eyes twinkling. "I don't remember anyone before you, Phae."

And that, he thought regretfully, *was another lie he'd told all too often.*

But this time, it was perilously near the truth. In fact, Tristan did not wish to contemplate just how far he had fallen. Particularly not here in this hellish, disgusting place. He did not want Phaedra surrounded by this filth. He did not want her to question, even for an instant, her own desires.

Struck with an urge to protect her, and to shut out his fears, too, Tristan drew her fully against him. Perhaps Phaedra was a little different, he thought, tucking her head beneath his chin. But there was nothing *wrong* with her, save that she was ashamed of her own passionate nature. She had been introduced to sexual desire in the worst possible way, by a wolf who'd preyed upon her youth. A bastard who'd seduced her when she was physically ready, but emotionally naïve. And that left a deep and ugly wound; one which could be healed but slowly, with trust and with patience—and with love.

He looked down to see Phaedra watching him, the deep blue of her eyes softer now.

"Phae, my dear," he said quietly, "when we leave this place—when all of this is over—forget this. And forgive me for ever letting you come here."

There is nothing to forgive," she answered. "You've done what I asked. And this place would be no less evil had I remained ignorant of it."

"Phae." He set his lips softly to hers in a kiss of reassurance. Her long lashes lowered in a sweep of velvet, and in his arms she trembled, not with passion or fear, but with something he could not quite name. Perhaps she, too, sensed the deepening significance of what lay between them.

Suddenly, the door flew open. Tristan broke the embrace, and looked round to see Mademoiselle LaFoy on the threshold, her eyes dancing with amusement.

"Oh, pray do not let me stop you!" The woman's lips twisted into a smile as she entered. "*Alors*, I have brought for you Sally and Flora—" Here, she paused to lift her hand toward the girls who followed her, "—but perhaps you no longer require their services?"

Without missing a beat, Phaedra resumed her surly pose. "We wanted girls with red hair," she protested, pointing at the smaller of the two girls. "Hers is blond."

Mademoiselle LaFoy's eyes glittered maliciously. "Flora has reddish-gold hair, Mr. Talbot," she said tightly. "And I can assure you, she will give total satisfaction."

"But her hair," said Phaedra slowly, "*is not red*. Take her away and bring us another."

Tristan held out a staying hand. "Harold, dear boy, she is a fetching chit," he said. "But have you anyone with darker hair, *mademoiselle*? We will, of course, keep Flora, too."

"We have no one else of that coloring," said Mademoiselle LaFoy tightly. "I can bring you a brunette, if you wish."

Tristan drew the girl called Flora to his side. The girl was terrified, her eyes shying wildly. "Thank you, *mademoiselle*," he murmured. "Flora will do nicely."

"*Merci*, my lord." Mademoiselle LaFoy bowed ever so faintly. "Ah, and here are your refreshments."

A maid set down a tray laden with bottles and glasses, bobbed a swift curtsy, and vanished.

"We shan't wish to be disturbed before daylight," Tristan ordered, already stripping off his coat. "See to it, *mademoiselle*."

"*Oui, bien sûr*," she said, inclining her head. "Good evening, gentlemen." Then Mademoiselle LaFoy withdrew, closing the slablike door with an awful *thud*.

The girl called Flora let out a little whimper. Her heart sinking, Phaedra let her gaze run over them, taking in their tawdry, low-cut gowns and painted faces. Until this moment, she simply had not accepted that Millie might not come. Certainly she had not expected these poor, thin, worn-down creatures, both of whom drew her sympathy. Neither remotely resembled Priss's mother. The smaller, Flora, was frozen in fear, like a spring rabbit caught in the garden, a pitchfork bearing down upon it.

Tristan poured two glasses of champagne and pressed them into the girls' hands.

Flora looked down at it, unblinking, as if she'd never seen such a thing.

"Wot would yer 'ave, sir?" asked the girl called Sally. "We can undress, the two of us, and lie wiv the both of yer together, if yer likes it that way?"

"Oh, let's not rush into anything, my dears." Tristan was pouring himself a brandy. "Sit down. Let us get to know you a little."

The girls exchanged uneasy glances, but they sat, clutching their glasses awkwardly. Tristan paced along the floor in front of them. "Tell me, girls, do you like your positions here?"

Sally hesitated. "Just come on two days past." She lifted a bony shoulder. "But it's a roof o'er me head, in't? And summink ter eat every day?"

The girl sat defiantly before them in her cheap, brightly-hued gown, her bosom exposed and her fingers bitten to the quick, and Phaedra wanted suddenly to cry. *Something to eat every day?* For that she had been compelled to sell her body into slavery? Oh, Phaedra knew, of course, as every upper-class Londoner did, that it happened. But to see it thus . . . dear Lord.

"Flora?" Tristan encouraged.

Flora did not answer, but instead seemed to curl inward on herself like a morning glory at day's end. The girl could not have been above sixteen years old. "I likes it fine, sir," she finally whispered, refusing to look at him.

Tristan knelt, and lifted her chin with one finger. "How long have you worked here, may I ask?"

But of course he could ask, thought Phaedra. He could do anything he damned well pleased. These poor girls were paid to indulge his every whim—and likely beaten if they did not.

Flora's wild eyes trembled. "A year September, my lord," she whispered.

"I see." Tristan stood, and tossed off what was left of his brandy, then turned to look at Sally. "My dear, can you make your way back to your quarters without being seen or scolded?"

Sally looked at him oddly. "We 'ave ter do it, 'ere, my lord," she said. "Vostrikova's rules."

"No, I mean you are dismissed," he replied. "My friend and I will amuse ourselves with only Flora tonight."

Flora gave a little cry, then slapped a tremulous hand over her mouth.

Sally looked as if she couldn't decide whether to be affronted or afraid, but she set aside her glass and flounced across the floor toward Tristan. She lifted one hand and stroked it slowly down his face. "Oh, but yer such a fine, big buck of a man, milord," she murmured. "Why would I wants ter leave?"

Tristan smiled faintly, lifted her hand away, and lightly kissed the back of it, as if she were a highborn lady. "Thank you for that heartfelt compliment, my dear," he said quietly. "But we have changed our mind."

The siren's façade fell away, and something like panic sketched over Sally's face. "No," she said abruptly. "I—I can't go. Madame will flay my backside for a week. I can give satisfaction, milord. I promise."

Tristan smiled and pressed some coins into her hand. "Look, you're a smart girl, Sally," he answered. "Find a quiet corner and put your feet up. I'm afraid I must insist."

Sally edged toward the door. "And you'll not tell old LaFoy?"

"She'll never know," Tristan assured her.

"Suit yerself, then." The girl cast them one last look as she went.

Flora, however, looked on the brink of tears. Tristan drew Phaedra aside, and tilted his head toward the girl. "Do you think she knows anything?"

Phaedra shrugged. "Perhaps, but you don't have time for this. Go. Leave me to question the girl. If she's been here a year, surely she must know what happened to Millie."

"My logic exactly." Tristan tossed Flora another glance. "But I don't like the look of her. She is not well. Whatever you learn, Phae, we are going to have to get her out of here."

Phaedra agreed. "Leave that to me," she answered. "You have until the clock at St. Anne's strikes midnight. One way or another, we'll be in the old scullery as planned. Now *go*."

His eyes filled with worry, Tristan lingered only long enough to interrogate Flora about the locations of closets, pantries, and servants' stairs throughout the house— things he'd been unable to ascertain from Vostrikova's customers. The girl answered him in a flat, monosyllabic voice, and if she cared why Tristan asked, one couldn't discern it. Phaedra got the impression that it had been a long time since Flora had cared about anything. Tristan was right. The girl had to be snatched from Vostrikova's clutches. Phaedra's only worry was for how many more there might be just like her.

At the door, Tristan tipped up her chin and kissed her hard. "Be careful, Phae, for God's sake."

Phaedra nodded, fighting down the fear that welled up in her chest, then pushed him out the door. She returned to the girl's chair. "Are you all right, my dear?"

The girl squeezed her eyes shut as if she expected to be hit. "Y-yes."

"Flora, we mean you no harm," she said, no longer bothering with her deep voice. "Listen, I haven't time to explain all this. Do you wish to leave here? To go home?"

Her face crumpling, she nodded. She was quite remarkably beautiful, despite her tears and her terror.

Phaedra took her hand, and gave it a squeeze. "Then we will take you away tonight," she said. "Vostrikova will not use you again, I swear it."

The girl was watching Phaedra oddly, as if wondering what to make of her. Phaedra rose and withdrew to the window. To her shock, the rain had returned, a downpour which slicked the cobbles with a yellowish sheen beneath the lamplight. The street looked gray and forbidding.

"Flora, I need information," she gently pressed. "We are looking for someone. I am sure she is here against her will. Her name is Millie Dales, and she is tall with red hair. Is she here?"

Mutely, Flora shook her head.

They were too late, thought Phaedra sickly. The events of the evening weighed down on her, and tears sprang to her own eyes. What a naïve fool she was! Tristan had been right.

"Not tonight," the girl whispered.

"What?" Phaedra's head whipped round. "What are you saying? That she *was* here?"

The girl snuffled wetly. "Bin gone a week, I reckon?" she answered. "Comes and goes, Millie does. Madame puts 'er out on loan."

Hope leapt in Phaedra's heart. "So she's coming back?"

The girl snuffled again and nodded. "Tomorrow, per'aps? I think that's right."

Phaedra crossed the room and grabbed both her hands. "Flora, listen to me," she begged. "We are going to get you out of here—and Millie, too. But first you must tell me *everything*."

It took Tristan better than a quarter hour to work his way back through the rabbit warren of corridors and stairs, sliding in and out of closets and pantries when he heard footsteps or voices. Some of the doors were locked, but devices Kemble had lent him—four long, slender bits of metal, worked infallibly—if a little more slowly than one might have wished.

It was Madame Vostrikova's habit, Tristan had learned, to play chess in the evenings with one of her bully boys. Her offices were on the ground floor of the last house, whilst her private rooms were two floors above it. To enter, he crossed over by way of the attic, through a sort of lumber room crammed full of old furniture, with plenty of places to hide.

Apparently he was not the only one who thought so. Near the exit, he stepped round a dark corner, almost stumbling into an old divan. A footman and one of the girls were putting it to good use, caught in the throws of passion. Impatient, Tristan slid behind a wardrobe and waited for the sighs to die down. He was not ordinarily the voyeuristic type.

When the girl had drawn her skirts back down, and both had slipped away, Tristan crept through, and let himself out onto a flight of narrow, dusty stairs. Sliding through the shadows, one ear constantly cocked, he made his way down the next three, far grander, flights which opened dramatically to the front hall below. On the last landing, he caught the sound of a sharp, feminine voice. The sitting room door above him opened, light spilling down the steps. Tristan sucked in his breath and pressed himself behind a potted palm.

"*Da*, my wool shawl, Lavrin," Vostrikova commanded. "And you, girl! Put more coal on the fire."

The door closed. A man moved past, going down the stairs. The same squat, thuggish chap who'd let them in, too well dressed to be a servant. In the gloom, he did not notice Tristan. He descended swiftly and crossed the hall, his heels ringing out on the marble floor below, then fading. In the distance, the clock at St. Anne's struck eleven, the sounds reverberating off the front of the town house.

Tristan exhaled, then eased down to the ground floor. Vostrikova's private offices were just along the entrance hall, the first rooms a visitor might see upon arriving. Working by feel alone, he snicked the first lock and let himself into a large, square antechamber. Gaslight fell through the window, casting a ghostly sheen over the chairs and settees which lined two walls. The room held a desk and a set of glass bookcases to the rear. Tristan made a mental note to riffle them if time permitted.

The next door took a little longer, but not much. This room was smaller, but richly appointed in shades of red and gold, with costly mahogany furnishings. The well-polished desk stretched to infinity. It held nothing but a lamp and an ornately carved rosewood box. Gently, Tristan lifted the lid. Cheroots—fine, sweet Cavendish, too, he thought, drawing one beneath his nose.

Behind the desk was a chest, four drawers deep, stretching from window to window. It took but a moment to spring the lock, then Tristan lit the lamp and set to work. The drawers held ledgers, receipts, and correspondence, almost all of it in English. After half an hour of meticulous searching, his suspicions were confirmed. Nothing of value there. He turned to the desk. Again, nothing save the usual clutter. Wax. Ink. Letter paper. A tidy pile of tradesmen's receipts.

Sighing, he made quick work of the rest of the room, lifting his lamp high to peer behind pictures and furniture, taking a calculated risk that no one observed from the street. Judging by the volume of rain which rattled through the downspouts, he thought it unlikely. He tried not to think of Phaedra, and of where she might be at this moment. He knew too well that losing one's concentration was the most fatal of errors.

Frustratingly, his search yielded nothing, so Tristan returned to the chest. On impulse, he extracted one of the bottom drawers and studied the cabinet's interior. He rapped on the bottom with the back of his hand. Yes, too high, and too hollow. He wedged his fingers between the frame and the wood skirting. *Ah*. The skirting was actually hinged; dropping down to reveal two, more shallow drawers—little more than trays.

Carefully, he drew them out, marveling at the tidy stacks of letters and ledgers. This, without question, was what he wanted. Tristan flipped through the correspondence. Most was in Russian, but what he could read was damning. Names, dates, all manner of schemes laid bare— years' worth. And far too much to be shoved beneath one's coat, unfortunately.

He looked about the room and saw the long fold of black wool tossed casually over the desk chair. *Madame's lost shawl.* The irony of it pleased him.

Hastily, Tristan spread it on the floor and piled his loot atop it. He rolled it into a tight bundle and tied it up with a long length of packing cord he'd seen in the desk. De Vendenheim's men were supposed to be watching the house. Tristan hoped to heaven they were awake.

He carried the bundle and lamp to a front window, threw up the sash, then thrust the lamp out into the rain, waving it back and forth three times. Hastily, he ran the cording out the window, lowering his bundle down the side of the house, the wool of Madame's shawl scrubbing along the brickwork.

At the ground floor balconet, he hesitated. He might manage to swing the bundle beyond it and onto the pavement, but a passerby might find it first. And then there was the rain. Best to go on as he'd begun. His cord, of course, was several feet to short. At the end of it, he cast up a prayer and let go. The bundle landed on the flagstone below the basement stairs with a *whump!*

He hung out the window another moment, wondering if anyone below had heard it. This section of the cellars was supposed to be used for coal, wine, and the like, with little traffic. And indeed, no one came out below to see what the matter was. Tristan withdrew, and shut the window.

At that very moment, however, a carriage came clattering down the street. A sleek black gig, moving fast. It drew up before the window. Swiftly, Tristan fell to a crouch. The driver leapt down, whipping his reins round a lamp-post. In the pool of weak gaslight, there was no mistaking the man's face. George Nebbett bounded up the stairs—the *front* stairs—looking as if the hounds of hell were on his heels. Softly, Tristan cursed beneath his breath.

This could not be good.

In an instant, Nebbett was pounding on the door like a madman. Tristan turned down the wick and considered his options. There were voices in the hall now; Nebbett's, followed by a servant's voice, stiff but politely solicitous. Tristan glanced about the room. If anyone came in, he had no way out, save for the windows, both of which over-looked the stairwell—easily survivable as falls went—but escape meant abandoning Phaedra inside the house. He would have to find another way.

He hadn't long to consider it. Footsteps were coming down the passageway; one set heavy, the other light and quick. Angry words were exchanged. The lock rattled in the antechamber door. *One more to go.* Tristan knew with a spy's instinct he was about to be caught out.

There was nothing to do save brazen it through. He turned the lamp back up, lit himself a cheroot, and threw his boot heels up onto Vostrikova's fine mahogany desk.

At the pounding which reverberated through the corri-dors, Phaedra froze on the back stairs, thrusting Flora be-hind her. If Tristan's intelligence had been correct, this part of the house should have been quiet now. It wasn't. In an instant, servants' voices rang out. Fast, light footsteps echoed beyond the door, heightening the urgency in the air. Phaedra hesitated, listening.

"I do not like my evenings interrupted, Mr. Nebbett."

It was Vostrikova's voice carrying sharply down the corridor. "Surely this is tomorrow's business?"

Phaedra leaned out. At the opposite end of the passageway, she could see Vostrikova descending the front stairs, her face tight with anger, a ring of keys clutched in her hand.

"Madame, it cannot wait." Phaedra could make out the profile of the thin gentleman who lingered in the hall, a sodden hat clutched in his hands. "I've just this instant received alarming news."

Vostrikova dismissed the servant, then motioned the man to follow her. "Come in," she said, rattling her keys. "But be quick." Her black silk skirts swished around the corner.

The man vanished after her. The sound of Vostrikova's key in the lock was unmistakable.

Good God, where was Tristan? From the diagram Tristan had shown her, Phaedra knew those were Vostrikova's private offices. Her heart was pounding in her ears now. Fleetingly, she closed her eyes. Surely, surely he had had time to get out?

But it was not likely. She knew it. Biting her lip, Phaedra reached into her coat pocket and extracted the little pistol Mr. Kemble had given her. Her pulse ratcheted up another notch. "Go on down without me, Flora," she whispered over her shoulder. "Hide in the old scullery until one of us comes."

The girl eyed the pistol and scurried away. Phaedra hastened across the open corridor and slid into the shadows, her back set to the wall. She eased toward the front of the house until the voices came clear. The weight of the gun was cold in her hand, like a dead, unnatural thing. She gripped it harder, remembering Kemble's instructions.

"I tell you that bastard's been at my papers!" The man's voice rang out, strained. "Twice he tricked my wife into leaving him alone in my library. She admitted it tonight, the cuckolding bitch."

"Was anything disturbed?" Madame demanded. "Out of place?"

"Well, no. N-nothing I could see." The man was blustering now. "But there's trouble afoot, I tell you. We are caught out."

Vostrikova's sharp laughter rang out. "You are such a coward, Nebbett," she answered. "Everyone knows Avoncliffe is nothing but a pretty fribble." But there was an uneasy edge to her voice.

Phaedra was near the foot of the stairs now. She flicked a quick glance up, the turns of the stairs fading into the gloom as they rose.

"You may think him a fribble, Madame," said the man. "But he was once sly enough to bed my wife under my very nose—and did it again yesterday, for all I know."

Hastily, Phaedra crossed the foot of the steps, and set her back alongside the open door.

"Half the *ton* has bedded your wife, Nebbett." Madame's voice rose. "My God, man! Does this domestic drama really warrant disturbing my chess game?"

Phaedra peeked round the corner into a sort of antechamber. "You've not heard the worst." The man called Nebbett had his hands clasped prayerfully before him. "Lord Hauxton refuses to see me now. The staff has been ordered not to let me in."

"He's ill," snapped Madame. "He'll be dead any day, you fool."

"You don't know Hauxton!" Nebbett cried. "He'll work until they pry the pen from his cold, rigored fingers and drive the nails into his coffin. No, Madame, I tell you— *I am found out!* Please, please, you must help me."

"Help you?" Vostrikova sounded incredulous.

"Madame," he said, clutching at her sleeve, "do you know what they do to traitors in this country?"

Vostrikova laughed richly. "I know what they do to traitors in *my* country, Nebbett," she answered. "In England, your death will be a luxury—swift and painless."

"At least give me back the letters," Nebbett begged. "You've had time to read them by now. They cannot mean anything to you."

Vostrikova shook him off, then relented. "Oh, very well, if it will rid me of you." She turned to unlock the door behind her.

"I need them all," Nebbett stressed. "I must replace them tonight."

"Be quiet, you fool," Vostrikova hissed. Phaedra watched a little sickly as the door swung wide. "Your letters are safe in my office."

"Not anymore, they aren't." Phaedra heard Tristan's voice ring out cheerfully in the gloom.

"My God!" Nebbett cried, plunging into the room, Vostrikova stalking after him.

Phaedra strained round the door, but could see only Tristan's boot heels—*propped upon the desk!* The audacity of the man! Emboldened, she crept in after them, terrified but determined, positioning herself to the left of the last door. Their attention was wholly focused on Tristan.

Vostrikova had paced to the edge of the desk. "My Lord Avoncliffe." Her voice was oddly calm. "You surprise me—and I do not like surprises."

"Neither does His Majesty's Government," said Tristan, puffing smoke from one side of his mouth. "By the way, Madame, these are damn fine cheroots. You must give me the name of your tobacconist."

Nebbett seized the madam's arm. "Kill him!" he hissed. "Call your bully boys! He has the letters!"

Phaedra watched as a grin curved Tristan's mouth. "Not anymore, I don't," he said. "Hell, I'm so witless I couldn't even read 'em—so I've sent them off to the powers that be."

"You lie!" hissed Vostrikova. She made the curious gesture of folding one hand over the other. "No one has come or gone from this house. The letters are still here, and *I will find them*, my lord."

"Have a look round, then." His grin deepening, Tristan uncurled himself from his seat and stood, planting one tall boot boldly in the middle of the chair, as if he owned the place. "Pull open your secret drawers if you wish. But you will find them empty."

Suddenly, Vostrikova leaned forward, whipping something long and glittering from her sleeve. "By God, I will not let you ruin this!" she cried brandishing the knife. "Nebbett! Seize him!"

"*Seize* him?" Nebbett cringed.

"Do it!" Vostrikova snarled. "Or I swear to God, I'll slit your throat next."

"No one," said Phaedra in her own voice, "is slitting anyone's throat." She stepped into the fray, the pistol held straight out in both hands, elbows locked, just as Kemble had shown her.

At last, Tristan's grin faded. His color went with it. Vostrikova turned, her eyes glittered wickedly. "Well, if it isn't *Mr.* Talbot," she whispered, the knife trembling. "You little bitch. I should have seen through you at once."

"Phae." Tristan was half turned from the door, one hand out. "Phae, I have it under control."

"But she has a knife," Phaedra whispered. "And I just—"

Everything happened in a flash then. Vostrikova glanced past Phaedra for an instant. Phaedra sensed rather than saw something lunge to her left. She was jerked back, a thick arm whipping round her throat. The cold kiss of steel brushed her windpipe below. "Drop the gun," a deep, foreign voice rasped in Phaedra's ear. "I assure you, my blade is far faster."

Nebbett fell back, his face ashen. "Lavrin! Thank God!"

"Just do as he says, Phae." Tristan's voice was utterly calm. "Everything's fine."

Across the desk, she watched him. Almost imperceptibly, he nodded, then winked with one eye. He had a plan. Phaedra flung the gun away. It skittered across the carpet and vanished under a low, heavy chest.

"Kill her, Lavrin!" Vostrikova's voice and her blade trembling with rage. "Kill her now!"

The man hitched his arm tighter, crushing Phaedra's windpipe. It was as if time leapt forward then. In one seamless motion, Tristan struck his hand across Vostriko-va's wrist, his opposite hand going to his boot. "Phae, *drop!*"

Phaedra went limp, taking her attacker with her. A blade of light came hurtling across the desk. The blade caught him—she knew not where—and he cried out. He fell over her like a dead weight. Nebbett shrieked and bolted from the room, slamming the door, snapping the lock behind.

Phaedra shifted, and a dark, thickset man rolled to the floor behind her, writhing in agony, the knife buried deep in his right shoulder. It had all happened in an instant. *It was over.*

"Tristan," she uttered. She sagged with relief, too witless to look for her gun. Suddenly, the wounded man—Lavrin—staggered to his feet, dazed with pain. Vostrikova seized the only weapon to hand—the lamp which burnt on her desk—and circled toward Phaedra.

"My papers, Avoncliffe!" she demanded, holding the lamp high, the glass chimney chattering. "Show them now! Or I swear I'll send her to a fiery death!"

Phaedra pressed herself back against the wall. Vostrik-ova was in front of the door now. If she sent the lamp crashing to the carpet, the whole room would soon be ablaze, trapping them. The madam's grip was unsteady, her eyes wide with rage.

Tristan held up both hands. "You win, Madame," he said, easing from behind the desk. "Just put the lamp—"

"Get back!" she cried. The flame flickered eerily up the walls, casting dancing, lethal shadows.

"Lilya, no!" Lavrin struggled to hold up one hand.

He lurched toward her, the knife still sticking from his shoulder.

Later, Phaedra could not have said whether he fainted, or merely lost his balance. But he tumbled into Vostrikova, striking her in the ribs. She lost her grip on the lamp. It crashed to the floor. Oil splashed, flames rolled across the carpet and onto her skirt. Vostrikova fell back against the door, screaming and beating at them with her hands.

Somehow, Phaedra found the presence of mind to grab Lavrin by the ankle. Then Tristan was beside her, pulling the other. They dragged him off the carpet, the knife jiggling in his shoulder. Vostrikova was screaming, flailing at the flames, making them worse.

"Roll!" Tristan shouted at her. "Roll on the floor!"

"No!" she shrieked, backing against the door. "No, noo!" Heat and light filled the room.

"Phae! With me!" Tristan dragged her to the window, and threw up the sash. "Crawl out," he ordered.

Phaedra did not hesitate, but sat on the sill and swung both legs through.

"Good God!" she cried, looking down.

Swiftly he kissed her. "It's not far, love. I swear."

But she did not have time to consider it. Tristan shoved her hard. Phaedra slid down the side of the house, brick scraping at her back. She landed at the foot of the stairs, collapsing onto something hard and fat, striking her head on the bottom step. Oblivion washed in around her, black and engulfing, then Phaedra knew no more.

Chapter 13

'Tis not the many oaths that make the truth,
But the plain single vow that is vow'd true.

Shivering and disoriented, Phaedra woke to a shaft of pale morning light cutting across her bed. Lifting her head from the pillow, she looked about the room, something nebulous and fearsome just beyond her grasp.

But there was nothing. Only Agnes, going about her usual morning tasks. Drawing her draperies. Pulling out her old slipper tub. In the street below her windows, the daily clatter of carriages and carts had started up, and the cooing of pigeons carried in from the sills.

Phaedra fell back into the pillow. *She was in her room. Her own bed.* And yet the darkness nagged at her. Her legs felt leaden beneath the bedcovers, her hands bloodless.

Tristan.

She rose up little, holding a hand to block the light. "Agnes—?"

Her maid tossed down the brush she was cleaning, and swooped down upon the bed, her brow fretful. "Awake, are you, miss?" she said, peering into Phaedra's eyes. "Oh, what a fright you gave me!"

Phaedra's brain felt swathed in cotton wool. "What happened?" she asked, rising onto her elbows. "I . . . I can't think."

Agnes settled herself on the edge of the bed. "You fell, miss. Do you not remember?" She stroked the hair back from Phaedra's forehead. "Ooh, what a nasty lump you have!"

Phaedra's hand fluttered to her temple. "A lump?" Yes, snatches were returning now. "Tristan?" she uttered, catching Agnes's wrist. "He is . . . safe?"

Agnes was smiling at her now. "Oh, aye," she said. "Lost a bit of hair in that fire, but still handsome as they come."

"Thank God," Phaedra whispered.

She knew, of course, that he was safe, though she wasn't sure how. But the vaguest of memories were beginning to stir. Tristan's hand soft against her face. His arms lifting her gently into a carriage. She'd felt his cheek pressed to hers. She had felt . . . tears. *Hers? Or his?* Both, she thought. Dear God. Her fingers fluttered to her lips, pressing hard.

Agnes cleared her throat a little awkwardly. "That Mr. Kemble came round this morning to ask after you, miss," she reported, tidying the bedcovers. "He said Mr. Talbot was quite the hero last night."

"He pushed me out a window," Phaedra said. "I remember that much."

"Trying to save your life," Agnes reminded her.

"Yes." Phaedra's gaze turned inward. "I—I think I hit my head on the steps."

"Aye, they said," Agnes murmured.

Phaedra remembered someone scooping her up, too. A very deep voice near her ear as they ascended from the gloom. The cool rain on her face. She could still feel the burn of smoke in the back of her throat. The cold terror which gripped her—the fear that something dreadful had happened to Tristan.

They had carried her up Vostrikova's front steps. And then she'd seen him, standing in a halo of charred and splintered wood, his face black with soot, an avenging angel battling his way through the gates of hell. Relief surged through her again, more vivid now than it had been last night. *He was alive.* She was alive. And they were bloody lucky, the both of them.

But the once beautiful Madame Vostrikova was beautiful no more. Phaedra closed her eyes, willing the vision away. The madam had lain upon the carpet Tristan had used to snuff the flames and carry her out; her hair a scorched mass, her face so badly burnt it was unrecognizable, the flowing silk gown cocooning her body in a crumbling, ashen sheath. De Vendenheim had cursed beneath his breath, and hastily turned Phaedra's face away.

That had been her waking dream. The thing she'd wished to escape. She remembered it now, and shuddered. Phaedra forced it away, and looked at Agnes.

"Lord de Vendenheim," she said, her heart sinking. "It was he who carried me up from the stairwell. And by now he will have told Stefan *everything*."

Agnes set a soothing hand over Phaedra's. "I fancy not, miss," she said. "He brought you here in his carriage. He and Mr. Talbot had hard words out in the alley, but I think they reached an understanding."

Phaedra closed her eyes. She could only imagine de Vendenheim's outrage at seeing her in Soho, and of course, he would have blamed Tristan for it. The knowledge sickened her. "What of our staff?" she whispered, scarcely caring. "Did anyone see me?"

"Oh, no, miss," Agnes reassured her. "I sent Cook to bed at ten with a strong, hot toddy and a bit of flannel for her throat. I thought she looked a trifle peaked, and I told her so."

Phaedra managed a weak smile. Cook was a notorious hypochondriac, and prone to watching at windows. "Poor woman. By now she must think she's dying."

Agnes shrugged. "Anyways, I was on the lookout, miss, when the carriage came round back," she said. "No one was about. But there was a girl—frightened little thing. Flora, they called her. De Vendenheim was taking her to mission house. Don't you remember coming up the stairs with me?"

"A little, yes." She felt gingerly at the knot on her head.

"By the way, I told Cook you tripped over the carpet last night," Agnes went on, pointing at the edge of Phaedra's dressing table. "That marble edge is frightfully hard. Anyways, I put you straight to bed. And here you've been from that moment 'til this—and I dare anyone to say different."

Phaedra dragged both hands through her hair. It felt filthy and matted. "Vostrikova—?"

Agnes's face softened. "That Kemble fellow said she was alive, but just. Very polite, he was. He said to tell you the other chap—the chap with the knife in 'im—was taken up by the magistrates." She gave a little shiver as she rose from the bed. "Ooh, miss, it chills me to think what went on last night."

"Yes, well, you're not the only one," said Phaedra dryly. "I made a fool of myself—and I almost got Mr. Talbot killed."

"Oh, miss, I'm sure you did not!" Agnes shot her a reproachful glance, then went to the bell pull. "Now you must put it all out of your mind. What you need is a good, strong cup of tea."

A few minutes later, the tea was poured and a parade of footmen carried in water for Phaedra's bath. When they were gone, she threw back the covers and rose, the teacup rattling in her hand. She had to see Tristan. Had to assure herself . . . of something.

But what? He was well enough; she knew that much. And what more was there between them now? He had done as she had asked. He had helped her find—

"Millie!" Phaedra set her cup down on her dressing table. "Oh, Agnes! I forgot to tell him about Millie!"

"Millie?" On her knees, Agnes turned from the tub, eyes wide. "Did you find her, miss?"

"Millie is supposed to come back today!" Phaedra threw off her wrapper. "Hurry, Agnes, lay out my blue walking dress. We must be there when she arrives."

Agnes looked doubtful. "I'm not to let you stir until Mr. Talbot comes, miss," she answered. "He said so last night. Said he'd come round this morning to check on you."

Phaedra drew her nightgown off. "Did he?" she answered. "Then I must hurry. Here, help me wash my hair."

An hour later, Phaedra was in the family parlor, alternately pacing the floor and staring out the windows across the garden. She remembered it now—coming up that path on Tristan's strong, solid arm, the scent of scorched wool sharp in her nostrils. The horrors of the night washed over her; the ugliness of all she had seen, and the sadness which came with the certain knowledge of how less fortunate women lived.

She thought again of Flora, and of Sally, so hardened, and so accepting of her fate. Of that dark, narrow, horrid room. But she thought most of all of Tristan; of how very much she owed him. Of how desperately she ached to touch him with her own hands and reassure herself that all was well. He had said he would call this morning—and he would. Above all else, he was a man of his word. And then she would ask him for one last thing—one last favor, though God knew she had no right to do so.

Moments later, she heard the knocker drop at the front door and knew with a woman's instinct that it would be him. Clutching her hands before her, Phaedra resisted the urge to rush down the passageway and answer it herself. It was time, she supposed, that she began to conduct herself with a little decorum—outwardly, at least.

She had already informed the footmen that she would receive Tristan here, for it seemed somehow fitting. In this soft, comfortable, familiar room, she had first begun to know him. Had first kissed him. And in this room, it was entirely possible she would now bid him good-bye. After all, what more was there to say? What more lay between them? He owed her nothing. Only her need to find Priscilla's mother had drawn them together, and today—one way or another—that ended. Phaedra had resolved it in her heart. If she did not find Millie this afternoon, she would search no more.

There was a noise, the soft sound of shoes on the carpet, and she turned round to see Tristan standing on the threshold. His face was fiercely red up one side, and a little of his hair was scorched away, but that irrepressible humor still lurked in his eyes.

"Mr. Talbot, my lady." The footman bowed, and stepped aside.

He entered the room as he always did; as if he owned it, with an easy, loose-limbed grace. He filled the room with his presence, making her mouth go dry and her heart hammer. For an instant, he stood looking at her, both hands set at his narrow hips, taking her in, something sharp and assessing behind his laughing eyes. He had been worried, she realized.

"Thank you, Stabler," she managed to say. "We require nothing further."

The footman bowed, and withdrew. Phaedra shut the door, and without fully grasping her own intentions, hurled herself at Tristan.

"Phae." His arms came around her, solid and strong. "Always on the edge of propriety."

She made a sound, a sort of choked sob. "Oh, do be quiet!" she said. "I am so tired of being proper. And I am so desperately glad to see you!"

He set her a little away, his gaze solemn and watchful.

"It was a hard, strange night, my girl," he said grimly. "And I'm dashed glad to see you up and around."

"Oh, Tristan!" She blinked hard, and gathered herself. "You are burnt!"

"Not enough to ruin my boyish good looks," he said, grinning. Then the expression faded, and he lightly touched the bruise at her temple. "Poor love," he murmured. "Does it hurt?"

"Like the devil," she answered. "And I deserve it. Tristan, I am so sorry for being so rash."

A wicked humor danced in his black Gypsy eyes. "You, Phae? Rash?"

Phaedra sighed. "That pistol!" she said. "Coming into that room. You knew what you were doing—and *I thought I was saving you*!"

At that, he threw back his head and laughed. "Oh, it was going to be a free-for-all no matter what," he said evenly. "Once old Nebbett turned up, my plan was out the window—and you with it, I'm sorry to say."

"Yes, my only regret is that I'll never be able to tell that story at dinner parties," she confessed. "Someday, when the terror has passed, it will likely seem hilarious."

He ran the ball of his thumb over her cheek, then let his arms fall. "Vostrikova died early this morning," he said quietly.

Phaedra was quiet for a moment. "And the house?" she finally asked. "The women and children? They are safe?"

Tristan shrugged. "Little damage was done by the fire," he admitted. "De Vendenheim's men are taking away those who wish to leave. His friend Lady Delacourt runs a mission in the East End."

"And what of you, Tristan?" She set her head to one side. "Was it worth the pain? Did you get what you hoped to find?"

His irrepressible grin appeared, but it was a little sideways. "Oh, my hair looks like a hedgehog cut it, and I blistered up one shoulder a bit," he said. "But yes, we found what we needed, and then some. It's as well Vostrikova died. It saves the Crown a hanging."

"Tristan." Lightly, she took both his hands in hers. "Oh, Tristan. I am so sorry to have dragged you into this."

"You did not drag me," he corrected. "My father did."

She lifted one shoulder lamely. "In part, perhaps," she agreed. "But I still wish to thank you for your help. And tell you that it's over. After today, I'm not going to search for Millie any further."

"After today?" He looked at her in puzzlement.

"Agnes and I are going back this afternoon," she said quietly. "Flora said Millie might return today. Did she tell you?"

He lifted one dark, slashing eyebrow. "No."

Phaedra snagged her lip. "I mean to try one last time to find her," she said after a moment had passed. "If we cannot, we will leave word for her. After that—well, I daresay we must all buck up, and move on. Priss included."

He squeezed her hands, his lips thinning with disapproval. "There's no stopping you from going, is there?"

She shook her head.

For a long moment, he simply held her hands and stared at her. There was an inestimable weariness in his gaze, and for the first time Phaedra noticed the deepening of the lines about his mouth and at his eyes. "Then I shall take you," he finally said. "God knows I oughtn't. But it is better, I daresay, than your going alone."

Phaedra felt the hot press of tears spring to her eyes. "You are too kind," she said, sagging with relief. She had not wished to face that awful place without him. "I thank you."

"Well, don't thank me yet," he warned her. "When we are done, Phae, you will owe *me* something."

"Yes, anything," she said. "You have only to name it."

He gave a bitter bark of laughter. "We are going to have a long talk, my girl," he said grimly. "Just the two of us. And you are going to hear out my every word without so much as a squeak. Are we agreed?"

She dropped her chin, and stared into the snowy folds of his cravat. "Yes, Tristan," she said quietly.

He folded his arms over his broad chest, and regarded her with his dark gaze. "Aye," he said quietly. "We'll see, won't we?"

They arrived in Soho to find Vostrikova's houses swarming with activity. Policemen in their blue, brass-buttoned suits were everywhere, taking statements, carrying out boxes, sending people hither and yon in hackneys, carts, and even on foot. Phaedra ordered Agnes to wait inside the carriage. It was one thing to know, intellectually, what a whore was, but an altogether harder thing to have it thrust in one's face, especially when the whore was your sister. She went up the stairs on Tristan's arm, thankful he'd forced her to wear a veil.

In the entrance hall, a police sergeant stopped him—

the same stout, florid man Phaedra had seen in Mr. Kemble's shop so many weeks ago. "My lord, above 'alf this lot already piked orf!" he complained, clearly believing Tristan in charge. "Wot are we ter tell the constables?"

"The truth, Sergeant Sisk," said Tristan. "De Vendenheim says we cannot hold anyone without evidence. Children will be taken in by the parish. As to the others, if they don't wish our help, we must let them go."

"Poor cows," said the man, shaking his head. "The beaks won't like it, neither."

Tristan paused to fish in his waistcoat for a card, then pressed it into Sisk's hand. "If any magistrate should question you, tell them the orders were Lord Hauxton's."

Lord Hauxton. That was Tristan.

Until this moment, the gravity of it had not quite registered with Phaedra. She realized in some shock that Tristan still had his father's funeral to attend to. And then he would have the responsibility of taking on the vast estates, and the many duties required of a peer of the realm. It was a sweeping, life-altering change—one which she knew he did not welcome.

But Phaedra lost that train of thought as soon as she looked up. Her gaze fixed at once upon the staircase, and on the people moving up and down it, and peering over the balustrades as if wondering what was to become of them. Women in all states of dress and dishabille. A pair of young boys—twins, by the look of them—stood barefoot on the upper landing, holding hands as they waited their turn. Three girls who could have scarce been above ten or twelve years were being led down by matronly women in gray serge gowns, bound, Phaedra feared, for the orphanages. And amongst all of them, a few haggard, hard-eyed women who clearly knew what they were about. The professional prostitutes, Phaedra supposed, but her heart ached no less for any of them.

Surveying it, Tristan uttered a soft curse. "I must be mad to have brought you back here."

One of the women pushed past them, carrying a cracked leather portmanteau, her chin high, as if daring anyone to stop her. Phaedra caught the woman's arm, and her eyes flared wide with alarm.

"Wait, miss," said Phaedra gently. "Do you need help? Food or shelter, perhaps?"

The alarm faded to a world-weary gaze. "I wish ter get on wiv me business," she said. "And 'oo are you ter stop me?"

"I don't wish to stop you," she said, as Tristan urged her forward. "I'm just searching for someone—for Millie Dales. Do you know her?"

The woman's gaze darkened, and she jerked her head toward the staircase. "Third floor, through ter the next 'ouse," she said. "The first room yer come to. But that one don't need no help."

They continued up the steps, Phaedra wondering at the woman's words, and at the barely veiled derision in her eyes. Millie's room was easily found. Phaedra peeked around the open door to see that a trunk sat on the floor, all manner of frothy garments hanging out of it.

Millie stood by the window in a pale pink muslin gown with puffed sleeves and a deeply flounced hem, a garment clearly meant for a girl just out of the schoolroom—an odd contrast in the tawdry bedchamber. A portly gentleman was clasping both her hands in his own, and looking almost rapturously down at her.

And thus ended Phaedra's mission of mercy—not with a bang, nor with even a fleeting moment of triumph—but with a whimper, and a sinking sense of the inevitable. "Millie?" she whispered without lifting her veil.

Millie turned slowly around. *"My lady?"* she cried, her eyes widening. "Is that you? Oh, lawks!"

Phaedra rushed to the girl, and seized both her hands. "Oh, Millie," she said. "Come, let me look at you! Oh, thank God. Agnes and I have been so frightfully worried."

But Millie's expression was oddly blank. "Why, I'm perfectly well, miss. Truly. But thank you."

The portly gentleman came away from the window, his brows in a knot. "Kitten?" he said sharply. "What's all this?"

Millie blushed. "My lord, this is a lady from my home village," she said. "She . . . why she is just paying a call on me, as she says, to see that I'm well, what with all the dustup last night. And this other gent—" Running an assessing eye over Tristan's expensive coat and polished boots, she made a swift curtsy. "I am afraid I do not know him."

"Oh, never mind me," said Tristan dryly.

Phaedra caught Millie lightly by the arm and glanced at the trunk, a shiny, leather affair with bright brass trim. It looked sadly out of place given the old portmanteaus and ragged bundles the other women had carried down. "Millie, I don't understand," she whispered. "This house is being shut up."

"Oh, I know that, miss!" she said. "But it's no matter to me now."

"But you won't need those things," said Phaedra, her voice strident. "We've come to take you home."

"Take her home?" said the portly gentleman, his voice sharp. "Whatever for?"

Millie bobbed again. "Oh, thank you, my lady, but with Madame out of the picture, me an' Lord Cotting have come to an understanding," she said. "I'm to go with him."

"To . . . to go with him?" Phaedra echoed. "But you do not have to. Millie, it is over. Madame is dead."

Millie wrinkled her nose. "Aye, so I heard," she answered. "Can't say as I'll miss the old cat."

"We've brought a carriage," Phaedra pressed. "Agnes is waiting outside. We want to take you back to Brier-wood."

But Millie was looking at her blankly. "What? And go back to scrubbing the taproom floors?" she asked, drawing back. "Oh, no, miss. Thank you. Indeed, I do thank you. You've always been ever so kind. But Lord Cotting is letting rooms for me, and I'm to pick out all the furniture."

Phaedra could scarce believe her ears. "But Millie, surely . . . surely you cannot enjoy this life? And what about Priss?"

"Priss?" The gentleman by the window swiveled his head to look at them, one eye narrowed suspiciously. "Kitten, who is Priss?"

Millie cut a low, swift look over her shoulder. "No one, my lord," she said hastily. Then she took Phaedra's arm and dragged her out into the corridor. Tristan followed, looking very much as if he knew where this was going.

Phaedra, however, was confused. She had expected—well, gratitude, she supposed. She had believed by now Millie would have seen the error of her ways. "Millie, I don't understand," she said. "What is going on here?"

"Listen to me, my lady," said Millie under her breath. "His lordship knows nothing of Priss—and you mustn't speak of her again, do you hear? Madame told him . . . well, she told him I was a virgin. And he paid good money to def—to defel—"

"To defile you?" Tristan dryly suggested.

Her eyes widened appreciatively. "Exactly," said Millie, turning to Tristan. "There's good money to be made in defiling virgins. Indeed, they're ever so popular with gents of a certain age, though I never would have thought it, would you?"

"Certainly I never would have," Tristan put in. "Always found 'em a nuisance, myself."

Millie tossed him an admiring glance. "Exactly," she said again. "But chaps in their dotage are right mad for 'em. And he thinks I am one—or was one, at any rate. And all it took was a bit of chicken blood and vinegar—well, that and a little shrieking and running around the room. 'Til he caught me, tore my clothes off, and tied me up, o'course."

Tristan was looking at Millie knowingly. "Oh, you're good at this, aren't you?" he murmured.

Millie drew herself up proudly. "Madame trained me to put on a proper show," she replied. "I got defiled thirty-two times." Then her face fell. "But only Lord Cotting here took a real shine to me. Still, his wife died last month—can you just imagine my luck? He's a *widower*."

Phaedra's brow was furrowed. "But what about Priss?" she said again.

Millie set a firm hand on Phaedra's arm. "Listen to me," she repeated, leaning near, one eyebrow arched in warning. "Priss will be fine. Aunt Kessie will see her raised up proper, I'm sure."

"Your *great-aunt?*" said Phaedra incredulously. "She's seventy!"

"And I'll send a little money when I can," Millie said hotly. "Really, miss. I'm sorry. But what else am I to do? Go back to Hampshire and wait for Mr. Hayden-Worth? No, thank you. Once the babe come, I thought as how he'd set me up proper, but he didn't—and now Cotting will."

Phaedra set a hand on her arm. "What, exactly, do you want, Millie? I—why, I'll arrange it if I can."

Millie's mouth turned into a pout. "What I *don't* want is to die of boredom in a poky old village," she said. "I'm a good-looking girl, miss, and I ain't about to waste it. You're very kind, I'm sure, but you can't help me."

Suddenly, a shadow fell across the corridor. "Kitten, do look at the time." Cotting had pulled a glittering gold watch from his waistcoat. "My carriage is waiting downstairs. Now put on your new hat, my little pet, and say good-bye."

Phaedra let her hand fall. And that was the end of it. No salvation, and no joy; just a feeling of utter helplessness, like watching someone plummet headfirst off a bridge into the cold and churning waters below, whilst praying fervently they could swim. Millie didn't want Priss, she wanted excitement. And Phaedra wanted to cry.

Tristan caught her elbow, and guided her gently back to the stairs. Together, they went out and back down the steps, his hand warm beneath her arm, Phaedra's stomach in a hard knot as she thought about Priss, and about going home to Brierwood empty-handed.

"Phae, I am so sorry," said Tristan when she was safely ensconced in the carriage again. "Agnes, I'm afraid we do not bring the best of news."

The maid's face went white with anger upon hearing Tristan's carefully-edited version of what had transpired. But Agnes knew, as Phaedra did, the utter impossibility of changing Millie's mind, and that there was always a chance that Millie—selfish and resourceful as she was—might actually land on her feet. Possibly even prosper.

In the end, Agnes accepted Tristan's offer to climb down and say good-bye to her sister. They waited in bitter silence until Millie came down the front steps, her hand on Lord Cotting's arm, a pink lace parasol swinging cheerfully from the crook of her elbow, her head tossed back in gay laughter.

"Always getting above herself, that one," Agnes muttered, climbing down. "And never a thought for the rest of us—especially not for Priss." At the last instant, she turned, looking back at them, her gaze wounded. "I should like to slap her senseless, miss," she said quietly. "But I shan't. I'll let her have the life she wants—much joy may it bring her."

Grief and a deep sense of failure pulled at Phaedra as she watched the maid dash across the lane. "I cannot imagine how Agnes must feel. Indeed, it must be far worse for her than for me."

"I am so sorry, Phae," said Tristan again. "All your effort—your concern for Priscilla . . ."

Phaedra's shoulders fell with fatigue. "There's nothing else for it," she said on a choked sob. "I must give Agnes up. Her aunt will need help raising Priss. I have been selfish."

Tristan scooted across the carriage to sit beside her on the banquette. "No, you have been trying to give Priscilla her mother back," he said, drawing her firmly to his shoulder. "And you feared for Millie as you would fear for any woman out of her depth with men set on taking advantage of her—because you know too well what that's like."

"But now I begin to fear who is taking advantage of whom," said Phaedra. "Am I really so naïve as all that?"

"Only in the sweetest of ways," he murmured. "But I am afraid, Phaedra, that Millie is simply not a fit mother for Priscilla. I'm sorry to have to say that."

"No, no, you are right." She tried to blink back the hot, urgent pressure behind her eyes. "Priscilla is the dearest, most precious babe *in all th-the w-world*." And then, appallingly, she burst into heaving sobs.

The tears seemed to swamp her utterly. She cried then as she had cried upon realizing she did not carry Tristan's child. She cried for Priscilla, and for her own foolish failings. Cried until Tristan's coat was wet and his handkerchief sodden. And he did not do her the insult of telling her that all would be well, or that it did not matter. He simply held her, his lips pressed to her fevered brow. He knew, as she knew, that she cried in part for a child lost long ago.

They sat in silence during the drive back to Mayfair, Agnes staring out the window, her hands clasped tightly in her lap. "Thank you, my lord," she said when Tristan helped her down at Brook Street. "You are very kind. Quite as kind as my lady—and that's saying something."

Blushing, Phaedra turned to Tristan. "Will you come in?" she asked. "Perhaps take some sort of refreshment?"

"Most certainly." He fixed her with a grim stare. "You've your end of this devil's bargain to keep now, my girl."

Phaedra remembered then what she had promised, and led the way back to the parlor. He followed her, his boots ringing heavily along the passageway, his height casting a long shadow in the afternoon light. It was odd, she mused, how swiftly a mood could turn. How two people who had just spent hours together—some of them perilously near death—could suddenly feel uneasy with one another.

Inside, the parlor seemed somehow smaller, and Tristan seemed so large. So imposingly *male*. Impulsively, she threw up one of the sashes. Tristan's presence seemed to crowd out all the air. Or perhaps it was the sudden tension in the room. He was going to say something he knew she would not like—she sensed it—though he still radiated utter calm. Absolute control. A pity she did not possess the same.

As if they might shield her emotions from view, Phaedra went to her reading table and put on her eyeglasses which, oddly, she'd scarcely worn of late. Then she rang for coffee. When it came, and there was no further delay to be found, Phaedra closed the door. This time he did not chide her—a bad sign, perhaps.

"You wished to have your say," she said, nervously slopping a little of his coffee onto the saucer as she passed it. "And God knows you've earned the right. All this effort. All this—this *madness* on my part. And now nothing to show for it."

But Tristan did not so much as lift the cup to his lips. Instead, he put it down and strode to the open window, gazing pensively across the gardens just as she had done that morning, one hand set at the back of his neck. A warm breeze blew in, shifting his dark, overlong hair like a curtain of wavy black silk.

She wanted suddenly to go to him. To touch him, and feel those powerful muscles shiver again beneath her touch. To let her hand slide up that broad, strong back, and beg him for . . . something. But what?

Her heart fluttered in her chest. The silence in the room was a heavy, palpable thing. Unable to bear it, she rose and went to him. "Tristan?" she said. But she touched only his arm. "Tristan, what is it?"

He turned and let his hand drop. "It's like this, Phae," he said, his eyes bleak. "I think we should get married."

She drew back an inch, her knees suddenly unsteady. "We . . . we should what?"

"Marry," he said tightly. "Us. I was not jesting when I said it in the alley last night. I have ruined, compromised, and thoroughly dishonored you—and both Kemble and de Vendenheim suspect it."

"No, no, you wait just a moment." But when Phaedra caught him by the shoulder, Tristan hissed through his teeth.

"Ah!" She leapt back, wincing. "Your burn."

He looked at her, chagrin and frustration in his clear, dark gaze. "I sometimes think, Phae, that you are going to be the death of me."

"No. I shan't be." She took a firm step back. "I've caused you enough trouble already. Certainly I'm not going to marry you. And you are *not* the man who ruined me."

At that, something dark and lethal passed over his visage. "No," he said softly. "Not like that, perhaps. But I'm sorry, Phae, that the man who did so is dead. In my quiet moments, I think of little else. I feel cheated of the opportunity to watch that bastard breathe his last."

This time she touched him gently. "Tristan, it's over," she lied. "It's so far in my past, I rarely even think of it. Certainly it has nothing to do with us."

"Damn it, Phaedra, don't you see?" His eyes glittered with frustration. "It has everything to do with us. That man hurt you. And I . . . Phae—I *love* you."

"You love me?"

For once, there was no laughter in his black, flashing eyes. "I wake up knowing it every day, Phaedra," he answered. "Knowing that I have an obligation to protect you—and knowing, already, that I can never make this one thing right, except to simply love you, and give you a good and happy life. Will you let me?"

She opened her mouth to speak, and felt the hot rush of tears against the backs of her eyes. Swiftly, she looked away. She knew pity when she heard it, though she knew, too, that he'd deny it to the last—and might not yet recognize that insidious emotion for what it was. But he would. Someday.

"Tristan," she said quietly, "I decided long ago not to marry. And I have been happy, by and large, with that choice."

"Phae, damn it, did you hear what I just said?"

"Yes, now *you* listen." She felt her impatience spike, and with it the ache in her heart. "You are an earl now—one of the most powerful men in England. You mightn't like it, but you *are* Hauxton. You have duties and obligations you have not had time to consider. You have not even sat down with your solicitors to see how things stand. You have not yet buried your father, nor had time to mourn his passing. How can you possibly know what you want? You don't even know what you have."

He closed the distance between them and set his hands firmly on her shoulders. "Phae, I have never wanted anything in my life," he said. "Nothing I could define. Not until I met you. Until now, my life was simple. My needs were simple. But there is nothing simple about *this*. About *us*."

She searched his face as she searched her mind for the right words—not to tell him how she felt, for that would never do. She searched instead for words of comfort, and of reassurance. For a way of letting him off the hook and sending him on to the rich and happy life fate was offering him, would he but give up this mad notion of saddling himself with a sometimes waspish—and quite probably barren—wife.

But he did not wait for her answer. Instead, he kissed her. Roughly. Possessively. He kissed her in a way he had never kissed any woman before, did she but know it, opening his mouth over hers and taking her without hesitation, possessing her. Claiming her. Tempting her to say *yes* until it seemed his embrace wrung tears from her very heart. She wanted him so desperately.

His hand fisted in her hair and his mouth ravaged hers until her knees shook and her scalp ached and until she wanted to crawl out of her skin and into his, melding with him as one. He slanted his mouth over hers again and again, kissing her without any pretense of grace or tenderness, raking her face with the faint stubble of his beard as he thrust deep and crushed her against him.

She wanted him—wanted him with more than simple lust. He was a part of her, and ever would be. He understood her. She let his tempest draw her in, almost losing herself in the dizzying rush of his rage and need. Her yearning drew her to him, and pooled in her womb with that old familiar ache as he trembled against her.

But her womb was still a cold, black void, and hope was a tenuous thread. All the passion in God's world would not make her whole again, and when the emotional storm raining round them slowed, and Tristan tore his mouth from hers, Phaedra held his dark gaze, shuddering at what she saw in his eyes.

"Now tell me, Phaedra," he gritted, his nostrils flaring, "that I *don't know what I want.*"

She looked away, too unsteady to answer. Too afraid to trust herself.

He gave her a little shake. "Do you think I give a damn

about a title, Phaedra? I don't—save for the fact that it makes it a good deal harder for your brother to refuse me."

She shook her head, afraid of how desperately she wished to fling herself at his feet. "This will not do, Tristan," she whispered, tears welling behind her eyes. "It will not."

"Phaedra." He caught her by the chin and forced her face back to his. "Phaedra, do you love me?"

"Oh!" she said softly. "Oh, Tristan. Please do not make me answer that."

"Phae, is this about children?" he whispered. "Because you do not know for sure. You *don't*. Sometimes miracles happen. And it doesn't matter to me, one way or the other."

But it would matter to him in the end, and she knew it. It mattered to all men—especially men of wealth and title. The laws of entail vested everything he had—everything he was or would ever be—on his ability to have a son. She would not take the risk of cheating him of that. Especially when he had scarce had time to grasp what fate and his father's death had thrust upon him.

"You will want children, trust me," she said quietly, steeling herself for her next words. "And if you love me as you say, Tristan, then you will not press me."

"You just don't want me, then?" he rasped, his face a mask of pain. "Is that it? Why, Phae? Is my blood too impure for the mighty Northamptons? No Spaniards, no Sicilians, and for God's sake, no Gitanos allowed climb that lofty family tree? Because if that's it—if it's just lust you feel for me and no more—well, I'm used to that. Just say it, and at least I'll—"

She cut him off, placing her fingers across his lips. "You are good enough," she said, her hand trembling against his mouth. "Good enough for anyone. Please, don't ever say that again. It's ugly and it's *vile*."

"You think I will change my mind." His words were cold.

"I fear it, yes." An almost overwhelming weariness washed over her then, and left her swaying on her feet. "And I will not be the reason you have no children, Tristan. I could not bear it."

He just shook his head. "Phaedra, *please*."

She wanted him to leave before she did something inestimably stupid. "Go home, Tristan," she said quietly. "To Wiltshire, I mean. Get out of London's filth and go see to your estates and to your earldom, and find yourself some pretty, biddable gentleman's daughter. One who won't drag you through the stews and doss houses of London, and make you wish to rip your hair from its roots."

"Thank you, Phaedra," he said icily, "for that most thorough advice."

She went to the window and stared out into the muted afternoon light, mottled across the garden by the shifting tree limbs and fluttering leaves. "Tristan," she said quietly, "until you are wed, if we are discreet, perhaps we could continue—"

"*No*," he interjected harshly. "Do not dare to suggest such a vile thing, Phaedra. If you want me, by God, *then you'll marry me*."

"I cannot think that wise," she whispered. "And once you grasp what your new life will be like, Tristan, you will thank me for this."

"And if I don't?"

She shook her head, opened her mouth, then shut it again. "Well, if you do not," she finally said, "give it a year. And then . . . and then . . . oh, I just don't know!"

"A *year*?" he sneered. Then he rammed a hand into his coat pocket, and closed the distance between them, slapping something down upon the windowsill without breaking his stride. "Your uncertainty is a damned cold comfort, Phae, and I am not a patient man. Now, if you will excuse me, I have a funeral to attend to."

She watched him leave, his gait no longer the lazy pace she'd come to love, but an angry, purposeful stalk. She had hurt him, and more than she'd imagined possible. Suddenly the chill deepened, settling over her and going far deeper than her bones. What if it was not just honor or lust or affection which drove him? What if Tristan meant what he said? What if she could have him, and know he would never, ever regret it? Was it possible? Dear God. What if she had just made the biggest mistake of her life?

But it simply *was not* possible.

Oh, he said he didn't care about children. But he would—and then he would begin to hope; quietly, and with a deepening despair. And she knew too well the awful burden regret could be, a burden which would weigh doubly heavy, she feared, when reflected in the eyes of the person you loved. When you had to watch it fester year after year, until it was nothing but a quiet look of hopelessness. Kingdoms had fallen for less.

Deep in the house, she heard the front door slam. She

exhaled on a ragged sigh, and bowed her head. And then she saw it. The thing he'd hurled down so angrily.

She picked it up, the yellow silk shimmering in a shaft of afternoon sun. Her garter—the little white rose still dangling by a thread—a little grubby from a life lived amongst a jumble of pocket change and house keys. She remembered then how long it had been missing—that the day she'd lost it had been the day she'd first kissed him.

First begun to fall in love with him.

And then her tears fell in earnest, the sobs dragged from her chest on a rising swell of grief.

Chapter 14

Thy love is better than high birth to me,
Richer than wealth, prouder than garments' cost.

"The potted palm?" Xanthia's voice was querulous as a child's, her mouth fixed in an uncharacteristic scowl. "Or the basket of gladioli?"

"The gladioli," said Phaedra swiftly. She motioned for Stefan's footman to take the palm away. "They are just the right height for a centerpiece."

Xanthia sighed, and fell into a chair, her gaze trailing across her ballroom, which admittedly looked a shambles. "Oh, why, Phae, *why* did I ever begin this?" she asked, plopping a hand high upon her now-rounding belly. "My feet hurt, my temper's short, and everyone knows my giving a gala ball is like a pig trying to waltz."

Phaedra sank down beside her. "You planned this ball to please Mamma, Zee," she said, gently squeezing her hand. "It was perfectly silly of you, of course. But you are trying to prove to her that you can do it all—raise a family, run a business, *and* be what she wants—Lady Nash, pillar of elegant society."

"*She* is Lady Nash, the pillar. In this family, I'm just the spindly fencepost—and soon everyone will know it."

"Nonsense," said Phaedra. "Now put your feet up on one of those empty chairs whilst I go downstairs and chide Monsieur René about the *mignardises*. Then Gibbons will help us decide where to hang the bunting, all right?"

"Yes, all right." With an exasperated *puff*, Xanthia blew a tendril of hair from her face, then cast her sister-in-law a grateful glance. "Thank you for all this, Phae, and for agreeing to stay," she said quietly. "I know you don't wish to. But Stefan has been so pleased to see you out a bit this season."

"I am happy to be here," said Phaedra.

But that had been a lie, she considered five hours later. Five hours which had been spent in frantic preparation, with vases to be filled, swags to be hung, silver punch bowls to be polished, carried up, and filled. All of her brother's servants—and half of Phaedra's—had worked tirelessly. And for what?

So that Phaedra's mother could brag to all her friends what a marvelous, talented, socially acceptable daughter-in-law Stefan had married. And so that Phaedra could put on another of her low-cut ball gowns and spend the rest of the night in misery.

Upstairs in one of the guest chambers, Phaedra dressed with the help of Evans, Xanthia's maid, having no maid of her own now. She had sent Agnes back to Brierwood almost six weeks past, and had missed her ever since. They had been grim, lonely weeks with no one save Zoë to talk to—and since Zoë knew nothing of Priss, and certainly nothing of Tristan's marriage proposal, there was limited solace to be sought there.

Zoë knew, though, that Phaedra was desperately, depressingly in love. Phaedra had not even troubled herself to deny it. It would have done no good at all.

"Will you have your dress on now, my lady?" asked Evans, drawing up the muslin sheath which covered it.

"Thank you, yes." Phaedra lifted her arms, sliding into the shimmering, deep green ball gown which had brought her an almost illicit amount of pleasure when Zoë had helped her choose it. She slicked her hands down the front, smoothing away the wrinkles, and wondering why the dress brought her no pleasure now.

Because Tristan was gone.

And because every garment she'd ordered—every scrap of silk or lace she'd worn through those heady first weeks of spring—had been bespoke for just one reason. Because, in her heart, she had hoped to see him wading through some crowded ballroom. Seated at someone's dinner table. Or relaxing at someone's card party, his long legs stretched carelessly out, those black Gypsy eyes dancing with laughter. She had gone out on Zoë's arm, forcing herself to be witty and gay, in the faint hope that he might notice her.

But Tristan had been occupied at the time with other, more important matters. She fully grasped that now. She wished she had grasped it then; wished she'd stayed home alone with her books and mending and her warm fire just as she always had done. For if she had, she would not now need to explain—to Zoë, to Mamma, and even to Stefan—why she no longer wanted to go out at all.

Suddenly her abdomen cramped, hard and fierce, and

Phaedra set her hand to her belly. She must have made a little sound, for Evans circled back around from doing up her buttons, her expression one of concern. "My lady?"

Phaedra forced her expression to relax. "My monthly," she said. "It will pass soon enough."

And it would. It always did. This, just as her last, had come like clockwork.

Thank God she had not acceded to Tristan's foolhardy wish to marry, she thought as Evans finished the last button. Otherwise she would have spent every fourth week of her life thus, one hand on her stomach, one hand on her heart, praying to God for something other than the inevitable.

Evans turned her around and smiled. "You look beautiful, my lady," she said. "You'll be quite the prettiest woman there, I am sure. Now sit, and I'll do up your hair—up very high, I think, to show off that long, graceful neck."

"Thank you," said Phaedra, taking the seat before the dressing table.

A short while later, there was a hard knock at the door and Zoë came in, dressed in her favorite purple ball gown. An amethyst pendant the size of a robin's egg hung from her throat, and her black hair was drawn into a knot which was pierced with a long purple plume.

"Phae, hurry!" she scolded. "Aunt Winnie and I were the second carriage to arrive, and now the queue's stretched up to Oxford Street."

Phaedra stood from the dressing table and smoothed her gown once again. "I'm ready," she said, not entirely certain it was true. "How do I look?"

Zoë scowled. "Like a ghost," she said, reaching up to

pinch Phaedra's cheeks, her purple plume bobbing with each squeeze. "There. Now you've got a little color."

They went down the stairs together, Zoë chatting gaily. "Robin is coming tonight," she said. "And his arrogant brother, too. They both asked if you would dance with them, so I accepted on your behalf. A quadrille, I think, for Lord Mercer—oh, and a waltz for Robin."

"Zoë, please. Not a waltz."

Zoë tossed her hand. "Oh, it's only Robin," she said. "Besides, you should—"

"Zoë." Phaedra jerked to a halt. "No more *shoulds*. Must we have this discussion again?"

Zoë rolled her eyes. "Lud, Phae, what a stick-in-the-mud you've become," she said as they strolled arm in arm into the ballroom. "But I think you might get rather a shock tonight."

"A shock? Of what sort?"

Zoë snapped out her fan, and plied it coyly. "I have it on good authority that Avoncliffe is back from the country," she said. "Excuse me—*the Earl of Hauxton.* He came up just yesterday—a whole entourage, mind, with two carriages, a baggage cart, and that big, black horse he adores—so I think it's safe to say he did not come alone."

Her knees suddenly unsteady, Phaedra followed Zoë to the punch bowl. "With whom did he come, then?" she asked, unable to stop herself.

Zoë took a cup from a waiting footman and eyed Phaedra across it. "I don't know," she said earnestly. "But I know he got a card for this ball."

Through the swelling throng, Lord Robert edged toward them. "Hullo, Phae," he said, grabbing Zoë's arm.

But Phaedra scarcely saw him. "Zoë, why would he?" she hissed. "Who would have sent it?"

But Zoë just smiled as Robin drew her away. "Now *that*," she said, melting into the crowd, "is a subject best discussed with your brother, I think."

Phaedra did not ask her brother. Indeed, she could not think how. What business was it of hers whom he chose to invite into his home? But why Tristan?

She did not have the entire night, however, to ponder it. She kept Zoë's pledge to Lord Robin, who galloped her around the room in a dance that was more an exuberant jig than a waltz. Lord Mercer, however, surprised her. Though she did not know him well, the young marquess invited her to stroll in the gardens rather than dance, and she accepted gratefully. In sharp contrast to his younger brother, Mercer was a solemn, almost austere gentleman. Quite the tallest man in the room, his dark hair and oddly colored eyes set him apart from the rest of the guests, though he made no effort to draw attention to himself.

Phaedra laid her hand upon his arm, which felt strong and solid beneath his evening coat, and passed a pleasant time conversing about nothing more exciting than the health of the king, which Mercer reported to be in sharp decline. They turned to books, and to their shared interest in the French and German philosophers, both of which Mercer read in their original languages, a fact he let slip casually, and without pretense. After that they talked of breeding bloodstock, a particular hobby of his.

She was almost disappointed when the music ended. But as was proper, Mercer returned her at once to Xanthia and Stefan, exchanged a few polite words, then bowed most formally. Phaedra watched him go with the strange sense that perhaps she had just met a kindred spirit.

Mercer disappeared into the crowd as the orchestra struck up Phaedra's favorite Haydn waltz. Ignoring it, she snapped open her fan to wave it gently over Xanthia, who had finally been persuaded into a chair, and was looking a little limp. "Oh, thank you, Phae." Xanthia cut another grateful glance up at her. "You are too kind."

When she straightened, however, Stefan was speaking to someone in a tone which was warm but a little formal. Perhaps it was her peripheral vision, or perhaps some sort of sixth sense, but she turned slowly, oddly certain of who she would see.

And she was right. Tristan stood before Stefan, more resplendent than ever she'd seen him. He was dressed in formal, flawless black, his linen almost blindingly white, his hair swept back off his face in a mane of ebony waves which did not appear to have been cut during his weeks of absence. With his strong nose and dark skin, his elegant attire could not alter the fact that he still looked barely civilized. Her medieval Sicilian prince, misplaced in time.

"Ah, Hauxton, I think you know my sister?" said Stefan, setting an arm round Phaedra's waist.

"I have had the pleasure." Tristan smiled, but it did not reach his eyes. "My lady, you are looking very well indeed."

"My lord." She made a deep, formal curtsey. "What a shock to see you here."

"And you do not shock easily, do you, Lady Phaedra?" There was a change in him; a wariness she'd not seen before, and it made her heart ache. His smile still guarded, he held out his hand. "I see you are not dancing. Might I have the honor?"

"Thank you, but—"

Phaedra felt a hard jab in the center of her spine. Stefan? Or Xanthia? She tried again, confused. "But you are in mourning," she blurted, then immediately wished she had not.

Beside her, Xanthia hissed.

Phaedra's face colored furiously. "I do beg your pardon. That was impertinent."

Tristan shrugged. "I never did have any sense of propriety."

"Oh, I think society affords a few exceptions, Phae," said her brother solemnly. "Perhaps Lord Hauxton has decided to do his duty by his title and look about for a wife? It is generally thought quite pressing under such dire circumstances."

Phaedra turned round to look at him. "I beg your pardon? Dire circumstances?"

"Yes, I hear his cousin Harold almost came to a bad end recently," said Stefan, his face perfectly straight. "Entangled in that brothel fire over in Soho, someone said. Russian spies caught out. State secrets exposed. It would not do for such a scandalous chap to inherit now, would it?" He lifted his hawkish black brows, and looked pointedly at her.

Dear heaven, thought Phaedra. *Did he know?*

But Tristan ignored the remark, and instead turned back to Phaedra. "Will you dance, my lady?" he said impatiently. "After all, we are *friends,* are we not?"

It seemed the only way to escape Stefan's glare. "Thank

you," she said, placing her hand in Tristan's larger, darker one. "I would like that."

Phaedra followed him through the crowd to the edge of the dance floor, then turned to face him, unable to stop herself from drinking him in. When he set his hand at the turn of her back, she laid her palm lightly on his shoulder, and allowed herself to be, well, *poured* onto the dance floor—for Tristan did not simply lead, he melted, taking her with him in an elegant, undulating ribbon of grace.

"I fear he's caught wind of that business in Soho," she whispered when she'd caught her breath and her nerves.

Tristan looked past her and shrugged. "He likely picked up a scrap of gossip somewhere and wished merely to make a point," he answered. "After all, Cousin Harold's exploits are tame in comparison to mine."

She flicked an anxious glance up at him. "Yes, I daresay."

They danced in silence for a long while, Tristan holding her closer than was strictly necessary, his big, warm hand set firmly at the turn of her spine. As always, his body possessed hers. Drew hers. In his arms she felt the stirring of passion remembered; of how it felt to have his long, powerful body stretched naked along hers. Joined with her. She had always believed Tristan danced as he made love—intensely, with perfect rhythm, and with the whole of himself. Tonight was no exception.

But that train of thought would not do. Ruthlessly, she shut it off. "I understand you've been in the country, my lord," she said stiffly. "How did you find it?"

He looked down at her with another faint smile, but for an instant, his dark, glittering gaze was unguarded.

"You speak as if we are perfect strangers, Phae," he murmured, his voice husky. "I liked it well enough."

"Did you?" He spun her smoothly into the next turn. "I am glad to hear it."

The smile fell away from his face then. "I am getting on with my new life, Phae," he said quietly. "I am going to do what is expected of me—well, not the Government bit, no. But the estates, the farms, the mines and the quarries—I'm going to do my best to make a success of it."

"And your best will be very good indeed, Tristan." She forced a tremulous smile. "I am quite sure of it."

He whirled her about again, and this time pulled her fully against him, causing glances to cut their way, eyebrows aloft. "Will you be at home tomorrow, Lady Phaedra?" he whispered, his eyes holding hers, his lips pressed scandalously near. "I have someone whom I should like you to meet."

Phaedra did not like the solemnity in his tone. "Someone special, I take it?"

Tristan's cheeks colored faintly, but he did not set her away. "I think she is very special, yes," he answered. "I met her when I was in the country. And I remembered your advice."

"My advice?"

"About finding a pretty gentleman's daughter," he said.

Something inside her froze. "Yes, I see," she managed, trying to keep her step. "And biddable. You did not forget that part, I hope?"

He flashed a chagrined expression. "Alas, she's not especially biddable," he said. "Still, I think . . . yes, I very much think she is going to be a permanent part of my life, Phae. But I should like your blessing first. Will you meet her?"

Phaedra forced herself to smile. "My brother was not wrong, then?" she said quietly.

Again the faint, tentative smile. "Nash isn't wrong about much, is he?"

Phaedra humiliated herself then by tripping over her own foot. "Bloody hell," she gritted.

Tristan caught her, smoothing over the error so gracefully no one could possibly have seen it. But Phaedra had seen it. And she had had quite enough. If she kept this up—her body pressed too near Tristan's, his rich, familiar scent teasing at her nostrils—she would most assuredly burst into tears.

Deliberately, she slowed, and Tristan drew her smoothly alongside an arrangement of palms. Then, when no one was looking, he swiftly kissed her cheek. "Your brother is looking daggers at me now," he said. "I had best bid you good night, Phae."

"Yes," she managed. "And thank you. Thank you, Tristan, for trying to help Millie. And thank you for catching me just now."

"With you, my lady," he said, "the pleasure—*always*—is mine."

Then, finally, he flashed a hint of that shameless grin she loved, and bowed with a great flourish, sweeping the floor with an imaginary hat, putting her very much in mind of the night she'd met him, when he'd very nearly toppled from his horse. Someday, perhaps, when the heat between them died down to ash, she would tell him about that. Perhaps they would be able to laugh together as friends.

"Until tomorrow, then?" he asked.

"Tomorrow, yes." Forcing a smile, Phaedra folded her hands together, her nails digging into her own flesh. "Shall we say half past two?"

He looked at her a little oddly. "Very well. Half past two it shall be."

Then he strode through the room, the crowd parting like the sea before him, and vanished from her sight.

The following afternoon, Phaedra was in the library upstairs keeping vigil by the bank of windows when Tristan's carriage came clattering down Brook Street. She had been there since noon, the press of tears hot behind her eyes, her entire body so rigid with the waiting her muscles ached. Again and again she went over the words Tristan had spoken last night, but she could ascribe no other meaning to them save for the worst.

He had met someone. A gentleman's daughter. Someone he wished to make a part of his life.

It seemed too soon, she thought. *She was not ready.* She had thought . . . *what?*

That she would have more time? That Tristan would wait, and press his suit again? Why should he, when she had turned him off so thoroughly? And what had changed? She was no more eligible a bride now than she had been two months ago. And now, her two months of misery were about to grow, she feared, into a lifetime of regret. He had taken her good advice. He was moving on with his life.

Rising onto her toes, Phaedra watched the carriage draw up, her hands clenched, her nails digging into her palms. She had resolved to wait until the calling cards were brought up, and then to receive them formally, in the withdrawing room. Now her resolve was weakening. She wanted to rush down and get it over with. Or at least receive them in her oasis of safety, the family parlor. But that room held too many memories, both happy and sad, of her time with Tristan.

The carriage was a fine one, an elegant, old-fashioned post chaise made for fast travel and privacy, with the Talbot family crest emblazoned on the side, and bewigged footmen posted to the rear. They wore the same gray and red livery she'd seen that day in Bond Street, their velvet knee breeches fastened with gold buckles. Having leapt down, they were now opening the door and dropping the steps.

And then she saw him. Tristan descended to the pavement wearing his usual tall, shining boots, a coat of midnight blue, his hair covering the collar. He turned, offering up his hand to someone. The lady took it, stepping gingerly down, glancing up at him almost deferentially as she did so, her broad-brimmed bonnet obscuring her face.

She was quite tall and wore a dress striped in shades of gray. A perfectly ordinary dress. An ordinary woman, too, by the look of her. Would it have been easier to bear, Phaedra wondered, had she been a stunning, round-figured lady dressed in the height of fashion?

Phaedra jerked shut the draperies and turned from the window.

She had thought that she could do this. And she could.

She would. But it would not be easy with her heart in her throat and regret bitter in her mouth. She paced the floor until Stabler came, his eyes solemn, the silver salver extended, the little patch of ivory taunting her atop it.

"The Earl of Hauxton, my lady."

Just one card. One name. At the time, however, it did not register.

"He asked, of course, for Lady Nash," said Stabler. "But since she is not in . . . ? "

Phaedra felt a moment of guilt for inviting Tristan when she knew her mother would be out, but she could not have borne this with her mother looking on. "Show them into the withdrawing room, please," she managed, taking the card. "And send for tea."

Stabler bowed, and quit the room. Going to one of the pier glasses which divided the windows, Phaedra dabbed at her face with her handkerchief. She did not have Zoë today to pinch some color into her cheeks. Besides, it would not have lasted. With one last steadying breath, she lifted her chin and swept from the room. She was Lady Phaedra Northampton, for pity's sake. She would bloody well act like it.

Her chin was still up, and her color perhaps a little higher when she reached the withdrawing room. The double doors were open to the passageway, and Phaedra swept through, a welcoming smile fixed upon her face. She had no sooner stepped over the threshold, however, when she was taken aback.

The woman in the gray striped dress was Agnes!

Tristan sat nearby, his elbows on his knees, his hands clasped as he leaned forward. On the floor before them a little child toddled, blond ringlets bouncing, her face lifted to Tristan's as if he were the sun, and she the sunflower.

"Dis is Bunnet," said the child, extending him a small stuffed rabbit. "Here. You take 'em."

Tristan smiled back, and suddenly, he looked himself again. "Thank you," he said. "I'll just tuck Bunnet in my coat pocket, shall I?"

"Priss!" Phaedra didn't even realize she'd cried out before she was on her knees, drawing the child to her breast.

"Oh!" squealed the child. "Phae, you squish me."

"Oh!" Phae set her a little away, and slicked a hand down her shining hair. "Oh, Priss, I did not mean to crush you."

But Priss just smiled, two rows of shiny front teeth beaming up at her. "Phae, me got a top," she said, turning. "I shows you." A basket sat on the Aubusson carpet by Tristan's shiny boot, brimming with toys. Priss toddled to it, and began to rummage.

Still on her knees, Phaedra looked back and forth between Agnes and Tristan, searching their faces for some explanation. "What has happened?" she asked breathlessly, her tangled rush of emotion not yet receding. "Where is your aunt, Agnes? What is going on?"

Agnes would not quite meet her gaze.

"It's complicated," said Tristan. "Just tell me, Phae, that you are glad to see her? To see us?"

"Of course I am glad!" Phaedra cried, her gaze returning to her maid. "Glad to see all of you. How could I not be? Agnes, what is going on here?"

Agnes cut a strange, somewhat dubious, glance at

Tristan, and rose. "I'm to let his lordship explain that one, and gladly," she said, bending over to pick up Priscilla. "Little Miss Mischief and I shall just stroll in the gardens, shall we, whilst he does?"

"But . . . I do not understand." Phaedra stood. "Why must you go?"

Agnes, however, just settled Priss on her hip, and tossed Tristan a parting glance. "Good luck to you, my lord," she murmured.

"Agnes, wait!" But Agnes did not wait, and Phaedra's gaze followed them from the room. When they vanished into the depths of the house, she turned to look at Tristan. He stood by the basket of toys, one hand at his slender waist, pushing back the front of his coat. In the other hand he held a sheaf of papers.

Phaedra jerked to her feet. "Tristan," she said sharply, "Tell me straight out. What is going on here?"

Wordlessly, he passed her the papers. Eyes wide, she opened them, shuffling from one page to the next. "But this . . . this is Millie's signature," she whispered. "Here. And here. And these seals—all these legal words—what do they mean?"

"They mean that Priscilla is now my ward," he said quietly. "The document was drawn by my solicitor in the City some days ago. And if you agree, Phae, I mean to petition the court to adopt Priss as soon as possible."

Phaedra lifted her gaze to his, mystified. Her relief at seeing Agnes instead of the future Lady Hauxton in her drawing room was giving way to utter confusion. "To . . . to adopt *Priss*?" she managed. "You . . . you cannot do that. *Can* you?"

Tristan lifted one of his dark, slashing eyebrows. "I can if Millie signs away her rights," he answered. "Which, for a price, she did—and pretty cheerfully, I might add."

"You . . . you bought her?"

"That sounds harsh, Phae," he said tightly. "But I am resolved, unless your brother means to step forward and claim his child? I shall do him the courtesy, of course, of waiting until he retur—"

"Oh, Tony will not claim her," Phaedra interjected, handing back the papers. "Tristan, you will not force his hand. Is *that* what you thought?"

Something dark and angry sketched across his face. "Hell and damnation, Phaedra!" he growled, snatching the papers. "Do you think me such a fool as that? I'll give Hayden-Worth the opportunity—to do otherwise would be ungentlemanly—but if he'd meant to do right by that child, he'd have long since done it. Isn't that how all this mess fell to you to begin with?"

Phaedra felt the tears well up again. "But Priss . . . I don't understand."

"The child needs a loving home, my dear," he answered, his tone softening. "With Nash's permission, I've hired Agnes to be her nurse. They are living at my estate in Wiltshire, not so very far from Brierwood."

Phaedra set one hand to her temple, unable to fathom it. Good God. What was Stefan's part in all this? Did he suspect Tony's guilt? Or *hers*? None of it made sense. "But Tristan, what will you tell people about Priss?"

"That it's none of their damned business," Tristan snapped. "They will assume the worst, of course—people always do. It will be whispered she's my by-blow, and that I adopted her as Lord Rannoch did Zoë."

"Oh," said Phaedra. "Oh, dear."

Tristan shrugged, and tossed the papers onto a side table. "Should it matter to us, Phae?" he asked. "She's a clever, sweet child, and I've never given a damn what people say. As to Priss—well, you tell me—is she better off as Lord Hauxton's pampered bastard? Or as the illegitimate child of a tavern maid? It's not a perfect world. I did the best I could."

Phaedra swallowed hard. "I—I see your point," she whispered. "But I know . . . oh, Tristan. I *know* you are doing this for me."

"Yes," he answered, his voice softening. "I am doing this for you—or I was."

"I don't understand," said Phaedra. "What do you mean?"

He shrugged a little shyly. "A funny thing happened, Phae, these last two weeks," he said. "Life was looking a little empty and a little bleak for me. But she's a taking little thing, Priss."

For the first time, Phaedra smiled. "Yes, she is."

At last he grinned, his square, white teeth contrasting sharply against his honeyed skin. "I've grown dashed fond of the chit," he admitted. "So, yes, I did it for you, and for her, and even for Agnes, perhaps. But I think, Phae, that in the end, it will have been for me."

"Do you?" Her voice was soft. "Oh, Tristan. I am so glad."

His gaze was focused on the door through which they

had vanished. "You were right, you know, about my needing a child," he said quietly. "I look at Priss, so smart and so vivacious, and I realize . . . well, that's she's worth a lot of effort. She brightens my life. Gives me a purpose, perhaps, mawkish as that may sound."

Phaedra did not remind him that what he needed was *a blood heir*, and no adopted child, certainly not a female, could ever be that. But the moment was raw, and his eyes were tender. There would be time enough for him to consider that later.

She clasped her hands tightly before her. "I am glad," she said again. "If your heart is set, then Priss is the lucky one."

His gaze fixed on hers, and he shook his head. "No, I think that perhaps I am," he answered. "And ever the gambler, I'm going to try my luck again."

"Yes?" Suddenly, her heart leapt. "In . . . In what way?"

He stepped a little nearer. Until that time, she had not seen the two packages which sat by his chair tied up with red ribbons, one atop the other. He turned and pulled the ribbon free, then with the smaller of the two in hand, he knelt before her.

"Lady Phaedra Northampton," he said quietly, "I did not do this properly the first time, so—"

"Oh, no!" she interjected, her hand out as if to stop him. "Oh, Tristan, please—"

"—so I mean to try again," he pressed on. "Phae, I love you more than life itself. I should have said so, very clearly, two months ago. Please marry me. Please be the Countess of Hauxton—be Priscilla's mother—and make me the happiest man on earth. Now, love, I am begging you. *Please marry me.*"

Phaedra was shaking so badly, she was compelled to collapse onto the settee behind her. "Oh, Tristan, please get up," she said. "Come sit by me. Let us talk of this rationally."

"No." He leaned into her, his eyes demanding, the box still in hand. "Let us talk of it *irrationally*, Phae. Let us talk of how we feel in one another's arms. Of how we understand one another. Of how we exasperate one another. Why, Phae, would I settle for something less, and live a passionless marriage? Is a child—an heir—worth that?"

"Tristan, you need—"

His lips thinned. "With all respect, Phae, I'm a little tired of your telling me what I need," he said. "I need *you*. And Priss needs *us*. You, me, and yes, probably Agnes, too. And how we'll work all this out, and what we'll say to people, I do not yet know. But I do know that our not marrying because you fear you cannot give me a child is just balderdash, Phae. We will have Priss to love. Let Cousin Harold inherit the rest of it. Whoever the hell he is, he'll no doubt make a fine earl."

Phaedra's hands were shaking now. "I don't . . . oh, Tristan . . . I can't think."

"Don't *think*," he whispered, his gaze level with hers. *"Just say yes."*

She closed her eyes, her hands fisting so that she would not reach out for him.

"Phae, I'll be a good husband, I swear," he said. "I'll never look at another wom—"

"No, you *won't*," she said sharply. "That, I *will not* have."

"Then you'd better say *yes*," he teased, "or you'll have no say at all."

"Tristan," she said, her eyes flying open. "Oh, Tristan. You are a fool."

His eyes were solemn as he shook his head. "No, I've never been a fool, no matter what people thought." Then his expression suddenly darkened to something far more intractable. "Now, I have a ring in this box, my dear. A Talbot family heirloom. Give me your hand, for I am done asking, Phae. You are marrying me. You can say yes. Or I can lay siege to your house for a year or two. Or I can go to Nash, and tell—"

"Tristan," she said warningly.

"Just hold out your hand," he ordered, "and say *yes*. Please, Phae. Because this is done. And because I love you—and because I think, perhaps, that you love me?"

Slowly, so slowly it quivered, she unclenched her fingers and extended her hand. "All right, then," she whispered. "*Yes.*"

He snapped open the box and slid the ring, cool and loose, onto her hand. She drew one last steadying breath, then looked down. A band of diamonds set with three large, perfectly matched emeralds winked up at her. A ring that must have cost a king's ransom two or three centuries past. She embarrassed herself then by bursting into tears.

"*Yes,*" she said again as he kissed away her tears. "Yes, *I love you*—and you know it, too, you wretch! I love you madly, and I have since the first time you kissed me."

"I thought," he said solemnly, "that you might never say so."

She laughed, and said it again for good measure. "Yes, I love you, and you are mad for doing this, but I have not the will to fight it," she answered, snuffling. "Oh, Tristan, I have missed you so! Now, what's in the other box?"

"Greedy puss," he whispered, rising and picking it up. He returned to sit beside her, laying it in her lap. "You may open this one," he said, his voice sultry, yet teasing. "It is for you to wear—or not—as it pleases you."

Her hands still shaking, Phaedra lifted the lid. Inside, on a bed of white satin, lay a set of purple velvet manacles fastened with long gold chains and tiny gold locks, and set at each corner with large teardrop pearls. "Oh, my!" she whispered reverently. She reached out, tentatively, and touched one. The fabric was soft as down.

"Only if you wish," said Tristan softly.

Then he turned on the settee, his hands coming up to bracket her face. He kissed her sweetly, as he had the very first time, but deeply. A kiss rich with the promise of years to come, and of passion unbound and eternal. And when he drew away, his black eyes were dancing again, and his irreverent grin was back in place. "Now, Phae," he said teasingly, "*you* have to give something to *me*."

"Anything." She held his gaze, perfectly serious. "You have only to name it."

"I claim my prize, then," he said. With a sudden twitch of his hand, he jerked her skirts up to her knees, making her shriek.

"Tristan, not here!"

"Yes, Phae. Now." The grin was back, brilliant and wicked. *I want my yellow garter back.*"

Epilogue

❦

Love is a smoke made with the fume of sighs,
Being purg'd, a fire sparkling in lovers' eyes.

WILTSHIRE, JANUARY 1833

The Earl of Hauxton was sweating—not perspiring, not merely damp with exertion—but sweating great rivulets that ran down his bare throat to settle in the vee of his collarbone, and from thence trickled into the light thatch of dark hair that graced his fine, broad chest.

"Oh! God!" he groaned. "That was—"

"—*exquisite,*" his wife finished.

Atop him, she bent forward and drew her long, purple feather down his throat, along his shoulder, and lower still. "*Now do it again,*" she whispered, gazing down at him. "Or this time I shall ply my plume without pity."

His black eyes flashing, her husband bucked his powerful hips, threatening to throw her off. But he wouldn't, and they both knew it. Instead, Phaedra held on with a little shriek.

"*Shh,*" he said gently. "You'll wake the children."

Phaedra lifted one eyebrow. "A good try, my lord," she replied, drawing the feather down his flank until he shivered. "But that pair could sleep through a thunderstorm." The feather came up again, teasing and tormenting. "Do you know, I'm glad we spent Christmas in the country."

He crooked his head to look down his chest at her. "Are you indeed?"

"Yes," she purred, drawing the feather lower. "I find this fresh Wiltshire air quite whets my appetites. Once more—then, I promise, I shall unfasten you."

The earl grunted. "That's what you said an hour ago," he answered. "Where the devil did you get that garish feather, anyway?"

Grinning, Phaedra twirled it. "It's just an old thing of Zoë's," she confessed. "I stole it from her trunk upstairs. She wears it sometimes in her hair."

Her husband grinned. "I think you should wear it in *your* hair," he said, lifting his dark eyebrows suggestively. "Untie me, love, and let's see how it looks, *hmm?*"

"Oh, no, no," said Phaedra. "You are my concubine. And I demand another performance."

The earl looked up at the purple velvet cuffs which bound his wrists to the bed and pulled down as if testing their strength. "Madam, I think you have me," he agreed. "Your tastes, I find, have altered."

She fell against him on a sigh of satisfaction. "Yes, I have mastered my passions," she murmured. "And now I mean to master *yours*."

"Witch!" he uttered.

She kissed his damp throat, reveling in the heat of his body, and of the scent of strong, lusty male. "Oh, you'll survive," she said, tossing the feather aside. "And I find I rather enjoy being the one in control."

He turned his face into hers. "My love," he said solemnly, "you have always been the one in control."

She peeked at him through a curtain of heavy chestnut hair. "Truly?"

He nodded, his hair scrubbing the pillow. "Aye, since that long-ago day when I kissed you behind the parlor door. Did you ever doubt it?"

She caught her lip between her teeth. "At first," she admitted.

He snorted in disbelief. Exhausted, the encore forgotten, they drifted off thus for a few moments, only to be roused again by a tentative knock at the door.

"My lady?" It was Arnolds, the butler. "My lady, I fear you are needed upstairs."

With a groan, Phaedra rolled herself gingerly away. "What is it, Arnolds?" she asked, scrabbling about for the key to the manacles.

The butler hesitated. "It is Miss Armstrong, my lady," he finally said. "No one is hurt, but I fear Miss Priscilla tied her to a chair in the schoolroom, and set her hair afire with an old tinderbox."

The earl grunted. "Wild Red Indians again," he said. "Didn't you forbid them that game?"

Phaedra sighed deeply. "Thank you, Arnolds," she said, snapping open the first lock. "Yes, I told them, but Zoë's as bad as Priss. I don't feel sorry for her in the least. But still, I daresay we'd best hurry."

The butler's heavy tread fell away, and in a trice they were dressed and rushing upstairs to the schoolroom. They arrived to find Miss White, the governess, already surveying the damage, her hands on her hips. Priss sat—

feigning contrition—in one chair, whilst Zoë sat in the other, looking much the same.

As usual, Tristan caved in first. "Oh, come here, Priss," he said, picking up the child, who was pretending to snuffle now. "I expect you've had a scare, *hmm?*"

Phaedra expected otherwise, but she held her tongue. It took but a few moments to elicit the full story, and to hear Zoë's apology for egging the situation on. The damage was to the tendrils at the nape of her neck, and the room still stank of singed hair.

"She's only five, Phae, for pity's sake," said their houseguest under her breath. "I never dreamt she could actually *strike* the bloody thing,"

"Yes, well, let that be a lesson to you." Phaedra borrowed Miss White's scissors. "Now look down, Zoë, and I'll snip out these burnt bits."

"I daresay you'll soon grow tired of having me," said Zoë sorrowfully over the *snick! snick! snick!* of the scissors. "I suppose I ought to just pack up my things and go back to Richmond and throw myself on the pyre of Papa's horrid demands."

"Yes, I'll believe that bit of drama when I see it, my dear." The hair cut away, Phaedra put down the scissors and motioned at Priscilla. "What of you, Priss?" she said warningly. "Have you something to say to Miss Armstrong?"

Priscilla turned her head into her father's shoulder. "I didn't mean it, Papa!" she said, settling her head on his shoulder. "I'm sorry! I didn't mean to do it."

"Oh, I'm fairly sure you did," said Tristan evenly. "Now, how would you like to go into the conservatory, and have breakfast with Papa, *hmm?*"

Phaedra sighed.

"Can the babies come?" Priss cut a doting gaze up at her father.

Tristan cast his wife an enquiring glance and she quickly nodded. After so many years of trying, the twins had been—well, nothing less than a miracle, really, and they rarely left Phaedra's sight. "We shall ring for Nurse to bring them," Tristan agreed. "*If* they are awake."

Half an hour later they were seated *en famille* in the conservatory, with Tristan wiping jam from Priscilla's fingers. Zoë was bouncing Caroline on her knee, whilst Christopher still slept in his basket.

Phaedra sipped her tea, and stared pensively out the windows. The snow was coming down hard now, cold and silent, blanketing the house's vast gardens in a mantle of white. Already Priss was wheedling to be taken out to play—and already Tristan was surrendering.

How much things had changed in just a few short years! After endless months of hoping—though she'd sworn she would not hope at all—Phaedra had conceived. Perhaps the Lord had doubly blessed her for her patience. The twins were beautiful, healthy babes, and some days, Phaedra still wept when she held them.

In Wiltshire, Priss had truly blossomed. She had stopped asking after her mother long before leaving her aunt's cottage, and Phaedra did not know whether that was good or bad. Immaterial, she supposed. Millie still lived under the protection of Lord Cotting, and though they had not married, he was fast growing old, and anything was yet possible. Agnes had shocked them in the spring by stepping out with Mr. Uglow, Tristan's valet.

They now lived on the grounds in a cottage where Priss had her own little bed when she visited, and yet a second collection of dolls and toys.

Which left only Zoë to be happily settled—an unlikely hope indeed, for though she claimed to envy Phaedra's happiness, she seemed as disinclined as ever to marry. Instead she lived a peripatetic life, moving from her father's Richmond mansion, her stepmother's family home, her aunt's town house and even spending weeks at a time with Phaedra and Tristan. It was as if she felt she belonged nowhere.

As if he'd read her thoughts, Arnolds came in at that instant, cutting short Phaedra's reverie and bringing fresh coffee with the morning's post. Today there was but one letter. Phaedra picked it up then, her eyebrows rising, pushed it across the table to Zoë.

"For you, Pocahontas."

Zoë passed Caroline to Phaedra and took up the letter, her smile withering. "From Papa," she muttered, slitting the wax with her butter knife. "Oh, Phae, this cannot be good news."

Tristan, who had been engaged in persuading Priss to eat her eggs, turned to face them as Zoë's gaze flicked over the page. "I trust no one is ill?"

"Only me," said Zoë dryly. Then she sighed, and lowered the letter to her lap. "Well, the ax has finally fallen. What day is it, Hauxton?"

"January twentieth," said Tristan. "Why?"

Zoë turned to Phaedra with a sour smile. "Papa says it will soon be time for The Talk," she said. "I'm to have only a little more freedom, Phae—five months and eleven days' worth."

Phaedra's gaze searched her friend's face, which was rapidly losing its color. "And then what, Zoë? You look as if you're headed to Tyburn."

Zoë lifted her chin, her eyes sparkling with anger. "I might as well be. The season is just weeks away, and Papa declares that if I cannot settle on a husband by the end of it, he is going to find one for me. Or I may go home to Scotland. Those are my choices."

Phaedra was taken aback. "Oh, my poor dear," she murmured. "Oh, that really is too cruel. But if you cannot find *anyone*, why, I am sure he will relent . . . won't he?"

"*Anyone?*" echoed Zoë bitterly.

"No, not *anyone*," said Tristan helpfully. "Here, let's make a list." When Zoë's eyes shot daggers at him, he clarified. "Of eligible bachelors, I mean. Why, there must be a dozen decent chaps I know who could use a good wife."

"Yes, what about Lord Robert?" Phaedra suggested. "You did once say, Zoë, that if you go round kissing someone long enough, you'll end up married to them. And Robin would do well to settle down, before he kills himself."

Abruptly, Zoë crushed the letter in her hands. "My God, just listen to yourselves!"

"I beg your pardon?" said Tristan.

Zoë fixed him with her darkest glower. "Why, not three years ago, Hauxton, you couldn't spell *matrimony*, let alone fathom it," she exclaimed. "And Phae! You were a confirmed spinster, you will recall. It took me a fortnight just to get you into a proper dress."

Tristan and Phaedra exchanged sheepish glances across the table. "Well," she said quietly, "we were wrong."

"Oh, bother!" said Zoë, shoving back her chair. "I'll find a way out of this, trust me. Papa is in for the shock of his life. Now come on, Priss. Get your boots and mittens. Let's go roll in the snow. I, for one, should like to cool off."

"Snow!" cried Priss, scrambling down from her chair.

Everything followed in a flurry of activity. Miss White swooped in to carry her charge off to be properly dressed for the outdoors, Zoë following. The nurse—a stout, dependable soul—declared it time for the twins' baths, then picked up their baskets by their massive handles and summarily carted them away. Arnolds motioned for the footmen to begin to clear the unused dishes. And in moments, Phaedra and Tristan sat by themselves, eyeing one another across the breakfast table.

"Well, my dear," he said suggestively. "Alone again."

"Yes, my love. What *shall* we do?" A myriad of possibilities passed through Phaedra's mind, then suddenly, she gasped and leapt from her chair.

"What?" Tristan jerked to his feet. "Phae, what's wrong?"

Phaedra felt her face flood with heat. "The velvet shackles," she whispered, grabbing his arm. "Oh, Lud! Please, Tristan, *please* tell me you put them away?"

At that, Tristan threw back his head and laughed. "Oh, Phaedra!" he said as she dragged him toward the stairs. "The servants will have plenty to gossip about now!"